THE MOON ALWAYS RISES

The Lycanthrope Protection Agency
Book 3

CJ Ravenna

Editing by Carta's Editorial Services

Copy and line edit by Jennifer Smith

Proofreading by Lori Parks

Beta reading by Rare Bird Beta Reading

Cover designed by Danielle Doolittle | DoElle Designs | www.doelledesigns.com

First edition 2023

CONTENT WARNINGS

- The first chapter contains on-page child abduction and torture

- Graphic violence

- Racism

- Predators hunting prey animals

- Amputation recovery

- Trauma recovery

Chapter 1

PAPÁ

When Gabe Reyes was a boy, he'd feared the dark and the monsters he was certain dwelled within the shadows. At thirteen, it was his turn now to laugh at his sister when she barged into his room and demanded he protect her from the things in her closet or under her bed.

"I saw something outside my window! I did! Shut up, Gabriel!" She stamped her foot and bared her fangs when Gabe chuckled at her.

"I checked, princesa," their father, Manuel, crooned, scooping the frantic seven-year-old into his arms. "There was no one. I promise." He kissed her on the nose and carried her to her room.

Just to humor his sister, Gabe peered out into the rain-washed streets. Nothing and no one. Only a crazy person would be out in that storm.

"Ay..." His father sighed. He'd returned to lean in the doorway.

Gabe laughed and snatched up his book on werewolf history. "She's such a baby."

"She's your sister, Gabriel. You should set an example. Laughing at her when she's scared isn't nice. Even if it's over nothing."

Shrugging, Gabe found his bookmark. He had so much to read before class tomorrow.

"Hey." When he looked up, his father was giving him The Look. Gabe knew he was in for a lecture. "Your mother told me an interesting story today."

Gabe barely swallowed a groan. "Papá—"

"She told you to keep an eye on Izzie today at the farmer's market."

He rolled his eyes. "I took my eyes off her for a second!"

"Anything can happen in a second, Gabriel!"

He winced as his father raised his voice. "I wanted to go look at the butcher's stall, and she wouldn't go with me."

"You could have let her look at what she wanted, then had your turn. But walking away from her wasn't the solution."

His father was right. A mixture of shame and anger burned Gabe's cheeks. "Why couldn't Mamá watch her? I'm too old to be a babysitter!"

"Yes, you are the oldest, which is why it's your job to learn some responsibility. A wolf protects his pack, mijo. Your pack is your family. Always remember that."

"Yeah, but big scary wolves don't let seven-year-olds boss them around," Gabe grumbled.

"No, but they look out for their younger sister and let their mother do her shopping. Fair?"

Gabe sighed. "Fair."

His father tousled his hair. "Get some sleep, mijo."

"When will you be back from your business trip?" Gabe asked.

His father grimaced and gave an exaggerated sigh. "In a day or so."

"I wish you didn't have to go."

Squeezing Gabe's knee, he said, "So do I, but... it's important. There's something Alpha Hanson needs to know, and some things should only be said face-to-face." He rubbed a hand over his stubble, a tell Gabe recognized.

"Is everything okay?"

His father smiled. "Yes." He spoke confidently, but his heart skipped. His father was lying. "Just... mijo, you need to promise me while I'm gone that you'll listen to your mother and be good to your sister."

Gabe frowned. "Okay." His father was being so weird. "I will. Promise."

"I know." His father drew him close for a quick squeeze before Gabe wriggled away and buried himself under the blankets.

"Goodnight, Gabriel." His father smiled at him from the doorway, then he turned and walked away. The door closed behind him.

It was the last time Gabe saw his father smile.

GABE WOKE SOMETIME LATER, shivering. The wind buffeted his blankets and pushed his hair into his eyes. It was cold for a summer night. The smell of wet pavement turned his head toward the window—and he found it open. He sat up, surprised to see rain pooling on his bedroom floor and flowing under the bed. He didn't understand; his mother had closed the window before the storm. He swung his legs out of bed, rubbing his eyes. Splashing under his bare feet, the water was cold and slicked the wood. He grasped the window and pushed down, only to freeze.

There were claw marks in the wood, deep enough for him to dip the tip of his pinky finger in. Where had these come from? Had his mother made them? He bent his nose, sniffing at the indentations in the wood. The hair on the back of his neck stood up. He smelled soil, cold and wet, like the mud in the cemetery during his abuela's funeral.

Rain spattered his arms, raising goosebumps. The smell hit him then, overpowering the whole room: dirt, sweat, and coppery blood. In the silence, the rain tapped like little fingernails on the windowsill. The floorboards creaked behind him. He felt like prey frozen in the underbrush, too afraid to even move.

He turned around—and a cold, clammy hand like a corpse's covered his mouth and silenced his scream. The man wore all black and blended seamlessly into the shadows. He was tall, bigger than Gabe's dad or anyone else. The streetlamp illuminated his gaunt face, and shadows pooled in the hollows of his cheeks. His hair was like a long, greasy curtain hanging over his eyes. They blazed yellow, the eyes of a predator.

"Hello, Gabriel." His voice crawled from the depths of his throat like unearthed worms. He bared sharp, pointed teeth, and Gabe couldn't stifle his whimper. The man's smile was a pleased thing, brimming with satisfaction. "Looks like I picked the right window to climb into. I'll admit I was nervous. Thought I'd get the wrong room. Looks like I hit the jackpot and found Daddy's favorite little boy. Too bad he's not here to save you."

He wanted to scream for help, but those razor claws tapping against his cheek like the rain on the windowpane silenced him. They were sharp and overgrown.

"I want you to listen closely. You're going to do everything I say, or else I'll slit your mother's throat before she can scream. While she's choking on her blood, I'll tear open your little sister's belly."

His words left Gabe too paralyzed to even scream.

He squeezed Gabe's jaw, his claws piercing the skin, and Gabe's own blood ran hot down his chin. "Do you understand?"

Bile rose at the back of Gabe's throat. He nodded.

"Good. Follow me. Don't make a sound."

Gabe's legs shook as he took one step, then another. He didn't want to go, but he also didn't want to be hurt or to see his family hurt. He had no choice. The door creaked as the intruder opened it. A cold, wet hand grabbed his arm and pulled him out into the living room. He passed his parents' room. All he had to do was scream, but he couldn't summon even a gasp of air.

He stumbled as the man shoved him toward the front door. The locks clicked; the door opened. His mom still hadn't come for him. Tears blurred his vision as the man shoved him out the door. It closed behind him.

The man led him to a car, rusty and weather-beaten. An icy wave of fear crashed over him.

Oh Goddess. I'm being kidnapped.

This couldn't be real.

The man shoved him into the car and slammed the door. It locked shut, and the man climbed in and drove out of the parking space. Tears blurred Gabe's eyes as his apartment got farther away.

"Please let me go. My family—"

"You'll never see them again."

Tears scorched Gabe's eyes.

"Why are you doing this?"

"I know," the man said, his voice almost pitying. "You're probably confused right now. After all, you're such a good boy, aren't you? Well-liked in school. A talented soccer player. A family who adores you. You probably think this isn't fair, and I'd agree with you. It isn't fair." Anger thickened his voice. "It isn't fair that hybrid *scum* like you, like your filthy family, get to be happy."

The breath tore from Gabe's lungs in gasps.

"Soon," he continued, voice thick with rage, "that will change. Impure filth like your father will never be an equal to pure-blooded wolves."

"W-wait. Please!"

He swerved violently to the right, and Gabe rolled off the seat and fell on the floor.

He stayed there for what felt like hours, too scared to move. The car screeched when his abductor slammed on the brakes. Then the engine cut off. The quiet buzzed in Gabe's ears. The man went outside, slamming the door behind him.

Gabe jumped out of his skin when the passenger door opened and rain soaked his clothes, making him shiver. Clawed hands dug into his arms. Gabe yelped in pain when the man hauled him from the vehicle.

"Walk," he snarled, hurling Gabe ahead of him.

"Okay, okay," Gabe whimpered. He had no idea where he was, but they sure weren't in the city anymore. Dark, empty woodland stretched on for miles in every direction. If he had to guess, they were somewhere upstate.

Gabe gasped when the man gripped his arm so tight, he cut off the circulation. "You so much as try to make a run for it, and I'll kill you. You'll never see your mom again. Your cute little sister. Your father."

Tears mixed with the rain on Gabe's face. He had no choice but to obey this monster. Maybe if he listened, just *maybe,* he could see his family again.

They crossed a knee-deep river, the icy water soaking biting at his toes. Wet leaves squelched under his bare feet. They walked through the trees, the branches rattling like bones. When a dilapidated house appeared, terror made Gabe freeze in place. He couldn't go in there. He would be trapped. He'd never get out.

"Walk!" the man snarled, fisting Gabe's hair and throwing him through the gaping doorway.

The air inside reeked like something long dead and forgotten. Wind and rain billowed through the shattered windows. The man clamped a cold, wet hand around his shoulder, his nails biting into his skin. Gabe gasped in pain but didn't dare tell the man to let go as he took slow steps down a steep stairwell. Dust and the sweetish reek of rotting wood clouded the air. The ground vanished beneath him, and he cried out as he crashed onto the floor, dust rising around him like smoke.

"Up, up, Gabriel." He yanked Gabe to his feet.

Stumbling onto a chair, Gabe felt cold metal cuffs snap around his feet. His eyes adjusted to the dark, but he wished they hadn't. Dead roaches lay belly up, and mice darted back into their holes in the walls. The stale odor of other wolves, their fear ripe in the air even though they were long gone, made his stomach churn.

The man yanked a lighter from his pocket and lit a lantern. Someone had scratched a symbol into the walls everywhere he looked: a circle with a lotus flower blooming in the center. The lotus was spattered with someone's blood. The light flickered as the man passed by him, kneeling before a tool bag in the corner. "Did your father ever tell you what you are, Gabriel?"

"I-I'm a werewolf. What d-do you mean?" His teeth chattered so badly, he could barely get the words out.

The man's lip curled in revulsion. "No. You're a *hybrid*. Do you know what that is?"

"My mom's a human. My dad's parents were a human and a werewolf. S-So what?" he stammered.

"It means your blood is tainted. You're impure."

Gabe didn't understand. He knew humans at his school who were afraid of werewolves, but he'd never met other werewolves who disliked him.

"That's why I'm going to hurt you." He drew a long, thin blade from the bag.

The sight of it pulled a scream from Gabe's throat. He struggled against the chains, but they wouldn't break.

Smelling his fear, the man bared his teeth. Gabe had never seen a man look so much like a wolf. He came closer, his bare feet stirring up dust. His smile never wavering, he knelt. "Humans take from us. They deny us our pride as wolves. Erase our culture and heritage. Folk like your mother and father, they want to defile the link between us and the goddess herself." Disgust made his lip curl. "Do you know the difference between hybrids and werewolves, Gabriel? You're weak. Want to know why? My kind can heal our wounds. We never suffer long. You?"

Tears blurred Gabe's eyes as the blade glided across his skin, so sharp the skin split at the slightest touch.

That gaunt face split into a grin. "Hybrids bleed. And they don't stop."

That night, Gabe learned monsters were real, and they didn't look at all like his sister's picture books.

The real monsters wore human skin.

The monster cut him, over and over again, until Gabe thought he'd pass out from the pain. He couldn't have been in the basement for more than a couple of hours, but time was distorted, stretching on and on into what felt like years. He missed his mother's kind smile and her warm hugs. He missed his father, the way he'd tousle his hair. He missed playing with Izzie, hearing her laugh...

"Want to go home. I w-want my mom and dad."

"Don't know what to tell you, Gabriel." The monster glared at Gabe from beneath strands of dark hair. "They don't want you, clearly."

"You're lying." Tears pricked his eyes. Why did those words hurt so much worse than the monster's knives?

"Then why aren't they here?"

Why *weren't* they here? Why couldn't they find him?

"'Cause they—they don't know where I am. They'll come. They'll get back at you. My dad's bigger than you, stronger than you. He'll hurt you."

The monster bared his teeth in a smile. "I'll tell you why your parents aren't here, Gabriel. They don't love you. Otherwise, they'd have found you by now. This is where they bring little hybrid boys no one wants anymore."

"Shut up," Gabe growled in a voice he didn't recognize. His gums itched as his fangs lengthened. The bone-deep ache of pain had awoken something within him, something that snarled and made his body thrum with fury.

The monster's eyes narrowed.

Fur blackened Gabe's arms, and a red haze fell over his eyes. "I hate you," he snarled in an animal's voice.

The monster's mouth curled. "Look at this. The little hybrid has bite."

A snarl pulled from Gabe's chest, and he lunged, fangs snapping the air inches from the monster's face. Those hateful eyes widened in shock. Gabe panted and strained against the bindings keeping him in the chair. His claws carved bloody marks in his palms that stung. He hated this man more than anything. He wanted to bite him, rip the flesh from his bones, bathe in his hot life's blood. It scared him, this fury surging from within.

The monster chuckled. "Look at you, losing control. You're damn near feral. Guess there is some wolf in you after all, mutt. What would your parents think if they saw you like this? They'd be so disappointed in you."

His words lashed at Gabe, and he recoiled, whimpering. He was a good wolf. A good son. He wasn't supposed to lose control. He closed his eyes tight, searching wildly for the bonds belonging to his father and mother and Izzie.

Nothing.

There was *nothing there.*

The fury of a feral beast swelled within him, hurling itself against his chest. His hands turned to clawed paws. Blood. He could smell it. His blood, but also the monster's. Hear it pumping in his veins. Lunging, he snapped at the monster with razor fangs. The monster jerked back, shock and awe bright in his wide eyes. Saliva flooded his mouth. He would lap up every drop of blood once he'd torn the flesh of the man's throat like paper.

The monster snarled, "No. No, no, no! You don't get to fight back!" The monster swung, and his ears rang as the monster's knuckles cracked against his nose. "You're weak. You're a mutt. You're nothing!" he screamed, eyes crazed and wild. "I will break you. You will know the despair all hybrids are due for defiling the goddess's gift!"

The monster's claws wrapped around his neck. With a gasp, Gabe broke free of the wolf's hold on his mind. What... what had just happened? He didn't know why his nose was throbbing. It was like he'd blacked out for a few seconds.

The monster was speaking, Gabe realized, but his words were fuzzy and made no sense. He held a phone in his hand, saying something. Then a voice so incredibly familiar brought Gabe out of the haze of agony.

"Stone?" The sound of his father's voice brought tears to Gabe's eyes. "Why are you calling me? What do you want, you damned traitor?"

Stone. *Stone.* The name of the man who used to work with his father. He'd turned his back on the Council when Gabe's dad became the first hybrid to join. He was a hateful fanatic.

"It's not what I want that matters, Manny. Listen closely. I have someone here who wants to say hello." He grabbed Gabe's hair and shook him, snarling, "Talk, mutt."

Gabe choked out, "Papá. Papá! It's me."

"By the goddess… Gabriel! Where are you? Tell me!" He'd never heard his father cry before.

"I don't know! Papá, come find me. He's hurting me. Please!"

The monster pulled the phone away from Gabe and snarled, "Manny, I'm warning you, if you say a word to Hanson, I won't hesitate to kill the brat."

"I won't. I haven't, John, I swear. I promise. I-I'm at the airport now. JFK. I'll come to you, okay? Just tell me where you are."

Laughter rumbled from the monster's sneering lips. "So pitiful! Not so high and mighty, are you now, crossbred dog?"

"John, please." Manuel's voice cracked and broke. "What do you want? Money? I'll give you whatever—"

"It's not money I want, Manny. I want to remind you and the human whore just what happens when you bring hybrid scum into this world."

The phone clattered to the floor. His father started yelling. Gabe gasped as spidery fingers locked around his wrist.

"Are you listening, Manny?"

Gabe thought he'd tolerated the pain the monster had inflicted. He realized he was wrong as his finger bent back and the bone snapped. Gabe screamed. He screamed until his throat was raw. All the hope that had flourished within him upon hearing his father's voice was torn away from him with each bone the monster broke.

"Stop it!" Manuel howled. "Please! John, I'm begging you, leave him alone!"

The monster cackled.

Gabe sobbed until his stomach ached and he vomited, unable to stop shaking.

"I've had my fill," the monster declared. "You want your brat, then come and get what's left of him. I'm in the house at Hackdirt Lane. Get here soon, won't you? The brat's sniveling is chipping away at my patience." He chucked his phone onto the ground and smashed it.

Gabe crumpled with his chin to his chest, tears blurring the bloody mess that was his hand. He couldn't feel anything. In that moment, he was nothing but an aching mass of pain with no room for anything else in his soul.

Time stretched on. It was impossible to tell what hour of the day it was in this dark basement. To Gabe, it was as if he'd been here for a thousand years.

A howl echoed through the forest. The wolf's song lit a spark in Gabe's chest amidst all the darkness, and the bond in Gabe's chest ignited.

"Son. My son. I'm here. I'm coming for you!"

Hope flourished within Gabe again.

The monster grinned. "Daddy's here, boy."

The basement door came crashing open. Sunlight poured into that dark room as a shape came hurtling down the stairs. The monster leaped with a roar and collided with Manuel. Both of them half-shifted, they wrestled, claws slashing and spattering the walls with blood. His father seized a chunk of brick and smashed it into the monster's head. Stone dropped, writhing in agony.

Gabe hardly recognized his father. His eyes were wild and dark, his face gripped by fury. Gabe had expected to weep at the sight of him. Instead he was afraid that if he so much as moved, his father would disappear and he'd be alone again. Then his father tore apart the cuffs binding him with clawed hands and gathered Gabe into his strong, warm arms. He shushed Gabe gently as he whimpered, his hand burning hot with pain.

His father was here. He still loved him. He'd come for him, and the bond between them surged bright, casting away Gabe's despair. Wrapped in the safety of his father's arms, Gabe broke down and clung onto him with his good arm, beside himself when he realized it was over. He was safe at last.

"Come on, mijo. I'm going to get you out of here. You're safe." His father's voice trembled, and he stood.

The monster yanked a pistol from beneath a filthy mattress.

"Run, Papá, run!"

An explosion deafened Gabe. Manuel spun to the right, turning his body to shield Gabe's. His father jumped up the stairs, carrying Gabe toward the dim light of the outside world. They stumbled out into the woods. Rain sprayed Gabe's body, falling so densely it was hard to see where they were going. The forest sprawled in all directions.

Manuel sniffed the air. "This way!" They ran through the woods, and the distant howl of sirens echoed. "We're almost there, mijo! Hold on!" Manuel's feet splashed through the waters of a swollen river. He froze, his face gripped by panic. His car was on the other side of the river, water splashing around the tires. "Shit…" The rain was coming down in torrents. "This wasn't flooded before…"

"Reyes!" Stone's voice was like the roar of a savage beast. He was getting closer.

His father held Gabe tight. "Hold on tight!" Gabe clutched at him, closing his eyes as they waded deep into the river. Waves surged against them, and his father latched onto mossy boulders to stay upright. The water came up to their chests, and the current was like gravity trying to drag them under to a watery death.

Bullets peppered the water behind them. Manuel grunted and stumbled, disappearing beneath the waves. Gabe choked on water and panicked, but his father resurfaced, still holding on to Gabe. Gabe gasped. His father's blood streaked the water. Stone's roar was triumphant. His father's face was pale, his shirt soaked in blood. Manuel held Gabe with one arm and dug his claws into the boulder to keep them both from being swept away.

Gunfire erupted on the opposite bank. The police had arrived and were shooting at Stone as they advanced on the river. Stone, teeth bared in a grin, turned and ran into the woods. Gabe wouldn't see him again for over a decade, but he would haunt Gabe's dreams for years to come.

With a grunt, Manuel heaved Gabe up onto the boulder. Gabe cried in terror as Manuel lost his grip and his father drifted downstream and crashed into another boulder, his claws scraping at the mossy stone. "Take him!" his father cried, choking on water.

"No!" Gabe screamed, struggling against the police as they grabbed his arms and heaved him from the boulder. The officers tried to reach his father, but the river's current was too powerful and his father was too far downstream.

"Get him!" his father called. "Don't let him hurt anyone else!" His eyes landed on Gabe, and he reached out. Gabe kicked and struggled against the officers pulling him from the roaring river. He reached out, screaming for his father.

This was a dream. He knew what would happen next. The river would drag his father under. Gabe would never see him alive again. His body would never be found, lost in the flooded woods forever.

Then the river faded. Gabe stood alone in a black void. His father lay facedown, bloated and unrecognizable. His father's face became a blur and then shifted. His hair changed from black to copper. Freckles mingled with the blood spattered on his cheeks. Gabe wanted to scream, to howl his despair, as before his eyes, his father morphed into Max Gallagher, broken and bloody. But he couldn't summon the strength. His voice was gone.

A pistol clicked behind his head. "It's so easy," crooned a voice that made his hackles rise in fury. "To take love and turn it into a weapon. He died for you, Gabriel. How many others will join him?"

Gabe whirled, and through his tears, Aaron McCready came into focus, grinning down as he pressed the muzzle of his pistol between Gabe's eyes. "So long as you have something to lose, I will take what you love and I will turn it against you."

A deafening bang pulled Gabe back from the depths of his nightmare. Eyes still tightly closed, he thought, *It was a dream. A dream. Thank the goddess.* His eyes opened, and he found his vision blurred with tears.

He blinked and saw a blur of orange and cream. His vision cleared and a wave of relief washed over him when he found Max standing beside the bed, his copper hair haphazardly swept back and still tousled from sleep. His pale and slender upper body was beautifully bare, and blue briefs clung to his hips. Max sighed. "Great." He knelt, and Gabe could hear the sound of ceramic scraping against something. Gabe smelled coffee.

"What happened?" he asked, rubbing his eyes.

Max jumped. "Did I wake you up?" The concern in his honey orange eyes soothed the frantic race of Gabe's heart.

Gabe shrugged. "Did you drop something?"

Max smiled guiltily. "I wanted us to have coffee in bed. I guess we could always shift and drink it off the floor..."

Gabe snorted. "Lie down. I'll make more."

Max shook his head determinedly. "No way! It's your birthday. Relax."

October first. In all the excitement of their mating ceremony, Gabe had forgotten. He sighed. What a great way to start the day. Max left and Gabe slumped against the pillows. Beyond the windows of their home in the countryside of upstate New York, the crows called out to each other. Otherwise, nothing shattered the idyllic quiet of the early morning. Gray clouds on the horizon warned of an impending storm. Gabe tried not to see that as an ill omen.

His fingers wandered over the scars on his arms. Most days, he hardly felt them. Today they itched, and the memory of Stone's blades made him cringe. To soothe himself, he ran his fingers over the mating bite on his neck, which was covered with a bandage and tender to the touch. He managed a smile. Not all scars were painful. Slumping onto the mattress with a groan, he tried to relax and let the tension in his body evaporate. He felt like a rabbit on the run, pursued by demons with fangs and claws that he couldn't shake no matter what.

It was a dream. A dream.

But it was more than that. It was a memory of the day of his father's murder.

I avenged him. Stone's dead.

He shivered, his fangs lengthening. He could still feel Stone's pulse under his fangs, the blood gushing hot across his tongue. The echo of the taste lingered in the back of his throat. Stone was dead and gone—Gabe had ripped him to pieces.

More than that, Gabe had become a monster to kill the monster from his past. He'd grown to twice his height, according to Max, sprouted claws several inches long, and had been built like a bodybuilder covered in black fur. A hulking, bipedal beast. Shifters could assume a full wolf form or grow claws, fangs, and fur in human form.

But that thing he'd become on that hilltop in Vermont... Gabe had never heard of any werewolf taking on a form like that. It hadn't happened since their return home, and Gabe prayed to the goddess that he'd left whatever that beast was to rot with Stone's corpse.

It's over. All over. So why can't I forget?

He'd thought that by taking Stone's life, he'd finally be at peace. The memory of his father's murder would finally fade away.

Because the hunt's not over, growled the wolf. A snarl rumbled in his chest. His claws lengthened, piercing the sheets beneath him. John Stone had been a rabid dog, but Aaron McCready was the one who'd held the leash. Stone and McCready's pure-blood supremacist goals had aligned, and they'd joined forces to rid the Council of its first hybrid councilman. And unlike Stone, McCready was—

"Surprise." Max smiled at him from the doorway. He looked so delectable with his beautiful copper hair artfully messy like he'd run his hands through it, ivory shoulders dotted with freckles, and cute pink nipples right at Gabe's eye level. He was carrying a tray with two mugs of steaming coffee. Gabe sniffed and scented strawberry pancakes and a side of bacon.

It's over, he told the wolf. *It's time to move on.*

Max was all that mattered to him. His father's murder had cast a shadow of vengeance over Gabe's life that had haunted the two years he and Max had been together. It was time to begin their future, time to remember his father as he had been and not as the man who'd been taken from him far too soon. Max deserved a peaceful life after all he'd been through. Gabe would be honest and say that he deserved a slice of newly mated bliss, too.

"Everything smells delicious," Gabe assured him with a smile, motioning his mate close. Max set the tray down on his side of the bed and leaned over. Nestling his nose into Max's neck, Gabe breathed in deep. "The food too."

Max laughed as their lips met and the sweet yet tart taste of strawberries danced across Gabe's mouth. He tongued a plump lower lip, craving more of the sweet taste that was so natural on his mate. It warmed his heart that Max had made such a gesture for him. Max hadn't even known just how badly Gabe had needed normalcy this morning. As always, his mate had caught him when he was falling.

"How many strawberries made it into the pancakes?" Gabe asked, sucking at Max's lower lip.

"Not many," Max admitted.

Craving a taste, Gabe's tongue wandered past Max's lips, licking into his mouth. Max sighed, lowering his hips so their bodies could touch. His skin warmed Gabe to the bone. Running his hands down Max's back, he dipped his fingers beneath the skintight briefs clinging to his hips. He squeezed handfuls of Max's round ass, enjoying the way his mate's tongue tangled with his in retaliation.

"Don't you want food?" Max panted, abruptly breaking the kiss.

Gabe didn't want Max's kind gesture to go to waste or be unrewarded. "Oh yes, mi corazón. Probably not the same food you're thinking of." He squeezed those perfectly round buttocks for emphasis. Max pushed his hips back and gave his ass an encouraging little wiggle. Gabe gave Max's ass a firm slap and the gasp he earned set his blood aflame. Closing his eyes, he felt his blood simmering as smiling lips fluttered over his neck, lingering on the bandage that concealed the mating bite Max had left there the night of their ceremony.

"Does it hurt?" Max asked.

"A little." Gabe's hand wandered over the scar on Max's neck where he'd claimed him as his mate. Max's bite had healed and scarred rapidly under the moonlight while Gabe's was still sore. He didn't mind feeling Max's bite. Hybrids healed much more slowly than pure-blooded werewolves, but Max differed from most hybrids. That was assuming Max *was* a hybrid.

Max was a child of the She-Wolf, Amaris, the lunar deity and creator of werewolves. That connection gave him healing abilities most hybrids lacked, among other interesting talents like the ability to control gravity and water. Gabe wasn't too surprised. He'd always known his mate was unique. It felt nice to confirm his beliefs. How many guys could say they were mated to the son of a goddess?

He paused, his lips parted against the mating scar on Max's neck. He squeezed Max's rear thoughtfully. Should he ask? He was burning to know. Their ceremony and the past two days had been wonderful, full of nothing but fucking like bunnies, eating when they were too tired to keep going at it, or running in the woods together as wolves... and fucking there beneath the stars. He didn't want to ruin it by potentially upsetting Max.

"Are you feeling okay?" he asked before he'd fully decided.

Max brushed copper curls from his forehead and smiled, sweet and dizzying. "I'm great." Then he understood. His smile slipped from his face, and the light in his eyes disappeared. He sat up out of Gabe's reach. "I'm fine, Gabe."

Sitting up as well, Gabe gripped Max's hips, caressing his hip bone with his thumb. "You have every right to be upset. It's not every day people are told they're adopted when they're twenty-one."

Max tried to smile. It came out as more of a grimace. "My mom did what she thought was right. Our lives were hard. I wish I hadn't asked. I could have gone the rest of my life not knowing my own biological mother abandoned me."

Gabe winced. He thought Max had just made it pretty clear how he felt. "You don't know that Amaris abandoned you."

Max snorted, his head rolling back to expose his slender throat. "She sure as hell wasn't there, was she? Amaris. My 'mother.'" He spat the words like they were poison.

"We don't know what the story is," Gabe said, trying to make amends for ruining the morning. He nuzzled into Max's neck, kissing and licking his soft skin.

Max wriggled away, straddling Gabe's knees. "Yeah, we do. Richard tortured me. The Moonborn cult abducted me. Amaris is a fucking goddess, Gabe, and she didn't do shit. If she'd loved me, she would have helped me." His voice trembled and broke. He blinked fast, his eyes gleaming. Gabe could hit himself.

"Max, maybe those powers you have are a gift from her?"

Max's nostrils flared. "I don't want to talk about this right now. Or ever."

"Yeah. Yeah, of course. I'm sorry, mi amor." Gabe's arms went around Max's shoulders, sighing his contentment as Max kissed down his neck to his chest. His mate's mouth was so warm, the sheets so soft beneath him. He closed his eyes, finally feeling at peace for the first time since his nightmare.

"Since we're talking about feelings now, are *you* okay?" Max frowned at him.

Gabe forced his eyes to open wider. "I'm fine." He didn't want Max to think he wasn't enjoying his attention.

"Now who's deflecting?" Max giggled at his wide eyes. "Did you have trouble sleeping?" Worried eyes flitted over his features as Max's chin settled on his chest.

"I'm *fine*." Gabe smiled to reassure him.

Max poked the bag under Gabe's eye. "A nightmare?"

His mouth went dry, remembering those vacant orange eyes, the blood pooling around him, Aaron McCready's slimy voice in his ear. He barely repressed a shiver.

Max nuzzled into his neck, his fingers intertwining with Gabe's. Their joined hands rose and fell on Gabe's chest with each breath. "I'm safe. We both are."

Gabe's arms went around his shoulders and held him tight.

For how long?

"It's Alpha Hanson. He's been killed." The memory of Ben's voice filled his mind and made his stomach churn.

Alpha Hanson had been leader of the Council of Lycanthrope Affairs, a governing body for shifters in the USA. Hanson's whole family had been killed, murdered by Aaron McCready.

Under normal circumstances with the Alpha dead, McCready, as Hanson's beta, would be set to inherit leadership of the Council after Hanson's funeral. But Hanson had been murdered, and McCready had the Wargs of the Apocalypse, a terrorist group, at his back. Until recently, McCready had lacked the numbers to challenge the might of the Council, but when he'd spread word of Max's divine powers among fanatics, bigoted werewolves had flocked to join his cause overnight. He planned to take control of the Council by force.

"I know you don't believe me." Max sighed.

Gabe planted a kiss on the milky skin of Max's neck, his lips drifting over the scar of his mating bite. "I'll believe it when the slimeball's dead."

Max leaned their foreheads together. "Let's not worry about it. The moonblade is destroyed. He can't hurt me... Well, not in the way he wanted to."

Gabe took some relief from that news. The moonblade was an evil weapon, created to carve out the soul of a werewolf without destroying it and take possession of it. McCready and John Stone had tried and failed to use Max's soul to open the way to the She-Wolf's realm and claim the power of a goddess's soul. But McCready had other ways of hurting them, especially if he took control of the Council.

Max's gentle lips brushed Gabe's mouth. The touch of Max's hand soothed the agitated growl in the back of his throat. "We're safe, Gabe."

For now, he thought but said nothing, caressing Max's lips with his own to keep from ruining the moment.

CHAPTER 2

THE HUNT IS OVER

To Gabe's delight, Max threw a party for him and invited their pack from the Lycanthrope Protection Agency. It was as much a birthday party as a housewarming party; Gabe and Max had only recently moved into a beautiful countryside home near the village of Millbrook in anticipation of their future together as mates.

Max grilled burgers in the backyard and Gabe chopped tomatoes and cut fresh cheddar into thin slices, both from one of the many local farms. His eyes lingered on the scars on his knuckles from the day when Stone had broken his fingers. He was lucky he hadn't been crippled for life or suffered any lasting side effects. At least, physical side effects. It was the scars below his skin that still ached at the memory whenever his nightmares forced him to revisit those agonizing hours he'd spent in the dark.

He breathed in deep and sharp, smelling the house and the smoky aroma of the grill outside.

I'm not in that basement anymore. I'm here. With Max.

And it was here he would stay. He wouldn't let anything come between him and Max again. He'd promised. Although he hadn't always been good about keeping his promises, this was one he would keep.

Gravel crunched in the driveway beyond the front door, and the rhythmic beat of hip-hop abruptly cut off. Gabe grinned. Ryan was here. He answered the door before his friend could buzz. Ryan Kelly was clad in a bulky sweatshirt with the logo of the Timber Wolves, his favorite football team, on it. "Hang on, I'll greet you when I can see ya," Ryan said, rubbing at the fog on his glasses that had accumulated in the crisp fall air. "Oh, there you are! Hey, man!"

Gabe pulled him in for a few hearty claps on the back.

"I brought the good stuff," Ryan said, handing over a bottle of peanut butter whiskey, Gabe's favorite.

"Knew there was a reason we're still friends." Gabe took the bottle away to open it.

"Right?" Ryan put his hands on his hips and surveyed the home. "Wow. I shoulda mated with you. Nice den."

Gabe snorted as he poured them both a splash of whiskey on the rocks. The whiskey was sweet enough to drink straight, but Gabe liked his with ice. "It is a beauty, isn't it?" He couldn't help being pleased with their choice, especially since Max loved it as much as he did.

"Where's Max?"

"Grilling. We got some elk burgers, steak, some salad." Gabe's phone buzzed, and he checked his messages. Izzie and his mom were on their way and Ben needed directions. Chuckling, Gabe called Ben. "Hey, Viejo. Lost?"

"Everything looks the same out here. Don't know how people can get around."

"Where are you?"

"Hell if I know. I'm starin' at a bunch of horses."

Gabe smiled. That described every house for miles.

"Helpful, huh? Hang on. I see a number. 3059."

"We're the next house over then, about fifteen minutes."

Fifteen minutes later, Ben Stroud was knocking on his door wearing a gray turtleneck under a leather jacket and a red skullcap on his bald head. Zach DeShawn loomed tall over his shoulder in a denim jacket. Gabe welcomed them in, and Ben shrugged off his jacket.

"Twenty-nine," Ben said, clapping Gabe on both his shoulders. "Feels like yesterday I was new to the city and your pa invited me over."

"Far cry from the kid you found in that dank alley nursing his wounds after a brawl, huh?" Gabe smiled, though the memory weighed on him. Ben had been a friend of Gabe's family, and he'd been there for him in the days after his father's murder. The older wolf had saved his life. "Let's be honest. I'm still alive because of you." He didn't know what might have become of him if he'd continued down the bloody path of angry vigilantism, though perhaps calling himself a vigilante was being too kind. Looking back, he'd been nothing but an angry kid filling the void his father's death had left in his heart with violence.

"Nah. You're still a bit of a punk ass." Ben smiled beneath his neat beard. He patted Gabe's cheek, his silver eyes as bright as moonlight on the still surface of a lake. "You've come a long way, kid. I'm proud of you."

Gabe leaned his cheek on Ben's shoulder as the older man pulled him into a brief but tight hug. His body was firm with muscle, and Gabe felt a sense of security. If the afterlife existed, he hoped his father was proud of him. He was glad his father hadn't seen what had become of him after his death. The lectures he would have gotten... the disappointed looks... He'd let his own mother down. Thanks to Ben Stroud, he was on the right path again.

"Have you heard from the Council?"

Ben untangled himself and brushed past. "Hey, where's the bathroom around here?"

Gabe didn't miss the way Ben dodged his question. "Down the hall over there."

Ryan offered Ben a whiskey, but Ben shuffled off to the restroom. Zach smiled and raised a big hand. He looked different somehow, but Gabe couldn't put his finger on it. Zach removed his beanie and Gabe groaned. "You cut your hair!" Zach had been growing his hair out in long, beautiful braids since their days as agents-in-training at the Lycanthrope Academy.

Now he sported a sleek buzz cut that was curly on top and short on the sides.

Zach grinned sheepishly. "Yeah. Did it myself too!"

"I can tell," Ryan said, then grinned to show he was kidding.

Zach frowned, touching his hair. "I don't have any razor burn, do I?" He circled so Gabe could get a look at the back where the hair faded cleanly.

"Man. You grew that hair out for ages. It's different, but I like it."

"I know, I know. You told me you liked it, so I thought I'd grow it out some." Zach shrugged. Gabe swallowed, suddenly warm all over. He looked away from Zach, his chest tight. They'd just started hooking up when Zach had begun growing his hair out. "Just… felt like a change, I guess. Time to move on, try something new. You know?" There was something melancholic about his voice. Gabe couldn't look at him, sensing so much more than Zach let on.

Before Zach could squeeze past, Gabe grabbed his arm. "Thanks for coming."

"'Course. I wouldn't miss it."

Gabe held tighter. "For everything, Zach. For dragging me home to my ma after all those stupid fights with lycanthrophobic jerks. For looking after Max while I was gone, keeping him safe. For loving me when it was too damn hard to do it myself." He wished he could have given this man everything he wanted, and he'd tried as best he could. But Zach was right. It was time for new beginnings, and he hoped to Amaris that Zach found real, lasting love this time around.

Zach smiled, his chiseled features soft and warm. For a moment, Gabe remembered why he'd believed he could fall in love with Zach. "I should thank you. If I hadn't met you, I never would have joined the LPA. I'd be stuck under my parents' thumbs and miserable."

"Huh. Guess I was good for something after all." Gabe slapped Zach's shoulder.

"Zach," Ryan called, waving a bottle of Gabe's favorite whiskey. "Pour you a glass?"

"Sure thing." Zach shot Gabe a smile and squeezed his shoulder before joining Ryan at the bar.

Gabe's sister, Isabella, arrived with their mother, Veronica, just as Max finished the burgers. Izzie had brought a housewarming present of tequila and margarita mixes. "Who wants margaritas?" she called.

Veronica had brought some fall vegetables they could plant in the backyard. "I know, you boys like your burgers and steaks, but the human in you needs a balanced diet." Gabe kissed her on the cheek. His mother frowned, poking at the bags under his eyes. "Have you been getting enough rest?"

Ryan hooted. "Not since he and Max mated, that's for sure!"

Gabe rolled his eyes. "Yes, Ma. Thanks for the veggies."

She smiled and Gabe couldn't help feeling grateful that he was still worthy of her smiles. There'd been a time when all he'd seemed to do was make her yell or cry. He hadn't been a good son after his father died. "Thanks for putting up with me."

Veronica cocked a brow. "Gabriel, you're my son. Putting up with you is my pleasure."

Still, there was a twinge of guilt in his chest like the jab of an icepick. That nightmare had made old buried memories resurface. He managed a smile, but before he could walk by, her hands on his shoulders steered him back into place. "Your father would have understood. What happened was hard on all of us, especially you."

Gabe shook his head. "He was your husband." His pain wasn't anything compared to hers.

"But you were hurt, Gabriel. Emotionally and physically. Sometimes, I wished I'd been more understanding."

"I wasn't exactly easy to live with." The nightmares had haunted him for months. He'd wake up paralyzed with fear, believing he was still in that basement at Stone's mercy. Some nights, he hadn't even been able to scream as fear had left him frozen beneath his blankets, certain Stone was hiding in the shadows of his room. When the fear had become too much to bear, his wolf had taken over, snarling at anyone who'd tried to breach the threshold of his room, unable to recognize even his own mother when the fear had driven him into a frenzy. He'd become especially protective of Izzie, sleeping as a wolf beside her bed and growling at any noises beyond their room.

She kissed his cheek, a twinkle in her eyes. "My handsome boy. You took a terrible tragedy and made something beautiful out of it. Your father would be proud of who you are, Gabriel. I know I am."

Gabe let her pull him into a hug and squeezed her shoulders.

Kendra arrived bearing a strawberry shortcake from Gabe's favorite bakery in Manhattan. The pack gathered around the table and devoured Max's elk burgers and filet mignon grilled to perfection. Gabe looked around at the pack: Izzie and Ryan giggling and raucous from enough alcohol to kill a normal human; Zach complimenting Max on the steaks; Ben nursing his whiskey; and Kendra and Veronica babbling about the days when Gabe, Max, and Izzie were pups. None of them brought up the upcoming funeral or McCready's imminent inauguration as Alpha of the Council. It felt good not to worry about it for now.

Gabe smiled, his heart warm with love for his rowdy pack.

After dinner, Gabe wanted to put on a cheesy horror movie to ring in the spooky season, so he picked a stereotypical werewolf horror movie. Everyone groaned at the portrayal of the wolf man.

"So stupid!" Ryan said, grinning despite his frustration. "They didn't even cast a real werewolf to play him!"

Izzie wrinkled her nose. "Look at that makeup. He looks more like he's suffering from some disease."

Max leaned his head on Gabe's shoulder. "Why were werewolves always villains in these old movies?"

"Because of medieval wolf-hating propaganda," Zach answered. "Real wolves aren't assholes. Don't know why everyone just assumes werewolves would be any different."

Veronica scoffed. "It's a product of its time, kids. There are tons of movies with good werewolves nowadays."

"I don't look that ugly when I'm half-shifted, do I?" Gabe asked, nudging Max.

Ben sighed beside Gabe. He'd noticed Ben had been doing that a lot tonight. "Need to put some more drink in you, Viejo."

Humming, Ben stared disinterestedly at the screen. "Tomorrow's Hanson's funeral service. Guess it's weighing on me. What will become of human and werewolf relations once McCready's in charge?"

Gabe hadn't known Hanson very well, and to be honest, a part of him still felt bitter toward the deceased Alpha for separating him and Max. Especially since Hanson had been ready to trade Max to McCready in exchange for his own family's lives. "The Council won't let him get away with Hanson's murder. They'll challenge his authority for sure."

"I bet some will be all too happy to embrace his bigoted ideology," Max murmured, clearly remembering the less-than-stellar welcome some councilmembers had shown him and Gabe when they'd visited.

Gabe's skin prickled. His claws lengthened and his stomach swirled with anticipation. What he wouldn't give to bring the man who'd arranged for his father's murder to justice.

"Sorry." Max clasped his hand. "I shouldn't have said anything."

Ben said, "There's nothing we can do about it. He'll be surrounded by councilmembers, many of whom likely support him openly now that Hanson is gone."

Gabe's mind drifted away from the movie, and he hardly felt the warmth of Max's thigh against his leg. He'd promised himself his quest for vengeance had ended with Stone, for both his sake and Max's.

But knowing that McCready had also had a role in his father's murder had changed things.

He couldn't go charging off again, not without Max. He'd made a promise that his place was here with him, no matter what.

"You okay?" Max's voice rumbled, warm and soothing in his ear.

Gabe forced a smile and dropped an arm around Max's shoulders. "Thanks for tonight. I'm feeling very lucky."

Max smiled, and Gabe closed his eyes as their lips met.

He had to be okay. For Max, for their future together.

The hunt was over.

Chapter 3

TORN IN TWO

Max turned his face to the moon above. Although it was two days after the full moon, it glowed, still nearly perfectly full. He rubbed the mating scar on his neck, the one scar he had that didn't hold a painful memory but a loving one. He had a wonderful life. He had the man of his dreams as his mate. A pack who supported and loved him. A mother who hadn't abandoned him.

A mother who'd kept secrets from him.

No. He couldn't do that. That wasn't fair. His mother had done the best she could in a trying situation. She'd worked several jobs at a time to keep a roof over their heads after his cowardly father... *adopted* father... ran out on them.

So what if she'd waited until he was twenty-one to tell him he was adopted?

Okay. That was a bit... strange.

Or maybe he was just stupid for not having known. They looked nothing alike; Max didn't have his mother's blonde hair or blue eyes. He looked nothing like his father either, who had been as dark-haired as the depths of his black soul. Max had never really questioned it. Besides, red hair was a recessive trait. Maybe his parents weren't redheaded, but maybe their ancestors had been.

He'd never questioned it because his mother hadn't kept *secrets* from him. Neither of them had, the one exception being that Max had hidden Richard's abuse from her. So really, how perfect was Max himself? He'd lied. So had his mother. They were both guilty of something.

So why could he hardly stand to look her in the eyes?

Max paced, the grass tickling his bare feet. He shouldn't be angry at her. She hadn't abandoned him like Amaris had. She loved him. And he loved her. Nothing could change that.

But she'd *lied*. She'd had no intention of telling him the truth.

A growl spilled from Max's throat. At a loss, he looked back up at the moon.

He couldn't decide what made him angrier: that she'd lied to him or that he knew. He knew the truth now, that he'd been abandoned in a field, unwanted, with never a thought spared for him by his birth mother. He knew, and he could never unlearn the truth.

Max closed his eyes tight. A lance of pain drove into his heart, and his eyes stung.

She hadn't wanted him. She'd left him without a second thought, just like his adopted father. He'd needed her when times had been hard, when he'd been hurting and suffering, and she hadn't been there. She was a goddess. Surely there was something she could have done.

And this is why Mom didn't tell me, Max thought, wiping his eyes stubbornly. *Because she knew I'm not mature enough to handle it.*

"Max?" He turned. Gabe slid open the door and waved. "Kendra's leaving."

Max nodded at the grass. Gabe's smile fell, and he closed the door.

In the sky above, the moon stared down at him, so near and yet so far away. Max squeezed his fists together. "Couldn't you have done something? Anything?" His voice echoed in the quiet of the night. The wind blew, whistling against the tree trunks. Coyotes howled. It was impossible to tell how close they were when sound echoed for miles in the quiet countryside. Max itched to howl with them. To shed his human skin and escape his angst-ridden thoughts.

The door opened and closed. Footsteps whispered through the grass. He smelled her before she came into view. Lavender perfume and coconut shampoo, his mother's signature scent.

His mother stopped beside him, wrapped in a quilted beige shawl. The wind stirred her blonde bob. She turned her face to the sky and breathed in deep followed by a long exhale. "It's so perfect out here."

Max hummed, managing a smile.

"I miss the country. I love the city. Everything's there. But the wolf in me always feels the happiest among nature." She gasped when the coyotes howled. "Isn't that amazing? You don't hear that in the city."

Max nodded, digging his toes in the cool soil.

She was watching him, her intense blue gaze prickling over his skin. "You're angry at me, aren't you?"

Max didn't know what to say. When she'd told him during the mating ceremony, he had felt nothing except guilt for being the reason his mom and dad—his *adoptive* parents—had drifted apart. Now he'd had a couple of days for the shock to set in, to really think about it. "Were you ever going to tell me?"

She closed her eyes, her face downturned toward the grass. She hugged her shawl tighter around herself. After a long moment, she said, "I was adopted, you know."

Max's heart skipped.

His mother stared up into the moon's cold, pale face. "The way I found out was... well, it was less than ideal. My mother, like me, couldn't have children. My father didn't want to adopt, but he went along with it for my mother. He never took to me as his daughter. Acted like I was lucky they'd even given me a thought."

"How did you find out?" Max asked, trying to ignore the stab of surprise. She'd never told him this either.

"My father told me when I was sixteen. Angrily." Her lips thinned. She brushed away a lock of hair from her face, trying for composure. "It was the most traumatic moment of my life, and I held on to that trauma for a very long time. He made it clear to me I was no daughter of his."

Max had never met any of his grandparents. Knowing why ached.

"I'm so sorry, Mom," he whispered.

She turned toward him, reaching out a hand, then thought better of it. "Max, it destroyed me for a long time. I was so scared that if you knew, it would destroy you too. That you would… see me differently." She blinked fast, her blue eyes glistening. Max swallowed the lump in his throat.

He felt so awful. Because he did see her differently. She was his mother. But she wasn't. Because his real mother hadn't wanted him. And knowing that hurt. It hurt like nothing else.

"Do you hate me?" she whispered. She sniffed and wiped her eyes with the back of her hand.

Max opened his mouth but couldn't speak. No, he meant to say. But he couldn't. Because he hated this. All of this. He hated Kassandra for telling him about the prophecy of his birth. He hated Amaris for abandoning him. And he hated his mother for telling him. Hated her for not telling him.

It was such a fucking mess, and he couldn't parse through it. Not right now.

"Max." She clutched his arm. "Please. You can be as angry as you want, but please tell me I'm still your mother."

He tried, but only a choked noise came out. She was. She *was*. She was his mother in the only way that mattered, because she'd loved him and cared for him. Because she'd stayed. She'd given him a home and a mother's love.

But why hadn't Amaris been able to do that for him?

He wished more than anything that he didn't know.

Knowing had ruined everything.

"I need to…" Max sucked in a gulp of air. He turned away. "I need to go. I can't, I—I can't."

Without another look at her wounded, tear-stained face, Max peeled off his clothes and dropped to all fours. The wolf burst from his skin, and he ran, leaving his clothes and his human thoughts behind. The wind tore through his fur and stung his eyes. The moon burned, bright and blinding. He wanted to rip his skin off so he could no longer feel the moon's caress. He wanted to burrow beneath the ground and disappear into the dark.

All his sorrow and confusion spilled from his heart in a howl that echoed over the treetops. Then the wolf took over and Max drifted in a sea of instincts. He drowned in the urge to sniff and hunt and run, let it wash over him like a wave and submerge him. Until all he cared about was—

A rabbit.

He smelled a rabbit! Soft and fat. So fast, so fun to chase!

It saw him and ran, and the wolf gave chase. He loved to run. He loved to chase and bite.

He caught it. Its neck crunched between his jaws. Its blood was hot and delicious. He ate until his stomach felt fit to burst.

Then he found himself a nice, cool patch of leaves to lie upon. He circled, kicking away leaves and stones, surveying the area for predators. Lying down, he listened to the sounds of the forest. The call of a bird. The scurrying of mice. They were too small to eat. The howl of—wolves? Pack? No. Not pack. Others. He growled.

The moon glowed in the sky above, bathing the wolf in its light. There came a tugging in his mind. Something sad. Something that ached. He ignored it and slept.

THE PARTY ENDED LATE after going well into the night. Gabe kept glancing at the door, wondering where Max had gone. His mate's mother had come inside about an hour ago, her eyes wet and red. Max hadn't returned. She said he'd gone hunting. Gabe sighed. Max wasn't taking the news of his adoption well at all.

The back door slid open. Max stumbled in, his eyes heavy and his hair bedraggled. He smelled wild, like the outdoors and freshly killed prey.

"Have fun out there?" Ben, the last to leave, was tying his scarf in the doorway.

Max picked a shard of bone from his teeth. He smelled like a rabbit.

Ben smiled warmly. "Thanks for the evening." He surveyed them, his eyes warm and full of affection. "Well. Goodnight." He opened his arms. Max jumped in for a hug.

"Jeez. What'd you roll in out there, Max?" Ben waved him away, pinching his nose.

Gabe chuckled. "Since when did you get so touchy-feely, Viejo?"

"Shut up and get in here."

Gabe put his arms around Ben and held tight.

"Know I don't say this often enough." Ben sounded guilty as he met their eyes. "But you and the pack, you're family to me."

"You too," Max said.

Gabe cleared his throat, looking down at his feet to hide his smile.

"And you." Ben punched Gabe in the chest. "I wasn't sure you'd last in the LPA. I thought you'd be here one day, gone the next. I'm proud of you and all the work you've accomplished with us."

Gabe wrestled Ben into a hearty embrace. "Thanks for giving me a chance."

"Best decision I ever made." Ben's eyes twinkled as he clapped Gabe on the shoulder.

He frowned, alarmed by how emotional Ben was getting. "You good, Viejo?"

"Yeah, yeah." Ben sniffed and wiped his eyes. "Birthdays get me all mushy. You should see me at my sons' birthdays." Ben grabbed his scuffed-up leather jacket and threw it on. "Night, kids. It's been real." Those silver eyes drank them in. Blinking hard, Ben shut the door with a sniff.

Gabe scoffed. "He's so cheesy."

Max chuckled as he locked the door. "He was a little dramatic." Max watched as Ben's headlights lit the way down the winding road, illuminating the trees. "He's probably just worried about the funeral tomorrow."

Gabe sighed, his arm winding around Max's shoulders. "I'd love to go, believe me, Lobito. But I guess it would be bad manners if I tore out McCready's throat at the service." The muscles in Gabe's arm tightened. He really wanted to go, was fighting with everything he had to contain his wolf's bloodlust for the man who'd ruined his family. As if sensing his anger, Max turned, his arms encircling Gabe's chest, his fingers curling in his sweater. "Stay. Ben's right—going after McCready now would be a terrible idea."

Gabe sighed but couldn't stifle a growl, and Max shivered, feeling it too. Gabe murmured, "I should try. For my father."

Max's claws came out, and he tightened his grip on Gabe's shirt as if fearing he'd run off. "Your father wouldn't want you needlessly risking your life, Gabe. Please. Don't be reckless. Stay."

Gabe chuckled, guiding Max's head to his chest. "Stay? I'm not going anywhere. Hell, McCready probably expects me to turn up. Gotta make things challenging for him, don't I?"

Max eyed him warily. "Don't make me tie you down to the bed."

Gabe barked out a laugh. "Careful. It doesn't sound like such a bad thing when you say it." He planted a kiss on Max's forehead. "Speaking of dramatics." He plucked a leaf from Max's hair and tried to tame his messy locks by running his fingers through them. "Where'd you go?"

Max's face turned surly. He sat on the counter barstool and let Gabe pick twigs and leaves out of his copper curls. "For a run." Max leaned in toward him, and he recoiled.

"You stink, Lobito. What *did* you roll around in?"

A shrug. "Beats me."

Max smelled like dirt and leaves, but he also smelled like roadkill. His wolf wanted to come out and roll around all over Max, cover them both in the scent of the wild. But the human in Gabe had a little more class than that.

"Sorry. I know, I stink. I really needed it."

Gabe believed him. Max hadn't looked so downcast in a long time. Everything he thought he knew about himself had been flipped on its head. Tilting Max's chin up toward him, he met orange eyes that lacked their usual spark. His mate shivered as Gabe ran his thumb over Max's plump lower lip. Max parted his lips, nibbling gently on Gabe's thumb. Heart aching, Gabe wished he had the perfect words to say to heal Max's pain.

"Did you know?" Max asked.

Gabe frowned.

"That she wasn't my birth mother. Did you ever suspect?"

He cast his mind back to the day he'd first met Kendra Gallagher. "I thought you two looked different, but I didn't think much of it."

Max sighed. "I feel so stupid."

"She loves you, Max. You know that, right?"

Max turned his head away and Gabe flinched. Yeah. Not the right thing to say.

"If she loved me, she'd have told me the truth. Or... or maybe just not told me at all."

Gabe frowned. "Which is it?"

"Both?" Max growled, running a hand through his hair and dislodging a twig. "I hate her for not telling me. I hate her for telling me. I... I wish I didn't know. I wish I could look at her and believe without any doubt that she was my real mother."

"She is!" Gabe grasped his shoulders. "Max, she's your mother in every way that counts. Just like this pack is your family in all the ways that matter. Because we love you. Because we stood by you."

Max blinked fast and bowed his head. "I know. Shit. I sound so ungrateful. I didn't mean to be."

Gabe framed Max's face in his hands, thumbs smudging away the tears on his face. "No. No, you have every right to feel the way you do. I didn't mean to imply that you don't. I'm sorry."

Max's long, slender arms went around Gabe. He opened his legs so Gabe could nestle close, their bodies touching, and parted his lips against Gabe's neck. The warmth of Max's body, as aromatic as he was, made Gabe heady with desire.

"Max, take all the time you need to process this. Hell, you could even get answers yourself if you really want to."

Max's breath hitched and he shook his head violently, pushing Gabe away. "No way. Like hell I'll ever go to Amaris for anything. She doesn't deserve a second of my time or energy."

Gabe raised his hands. "Fine, Max, fine!" Max was stubborn as all hell, and everything Gabe said was the wrong thing. "I don't know what the hell to say, all right? I don't know how to fix this."

Max laughed softly. He hopped off the barstool and put his arms around Gabe. "You can't, love. You can't fix this. I'm going to be pissed until I'm not anymore. Things will be awkward as hell between Mom and me. But it'll pass. Eventually." He sighed. "Everything's changed."

Gabe took his hand and kissed the back of his elegant fingers. "Not everything."

Max managed a smile. Leaning in to kiss the crook of his neck, Gabe enjoyed the sigh he coaxed from Max's lips and the way he angled his neck, silently asking for more. Gabe's hands were cold, so he warmed them beneath the front of Max's sweater. Gasping when Gabe's cold fingers pinched and tweaked his nipples, Max whined and rocked his hips against him.

"Come here. It's time to unwrap my best present yet."

Gabe gripped the backs of Max's thighs, and he jumped, twining his legs around Gabe's waist. Their lips collided, noses bumping, and he groaned deep into Gabe's mouth. The sound ignited Gabe's blood, and he parted his lips and swallowed it down, pushing his tongue into Max's mouth to taste him. He tasted like blood.

Gabe pulled away and made a face. "Mi amor, don't take this the wrong way, but..."

Max grinned. "I'll shower. Join me?"

Oh, Gabe loved Max with every fiber of his being. "Hell yes." He set Max down. Taking his hand, Max led the way to the en suite bathroom upstairs. The tile was cold under their feet but when Max turned on the showerhead, heat filled the room.

Max brushed his teeth, spitting into the sink, then rinsed. Gabe was already sweating as the warmth of the steam seeped through his sweater, but his temperature climbed even more as Max caressed the hollow of his throat with his warm velvet lips, licking a wet stripe up his Adam's apple.

Soon Max was pressing a smoldering kiss to Gabe's mouth, his eager hands bunching up the hem of Gabe's sweater.

He hated to undress Max—he'd looked so good all evening in his indigo sweater that complemented his orange locks—but he still peeled Max's sweater over his head. "Too many clothes," Gabe chided, biting Max's lower lip in punishment.

"You're no better," Max growled, tugging Gabe's jeans down to his knees.

Gabe chucked his sweater over his head, leaving his upper body exposed to the warmth of the shower steam. He'd love to banter with Max, but there was a better use for his mouth and tongue. Once they were both naked, Gabe led Max beneath the blissfully hot shower spray, pushed him up against the tiled wall, and claimed his mouth.

Whimpering into the kiss, Max rocked his hips, dragging their erections together. A shudder racked Gabe's body, and he squeezed Max's ass in reward. Gabe broke the kiss to catch his breath, then grabbed a bottle of shampoo, applying a dollop to his fingers. He worked his hands gently through Max's hair, massaging his scalp. Max tilted his head back, his heavy-lidded eyes gazing into Gabe's. Soapy bubbles ran down Max's gleaming chest, catching in light ginger fuzz.

Grabbing a washcloth, Gabe liberally applied some bodywash and ran the cloth over Max's chest and perky nipples. He claimed Max's mouth, growling when Max claimed his mouth in return, fucking into it with his tongue in hungry, possessive swipes. Max curled his fingers in Gabe's hair, claws pricking his scalp. He rocked his body against Gabe's, urging him to give him more. Not wanting to deny him, Gabe slid the washcloth down Max's chest and over his stomach until he was kneeling in front of him.

Panting, Max leaned his head against the tile, gripping tight to Gabe's hair. The tile was hard beneath Gabe's knees, but he had an eyeful of Max's cock and the view was worth any discomfort. "Turn around," Gabe rasped.

Moaning, Max obliged and rewarded Gabe with his second favorite view. Grabbing handfuls of his ass, Gabe squeezed hard, enjoying the way Max clenched his buttocks under Gabe's hands. Gabe spread him wide, unable to stifle a groan at the view of Max's pretty hole. Max's hips arched off the tiled wall, and he barely stifled a whimper as Gabe put his head between his cheeks, licking his tightly puckered hole while massaging Max's heavy testicles.

The sounds Max made were filthy. Enjoying his little moans and breathless sighs, Gabe entered him with his fingers, swooning at the tight heat that enveloped them. "Fuck. I could watch this forever, mi amor. I love the way your greedy hole takes my fingers, my cock." Gabe spread his fingers wide, stretching him open. Max's body quivered. He was stroking himself, enjoying this every bit as much as Gabe was.

His mate was close. He was making those noises he made before he came, desperate and unhinged. Gabe withdrew his fingers and gripped Max's hips. "Turn around. Let me see you when you come for me."

Max turned. His eyes were dark and glassy, his face flushed a beautiful pink. One hand worked his cock while the other played with his nipples.

Gabe leaned in and opened his mouth, moaning at the taste of Max's cock. He loved the way Max filled his mouth, loved his earthy taste.

Shuddering, Max's fingers curled in Gabe's hair, his claws biting into his scalp. Max rocked his hips, pushing himself in and out of Gabe's mouth as Gabe moaned, loving the way Max used him in wild, mindless thrusts. His mate panted, honey orange eyes dark and lustful, and his head fell back against his shoulders, his nails driving into Gabe's scalp. Biting his lip, Max stifled his breathless moans as he finished. With one long final suck to Max's softening cock, Gabe swallowed, enjoying the beautiful flush on Max's cheeks.

They left the shower wrapped in towels and shivered. Gabe had forgotten to turn on the heat. Seeking warmth, they lay down on the faux fur rug in their bedroom while Gabe threw some logs in the hearth, lit the fire, and filled the room with the smoky aroma of burning wood.

They sprawled on the soft rug together, warmed by the crackling flames nearby. Max smiled. "Your hair is graying." He ran his fingers through Gabe's hair for emphasis.

He planted a kiss to Max's inner thigh. "Used to think I'd rather die than turn thirty." Now he was just excited for the future they'd share. "Still gonna love me if I go silver?"

Max looked hurt he'd asked, even as a joke. He pulled Gabe to him and kissed him hard on the mouth. "Of course."

"Even if I'm bald, like Ben? You know that's why he shaved his head, right?"

Max snorted. "He said he did it because it was stylish."

"Nope. His hair was going silver when he was forty, so he shaved it all."

"I'll love you if your hair's all gone, if you get wrinkles, or nice and soft in the middle... It just means I'm lucky enough to watch us grow old together."

Gabe sighed, all warm inside. "Never thought of it that way before. I'll miss your copper curls, though."

Max drew him close, rubbing the tips of their noses together. "I hope it's always like this between us. Even when we're both old."

Gabe chuckled and stood to go get the lube from the end table. Lying back down, he coated his fingers and pressed inside his mate's heat, swirling them around and slicking him up. "I'll be breaking my hip trying to fuck you against the fridge. Just watch."

Max laughed, breath hitching when Gabe caressed his prostate.

He smiled, enjoying the way Max's eyes widened. "You don't think I could?"

Smiling dangerously, Max shrugged.

"Then I'll just have to have you now, before my cock can't stand up on its own."

Max gasped, his hips arching off the rug as Gabe sheathed himself inside. The fire scorched his back, and he was hot enough to burn alive from the inside out. The sweat left their bodies slick and glistening, gliding easily together with each hard thrust. Max's legs locked around Gabe's waist, and Gabe fucked him until his thighs ached from exertion.

Their lips collided, stifling each hoarse moan and cry. Gabe groaned as his knot expanded with every thrust, loving the way Max's walls stretched around him. A primal growl escaped Gabe when Max's nails bit into his back. Tied together and buried in his mate as deep as he could go, Gabe felt the impact of each thrust reverberating like an earthquake from his pelvis to the pit of his stomach.

He worried he was hurting Max, but Max wouldn't stop kissing him long enough for him to ask. Gabe thought his heart would burst as he finished, coming so hard he swore he'd emptied his soul into Max's body. Satiated, he rode out the waves of his release until Max contracted around him with a desperate cry.

Gabe collapsed against Max's heaving chest, ready to pass out and sleep. His lips caressed the salty skin of Max's shoulder, closing his eyes as warm, damp fingers curled in his hair. Draping his leg over Max's thigh, Gabe nuzzled into the crook of his neck. "Te amo, Max." He sighed, unable to keep his eyes open a minute longer.

Max's smiling lips brushed his forehead. "Te amo," he whispered back, and he was asleep in seconds.

A FIELD OF WHITE flowers blinded Max with their luminance. He pushed himself up, naked as the day he'd been born and alone. He was lying in a vast field of lunar flowers dancing in the gentle night air beneath a full moon. It hung low on the horizon, so close he thought he could reach out and touch one of its many dark pockets. His skin itched; his gums were sore. He ached to shed his human skin and run as a wolf through the sweet-smelling field of flowers.

Instead, he lay alone. The grass tickled his bare skin and cooled his body. The moon's silver light bathed his skin. Above him the stars winked, illuminating the sky, so close yet so out of reach. Loneliness crashed over him in waves and brought a lump to his throat and tears to his eyes.

Wolves sang and their song cleaved him in two. He couldn't put a name to any of their voices or why they were so achingly familiar. Another chorus of howls rent deep into his chest. These voices he knew down to the marrow of his bones. Ben, Gabe, Izzie, Zach, and Ryan. Kendra. His mother. Not in blood but in bond.

The two pieces of his soul didn't know which song to answer, though the choice should have been obvious. So why was he torn apart? How could he desire anything more than the pack who'd saved his life and given him a family?

"Max." A woman's voice. Warm and sweet as mother's milk, comforting and devastating as it twined around his heart and pulled, dividing him. "Come and find me. Find me, my love."

"No..." The tears slipped free, hot and wet down his cheeks as they dampened his hairline. "You're not my family. I have a family. I have—"

The family he'd never known sang to him, and Max ached with how badly he wanted to know them. To know himself. All the pieces of himself that he hadn't realized were missing.

But his pack was calling him.

He couldn't leave them. He wouldn't. But—

Max woke beside the dying fire. Tears were damp on his cheeks and his chest ached. Gabe snored beside him, his back to Max, who was facing the fireplace. He covered his mouth, his shoulders heaving. Guilt and sorrow tore into him. Sorrow for the family he'd never known and lost. Guilt for desiring anything more than the life he'd been blessed with.

Anger came then, steeling his jaw and driving away any other feelings.

When he was a baby, the man he'd thought was his birth father left him. Richard left him in the dark. For all he knew, Amaris had left him too. He'd been left on his mother's doorstep, unwanted and alone. When he'd been hurt and at Richard's mercy, Amaris hadn't come for him. Kendra had been there for him. Gabe and the pack had been there for him.

They'd saved him, and his own birth mother hadn't bothered to so much as look for him. He owed nothing to Amaris or her pack.

Max rolled over and nestled close to Gabe's back, breathing in his mate's scent.

He had all the family he would ever need.

He closed his eyes against the ache in his chest and tried to forget the song of the pack he'd never know howling for him.

Max was home. Home was wherever Gabe Reyes dwelled.

CHAPTER 4

A WOLF PROTECTS HIS PACK

WHEN HE WOKE UP smelling like sweat and dry, crusty spunk and with a burn on his ass, Max learned the hard way that having—awesome—sex in front of an open flame wasn't one of the brightest ideas. But man, was it worth it. He took a much-needed shower with Gabe and joined him for a quick breakfast where he realized sitting was going to be difficult during class. He and Gabe said goodbye; Gabe had the day off from the agency and was staying home, so Max went on his way to the academy in the city.

Just as Max's training got out for the day, he received a text.

Zach: Pack meeting today. Come by HQ. I need to talk to you.

Assuring Zach he would come, he only wondered what he wanted to discuss.

Zach replied with a request that made Max freeze in place.

Zach: Come alone. Don't bring Gabe.

Max reread the message, confused and concerned. The pack never excluded one another. Whatever Zach needed to talk about, it sounded secretive. Unease extinguished the afterglow of a hard day of studying and training.

Once Max arrived on Fire Island, he made his way to the estate and the gate opened at his approach. Max hadn't been to HQ since they'd returned from Vermont. Life had gone on, business as usual, as if John Stone hadn't almost torn the world apart trying to kill the goddess of lycanthropy. Agents bustled about carrying caged feral wolves from vans, showing patients around the estate, or eating lunch on the wraparound porch.

Max had spent a whole summer here while Gabe was away hunting Stone, doing volunteer work around the manor, studying for exams and quizzes for the academy, and training in the gym. He sighed, still remembering the many days he'd spent on Fire Island during the summer while Gabe, Ryan, and Ben were away in Italy.

Guarding the door were two new but familiar faces: Vicenzo Salvatore, tall, olive-skinned and brooding with narrowed blue eyes and a sharp buzz cut, and Eddie Turner, platinum blond with sun-kissed skin, his silver collar gleaming in the sunlight. As per usual, just because they were on guard duty together didn't mean they'd pay the other any attention. Max wondered if their painful pasts would always come between them.

"Mornin', Max," Eddie greeted, his voice soft and Southern as he tipped his weather-beaten hat. He smiled bright as sunshine, contrasting Vicenzo's scowl.

"Yo." Vicenzo's brash voice was in such opposition with Eddie's it made Max jump. Vicenzo spared him a brief, bored glance. "Zach's waiting for you upstairs."

"Thanks!" Max was pleased with how they were settling in. Eddie, a werewolf and former werewolf hunter, used to get flustered if he so much as looked at the pack but was so much more at ease now, and Vicenzo appeared to be getting used to life outside the wilderness. Max knew Ben had been giving them different jobs around the estate. Eddie sometimes worked the gardens, and Vicenzo was an excellent cook when he wasn't on door duty.

Zach hadn't mentioned where they were meeting, but all Max had to do was follow Zach's scent. He was in Ben's office. Max wondered why Ben hadn't been the one to schedule the meeting like he usually did. Zach only took charge when Ben was absent. Closing his eyes, Max felt among the pack bonds. His heart lurched when he realized Ben's thread was missing. Something wasn't right.

Max's unease only deepened when he opened the door. Inside the office, Zach was pacing up and down behind the desk, his arms crossed tightly on his chest. The scent of his worry made Max close the distance and grip his arm. "Hey. What's wrong?" Max touched the side of his neck, hoping to comfort him by mingling their scents.

Zach breathed in deep, his heart rate slowing only slightly. "Not yet. We need to wait for everyone else." His eyes flared when he said through the bonds, *"Max is here. Come to Ben's office now."* Izzie's and Ryan's threads pulsed in answer, and Max realized they were worried too.

Sighing, Zach dropped into the armchair. The chair, Ben's chair, looked too big for him. The whole office smelled of Ben. Pictures of his sons, two blond teenagers with Ben's silver eyes, adorned his desk.

"Why wasn't Gabe invited?" Max asked, sitting across from him.

Zach sighed, running a hand over his buzzed hair. "Sorry. I know—you're mates. Where you go, he goes. But this is important. What I have to say—"

"I'm here!" Ryan hurtled into the room, banging the door against the wall. Zach startled, one hand flying to his chest. Max had never seen him so jumpy before. "Sorry, Zach! I was organizing those new tomes we ordered—well, reading. They're dope and... you're gonna hit me, aren't you?"

Zach sighed. "Just sit down, Ry. We're not in a rush. It's fine."

"Hey, Max. Is Gabe around?" Ryan put his dirty sneakers up on the desk.

"Could you not, man?" Zach swept dirt off the sleek surface of Ben's desk.

Concern puckered Ryan's brow. "Hey, what's eating you?"

"Not yet, we need to wait for—"

Izzie stormed in, and the door crashed against the wall again.

"What did the wall do to you guys?" Zach groaned as Ben's framed diploma came crashing off the wall.

"I don't want to talk about it, Zach. Okay, fine, I do. Just be lucky you're all cis men and that you don't have a stupid uterus!" Izzie snapped, her voice clipped. She threw herself into a seat. "Ugh." She rubbed her abdomen and slouched. "Stupid periods," she muttered.

Zach looked around as if surveying an active volcano. "Can I talk?"

"Yeah, man, hit me," Ryan said, spreading his legs on the desk. His foot knocked over a picture and Zach caught it, his nostrils flaring.

"Go ahead," Izzie said, shrugging as if she didn't care either way.

Zach exhaled, looking around at the pack. "Okay, I—"

"Wait, someone go get Gabriel," Izzie said. "Why isn't he here?"

"I didn't want him here," Zach said through gritted teeth. "What I want to talk about concerns him."

It was just as Max had feared. "What do you mean?"

Zach scratched at the back of his head. "I don't know where to start. Here. Read this." He handed Max a letter from Ben's desk drawer. It was addressed to Zach. Max unfolded it.

Zach,

It's been one hell of a ride, kid. You've got a good head on your shoulders and a big heart, so I'm entrusting the future of the LPA to you.

Max's jaw dropped.

"Keep reading." Zach slumped in his chair.

Max read aloud, "I'm entrusting the future of the LPA to you. You've proven yourself reliable time and again. It's a heavy burden, but you're right for the job. I'm never... coming back."

All of a sudden, Ben's heartfelt goodbye the other night made frightening sense. He hadn't been saying goodbye for the night, but for good.

Ryan ripped the letter out of his hands and continued reading. "McCready's got to be stopped. If he takes control of that Council, it will be the end of the shifter world as we know it. I've gone to challenge him, as is customary when any beta is set to inherit. Someone's got to stop him, and it falls on me to protect the pack. Please, don't try to stop me. I've made my peace with it. Don't tell Gabe. He told me what he became in Vermont. His rage turned him into a monster I've only ever heard about in legend. I won't risk him losing himself like that again. I don't have time to explain what he is, but I need you to promise me that you won't tell him. Gabe can't be anywhere near McCready. He's... he's like a son to me, and I won't let him be hurt anymore. A wolf protects his pack. I hope you all can understand." Silence fell. Ryan crumpled the letter in his fist and chucked it across the room. "Like fuck we understand!"

Izzie paced the room. "I can't believe it. After all these years we've known him, he takes off without even telling us! I thought we were done running off on each other. Goddess, why are all the men in this pack self-sacrificing assholes?" Her scowl softened to a worried frown. "Gabriel didn't say anything to *me* about becoming some kind of monster. What has he been hiding?"

Max squeezed his fists together until his nails bit into his palms. "What about his sons? How could he do this to them?" It seemed selfish, but knowing Ben, he likely thought he was giving his life so his sons could have a future free of McCready's tyranny.

"He seriously thinks we're gonna sit around and let him die? We've gotta stop him! That's why we're here, right, Zach?" Ryan looked to Zach, wide-eyed and desperate.

Zach nodded. "I can't do this by myself. I don't know much about the Council or what we're up against. I need you, all of you."

"Except Gabe." Max sighed. He already knew Gabe would be hurt and furious if Max went to the Council's HQ in Montana without him.

"Right." Zach sighed. "I'm sorry, Max. I don't like it either, so I wanted to ask for your perspective. You were there when Gabe killed Stone. Is Ben right to exclude Gabe from this?"

A shiver ran down Max's spine when he recalled the beast Gabe had turned into during his fight with Stone. He hadn't known Gabe had talked to Ben about that. "It was terrifying. At first he was in control, but he almost lost himself when he killed Stone. I thought he wouldn't come back. But he did," he added when a frown creased Zach's face. "It was… it was bad."

Horror widened Izzie's eyes. "And no one thought this was something we should all know about?"

Wincing, Max couldn't meet her gaze. "There wasn't time. I'm sorry."

Blowing out a breath, Zach nodded decisively. "Ben seems to think Gabe will lose it if he and McCready fight, and based on what you just told me, then I'm of the decision that Gabe can't know."

Max wanted the floor to open up and swallow him as Izzie and Ryan looked at him. He wanted to help, but Gabe would never forgive him. Gabe wanted to be the one to confront McCready, and it was his right to do so after all the harm the beta had brought to his family. If Max put himself in harm's way by confronting McCready without telling Gabe—it would tear Gabe apart. How could Max go while Gabe stayed? It wasn't right.

But this was Ben. Ben who was the father Max had never had, who'd changed Max's life when he'd welcomed him into the LPA. Ben was like a father to Gabe too. Gabe would be devastated if Max knew there was a threat to Ben and said nothing to him.

"I don't know what to do," he confessed.

Izzie touched his arm. "You have to tell my brother, Max. If we do this without telling him, this will kill him."

"Or McCready will," Zach growled. "An Alpha of the Council is chosen by strength alone, that's what Ben told me once. And McCready's no regular Alpha. He's got the Wargs of the Apocalypse at his back. Max, we've gotta honor Ben's wishes on this one. He was concerned for Gabe's safety. We should take that seriously."

"That should be his choice, though," Ryan said. "This is important to him, Zach. We can't keep him in the dark."

Zach paced, running a restless hand over his hair. "Look, this is something Ben's asked us to do. He wants to protect Gabe. He clearly thinks Gabe's in danger if he goes after McCready. We should listen to him."

Ryan nodded glumly. "He's never gonna forgive us for this, Zach. I mean, not letting him go after McCready is one thing. But not telling him Ben's in danger? And if Max and Izzie go and put themselves in harm's way, that'll just be adding insult to injury. What if something happens and Gabe finds out later?"

For a moment, Zach's composure cracked and Max saw what this was doing to him as his eyes glistened and his lips trembled. "I... I have to follow Ben's wishes on this one, guys."

Max's stomach felt full of worms. Gabe would be devastated if something happened to Ben. He would blame himself, wishing he'd been there to defend Ben with everything he had and furious that they'd denied him that right—that *Max* had played a part in denying him the right to be there for the man he considered a second father.

"Max, you don't have to do this," Zach said. "You and Izzie should stay and be there for Gabe. What about you, Ry?"

Ryan sighed and nodded. "Yeah. I'll go."

Izzie squeezed her fingers together. "I hate knowing you'll be running off into danger, Zach, but I know my brother. If he thinks Ben's in danger, he'll throw himself at McCready. Keeping this a secret might be the only way to keep Gabe safe."

"Can you and your mother keep him distracted? He'll notice when we all leave without him. Maybe we can't stop him coming if he finds out, but if you can hold him off while we're leaving, that may buy us enough time to rescue Ben," Zach said.

"I... I can try." Izzie worried her lower lip.

"I guess I could come up with a cover story," Max said, but his heart ached at the idea of lying to the man he loved, even if it was to keep him safe.

Zach tried to smile. "That's fine. Max, don't worry about coming with us, okay? I bet Vicenzo will wanna come. He's always complaining about how boring it is watching the door. Bet he'd love to get away from Ed for a bit."

Max just nodded, unsure what to say, torn between the urge to protect the man he considered a father and keeping the trust of his mate.

LATER THAT NIGHT, MAX couldn't sleep. Usually, he slept like a pup in their bed in their Park Avenue apartment. Tonight, his mind tossed and turned, anxiety making a mess of his stomach.

What if Ben dies?

His breath caught.

How will I explain that to Gabe? He'll hate me. He'll hate himself. He'll blame himself for not being there, for not doing everything he could—because I lied to him.

His jaw tightened, just imagining the look of devastation on Gabe's face, the fury and hurt twisting his features.

And if he goes, then what? Gabe could lose control and turn into that monster again. If he did, would he be able to come back from that?

The uncertainty made Max feel sick. He rolled over and punched his pillow, letting out a growl between his teeth. He and Gabe had been through difficulties, but Gabe would be so hurt if Max kept him from saving Ben. He should wake him up right now and tell him. Together, they might have a better chance of saving Ben.

What if I lose him? What if I lose them both?

Gabe slept beside him, his wavy ebony hair askew against his cheek, his lips parted. It looked like a peaceful sleep. No nightmares yet, but if he lost Ben, the grief and guilt would eat him alive.

If I told him, he'd go to Ben without question. It's his right to know.

Tears pricked his eyes, and his throat ached. If anything happened to Gabe, he would be lost.

"Max?" Gabe blinked bleary eyes at him. "What's wrong? I can feel your distress through our bond."

Crap. Max shook his head. "Nothing. It's nothing." Feeling guilty, Max leaned over and kissed him. "Sorry."

"Well, we're awake now," Gabe murmured, pushing his lips up against Max's. "Wanna talk about it?" His hand smoothed over Max's side, warm against his bare skin.

Max didn't know where to start or if he should speak at all. Fear kept his words locked away.

Gabe grabbed his phone and idly scrolled. He frowned. "That's weird."

"What?"

"Izzie just invited me on some last-minute road trip to Vermont. That's weird."

"Izzie's pretty spontaneous," Max said as he squeezed the sheets.

Gabe glowered at the screen. "Yeah, but still. This is impulsive even for her."

"Maybe you should go," Max blurted out. "It could be good for you to get some country air, you know?" His palms were damp, and Max wiped them on the sheets. He had to stay calm; otherwise, Gabe would feel his anxiety through their bond.

Gabe snorted, setting down his phone. "I've gotten plenty of fresh air upstate with you this past week."

Max's mouth went dry. "Yeah, but maybe the Vermont air is... different? Maybe it smells like maple syrup? Yeah. You should totally go."

A frown creased Gabe's brow. He wet his lips. "Okay. Something's up."

Shit. Fuck. *Shiiit...* "No. Nothing's wrong!" Max waved his hands. "I just think you've earned a break, you know? That big fight with Stone, traveling around Rome... You deserve a vacation."

"Max, why are you trying to get rid of me?"

Max winced. "I'm not."

Gabe sighed, working a hand through his sleep-tousled hair. "Is everything okay... you know. With us?"

Whoa. Not the heavy conversation Max wanted to have at three in the morning.

"Why would you think that?"

Gabe shrugged, not meeting Max's gaze. "I don't know. A lot's changed so quickly. You found out about your lineage. We mated. Things are weird between you and Kendra. I just hope you aren't having doubts about me. Us."

Oh no. Max couldn't have Gabe thinking he was trying to get rid of him. He'd tried. He had. But he had to tell Gabe the truth.

"Gabe, you need to promise me something."

Gabe's expression darkened, his brows knitting in concern. "Yeah. Anything." He stroked Max's hair.

Max couldn't take comfort in the gentle touch weaving through his hair. He felt sick, realizing that the next words he uttered would set in motion something that couldn't be undone. "Promise me you won't go after McCready. Not until we have a plan to stop him. Okay?"

Gabe's lips thinned, his face turning stony. "What happened, Max?"

"Gabe, promise me. Or I can't tell you." He wouldn't send Gabe to his death and betray Ben's final request all at once.

Gabe sat up, the sheets pooling around his torso. His jaw tightened, his eyes dark and unreadable. Max held his breath, wishing he had said nothing at all. Gabe exhaled shortly and took Max's hand. "I promise."

Max's shoulders loosened as he relaxed. Now, where to begin?

GABE LISTENED WITHOUT INTERRUPTING, his insides tossing and turning as Max's story went from bad to worse. Ben's behavior the night before made sense now. He'd known something was wrong, and he'd said nothing. If he'd been more observant, Ben wouldn't be in danger.

And Zach... Gabe growled.

He was just doing what Ben told him. Honoring his wishes.

Still, that Zach had wanted to keep him out of the decision-making infuriated him.

Max had fallen silent. He'd finished talking. Those wide honey eyes gazed at him, his teeth worrying at his lower lip as he awaited Gabe's response.

When he'd confided in Ben about the monster he'd become shortly after their return from Vermont, he'd done so thinking Ben could offer advice and understanding. Instead, he'd used that information to make a decision behind Gabe's back. Maybe it was the right decision, but it still hurt. "Ben really thinks I'm dangerous? Is that what you think, too?" He couldn't keep the hurt from his voice. "I'm not some explosive asshole on a hair trigger."

Max rubbed his shoulder. "Hey. I know that. Ben's just being cautious. He wants you to be safe."

From McCready... or from himself? Gabe's stomach twisted. When he'd become a monster to kill Stone, he'd nearly lost himself in feral fury. On top of that, when he and Max had been separated, he'd struggled with controlling his wolf. His wolf had only recently settled down when he and Max were reunited after a month apart in Italy. Was the monster in him gone for good, or only slumbering? Gabe balled his hands into fists, afraid of losing the control he'd found when he'd killed Stone, of losing himself in bloodlust for good and never coming back.

"I shouldn't have told you." Max sighed.

Gabe's chest warmed, and he smiled despite it all.

This was what his sweet Lobito had been torturing himself over for the last few hours of the evening. He wished Max had just come out and told him right away, but he understood Max's reluctance. "No, mi amor. I'm happy you told me." His mate had gone against Zach's wishes, and Ben's, for Gabe's own peace of mind. He tipped Max's chin up and leaned in, counting the freckles that dotted his cheeks. Their lips met, and the intensity with which Max held on to him took him by storm.

Max threw his arms around Gabe's shoulders, his fingers curling in his hair. His lips trembled against Gabe's, his chest rising and falling to the rhythm of a shaky sigh. Gabe was woozy when they broke apart, and he held Max tight as he nestled his face in Gabe's shoulder.

"I didn't know what to do," Max confessed, his hands warm as they framed Gabe's face. "I thought you'd hate me if I kept it from you. But now—love, promise me you won't be reckless. We don't go there to fight, not if we can help it. We rescue Ben, and we get the hell out. Got it?"

Gabe tried to speak, but the words wouldn't come. McCready could not be Alpha. Knowing about his affiliation with the terrorist organization the Wargs of the Apocalypse and about his twisted vision of a new world where humans and hybrids were at the bottom and full-blooded wolves at the top, how could Gabe sit back and watch him claim the power he needed to bring about the destruction of their world?

"Gabriel Reyes." Max's eyes blazed and his fangs gleamed. "I didn't tell you this so you could put your neck between McCready's jaws! If you don't swear to me you'll behave when we confront McCready, then he isn't the one you'll have to worry about."

Gabe smiled. Max hardly ever raised his voice, but that he could do so with Gabe made him feel stupidly proud of the progress Max had made over the years.

"Being killed by my mate doesn't sound like fun," Gabe admitted, biting Max's chin. He couldn't say no, even if he doubted his own ability to keep such a promise. "Fine. I'll be a good boy. But if McCready's hurt Ben, Max—"

Max growled at the very thought. "Then we'll show him what happens when he fucks with our pack."

Grinning, Gabe tugged ginger curls as he brought Max close. His blood simmered as Max's breath blazed against his lips. "Sounds like a plan, mi amor."

CHAPTER 5

RETURN TO WOLF POINT

Early the next morning, Gabe and Max packed lightly in preparation for their flight. They'd snagged two tickets for a flight out of New York, departing on the same plane as Zach and the others. They jumped in a cab and left the city behind, pulling up outside JFK. Max called Izzie and told her Gabe knew so she could join them in Ben's rescue.

Sniffing the air, Gabe caught the scents of the pack right away. Max's grip on his hand tightened, and the smell of his worry made Gabe laugh. "What's wrong?"

"Just worried Zach will kill me for telling you," Max admitted.

Gabe put his arm around his shoulders. "I'll protect you."

His mate snorted, his cheeks reddening.

They passed through security and went in search of their gate. Zach was impossible to miss, standing taller than most anyone else in the crowd. Gabe quickened his pace, his heart racing as he went up behind Zach and tickled the back of his neck. Zach chuckled, no doubt having sensed Gabe before he approached. Guilt soured his scent. "Gabe, I... I'm sorry."

"I tried, Zach." Max folded his arms over his chest. "I couldn't keep him in the dark."

Gabe stepped in front of Max, glaring Zach down. "And you shouldn't have asked him to." He couldn't keep the anger out of his voice.

"No, I shouldn't have. I'm sorry to you too, Max." Zach bowed his head, his eyes remorseful. "I was doing what Ben asked me to, Gabe."

"And you bet I'm gonna have a talk with him too." Tiring of Zach's kicked puppy look, Gabe squeezed his shoulder. "Where's everyone else?"

Zach led the way to the seating area where Ryan snored with his head back against the seat and Izzie sipped coffee from a paper cup. Vicenzo raised a hand, looking shell-shocked as his eyes darted around the bustling terminal. He glowered down at his lap. "Don't know what's worse, this place or the subways. God damn, humans stink." He covered his nose, looking green.

Gabe clapped his knee as he sat beside him. "Still, nice to get away from patrol duty, right?"

Vicenzo rolled his shoulders and smiled. He usually had such a scowling face, but his smiles brightened the room. "Couldn't say no to a chance to get away from Eddie for a change. Even if it means packing into a flying tin can with a bunch of humans."

Although Gabe didn't see why he and Ed still couldn't get along, he didn't want to push it. Complicated didn't even begin to describe Vicenzo and Eddie's relationship, and Gabe felt he'd only brushed the surface of their past. Something about fire and werewolf hunters. "Come on now, humans aren't that bad."

"You can't trust them. Any of them," Vicenzo growled in response. "I just said yes to get out of the city, be back among nature. I like the estate 'cause it's secluded. This place, forget about it."

Izzie narrowed her eyes at Gabe. "Remember, we're rescuing Ben. We're not challenging McCready and his wargs."

Tousling her hair, Gabe nodded. "Yeah, yeah. I got the message."

Zach shook Ryan gently, jolting him awake. "Guys, they're boarding. Let's go. We've got a foolish but well-intentioned friend to save."

Max sighed, lacing his fingers through Gabe's. "We really need to visit Montana under better circumstances."

Yeah, Gabe couldn't argue with that.

Once they found their seats on the plane, Gabe switched on the Lycanthrope News Network, or LNN. The reporter was broadcasting from Wolf Point, Montana, the domed town hall visible over her shoulder.

"The Council of Lycanthrope Affairs is in disarray after the shocking death of Alpha Hanson at the hands of his own beta. McCready claims he traveled to the former Alpha's home in Vermont where he challenged Hanson for his position and bested him, a brutal and archaic but legal practice among the Council."

"That's what he's claiming happened?" Gabe scoffed. "Like hell."

"I was there when McCready killed Hanson's family. He didn't challenge him at all, and it wasn't a fair fight. He set his wargs on him." Max bristled with anger.

The reporter went on. "However, many humans and wolves have expressed their disapproval of Beta McCready's actions. As is werewolf tradition, any dissenters are welcome to challenge Beta McCready for the position."

Gabe growled as McCready's face filled the screen. He looked the same—pallid but well-kept with not a strand of dark hair out of place, his goatee immaculately trimmed, and his suit perfectly pressed. Gabe wasn't fooled by his grooming; he knew too well the monster hiding beneath that well-kept façade. When McCready smiled it was all teeth, like a wolf baring his fangs just before the strike.

"Alpha Hanson was weak, and the time has come to move forward. To rise from the ashes and begin our future. As Alpha, I will lead all werewolf kind into a new future, and we shall be greater and stronger than ever." His snakelike eyes narrowed as he surveyed the gathered crowd as if looking for weaknesses. Gabe wondered if Ben was among the thousands of shifters who'd turned up to pay homage to Alpha Hanson. His stomach twisted in fear. "But of course, there are those of you that believe you could do better, that your vision for a new world is greater than mine. Challenge me, then! Turn your words into actions, and whoever still stands will be the one truly deserving of the title of Alpha!"

Gabe squeezed the armrest of his seat. Goddess, he hoped they got there in time.

Then Max's hand settled on his arm. "We'll make it, Gabe. Ben will be okay." He knew Max well enough to know he was trying to be strong for him despite his own doubts.

Gabe swallowed, blinking hard.

He wouldn't lose his father, not again.

WHEN THEY ARRIVED IN the Elderwoods, the pine forests that surrounded the town of Wolf Point, the silence rang in Gabe's ears. They walked among moss-eaten graves cast in the shadows of dense clusters of pine trees. Ravens cawed deep within the woods, and paw prints mottled the ground. The scents of other wolves still clung to the air, but Gabe couldn't make out Ben among them.

He must be here. He must be safe.

A growl rumbled in his throat. If Ben was hurt, if he was—

Hunt. Must hunt. Must kill. Kill them all. Protect Ben. Protect pack.

He inhaled and exhaled slowly, forcing his fists to uncurl and wincing as his claws withdrew from the palms of his hands. He couldn't lose his head. This was about Ben. He had to find him and get out. They could plan back in New York.

Beside him, Max rubbed his shoulder, holding on tight. To comfort him, or to keep him from running off into the woods?

Vicenzo breathed in. "Ah, this is more like it. Reminds me of the territory I grew up in."

A scream cleaved the silence in two.

Vicenzo's eyes widened. "Never heard that in my territory. Looks like we're gettin' some action!"

Ryan stopped, a gasp spilling from his throat. "Tell me you guys heard that."

Gabe thought he'd heard something. It was hard to tell when his heart was pounding in his ears, when all the sounds of the forest were blending: the snapping of twigs, the racing heart and pumping blood of a rabbit, the calling of birds.

They stayed quiet, waiting.

The scream came again, but there was something… off about it. It wasn't a scream of pain or fear, and it was unlike any animal he'd ever heard. No human could replicate such a sound. It made the hair on the back of his neck stand on end, had him baring his teeth in reaction to the threat.

"What the hell is that?" Ryan whispered.

Vicenzo shoved him. "Don't be a baby. It's a bear or maybe a mountain lion."

"No," Gabe growled. "It's not." Whatever it was, the scents of other wolves were gravitating toward it.

Ben. He's in danger.

Gabe took off, his sneakers pounding the forest floor and throwing up leaves and dirt.

"Gabe, wait!" Max cried.

Wolves howled, their eerie, haunting voices echoing through the forest like a siren song, urging him onward. Their scents became overpowering, and so did the smell of blood. That scent was fresh while others were as old as the trees themselves. The ground was stained red with blood, soaked so deep into the earth no rain could hope to wash it out. Bones snapped under his feet, old and yellow.

This was a battleground. How many had fought here, *died* here, challenging Alpha after Alpha for centuries?

A bellow pierced his ears and sent his heart into a wild gallop. The trees shuddered as if in revulsion, the branches quaking from the roar.

His human instincts screamed at him to run while his wolf struggled for control, desperate to take the reins. His claws came out, his fur growing coarse on his body, his clothes straining.

No! Let me find Ben. Then you can do whatever you want with me! Just let me—

He stumbled to a halt, gasping, his heart slamming against his ribs. He stood in a glade where the surrounding trees grew so tall, they choked out the sunlight. Gabe breathed in and choked on the scent of blood, so pungent he could taste it.

Let me out. Let me out, the wolf snarled, pacing back and forth, his ears pulled back, his fangs bared. *Let me fight!*

His stomach lurched as the smell of voided bowels and bloody fur, fear and pain, overwhelmed his senses.

The Council wolves lay broken and bloody, some a mixture of human and wolf, others fully shifted. There were too many dead to count. Deep claw marks split a woman from her torso to her throat. A wolf lay on his side, his eyes wide and vacant, intestines crawling from his gutted belly like gray snakes. Gabe swallowed, willing himself not to be sick. Was McCready responsible for this carnage?

From within the trees, there came another hoarse bellow. Gabe stepped on something. It was a leather jacket, ripped and soaked in blood. A familiar paw-shaped badge was pinned to the fabric, Ben's name engraved into the metal. His heart sank.

"Ben! You there?" His voice echoed through the trees and went unanswered. Fear tightened his throat. What had happened to Ben? Closing his eyes tight, he felt for Ben's bond. A pulse rippled through his chest, but it was weak. Ben was alive but he was hurt. Badly.

From the depths of the woods, it came, the smell of blood and death hanging from it like a shroud. Yellow eyes glimmered like twin flames, wide and crazed with bloodlust.

McCready strode toward them as a wolf, his brown fur matted with blood. Gabe growled. He was so unassuming in this form, slender and thin.

How could a wolf like him have defeated so many? In his jaws he dragged the broken body of a gray wolf by the ankle, silver-tipped fur matted with blood and dirt.

"Ben!" He ran to the wolf's limp body. The wolf's silver eyes were barely open, and Gabe could scarcely breathe as the wolf's ribs rose and fell slowly. Ben was still alive, for now.

Aaron McCready shifted and walked toward him naked and bloody, teeth bared in an eerie smile.

"Gabriel, welcome."

"Pendejo!" Gabe didn't realize he'd swung at McCready's stupid, smug face, not until he was gnashing his teeth to keep from howling as McCready trapped Gabe's arm in a bone-crushing grip.

"Come to challenge me? You'll fail, just like your foolish friend here."

Gabe bared his fangs as rage curdled his insides. "I'll kill you, McCready." He grunted, the pain in his arm bringing him to his knees. "I'll rip you apart!" This man had hurt the ones he loved for the last time.

"As if a mutt like you could stand a chance against me."

"Gabe!" Max burst into the clearing, his eyes going wide at the sight of Gabe on his knees before McCready. "Get away from him!"

McCready relinquished his grip on Gabe's arm, and the blood came rushing back, restoring feeling to his numb fingertips. Max clawed at Gabe's shirt, his hands pressing at Gabe's chest as he ushered Gabe behind him. Though Gabe was a few inches taller than Max, his mate was ready to defend him to the death.

"Oh, what a joy this is. The whole pack's here." McCready's smile grew as Ryan, Zach, Izzie, and Vicenzo came thundering up behind Max.

"Did not need to see that." Ryan grunted, looking away from McCready's naked form.

Zach raced to Ben, heaving the wolf into his arms.

Her eyes blazing, Izzie leaped out in front of her brother. "Gabe, Max, get away from him!"

Vicenzo and Ryan came closer, standing shoulder to shoulder with Max and Gabe.

Gabe clenched Max's shoulder, urging him to stand aside. "Max, get out of my way."

"No," he growled.

It could be over in seconds. All he had to do was tear out McCready's throat, and the nightmares would end. He'd never have to fear for the lives of those closest to him again.

McCready's black gaze dropped to Max's neck, eyeing the bite Gabe had given him. "What's this? Gabriel's, I assume?" A repulsed shiver rippled through Gabe as McCready's eyes landed on his own mating bite. His skin wanted to crawl off. "I suppose I should be glad you half-breeds have each other so you can't taint our species by contaminating the blood of a pure wolf." He reached out a thin, pale finger and caressed the bite mark on Max's neck. "Enjoy this petty victory while you can. It won't last long."

Max raised a hand to throw him off, but Gabe was one step ahead. The blood roared in his ears as his hand snapped around McCready's wrist, his shoulder ramming into his chest, and they stumbled until McCready's back was up against a tree.

"Touch him again, and I'll rip your hand off," Gabe snarled.

McCready's smile only widened, as if he enjoyed getting under Gabe's skin. "Disgusting. The both of you. Makes me want to rip you both to shreds."

Gabe's jaw tightened. Memories of Max lying in a pool of blood, lifeless and bleeding out right before his eyes while the smoke curled from Mc-Cready's pistol, surfaced in his mind. His arm trembled.

Lunging, Gabe dug his claws into the pale skin of McCready's throat. "You want him, you go through me."

McCready choked on laughter, baring crimson-soaked fangs. "Change is coming, mutt, and you won't be strong enough to stop it!"

The man's bones snapped and cracked, his back hunched, his legs grew longer. Gabe lurched away from him as McCready's body grew bulky with muscle and coarse fur sprouted from his skin. His roar shook the pines and left Gabe's ears ringing. The beast towered over him on its back legs, enormous arms spread wide. This thing was taller than any man alive, more hideous and terrible than any monster Gabe's worst nightmares could conjure. A beast unlike any he'd ever seen, a fearsome conjoining of man and wolf, with a body of tightly coiled muscles.

An enormous claw struck the trunk of a pine tree, and the earth shuddered as the roots tore free from the soil. Another slam, and the tree came crashing to the forest floor, shaking the earth.

"There'll be nowhere you can hide!" McCready roared.

Ryan ran, hurtling behind the cover of a tree. Seizing Gabe's shirt, Max pulled, urging him away from McCready as he came toward them, his thunderous steps shaking the ground. Gabe shoved Max ahead and turned to run, but the ground vanished beneath him as a clawed hand curled around his ankle. He flew across the forest floor, and wound up sprawled beneath McCready.

"You have one chance to stop me, agency wolves," the beast snarled, splaying two huge paws on either side of him. Hot strings of spit dribbled on Gabe's face, and he shuddered as he stared up into the darkness of the wolf's throat. "If you fail, I will make you all watch as I break and remake this world into what it was always meant to be: a utopia for the pure and a hell for those who defile this land and our bloodline."

His words reached a clawed hand deep into Gabe's chest and grabbed hold of his racing heart. He could not be helpless again. He wasn't a weak little boy anymore, forced to watch as those who protected him lost their lives. He wouldn't sit back and take abuse or tolerate threats to those he loved.

Gabe squared his jaw and stood to look the beast in the eyes. McCready towered over him, razor claws long and sharp enough to disembowel him with a single slash. If he challenged McCready, he had no doubt he would go to his death. But if it meant putting an end to the man who'd shattered his family as well as protecting those he loved, then what choice did he have?

But he'd promised Max he wouldn't be reckless. He'd promised he wouldn't give Max reason to fear for Gabe's life. Gritting his teeth until he thought they'd crack, he balled his hands into fists to keep from lashing out at the man who'd hurt his friend and had a hand in his father's murder.

"Challenge me, agents," McCready growled. "I'll wait for you here tomorrow." Hoarse laughter crawled from his throat. The beast bunched his muscles and sprang, tearing away into the trees. Gabe turned to the pack and found them wide-eyed and afraid.

"We can't do this," Ryan snapped. "That thing will kill us all in seconds!"

Gabe brushed past him. "Someone has to stop him!"

"Gabe." Zach's deep voice pulled at him, but Gabe ignored him. "There are other ways! Let's wait until Ben's recovered. Then we can plan something else!"

Gabe quickened his pace.

"Gabriel, you can't do this! Father didn't risk his life so you could commit suicide!" Izzie said, jogging to keep pace with him.

"Gabe's right. We've gotta stop him here and now," Vicenzo growled, keeping stride with them. "If he takes over the Council, hybrids can kiss their rights and protections goodbye. We can't let that happen."

"Everyone just let me think!" Gabe roared, silencing his friends.

The only one who stayed silent was Max, and somehow that hurt worse than if Max had scolded him outright for even considering accepting McCready's challenge. Max was only silent when he was hurting, and Gabe's insides twisted into knots. He didn't know what to do.

Vicenzo and Zach helped Ben into the bed of the rental truck and covered the wolf with Zach's sweatshirt. Max stayed silent during the drive back to the motel. Once they got there, Zach and Ryan sped off with Ben to the nearest hospital. Gabe went upstairs without looking at Izzie or the others. He needed peace and quiet so he could plan his next move. The door to their room closed behind him.

"Gabe," Max began.

Gabe flinched. "I know I made a promise to you, mi amor. You know that's all that stopped me from ripping that son of a bitch to pieces. Or throwing my life away trying to."

"Gabe." Max's voice quaked.

Gabe turned and his breath caught. Max was shaking, his shoulders rising and falling fast. His hands were clenched so tightly at his sides that the knuckles had whitened and beads of blood oozed between his fingers from where his claws had dug in.

"Fuck our promise." Max's fangs were sharp. "And fuck me for asking you to hold back from tearing that monster to shreds. I just watched that thing hurt my friends. Threaten you. Threaten everyone like us who is different. He needs to be stopped. He cannot take control of the Council." Max's orange eyes blazed. "If you wanna kick his ass, then I'll stand with you."

Gabe grinned. "Yeah?" Fuck, seeing Max so enraged sent blood rushing to his dick.

"Hell yeah."

A part of Gabe was terrified Max would get hurt, and he surely would. They were in for the fight of their lives, but if he knew anything, it was that no good ever came from trying to take on all their problems alone, even if it was out of a desire to protect Max. They were stronger when they stood together.

Gabe lunged for Max, crushing their mouths together as he hauled his mate into his arms. "Yeah, Max. Okay. We're doing this together."

A growl vibrated in Max's chest, and he brought his lips to Gabe's ear and bit down. "Together," he growled.

CHAPTER 6

BERSERKER

WHILE THEY WAITED TO be let into Ben's hospital room, Max squeezed Gabe's arm. "Back there, McCready looked familiar."

Gabe hummed, his eyes closed and his head resting back against the wall.

Max wet his lips, unsure how to broach the one thing they hadn't discussed since their last confrontation with Stone. "Gabe, that form you assumed when you fought Stone... it looked a lot like McCready."

Slowly, Gabe opened his eyes, sighing through his nose. His brows furrowed. He opened his mouth, then shut it.

"What do you think it means?" Max wondered, not really expecting an answer.

Gabe shrugged. "I think... It was just a lot. You know? Stone and Mc-Cready coming at us. Being reunited with you. I was so desperate to leave with you and go home. This rage came over me..." He trailed off, his limbs slackening in his exhaustion. Max brushed his hair away from his forehead. Fear soured Gabe's scent. "You think I'm a monster. Like him."

"No." Max squeezed his hand. "No. Never. I'm just wondering what it all means. If you could do it again, then maybe we could win?"

Gabe's jaw tightened. "I don't know."

The nurse let them in to see Ben. The other wolves had been by, leaving him flowers and get-well cards. Someone had left a pink balloon that said,

66

It's a Girl! Probably Ryan's idea of a joke. The man himself lay propped up. His wounds had healed overnight, and his eyes were alert.

Gabe glowered at him. "I don't know whether to hug you or hit you."

With a sigh, Ben opened his arms. Gabe and Max went to his side and took turns hugging him.

"You left without saying anything to us," Max said, unable to help but be annoyed.

"I know." Ben's shoulders slumped. "I wanted to keep you all safe. Instead, McCready wiped out any councilmembers that opposed him. Most of them, anyway. The few he spared, he... did something to them."

"What do you mean?" Gabe asked, sitting at Ben's bedside.

Ben shrugged. "Their eyes were all wrong. Empty. They obeyed his every command."

Max did not like the sound of that.

Ben slumped against the headboard. "Fighting him is hopeless."

"No, it isn't." Gabe sat at the foot of his bed. "The pack and I are going to face him together. Like we *should* have done."

Ben winced. "Guess I deserved that one." Before Ben could offer any input, a nurse came in with a tray of food. He took a bite, made a face, and pushed aside his hospital food.

Frowning, Gabe said, "It's no good? I can run out and get you something from the diner, Viejo."

Ben glared at him in response. "No. I was thinking about this plan of yours, and it made me sick. Seriously? I expected this dumb shit from Gabe, but you, Max? Are you both suicidal?"

"That's rich, coming from you. Aren't you the one who ran off without a word and threw himself at McCready?" Gabe growled.

Ben scowled, gnashing his teeth. "That was my decision. At least I knew what I was getting myself into."

Max said, "I know. It's crazy, but this is our only chance to stop McCready before he seizes power. We'll be stronger if we stand together as a pack."

Gabe smiled, and Max's chest warmed. Gabe looked proud.

Muttering something, Ben shook his head. "You saw that... thing he became. How can you possibly think you have any chance against him?"

Max thought back to McCready's wolf. He'd never seen something so monstrous, even for werewolves. Werewolves could take many forms. They could go full wolf, or they could grow fangs and claws in their human form. Whatever McCready was, he was nothing like Max had ever seen. Except Gabe, back on that hilltop in Vermont under a blood red lunar eclipse. Max shivered and pushed the memory away. McCready had stood at least eight feet tall, his body bulky with muscle, and he'd been able to walk on two legs and even speak, something no werewolves could do as wolves unless they communicated telepathically through their pack's bonds.

"What is he?" Gabe asked, his scent sour with dread.

Ben's eyes darkened. "There's a long history. In the days of the Vikings, warriors would wear the skins of bears, boars, and wolves into battle, believing the spirits of the beasts would give them an edge in combat. Vikings called such warriors Ulfhednar, which means wolf-coat. Nowadays, berserker is more commonly used."

Beside Max, Gabe swallowed, his body going tense. They had a word now for what Gabe had become in Vermont, only Max still didn't understand why or how it had happened.

"Alphas can pass the power of the berserker down to those they trust the most when they die. After what McCready did to his family, I doubt Hanson handed over the gift willingly. The only way to steal the power of a berserker is to carve the Alpha's heart from his chest and—"

Gabe blanched. "Skip the details, Ben. I just had lunch."

The sandwich he'd eaten for lunch sat heavily in Max's stomach. "How is Gabe able to become a berserker?"

Lifting his shoulders in a shrug, Ben said, "Who knows. Outside of the Council, berserker abilities come from a rare genetic mutation. Only one in ten lycanthropes may be born with it. I'm sure if more werewolves out there have the gene, they hide it all their lives. Humans have enough reason to fear us, after all." Ben sighed, the sound long and bitter.

Furrowing his brows, Gabe said, "So that would mean someone in my family was a berserker. I wonder who."

"You know a lot about these... berserker things," Max said.

Ben chuckled. "'Cause I was one. Once. I inherited the gene from my great-grandmother's side of the family."

Gabe's jaw dropped. "You mean... you could be like McCready? Go all Furry Hulk on your enemies like that?"

Ben nodded. "I thought I might still turn into one. That's why I went. I thought fighting another berserker might wake it up. Instead, I just got my ass gnawed on." Ben's smile fell away and for a moment, he looked lost and defeated. "The gene activated when I was desperate to protect... someone. A long time ago." He compressed his lips like he'd eaten something sour. "But now, it's gone dormant. That determination, that drive to protect... it's just not strong enough to activate the gene."

"Why?" Max asked. "What happened?"

A shadow darkened Ben's eyes, and the sheets bunched in his fists. Ben blinked and relaxed his hands. "It doesn't matter anymore. The point is no one stands a chance against McCready in a fair fight. We need to step back and come up with another plan, even if it means McCready gets his victory for now."

Disappointed that Ben couldn't, or perhaps didn't want to, offer guidance, Max bowed his head. His stomach twisted, and he was afraid of what might happen if they backed down and let McCready have control of the Council. Though it might be futile, Max asked, "Do you know anyone else who might know how to fight a berserker?"

Gabe turned to Max, excitement lighting up his eyes. "Ed would know! He was a werewolf hunter!"

Max hadn't thought of that. "Let's call him!"

"Or we could all forget about this and go home!" Ben snapped. Max pulled out his phone and dialed Eddie's number. Ben growled, "Or you could ignore me. For fuck's sake…"

Max put Eddie on speaker. "Eddie, it's Max."

"Max, hey. How y'all farin'?" Eddie sounded like his mouth was full.

"Sorry to bother you."

"No, no! It's fine. I was on break anyway. Nice to have some peace and quiet from Vico's grumblin'."

"Ed," Gabe said, "have you ever heard of a berserker? Real tough and big, ugly, really strong—"

Eddie had some kind of coughing fit.

Gabe grinned. "Guessing you have."

"You guys met one? And I wasn't there?" Eddie sighed his disappointment. "Yeah. I'm familiar with 'em. It's hard to forget when you've fought one. My unit and I once tracked one. A murderer who'd gone on a killin' spree in Dallas. It slaughtered my entire unit before I brought him down. I've still got the scars from when the thing gored me with those claws. Wait. Don't tell me you two are planning on fightin' one! I even need to tell you why that's a stupid idea?"

Ben motioned toward the phone. "Thank you!"

"Be prepared if you take on one of those fuckers. They're not like normal werewolves."

Gabe snorted. "Yeah, we figured that one out. That's why we called you. We wanna know what we're up against."

"Everythin' you know about werewolves—forget it. All of it. A berserker's got skin like stone, and a bite force that can take off your arm. Their claws alone could kill you in seconds. The one I fought ate silver bullets for breakfast. I mean, I emptied two magazines into that thing. Regeneration? Forget it, their wounds heal so quickly, it's damn near impossible to maim them enough to slow them down. Aconitum just makes them angry. Their immunity to poison is through the damn roof."

Eddie was so riled up, his Texas drawl was more apparent than ever. Usually, he was soft-spoken. Max's spirits plummeted. "So, we have no chance against him?" If they couldn't hope to defeat him in a fair fight, then what chance did they have of stopping McCready with the Council at his back?

"Well, I didn't say that. I'm still alive, ain't I? They still bleed; they can be killed. Penetratin' their defenses is the hardest part. Don't fight one during the night. They're at their strongest in the moonlight. Silver can still weaken some of their strong regeneration abilities as long as you use it right."

Ben cut in. "There's a problem, Ed. Guns aren't exactly permitted in the fight."

Eddie laughed. "Who said I was talking about guns, boss? Montana's big on their guns but many gun shops also carry items of protection against werewolves. There are tons of variety, so you don't need to worry about permits. This is gonna be a physical fight, so buy yourselves some finger claws. They're like brass knuckles, but they fit over your fingertips, and they're made of silver. They sell some that fit most paw sizes, too. Go with those, have someone fit you just before the fight. Keep slicing him and let the silver get all up in his bloodstream. You'll start seein' results. Oh! And buy some silver dentures for your fangs too. That'll make him real mad."

Max's head spun. He'd had no idea such items even existed. "So silver claws and fangs. Thanks, Ed."

"No problem. I'll do some research on who stocks silver weapons in Montana. One more thing, and this is important, guys, so listen. The most dangerous thing McCready can do is howl. These things can control a battlefield with their howl and make soldiers enter a bloodlust that turns even friends against each other. That happens, you're finished. I've seen it. Remember that."

Max swallowed, his heart pounding. "So, what do we do?"

"I'd recommend wearin' earplugs to block out the noise. They could always fall out, but they'll be better than nothin' once that beast starts howlin'."

Gabe clapped Max on the shoulder. "Thanks, Ed. We owe you one. First round's on me when we get home."

"Be safe, y'all."

Max hung up and exhaled. He felt more hopeful than before.

Slouching in bed, Ben furrowed his brows. "A berserker can control the minds of lesser werewolves, huh? Guess that explains the councilmembers I saw with glowing eyes. Great."

Max asked, "This fight... are there any rules?"

Ben pursed his lips. "I'm trying to remember. Gabe's dad explained this all to me once. From what I remember, it's a free-for-all. The fight ends when the loser submits to the new Alpha, the Alpha is killed, or when no one is left alive to oppose the Alpha's rule. As is custom, the one who submits may live, but he is banished from the territory forever. Disgrace to some wolves is a worse fate than death."

In the silence, Gabe glowered at Ben. "You knew all this shit about berserkers, but you seriously thought you could do this alone."

Ben winced. "Like I said, I was desperate enough that I thought I could still shift into one."

A growl rumbled from Gabe's chest. "I told you what I became in Vermont. You knew I could shift to one. We could have faced this together!"

Sighing, Ben said, "You told me you lost control. I couldn't risk that happening."

Gabe deflated, scent souring with hurt. "You didn't trust me to be there for you, Ben."

Another wince. "Gabe, I didn't want you to risk getting hurt."

"I could have lost you!" Gabe's roar filled the room. "You fucking asshole. You could have died, and you didn't even give me the option of being there to help you. I already lost my father, I can't fucking lose you, too." Beneath the scent of fear and hurt was the salty sting of tears. "Screw you.

Why the fuck would you do that to me?" Shoulders rising and falling fast, Gabe looked away.

A wounded noise escaped Ben. "I'm sorry, kid."

A harsh laugh escaped Gabe. "Like that makes it okay."

"It doesn't. I'm… I'm so sorry. I just—" His voice broke, and Ben cleared it. "I didn't think any of us would leave Vermont alive. I thought I'd have to watch all of you die. Do you know what that's like? You're my agents, and you signed on for the job knowing the risk. But… Gabe, I'm so tired of worrying that I'm going to lose you. I couldn't ask you, any of you, to throw away your lives. It's on me to leave the world better than I found it. For the younger folks like you. Like my sons."

"Ask me. Ben, you can always ask me. I'd… I'd do anything for you. You know that."

A single tear spilled down Ben's cheek and disappeared into his beard. Clenching his jaw, he opened an arm. Gabe went to him in seconds and buried himself in Ben's side. Averting his gaze, Max decided to give them the space they needed.

After a few minutes, Gabe walked out with an awkward clearing of his throat, head held high as if his posture would hide his red eyes and damp cheeks. They left Ben alone to rest. Max gripped Gabe's arm. "Gabe, if you could become a… a berserker again, we could kick McCready's ass."

Gabe punched the button to call the elevator. "I don't think I can!"

"Could you try?"

"I don't know, Max. For all I know, it was the blood moon's influence on me that messed something up in me. Everything was inside out. The portal to the She-Wolf's realm had been opened. The blood moon was pulling at me. You were in danger. The monster from my past was there. I'm not a berserker. It was just a combination of a thousand different things happening at once."

Smelling Gabe's distress, Max frowned. "Gabe, this could be a good thing."

Gabe scowled and marched inside when the elevator doors opened. "It's a *good* thing that I can turn into a werewolf version of the Hulk? I'm already dangerous enough as a regular-sized wolf!"

Max reined in his excitement. "You're not dangerous. Look, if you feel like hulking out tomorrow, will you consider doing it?"

Gabe pursed his lips, his eyes narrowed. "And kill how many bystanders in the process? Ben was worried about the damage I could do. He was an idiot, but he knows me. Stopping McCready at the cost of losing myself is not worth the risk."

Max sighed, leaning against the wall. "Fine. Okay. You're right." He took his mate's hand. "We can do this, love. You don't need to go all berserker mode. Hey." He took Gabe's face in his hands when he continued to frown. "Maybe we don't need it. We're so much stronger together—"

"—than we are apart." Gabe managed a smile and pressed his lips to Max's forehead. "Let's do this, mi amor."

McCready's wolves gathered in the depths of the woods, pawing over earth dyed red with centuries-old blood. The smell of their excitement and anticipation fueled Max's heartbeat as he and Gabe led the way toward the grove. Ryan and the others came along, each wearing earplugs. They would challenge McCready's council wolves while Gabe and Max focused on McCready.

Ben took them aside and opened his bag. "Earplugs. Fangs. Claws." He sighed, silver eyes dark as he met their gaze. "Shift, and let's get you ready."

Max's stomach churned as Gabe looked into his eyes, then asked, "Ready?"

He nodded, swallowing. "Yeah. Let's do this."

Gabe peeled his shirt over his head and kicked off his jeans. He dropped to all fours as the change came over him and within seconds, an amber-eyed black wolf stood beside him. He thrust one enormous paw forward and Ben strapped on the silver claws one paw at a time.

"Open up," Ben said, holding out the silver dentures, each canine as sharp as a blade. "Careful now, don't want you to cut yourself."

The black wolf opened his maw and Ben carefully placed the dentures. "They fit okay?"

Gabe wagged his tail in response. Ben squeezed the earplugs and inserted them into each pointed ear, and Gabe flicked them in protest.

Max had already undressed and shifted by the time Ben was ready to suit him up. The dentures were uncomfortable and pricked him, but they fit snugly. The claws felt unnatural, but he hoped they worked. Once Ben inserted the earplugs, the sounds of the forest were muted. Max whined, not liking that one of his vital defenses was dulled.

"Don't be worried, mi amor."

Max jumped, his ears flicking. The voice had come from within his mind as clearly as if Gabe were speaking right into his ear. He turned to his mate and found his tail wagging.

"I'm here. I'll be your eyes and ears."

Within Max's heart, the golden bonds of *love* and *pack* and *mate* filled him with warmth and drove away his fear. *"We will. We'll be stronger together."* Despite his fears, Max's tail wagged too.

The black wolf's eyes seemed to sparkle with delight.

Max nuzzled underneath Gabe's chin, licking the fur on his cheek. *"Let's go. McCready's expecting us."*

Ben helped suit up the other agency wolves with silver fangs and claws, then popped in his own noise-canceling earplugs and shifted.

McCready awaited them, lanky and naked, his skin so pale he glowed in the darkness of the woods. His lips split into a smile at the sight of them. "Maxwell. Look at you, so cocky and sure. Not afraid of me now that the moonblade is gone?" Anger thickened McCready's voice to a growl as if Max was just a reminder of the power he'd almost had within his grasp.

Narrowed eyes crawled over Max's skin. He fought back a growl, unsettled by the way those eyes seemed to delve under his fur, seeking his every weakness. McCready clicked his tongue dismissively. "It's no matter. I can bend this world to my will even without the She-Wolf's power. You really think you dogs have a chance in hell against me? Come on then! I'll show you the might of a pure-blooded werewolf!"

McCready doubled over. His arms extended and bulged with muscle, and coarse brown fur burst from his pores. His euphoric cry became a guttural snarl as his face distorted. A snout grew where his nose used to be. His fingers became paws, each with razor claws.

When McCready looked up, the face of a monster stared back at them. It was hard to imagine he had ever been human at all. The beast threw back his head and a hoarse bellow rippled the leaves on the trees and sent birds fleeing into the gray skies.

Max's tail drooped and his ears flattened. He was prey.

"Lobito, stay with me!" Gabe's voice commanded. *"Let's do this, Max. Together!"*

Max turned and found his mate standing tall, fur bristling, lips pulled back from his fangs. Gabe's tail hung low, but before Max's eyes, he raised it high in defiance.

The whine at the back of his throat turned into a snarl, as loud as he could make it, until his body thrummed with fury. He raised his tail high and took a step forward, coming to stand beside his mate, their fur touching.

"Together," Max promised him.

The ground shook as the beast came toward them.

"I'll hit him from the front," Gabe said through their telepathic bond. *"You circle around and flank him."*

Max growled his response.

Around them, Gabe and Max's friends shifted and prepared to face off against McCready's wargs and ensorcelled councilmembers. Ben led the charge with Zach, tackling an enemy wolf to the ground. Ryan and Izzie watched each other's backs as McCready's pack closed in.

In a blur, Gabe dashed forward, and he and McCready stared each other down. Neither attacked, growls vibrating their bodies. Gabe snapped at the air between them, egging McCready on. The beast shot forward, his jaws lunging for Gabe. Gabe got in a bite, his fangs slicing at McCready's wrinkled snout. Blood dotted the ground. An enormous paw came flying at Gabe, claws slicing the air.

With McCready's back to him, Max charged, spraying dirt behind him as he ran. Max lunged for McCready's haunch, digging his fangs into the hardened hide and ripping away fur. Despite the sharpness of his fangs, he tasted no blood as he dashed away.

Gabe attacked McCready's blind spot, clinging by his jaws to the beast's side.

"Now, Max!"

Max hurled himself into the beast's bulky body, digging his fangs in deep and slashing at his hide with his claws.

Gabe's yelps filled the woods. McCready fastened his claws into Gabe's hindquarter and pulled the black wolf free of his grip on McCready's flesh. Max bit down with all his might, shaking and ripping, but Gabe only screamed louder.

"I'm trying! I'm trying!"

Max charged at McCready's head and his jaws snapped around a short, pointed ear. McCready released Gabe, and Max saw white when a claw caught him across the side of his head. He toppled over, tumbling in the dirt. His ears rang, his whole body aching. When he looked up, the beast was tearing toward him, shaking the earth under his paws. McCready yelped when Gabe tackled him, his fangs embedded in the beast's back leg. McCready whipped around and his jaws snapped closed on Gabe's neck, sending him flying. He tumbled in a tangle of claws and lay limp in the dirt.

"Gabe? Gabe, are you all right?"

The beast came toward him, and Max retreated, coming to a stand in front of Gabe, digging his snout underneath matted fur, and nudging him.

"Gabe, get up. He's coming!"

Gabe whined weakly in response, his breathing labored.

A growl compelled Max's attention. McCready, his fangs bared in a hideous smile, threw back his head.

"He's going to howl, Gabe. Get ready!"

It wasn't a howl that tore from McCready's throat but a roar that could shatter glass. It left Max's ears ringing and made his head throb. Gabe yelped and pawed at his ears.

Max's eyes watered when he opened them, his paws unsteady. He was still under his own control. He huffed. *Nice try.* He lunged—and fangs carved into his back leg. Max fell, kicking and squirming, yelping in shock and pain. He turned and looked up into Gabe's blazing yellow eyes, the pupils so constricted they were pinpricks. The golden bond between them shuddered and strained, on the verge of breaking as McCready twisted it to his whims.

Gabe's furious voice boomed in Max's mind. *"Die! You must die. For Alpha McCready!"*

"Gabe? No, fight it!"

The black wolf shook him in his grasp, fangs carving through flesh and muscle. The silver only made it worse, like he was being burned and bitten all at once. The pain left Max paralyzed.

"Gabe, stop!"

Panting, Max struggled to stand, and the throbbing pain brought him back down. The silver was in his bloodstream. The black wolf came toward him, his snout wrinkled in a hateful snarl.

"Kill, for Alpha McCready," Gabe's voice snarled, so hateful it was unrecognizable. He whined, shaking his head, his eyes flashing from feral yellow to fiery amber. Gabe's human voice, tortured and anguished, cried out to Max. *"I can't stop it, Max! Run, get away from me!"*

McCready growled as he advanced on Max, coming to stand beside Gabe. Max forced himself to stand, wobbling as he avoided putting weight on his back leg. He stepped on something—one of Gabe's earplugs. Despair made him tremble. Around him, McCready's pack was overwhelming Ben and the others.

It was over. They'd lost. There was no way they could stand against McCready. Max ran as fast as he could, panting through the pain as Ben and the others grew closer and closer. Hot breath blazed on his heels, fangs snapping as Gabe pursued him. The ground shook and Max's paws scrabbled in the dirt as McCready landed before him, barring the way. The beast snapped his frothing jaws, eyes wide and hungry.

Something hurtled past him. A whip cracked, gleaming silver. McCready toppled over with a howl, blood bursting from his hide. Max's jaw dropped.

Veronica Reyes stood before her son's bristling form, brandishing her silver whip. "Get the hell away from my son." She snapped the whip across the ground in warning.

The surrounding wolves barked and snarled but didn't attack, their yellow eyes fixated on McCready. Waiting for his instructions.

McCready froze in his tracks, regarding her. He growled but did something Max hadn't anticipated. Bowing his head, the beast lowered himself to the ground. He shifted, turning from wolf to man.

Max returned to human form and ran, darting to Veronica's side. He spat out his silver dentures and said, "V, what are you doing here? It isn't safe!"

"Izzie called. Someone had to talk some sense into my son's head," Veronica growled.

Max felt such shame he could hardly look at her. He thought he'd been doing the right thing by fighting alongside Gabe. Gabe would have fought alone otherwise. Now, he wished he'd fought harder for them to go home.

"Reyes. You're human." McCready bristled with contempt. "You have no place here." He closed in on her, but Ben and the other wolves flocked around her, shielding her.

Veronica's eyes hardened and her lip curled. "Do not speak to me. Max, help Gabriel up. We're leaving."

"You're as meddling as your husband," McCready sneered. "And we all know what happened to him, don't we?"

Izzie shifted, blood staining her olive skin. "Touch my mother, and I'll take your fingers off." She snapped her fangs at him.

"Ben," Veronica said, her voice shaking, "tell everyone to back down while you still can. I'm not losing another of my family to this son of a bitch."

Max knelt, grabbing onto Gabe's arm as he reverted to human form, too weakened to keep his wolf form. The silver dentures fell out, and Max tugged off the claws stuck on Gabe's fingertips.

McCready's wargs closed in on all sides, caging them in.

"Wolves of the LPA," McCready said. "Submit. I will make your deaths as painless as possible. Resist, and my wargs and I will rip you to pieces."

Izzie wiped away a smear of blood from her eye. Ryan growled, his white fur stained red, and Zach flattened his ears and went on licking Ryan's wounds. Vicenzo, bloodied and covered in sweat, flipped McCready the middle finger. Panting, Ben held a paw to his chest.

"Ben. What do we do?" Max asked through the bonds.

Ben whined low in his throat. *"If anyone wants to retreat, I won't stop you. I'll do all I can to hold him off long enough for you guys to escape."*

Zach whined. *"Ben, we won't leave you."*

Ben whipped his head toward him, an anguished sound spilling from his throat. *"The agency has to go on. The wolves of NYC will need our help more than ever. Please. Run, all of you!"*

Gabe's bond pulsed and burned in Max's chest. "No," Gabe snarled, and there was an edge in his voice that made Max shiver. His mate's body burned hot against Max's side.

Veronica gasped. "Gabriel, what are you doing?"

One look at Gabe's face, and Max's heart sank. Gabe's eyes blazed feral yellow. Black fur thickened on his face, which was contorting into a wolf's by the second. Max gasped and let him go, unable to stop himself. His chest burned and ached, and he struggled to breathe as Gabe's bond blazed.

"Gabe, stop. Stop, you're losing control!"

"Won't let you." Gabe panted, his voice deepening until it was bestial and unrecognizable. "Won't let you hurt my pack. My family. Not again!" Gabe's bones creaked, and a snarl of pain and fury tore from him as he grew taller by the second. He was going berserk like in Vermont, but this time it was different. Max could feel it. Gabe wasn't in control because he was terrified. Max could smell it, feel Gabe's terror thundering through their bond and spinning his own heart out of control.

"Gabe, don't!" Max implored him, gripping his hairy arm.

McCready took several steps back. His wargs growled, lashing their tails and baring their teeth.

"This again?" McCready hissed. "Ready yourselves!"

"Run," Gabe croaked, his voice quaking with terror. "Run, all of you! I can't—I can't control it. I can't fight it!" He'd shifted entirely to a bipedal wolf, casting his shadow over them as he towered above.

Ryan stumbled back, and Zach crowded in front of him as Ben tucked his tail in terror. Max's heart sank when he looked into that bestial face. There was nothing he recognized about Gabe in this form, not even his eyes. They were overrun by feral light.

Gabe threw back his head and his roar rattled the trees to their roots. A piercing pain stabbed into Max's brain. Next to him, Ben howled in agony. Whining, Ryan pawed his ears. Zach's eyes flashed from his human shade to pure yellow, and Izzie dropped to her knees, clawing at the grass and arching her back.

"Kill," Gabe commanded, his voice monstrous and all-consuming. *"Kill him. Kill them all!"*

Fury overtook Max. The earplugs were useless. All Gabe had to do was grab hold of the bonds tying them to one another and poison them with his rage. His mouth flooded with saliva and his claws lengthened. He couldn't distinguish between friend and foe. He wanted blood. His pack's blood. McCready's blood. Max rounded on Ryan, who stared him down, fangs bared. Ryan hurled himself upon Max, crushing him into the dirt.

Izzie yelped in agony when Zach threw himself into her, fangs ripping into her fur. Ben collided with Vicenzo, fangs and claws tearing at each other. McCready's wargs fought among themselves, spilling blood.

"Gabriel, stop!" Veronica roared, and she charged. She swung her silver whip, and Gabe bellowed when it sliced across his snout. Her son stumbled, his eyes flickering. "This isn't you!" Veronica's voice shook, and tears were caught in her eyelashes. "I've already lost a husband. I won't lose you too! Find our bond and use it! Come back to me."

The fury pounding through Max flickered and died.

Gabe slumped over, shrinking down to his normal size. "M-Mamá," he croaked. The fire blazing through Gabe's bond simmered to a flickering flame. His horror and remorse crashed over him, threatening to buckle Max's knees.

McCready rose, shaking his fur as if to throw off the force Gabe had used to attack them. He snarled, "Now! Strike!" His wargs obeyed, rushing at Gabe.

"Run!" Veronica screamed. "All of you, run!"

No one needed telling twice. Ryan's wolf nudged Max to his feet and shoved him in the back. Shifting to a man, Ben hoisted Izzie into his arms and carried the black wolf away. Vicenzo ran, Zach at his heels.

"Gabe, come on!" Max shouted, unwilling to go any farther.

Gabe and McCready were locked in combat, shaking the earth every time they collided. The wargs hurled themselves on Gabe's body, swarming him. Veronica swung her whip at them and made them fall to the ground thrashing as their flesh and fur burned. Gabe lifted McCready off his feet and threw him into a tree, the roots groaning as they ripped free from the earth.

Gabe picked up his mother as if she were a doll. "Hold on to me," he growled, and she clutched onto his shoulders. Bunching his muscles, Gabe sprang, tearing into the trees away from the pack and McCready. Max called out to him, but the howls and snarls of McCready's wolves drowned him out. McCready sent a few wolves after Gabe and Veronica, then rounded on Max and the pack.

"Move! Now!" Zach grabbed Max's wrist and hauled him after the pack. They ran, feet and paws thundering over the blood-soaked earth. The trees thinned, revealing the main road back to town. Zach leaped into the rental van, and the pack piled in as McCready and his wargs burst through the tree line and charged at the vehicle.

"Fucking drive, Zach!" Ryan shrieked as several wargs lunged at the vehicle, bloody paws smearing the windows.

"I'm trying!" he hollered, slamming on the gas.

McCready pounced, slamming down where the vehicle had been only seconds ago. Pushing the speed limit, Zach drove them away toward town. McCready and his wargs howled, their voices cruel and mocking.

Frustration overwhelmed Max, and he slammed his hand against the window.

This wasn't over, not by a long shot.

Their fight with Aaron McCready had only just begun.

GABE CARRIED VERONICA THROUGH the woods until the howls and roars of McCready and his pack faded. The shift lost its grip on him and he shivered as the crisp air rolled over his naked skin.

"Here. I brought you a change of clothes." His mother opened her backpack and handed him some fresh clothes.

Exhaustion wore at him, but Gabe knew they had to keep moving. McCready would be tracking them. Wordlessly, they walked until the town came into view and followed the road that led to their motel. Gabe's stomach clenched at the sight of the rental van parked outside. The pack awaited them.

Veronica rubbed his shoulders. "Go on. Talk to them."

Acid was bitter in the back of his throat. "I... I can't face them."

Rolling her eyes, Veronica grabbed his shoulders and steered him toward the motel. "Come on, Gabriel. Which way is your room?"

The scent of the pack compelled him onward until he stood outside the door. Just as he raised a shaking hand to knock, the door opened. Wide honey orange eyes took him in.

"Gabe?" Max's voice quavered. There was blood in his hair. Cuts on his arms. Some of them were from the fight with McCready, but the other bites and scratches... Gabe had done that. Bitten him. Controlled his own friends and made them fight each other.

The reality of what he'd done ripped into him, guilt and horror bleeding out of him in waves he couldn't fight. "I... Oh Goddess." Shaking, he bowed his head. The pack was gathered around him. Their scents soured with uncertainty, and he didn't miss the way Vicenzo took a step back. Tears burned Gabe's eyes. "I'm... I'm so sorry."

Goddess, he'd used their bonds against them, used their friendship, their love, their trust, to turn himself into a killing machine. And the terrifying part was he hadn't been in control of it. Taking from them, using them in such a monstrous way, had been as instinctive as breathing.

"Gabe," Max whispered, the scent of his tears burning Gabe's nose.

Unable to face them, Gabe stumbled past them to the bed and collapsed at the edge.

Gasping, Gabe doubled over and hid his face in the sheets. "I'm a f-fucking monster." He sucked in a gasp, sobs rattling his body.

"You're not, mi sol. I know you," Veronica whispered. She put her hands on him. Gabe wanted to throw her off, to scream at them to get away from him before he lost control and hurt them.

"I'm no better than McCready. I'm worse!" He clutched at his mother's ripped blouse and buried his face in her stomach. She stroked his hair like she'd done when he was a child, whispering to him.

"That wasn't you," Ben said, his voice hoarse and trembling. "You weren't in control."

Gabe gulped frantically. "S-Stop it, Ben. Stop defending me!"

Ryan sniffed hard. "We'll always defend you, you idiot." His arms went around Gabe, squeezing too hard for Gabe to shake him off.

Gently, Max leaned his forehead on Gabe's shaking shoulder. Zach sat on the bed and touched his knee while Izzie sat on his other side and hugged him tight. Their bonds glowed warm in Gabe's chest, soothing him. It was too much. He'd just shown them the absolute worst side of himself, and even so, they stood by him. He didn't deserve it, but he was too selfish to reject them.

Once his shaking had subsided, Veronica dried the tears from his face, her own cheeks damp.

Vicenzo stood behind her, watching the streets outside the window. "We can't stay long," he said, ever the bearer of bad news. "We've got to get back to New York and get ready for what's coming."

They'd had one shot at preventing McCready's ascension to Alpha and they'd failed. Before the day was over, the news would spread of the Council's new leader. What would happen next? What kind of damage would McCready do to the years of progress in werewolf-human relations? It made him sick with uncertainty.

Ben sighed. "I'm going to pack for the trip back. We should clear out sooner rather than later."

The rest of the pack dispersed except for Max, Veronica, and Izzie. Max collapsed into a chair by the window, putting his head back and closing his eyes.

Veronica's gentle hand settled on Gabe's cheek. "How are you feeling?"

He slumped into the bed. "Terrible."

"I meant your wounds."

Gabe jerked his shoulders. "Fine, I guess. Mamá, you could have gotten hurt by interfering. Izzie, what were you thinking? Did you want us to lose another parent?"

Izzie reeled back as if slapped. "Screw you, Gabe! She had every right to know the danger we were in. What if you'd died?"

"What if our *mother* had died?" Gabe spat.

Veronica snapped, "Enough! Izzie, go and pack. Now. We can't waste any more time in Montana. We must get out while we can."

With a huff, Izzie stomped off.

"For the record, your sister is right. You were reckless. And I've had it up to here with reckless behavior from you."

Gabe's ears burned. "Ma. I had to. McCready needs to be stopped."

"You never should have agreed to fight him. I understand what is at stake, but this was a death sentence."

Gabe folded his arms. "Ben went rushing recklessly into danger too."

"And he'll get a lecture from me. You can count on that." Veronica slumped, pushing her hair away from her face. "This is my fault. I know it."

"Mamá, no."

"Yes, it is. After Manuel died, you took on so many of his responsibilities. Whether it was looking after Izzie, working all those jobs during high school, or even making me coffee in the morning. You were already working so hard, even harder than I was. I hope you know how much I appreciated it when you stepped up and became the man of the house."

Gabe nodded.

"I tried to help you cope after Manuel—but there was so much guilt, so much anger and pain, and all those feelings, coupled with all the responsibility you felt toward our family... it changed you."

Gabe stared down at the sheets. "I was a lost cause for a long time. You did all you could. I just wanted to fill Dad's shoes."

And he'd failed miserably. A part of him wished he'd stayed and fought. If he'd died at McCready's hands, at least he would have died as his father had, trying to keep those he loved safe. Now, McCready would come for them, and Gabe didn't know if he was strong enough to stop him.

"Gabriel. Breathe." Her hand settled on his trembling arm.

"I'll kill him next time, Mamá." Fury left his voice choked and trembling. "He won't break our family apart again." He would die before he saw his family divided by McCready.

His mother blinked back tears and looked away. Her hand fell away from his arm.

CHAPTER 7

WORLD GONE MAD

THE PACK PREPARED TO leave the motel and drive to the airport. The clouds darkened and stars lit up the sky. Gabe was silent, trailing behind Max. Max felt the same disappointment and frustration; they'd failed today. McCready would take power, and what would happen then was shrouded in uncertainty.

"Chin up, kid," Ben rumbled. He squeezed Max's shoulder. "We gave it our all. I'm damn proud of both of you."

Max managed a smile. "Even though you told us to stay?"

"Yeah, even if you went against orders." Ben's mustache twitched as he smiled.

Once they were packed, they loaded up the rental van. Max threw his bag in the trunk and stared back up the road toward Wolf Point.

Gabe dumped his bag and sighed. "We did our best, Max." He didn't sound fully convinced.

"We can still stop him. We'll think of something else."

Gabe heaved his shoulders up and dropped them. "Like hell I'll be sitting around waiting for McCready to make us a target." He slammed the trunk and walked away.

Ryan scowled, holding his heavy suitcase. "Thanks, I was just gonna sit on my bag, Gabe."

Max opened the trunk for him and then followed Gabe inside the van. The pack piled in, and Zach sped the car toward the airport. The headlights illuminated the road and the trees as they hurtled through the night. Max was looking forward to returning home.

How long will it be home? How long will we feel safe there?

He leaned his head on Gabe's shoulder and crossed his arms, exhaling as a strong arm wound around his shoulders.

BY THE TIME THEY arrived home, the news had broken: the Council had a new Alpha. On national TV, Alpha Aaron McCready accepted the title before the eyes of the surviving councilmembers who'd allied with McCready as well as the entire shifter world. Gabe, Max, and the pack watched from the TV in the agency's living room.

"A new day dawns for the werewolf. For too long, we've been hated and feared. Too long we've been abused, shunned—hunted! The war between humans and shifters ended long ago, and still, we are not free of human prejudice and persecution. The time has come to rise, rise and welcome the new world that we shall create together. A world where we don't have to be taught to hide who we are. As of today, the Council is ending all negotiations with human governors."

Max's stomach turned over.

"Any werewolf who continues to hide inside human cities with our oppressors will not have the protection of this pack. I will not support any treaty that makes us live alongside humans after all they've done to our kind. So it is my greatest pleasure to welcome all werewolf kind to Crescent Cove. It is, by far, the biggest pack territory in the country, an island off the coast of Alaska, just for our kind. Humans are not permitted, nor is anyone who shares human blood, such as hybrids. To all who've lived your lives in fear just for being what you are, you and your family will be safe here. This is only the beginning of the new world we will create together." There was genuine emotion in McCready's voice. The man actually believed he was the savior their kind needed. When applause erupted, Max felt sick as he realized that others saw this monster as the hero they'd been waiting for.

Gabe's shoulders were tight as Max put his arm around him.

"Ben, what will happen?" Max looked over the back of the couch at him.

Ben collapsed into an armchair. "Shifters coexisting with humans won't be protected from discrimination." He scoffed. "So much for liberating werewolves. Then there's the fact that the Council was formed to act as peacekeepers between human governors and shifter society. With the Council doing away with the negotiations, there's no one to represent werewolves in government, no governing body to uphold the peace treaties we established with humans all those years ago. McCready might as well have declared war on the humans of America."

Max felt sick. "Will humans see it that way?"

Ben pressed his fingers into his temple, letting out a growl. "Things are gonna get tense between shifters and humans, Max. You know how many assholes like McCready have been waiting for a fucking war against humans? Too many. So we need to watch our backs. All of us." He shot looks at the pack seated throughout the living room, their faces etched with worry.

Vicenzo paced on the carpet. "Right. So smile and wave at the scared little humans so we don't hurt their fragile feelings? What shit."

Max's chin touched his chest, his stomach swirling with uncertainty. He'd never considered the Council's greater purpose. They'd been one-half of a bridge in the relationship between werewolves and humans. Now that bridge was crumbling, creating a divide between their kinds. All that remained to be seen was who would attempt to cross that divide first and with what intentions. Would it be for good or evil?

"What happens to the agency?" Izzie asked.

"Nothing," Ben said, eyes narrowing. "The city will need us now more than ever. We keep fighting the good fight and helping others. No matter what."

"You know," Gabe murmured, his voice hesitant. "Max, if things get too dangerous, you can always leave this world for a better one."

Max's stomach lurched. As the son of a deity, he could open a path to the She-Wolf's realm. "You want me to leave?"

Gabe winced. "No. But you might be safer in the She-Wolf's realm. It's something to consider."

He felt an unexpected sting of anger. "I'm not leaving you. Not ever."

"But don't you have questions, Max? About your birth mother? About why you were left on Earth? I don't want you to feel deprived of that knowledge. You deserve to know. Don't let me stand in your way."

Max's throat clicked dryly. He did, but anger stirred in him just from acknowledging how badly he burned to know. It didn't matter why he'd been left, only that it had happened and Amaris had never come for him when he'd needed her. But Gabe and Max's adoptive mother had been there for him.

Max pressed his lips to Gabe's forehead and looked him square in the eyes. "You are my way, Gabe Reyes."

If Gabe sensed any doubts, he only smiled and nuzzled their foreheads together.

Ben faced the pack. "Be on alert, all of you. Things will get rough. The city will need the agency more than ever, but there's no doubt in my mind McCready's people will continue to target us. Be watchful. Be safe. This is going to get worse before it gets better."

If it got better at all.

Not long after their return to New York, the tension between humans and werewolves shifted.

When Gabe, Ben, and Ryan had gone away to pursue John Stone to Italy, Max had been forced to take time off from The Lycanthrope Academy, a training center for aspiring agents. Now that his time off for his mating ceremony was up, it was time to get back to work. Max had three more years of training ahead and with tensions as they were between wolves and humans, he was more determined than ever to graduate and do his part to contribute to society.

Dressed in his tight-fitted black training apparel, Max roamed the halls in search of his next session. They would practice subduing a feral wolf today. In the training room, people paired up on the mats with their four-legged partners. Scents clashed in the training room. The students were a diverse mix of full-blooded wolves, hybrids, and even humans who wanted to learn more about werewolves and help them as allies.

Max fitted his utility belt with a tranquilizer gun and a catch pole among others items he might need. Behind him, a wolf snarled and a woman screamed, and Max whipped around. A wolf towered over their human classmate Tanya, fangs bared close to her neck.

Max and a few others charged in. Catching the wolf with his catch pole, Max yanked, tugging him off Tanya.

The instructor stormed over, shouting, "What in the goddess's name is going on here?"

The wolf shifted to a human and freed himself from the noose. He shoved Max out of the way and marched up to the instructor. Max swallowed his growl and checked on Tanya, who was shaking but not hurt.

"Humans don't belong here!" the shifted man shouted. "They're our oppressors!"

Max snapped, "Not all of them. Tanya's our classmate. She's on our side!"

"Shut up, mutt! No one cares what some half-human thinks." A bark of a laugh tore from the shifted man's throat. "Alpha McCready's got the right idea. I don't want to live among the people who oppress and muzzle us. Fuck the LPA for encouraging this crap." He grabbed his clothes, dressed, and marched out.

To Max's dismay, a handful of disgruntled-looking men and women followed him.

Max's stomach soured as he watched them leave. He'd thought the aspiring agents had been united in their ideas of a future for werewolves. Maybe all the werewolves at this school had needed was someone to embolden them to be open in their hateful thinking.

Someone like McCready.

"Take a seat on the table," Dr. Luke said.

Gabe sat on the exam table and removed his shirt. His heart quickened when Luke dipped a syringe in light purple liquid. Gabe's nose wrinkled at the potent odor. Aconitum, or wolfsbane as it was more commonly called. "Try not to poison me, Doc."

Luke pushed out some air bubbles from the syringe and turned to face him, smiling pleasantly. "Believe it or not, I have done this before, Gabriel. Many times."

"Will it help?" Gabe asked.

"It should, yes. I've used this treatment on a few berserkers before with some success. It will act as a sedative and suppress your wolf."

Gabe nearly jumped off the table. "Completely?" How would he protect the pack if he couldn't shift?

"Oh no. You'll still be able to shift, but you'll be much less likely to lose your control, provided you don't skip any doses."

"Good." Gabe sighed, twisting his fingers together.

"You might feel some side effects after the first dose. Weakness, irritability, dizziness. It will pass, but call me if it doesn't."

"How often should I take the dose?"

Luke stopped beside the exam table. "Let's start with twice a week and say after two weeks, we'll bump you down to once a week. Deep breath in and out for me."

Gabe did as he was asked and Luke jabbed him in the shoulder. He grimaced at the sting. The injection site tingled.

"You should feel tingling and numbness in the area for twenty-four hours. This is completely normal."

Gabe hopped off the table and pulled his shirt on.

"Have a good day, Gabe. I hope this helps."

Gabe hoped so too.

After his doctor's appointment, Gabe and Max made plans to meet with the pack at their favorite bar, The Slaughtered Lamb. The leaves around the city were changing, and the sky was an indigo blue as the moon rose.

"How do you feel?" Max asked.

Gabe yawned. "A little tired. I hope this treatment works."

"It will." Max squeezed his hand. "What do you want to order at the bar?"

"I'm craving their rabbit stew. Think I'll get a boozy hot chocolate too. What the—" Gabe stopped in his tracks, his smile sliding off his face.

Strings of caution tape warned customers away from the bar. Lights flashed from a parked police cruiser and police officers investigated the smashed windows of the bar. Gabe let go of Max's hand and jogged to the storefront where Ben, Ryan, Izzie, and Zach were standing.

Ben combed a hand through his beard. "Fucking hell."

Next to him, Ryan stomped his foot. "Are you kidding me? They had to target The Lamb?"

Glass crunched under Gabe's boot. The windows had been smashed. The wooden sign with a werewolf howling at the moon had been splashed with paint. One window hadn't been broken but spray-painted on it was the sentiment COLLAR THE DOGS.

Izzie grimaced, her jaw tight. "The Lamb has been a safe place for werewolves for as long as it's been around."

Gabe touched her shoulder. "They can fix a few windows and clean a sign."

Izzie shook her head. "It's more than that. I don't know if I'll feel safe here again."

Neither did Gabe.

Gabe killed the engine on his bike, and checking to be sure his tranquilizer was fully loaded, made a dash for the grocery store. Red lights flashed in his eyes. Police officers hurried in and he followed them toward the produce section. Gabe slipped on spots of blood dotting the floor and grabbed onto a shelf full of apples to keep from falling.

"This fucking thing was sniffing me! It was gonna attack me!" a mustached man shrieked, motioning an arm toward something.

"LPA." Gabe showed the cops his badge. "Let me through."

The cops stepped aside and revealed a gray wolf huddled against a bin full of produce, bleeding from the top of her head. She shivered but didn't display her fangs as he came closer. Her eyes were wide and fearful, her ears flattened back as he knelt before her.

"Hey. You're okay. Tell me what happened."

The wolf whimpered. She wasn't growling or showing her fangs, and her eyes were a human shade. She was only scared and needed comfort.

Gabe reached out and touched her head between her ears. "You're safe, I promise. Can you tell me what happened to you? I'll give you a ride home if you need it."

The wolf became a woman, blood dripping between her eyes. She wrapped her arms around her chest and Gabe shrugged off his leather jacket and offered it to her.

"I was j-just sniffing the produce. That man, he... he screamed and started attacking me. I didn't bite him, I swear! The shock, the fear, it made me change. Please, don't let them take me to jail." Tears leaked out of her eyes. "My pups need me."

"You won't go to jail. I'll tell them what happened."

Paramedics came to check on her and Gabe filled the police in.

"Bullshit!" the mustached man snapped. Gabe's fingers curled. "That thing was gonna take a bite of me! Bitch should be locked up like the animal she is!"

"She was doing her shopping, same as you!" Gabe's temper flared to the surface, his fangs stabbing at his lower lip.

Beady eyes narrowed as the man glimpsed his fangs. "You animals should have stayed in the fucking woods."

Later that evening, Zach invited Gabe out for a much-needed drink. "I'm telling you, Zach, I wanted to hurt him." Gabe slumped in his bar seat, exhausted.

"I feel you. Here. This one's on me." Zach called the bartender over for another whiskey, on the rocks like Gabe preferred it.

"Thanks, man." Gabe closed his eyes tight. He couldn't get the frightened eyes of the she-wolf out of his mind. "Does it feel... worse than usual?"

Zach gulped his beer and made a face, as if the drink were too bitter. "Yeah. We've been busy lately. Violence is up. More ferals, more clients. Full-blooded werewolves are harassing hybrid wolves, werewolves prey on humans, and humans retaliate."

"Humans have always feared our kind."

"Yeah, but this feels different. People are scared, Gabe."

And Gabe was too.

"Whoa, careful!" Max's laughter was like music to Gabe's ears. He stumbled, latching onto Max's shoulders to keep himself steady. The city spun around him, and his knees were weak. His head would punish him dearly for their drunken night out, but the sixth mojito still felt like a good idea. The Woolen Wolf wasn't as homey as The Lamb, but they knew how to make a mean drink.

"Come on, let's get—*hic!*—home." Max fumbled with his phone, trying to call an Uber.

Gabe nestled his face in his mate's neck, breathing him in. He smelled like a bar, but underneath the other smells clinging to him was Max's unique scent. "Wanna smell more of you when we get home." He wanted to smell Max's most intimate scent, the scent only he knew, wanted to make his body smell like Gabe's and no one else's.

He parted his lips against Max's neck, his tongue smoothing over the mating bite in his warm skin. Max shivered and angled his head, though he kept his eyes on his phone. Determined, Gabe wrapped his arms around Max's chest, bundling him up in the warmth of his body in case he was cold.

"Cold, mi amor?"

"A little," Max confessed. "It's windy tonight."

"I'll warm you up once we're home."

Behind them, there came a loud sniff. A growl rumbled. Gabe reluctantly removed his lips from Max's skin, barely stifling a growl of his own as he encountered the predatory leer of a bulky shifter standing behind them, fangs bared.

"Disgusting. Look at you two," the shifter growled.

Max's shoulders tensed.

"Fucking mutts."

A shock went right through Gabe. He lurched forward and stumbled, crashing headlong into the werewolf and slamming him up against a wall.

"Gabe, no!" Max pawed frantically at his back.

Growls and snarls split the air. Gabe had zeroed in on his target, neglecting to notice he wasn't alone as two other bigoted losers bared their fangs and exposed their claws.

"Call us mutts again," Gabe said, seething. "Fucking dare you!"

He wished he'd kept his mouth shut, but the crushing blow across his jaw was worth watching the bigot's face seize up in fury. Gabe hurtled into one of the bigot's friends, who hurled him away. The wall came flying at him and Gabe braced himself, pushing off with his hands and swinging around. His knuckles bounced off someone's nose, and a roar of fury split the night.

"Get off him, assholes!" Max roared. He tackled one of the bigot's friends and wrestled him away from Gabe.

Gabe saw white as his head struck the wall. He crumpled to the ground, and the wind went out of him as a boot plowed into his gut. Acid scorched his throat, and he doubled over, retching until his stomach ached and his vision blurred.

"Get off me! Get off!"

His heart flew into his throat. The pack had surrounded Max.

"Let's show these mutts just who this city belongs to!"

Max shouted in dismay as one shifter seized him under the arms and restrained him.

Something gleamed in the dark. The blade of a knife. They'd baited them for a fight, and Gabe had taken it. Max would suffer because of him.

"Leave him alone!" He threw himself to his feet and ran, ready to tear them to pieces.

His back collided with the wall, a clawed hand clamped around his throat. Fangs leered at him in a hateful smile.

"We'll make him nice and pretty for you," the shifter sneered.

Gabe struggled, but the shifter was just too strong. He had the strength of a pureblood. Gabe? He was just a weak hybrid. Weak and helpless. They would torture Max and all Gabe could do was watch.

Next thing he knew, the shifters were howling in fear and confusion as they hurtled into the air and floated above the street. The moonlight shone down on Max as he kept them levitated at the level of a streetlamp.

"Apologize!" Max shouted. "Now!"

"We're sorry! Don't hurt me—I mean, us!"

"For what?" Max bared his fangs in a grin. Gabe didn't know whether to be turned on or frightened.

"F-for attacking you and stuff? For calling your lover boy a mutt? All of it! Let us down!"

Max lowered his hands and they dropped, crashing onto the pavement. They groaned and grunted, twitching. Something in Gabe snapped. He lunged, grabbing hold of Max's hand, and ran with him. The wind roared in his ears as his feet slammed the pavement. He hardly heard Max's voice. All that mattered was getting him away, getting him out of there—

"Gabe, stop!" Max ripped his hand away, gasping for air.

Gabe's stomach twisted when he realized blood glimmered on Max's cheek. He'd been scratched. Was he hurt anywhere else? His hands shook as he rolled up Max's sleeves, checking for cuts. He sniffed Max's neck but only smelled sweat and the foul odor of those other werewolves.

"Gabe, Gabe, I'm fine." Max shied away from his touch.

But Gabe couldn't breathe, his arms shaking as they clamped around Max and cradled him to his body.

"Gabe, I'm all right."

His throat closed and his eyes burned. His body trembled so badly he could hardly stand.

But you could have been hurt. They wanted to—

Max could have been tortured until he went feral, like the werewolves in the kennels at the estate.

"Shh. It's okay." Max's arms held Gabe tight. "I'm okay. We both are." His hand was unsteady as it glided over Gabe's hair.

Gabe's throat ached as he sucked in a shuddery gasp, burying his face in Max's neck and breathing him in.

He didn't stop shaking, not until they were home.

CHAPTER 8

SOLACE IN THE STORM

Gabe couldn't sleep. All night long, his mind tormented him with images of what-if scenarios involving Max and those shifters.

I was helpless again.

He wanted to cry at the realization, blinking hard as he stared up at the ceiling. He'd been staring at the ceiling for hours. Max slept beside him, breathing softly, his lashes resting against his freckled cheeks. He kept hearing Max's voice demanding they let him go while the shifter held him up against the wall.

Would Gabe be helpless when McCready came for them? Would he be strong enough to protect Max then? If he tried to protect Max, would he lose all control again? Was he the one he should be afraid of, the real monster? He didn't know what to do, how to trust in himself.

The uncertainty brought bile to the back of his throat. No. He wouldn't be weak again. It was time to take control. He kicked off the sheets and stood, wincing as his stomach ached from where he'd been punched. He eased open the bedroom door, listening, his eyes straining to penetrate the darkness. Seeing and sensing no one, Gabe flicked on a lamp and approached the front door. He'd locked it the moment they were home but double-checking it made him feel more secure. He checked the bathroom, pulling back the shower curtain to make sure no one was hiding out of sight. It was stupid, but he didn't care.

Returning to the living room, he discarded his clothes and shifted to his regular wolf form. He was in control. He padded across the living room carpet to their bedroom door, circled twice, and lay down. The wood was hard and uncomfortable, but he lay there for hours until the first light of dawn cast away the shadows of the living room.

Only when he was sure his mate was safe did Gabe close his eyes and finally find peace.

THE NIGHTMARES RETURNED AFTER their encounter with those shifters. In these nightmares, Gabe was helpless as the city burned, as his friends were brutalized by humans or hybrid-hating werewolves, as Max was taken from him before his eyes. As Gabe tore his own friends apart, his good intentions turned to feral madness by the berserker that snarled under his skin.

Gabe woke in the night, covered in sweat. He shivered, cold all over. Bits and pieces of the nightmare were fading. Max's screams still haunted him. He rolled over and the sheets ripped, clinging to his claws. Max slept peacefully beside him, alive and unhurt. For now.

He didn't sleep the rest of the night. Instead, he got up and watched the door, prowling the living room on all fours. He listened to the silence, fearing the moment it would break.

It never did, but that meant nothing. The hunt was coming eventually.

When he woke, he prepared breakfast and tried not to fall asleep in the pan of eggs he was scrambling.

"Are you sleeping, love?"

The sound of Max's voice made him jump as his mate came up behind him. A gentle hand touched his face, the thumb rubbing at the bags under his eyes.

"Guess not." Gabe tried to smile. He knew he looked hideous.

Max frowned. "Is everything okay?"

He angled his head and kissed Max's palm. "Yeah." Gabe couldn't tell him, not about the nightmares, not about his unusual nighttime patrols through their own home. Max would worry about him.

A wolf protects his pack.

He wouldn't burden Max. His mate had his own worries. Gabe would be strong enough for them both.

He snapped.

Of course he did.

He'd barely slept in weeks. Maybe four hours each night, maybe less.

He forgot to close the front door. Of all the things he could forget, it was the door.

Nothing happened. Nothing happened. Nothing fucking happened.

He repeated those words like a mantra, but they were meaningless every time. Because something could have happened. His heart had dropped when he'd rounded the corner from the elevator, groceries cascading from his arms.

The door was wide open.

I locked it. I locked it!

Where was Max? Was he home? Was he hurt?

In hindsight, all he'd needed to do was sniff the air and he'd have known at once that no one unfamiliar had been through these halls. But something in his brain sounded an alarm bell, and he couldn't hear over it. He crept on his toes from the elevator to the front door.

Holding his breath, he peered into the apartment. Nothing seemed out of place and no one was in sight, but still his heart pounded. The familiar scents of the apartment, of him and Max, did little to calm him. He tore through the house, ripping open the shower curtain, throwing open closet doors, burning his knees on the carpet when he checked under the beds. No one. Nothing. So why couldn't he stop shaking?

Max. Where was he?

Gabe's hand shook so violently he almost dropped his phone when he called Max.

His mate didn't answer his phone. Just like he hadn't answered his phone the day John Stone had attacked Izzie and taken Max away right under Gabe's nose.

"Come on, come on, pick up."

The call went to voice mail. He tried again and got the same result.

"Max, pick up. Pick up!"

Where was he? He didn't have academy training today. Where would he disappear to? Why wasn't he answering his phone?

"Fuck. *Fuck!*"

His phone smashed against the wall, narrowly missing Max's head as he stumbled through the door carrying the groceries Gabe had dumped in the hallway. Wide-eyed, Max looked from the phone to Gabe. "What's wrong?"

Gabe's throat closed at the sight of him. He didn't know whether to be relieved or furious. "Why didn't you answer your phone?"

Max arched a brow at Gabe's tone. "Because it was charging? What's with you?"

Where did he even start? Because what in the hell *was* with him? Since when did he blow up at Max over something so stupid? Since when did he blow up at Max at all?

"I... I left the door open." He sounded crazy. The revelation made him feel sick. Was he losing his mind?

Max's eyes widened. "Did anyone steal anything?"

No, but someone might have. He'd left the door wide open for anyone to come into their home and invade their privacy as easily as John Stone had climbed in through his window.

"No," he mumbled, but his hands were shaking.

Max exhaled. "Then everything's okay."

How was anything about this okay? "No, Max. It isn't okay. I don't do that. I don't just leave the fucking door open when I leave the house." Needing some space, he paced to the kitchen. His chest tightened and his heart raced until he thought it would burst in his chest and kill him on the spot.

"So you forgot. It's okay. Nothing bad happened."

"But it could have!" All the oxygen felt as if it were being sucked out of the room. He tried to breathe and only brought in a pinch of air.

"Gabe." Max's voice trembled. "What is going on?"

"I left the door wide open! Anyone could have come in. You could have—" He couldn't speak. The need for air was too much, so he sucked in short, shallow gasps. Why couldn't he breathe? He was going to fucking die. His stomach lurched and he thought he'd be sick. Tears stung his eyes.

Max could have been attacked. Killed. Abducted. It could happen. This was the world they lived in now—Aaron McCready's world, where hybrids could be killed walking down the street. Or attacked leaving bars, too drunk to defend themselves.

"Gabe." Max's voice was quiet, but the anxiety radiating from him amped up Gabe's frantic heartbeat. "Sit down, okay? You're hyperventilating. Nothing bad happened. We're okay."

But they weren't safe. They'd never be safe again.

"We have to"—he sucked in a gasp—"go. Get out of the city. Go far away."

"Okay. We can do that. Can you sit down first? We can talk about it."

"No! We have to go right now!"

"Can you tell me why?" Max's voice broke, tears glistening in his eyes.

Before Gabe lost him. Before he was forced to watch as another person he loved was ripped away from him and he was helpless to do anything about it.

"I won't be helpless again, Max. I won't. I won't. I won't." His voice warped, deepening into a snarl. Fury blazed within him. Fur sprouted on his arms, his fangs sharpening to points. He would kill anyone who threatened his pack, his mate, rip them to pieces and—

Two shaking but powerful arms went around him.

"Gabe. I'm safe. You're safe. We're okay. I'm okay. I promise. I promise."

Waves of soothing comfort washed over him, casting away the darkness of his feral fury. The berserker's rage faded much more quickly than the last time thanks to the treatments, but it felt so fucking temporary, just like everything else in life right now. Goddess. He was so *tired*. Tired of waiting for the worst to come. Tired of wondering how long it would be before he lost control.

His throat ached, and tears burned his eyes. His knees hit the kitchen tile, and he wrapped his arms around himself and hid, knees to his chest. His gasps turned to pants as his claws pierced the flesh of his leg. Like it always did when he was too weak to stop it, his wolf wanted to come out. He wanted to let it. He'd surrender himself to the beast if it meant he never had to be helpless again.

"Gabe, can you talk to me?"

A growl responded.

"Okay. You don't have to. Can you listen?"

He couldn't speak.

"You're not helpless. You're not weak."

Trembling hands clasped his. They were so warm while his were like blocks of ice.

"Gabe, the minute I met you, I wanted to be just like you. You've been through hell. I can't even imagine. The minute I saw your scars, all the shame I felt about my own scars didn't matter anymore. Because, to me, you were so strong. I thought, if he can go through hell and back and still smile and laugh and love, then I can too."

Max sat beside him on the tile, his back against the oven. Tears clung to his lashes, but his watery smile was radiant. "We're a pair, the two of us. Someday, we'll be fathers of our own pack. It's okay. You don't have to be strong all the time, because when you falter, that's when I'll come in. Like now. And I'll be strong for you too."

Their shoulders touched, then their sides. The steady rise and fall of Max's ribs against him helped Gabe find the rhythm in his own breathing. Max's arm wound slowly around his shoulders, and he sat with him on the kitchen floor until Gabe's breathing slowed and his heart beat in time with his mate's. Then came a lump in his throat, painful to breathe around. He wished he could tell Max how much he loved him, that he didn't deserve him, but he was crying too hard.

He didn't even know why. Exhaustion? Definitely. Relief? Yes, because he knew Max could see him at his absolute worst and still see the best in him and remind him that this was just a truly awful day and not who he was. He could get better. He wanted to get better. For Max, for himself.

Max's chest shuddered with a sob as he pulled Gabe close, guiding his face to the crook of his neck. "We're gonna be okay. We'll get through this."

WHILE GABE CURLED UP on the sofa, Max took a quick trip to the pharmacy nearby.

"It sounds like you did everything you could, hon," his mother assured him through the phone.

"I don't know if I did." Max blinked hard, keeping his voice low as people shuffled past him with shopping carts.

"You calmed him down. That's all that matters. How's he doing now?"

Max browsed some bath soaks specially made for werewolves. "Exhausted. He hasn't been sleeping. I should have seen this coming."

"We're all scared right now, honey. There's so much fear and uncertainty. It would give anyone a panic attack."

Max took a whiff of the bath soaks and sighed. It smelled like a pine-scented forest, and the packaging claimed it would relax and appease one's inner wolf. Maybe it was just marketing, but Max was willing to give it a shot.

"I've just... never seen him like that before. I wish he'd just told me before it got so bad."

"He loves you. Knowing Gabe, he didn't want to worry you. And if I know you, you'll nurse him back to health in no time."

"I'll try my best. Gotta go, Mom. Thanks."

Before he left the store, he bought some floral-scented candles and some fragrant body oil.

Once he was upstairs, he glanced at Gabe and found him still lying motionless on the sofa, eyes closed. His body radiated tension. Max set the bathwater running.

He returned to check on Gabe and found him staring blankly at his phone where he was watching a... Japanese game show? "Go take a bath, sweetheart."

Gabe managed a tiny smile. "I'm not a dog. I don't take baths."

"Today you do. Go relax, I'll cook tonight."

Gabe sighed and shut off the TV. He lugged himself off the couch and shuffled to the bathroom. "Whoa." Max grinned at his slack-jawed reaction. He'd lit candles around the edge of the bath and on the sink and toilet tank. The air smelled sweet and mystical.

"This is nice and all, but I really don't..." Gabe breathed in deep and sighed dreamily. "Fine. Just one bath." He peeled off his shirt and kicked off his jeans, his briefs pooling around his ankles. He took another whiff and sighed. Before Max's eyes, he shifted to a great black wolf and leaped into the tub, splashing water everywhere. He lay down in the bath, chin propped on the edge and amber eyes closing. His fur floated like a cape around him.

Max closed the door before he could laugh. He supposed the bath soaks really did influence the inner wolf.

While Gabe bathed, Max prepared dinner and relaxed on the sofa while the enchiladas baked. Gabe always ordered enchiladas when they ate out at their favorite Mexican restaurant. Max was pretty sure it was all he'd eat if he were allowed to. By the time Gabe emerged from the bath clad in a white robe, his hair sleek and damp, Max had dinner on the table. He stopped by Max's chair and leaned down for a kiss. Max laughed when his stubble tickled his neck. Warm lips caressed his skin, and arms wound around his chest and squeezed.

"Thank you, mi corazón." Affection and love flowed through Gabe's bond and into Max's heart.

"My pleasure." Max squeezed his hand.

Gabe kissed his cheek and settled into the chair opposite him. They ate in pleasant silence. Gabe cleaned his plate in seconds and went for another serving. After dinner, they retired to the bedroom and Max offered to give him a massage.

Gabe slid his robe off in approval and sat on the edge of the bed. Max knelt behind him, spreading some oil over his fingers. It smelled like lavender. Max glided his hands over broad shoulders. Gabe's muscles were still tight, even after his bath. Kneading gently, Max pressed in with his thumbs. Gabe sighed his approval, and Max lowered his nose to Gabe's neck and breathed him in. His mate smelled delectable, his skin soft and slick and warm. He parted his lips, nibbling at his skin.

Gabe's breath hitched, his chest expanding beneath Max's hands as they departed his shoulders and squeezed the firm, soft muscles of his chest, pinching and squeezing his nipples until they hardened under his touch.

Abruptly Gabe turned around so their lips could meet, his warm, eager hands gliding beneath Max's shirt. The sheets puffed up around them as Max brought Gabe back down to the mattress with him. Max breathed in deep, his arms and legs wrapping around Gabe, trying to bundle himself up in his scent and warmth as much as he could.

Gabe's warmth seeped through his robe as it fell open, his body heat blazing like a furnace through Max's clothes. Every touch of Gabe's mouth against his skin burned hot and left the front of Max's jeans unbearably tight. Gabe was even worse, rocking his swollen member against Max's hips and stifling his groan by biting down on Max's lower lip.

He supposed he'd done a very good job tonight in his duties as a mate. He rocked his hips, hoping to give his mate the friction he craved, and was rewarded with a nip to his neck. Gabe's lips descended, leaving a trail of scorching heat, and his teeth nibbled at his collarbone. His arms encircled Gabe's shoulder, and he suckled at his neck to encourage him—but then Gabe slowly fell still. His breath came in warm, peaceful puffs against Max's neck, his eyes closed.

Max smiled and kissed his forehead. "Sleep well."

GOLDEN STREAMS OF EARLY morning sun glimmered through the curtain. Beyond the windows, the city was sleepy and still, the leaves of the trees in Central Park swaying in the breeze. Max rubbed sleep from his eyes to better take in the view, sighing in the blissful quiet of the morning. The sheets rustled behind him, and his mate's warmth soaked into his skin as a strong arm encircled his chest.

Barely there stubble tickled his skin as hot lips fluttered across his neck. "Morning, Lobito."

Max rolled over, smiling at the sight of Gabe's face, his wavy hair tousled and a warm, sleepy smile on his lips. Max nestled into Gabe's robe, which drifted open to invite him into the warmth of his mate's body. The heat of Gabe's bare skin seeped through Max's clothes and made him wish they weren't there at all.

"Sleep well?" Max asked.

Gabe nodded. "Like a pup." He closed his eyes as gentle fingers carded through his hair. "Thank you, Max. For everything."

Max kissed him in reply. Gabe's tongue slipped past his lips, sharing languid strokes. His mate rocked his hips against Max's, and Max shivered as a sharp canine nipped at his lower lip. Slowly, he trailed his fingers over the expanse of warm, hard abs, sinking into the wavy curls between Gabe's thighs.

Gabe's hips swayed out of reach and Max flashed him a questioning smile. His mate's mouth curled into a mischievous grin. "You did enough yesterday. I think I owe you a good turn now." Max's heart raced as Gabe pushed him onto his back, throwing a long leg across his hips. As Max raised his hips, Gabe wiggled Max's sweatpants down to his ankles.

His mate sighed his approval, his hand skimming the outline of Max's cock. Max's breath hitched, his hips rising to meet Gabe's touch. Even the slightest caress was overwhelming. Gabe squeezed him, his lips curling into a smile that ignited Max's blood. He loved how confident Gabe looked when he was in control. His mate's robe parted, allowing Max an unrestricted view of smooth, chiseled skin, of his cock hard and ready for their union. Max could get off to the sight alone.

Gabe slipped a single finger in the waistband of his boxers and tugged. Wriggling, Max kicked them off somewhere on the other end of the bed. Gabe chuckled. "So impatient. Relax. Let me take care of you." He reached for the vial of lavender oil on the dresser. Max expected the oil to be cool, but it was room temperature as it drizzled across his chest and trickled over his abs.

He sighed as his mate massaged the oil into his skin, his large warm hands working away any knots in his shoulders. "Close your eyes. Relax." Smiling, Max obliged. Gabe's hair tickled his cheek, his warm lips parting to lap at Max's neck. Sharp fangs nipped him, and Gabe squeezed his chest with oil-slick hands, tugging and pinching his nipples until they hardened.

Max bit his lip, his breath growing shorter with every pinch and pull. The musky, earthy smell of Gabe's arousal mingled with the aroma of lavender. Gabe rubbed in slow circles, spreading more of the oil across his skin. Max could only imagine how those fingers would feel around his cock or curling inside him. The thought made him moan, his cheeks burning hot.

"Good?" Gabe asked.

Max practically purred as those hands returned to his nipples, squeezing and rolling them between his fingers. "So good."

Gabe chuckled and claimed his lips as Max squeezed a fistful of his soft, wavy locks. Their teeth bumped, which gave them both an excuse to laugh before busying their mouths again. Oil-slick bodies glided together, and Gabe's chest rose and fell faster against Max's. When their tongues tangled, Max lost track of which was his as they plundered each other's mouths. Gabe's fangs left Max's lips hot and swollen.

Slick fingers curled around Max's cock, and he arched off the bed. Gabe's lips stifled his gratified moan as his mate's tight, hot fist worked him easily from his knot to the tip of his shaft. Max whimpered, amazed by just what a little oil could do as Gabe's hand glided effortlessly up and down his shaft, faster and faster.

Needing more, Max bucked into Gabe's fist, praising him with breathless moans and whimpers. But the hollow ache between his thighs grew harder to ignore by the second. "Fuck me, Gabe. Now." It wasn't exactly romantic, but he needed it.

"On it."

Max fisted the sheets, his eyes closing as inch by inch, his body surrendered to his mate's girth. Gasping above him, Gabe gripped his hips and Max arched off the bed, making them both moan when Gabe's pelvis smacked his buttocks.

"Look at me." Gabe's breath warmed Max's lips. "Max, look at me."

He did, his heart pounding fast as their eyes met. Squinting at him through dark eyes, Gabe smiled. Max gasped, clutching onto his shoulders as Gabe rolled his hips. His mate groaned, a dazed smile lighting up his face as he filled Max completely. As a sigh fell from Max's lips, his arms wound around Gabe's neck and he held on tight as their bodies came together in swift, deep thrusts.

Clasping Gabe's neck, Max pulled him down for a kiss. Gabe whispered his name between each hungry kiss. Max reached between their bodies, stroking himself and gasping when Gabe pegged his prostate. "So good, baby. You're so good to me," Max whimpered, closing his eyes when Gabe sucked on his neck and kissed him as if he were something precious and revered.

Gabe grunted above him when his knot expanded, tying them together, and Max tipped his head back, pleasure arcing through him as he came. "Gabe. Fuuuck. *Yes.*"

His name spilled breathlessly from Gabe's lips as he finished. Max caught Gabe when he crumpled into his arms. Their bond glowed like so much sunshine between them. Tears prickled Max's eyes when his mate nuzzled into his neck, his trembling lips kissing his skin. Max closed his eyes, listening to the rhythm of both their hearts, Gabe's breath warm and damp against his neck.

"I love you so much," Max whispered. He knew Gabe could feel it in their bond, but he couldn't have stopped the words if he wanted to.

"Love you too." Gabe took his hand and kissed his fingers. "My sweet, sweet Lobito."

In the storm of uncertainty that clouded their lives, he found solace in the surety of their joining. The familiar way their bodies fit together cast away every doubt, every breathless kiss communicating a promise that, even in a world so hurtful and confusing, they would always find their way back to each other.

Chapter 9

IT HAS BEGUN

It started off as a quiet day at the agency. Max had the day off from his academy training, so Gabe invited him to the agency for the day while he worked. Gabe couldn't wait until Max graduated and they could start working together.

Gabe and Ryan were in the gym sparring. Through the window he had a view of the courtyard and the main entrance into HQ. A white van pulled up to the gates. The door opened and a woman got out and approached the security booth, smiling at the gate guard within.

"What's up?" Ryan asked, arms raised to block Gabe's blows.

He shook his head. "Nothing." He threw a punch into Ryan's gloved hand.

Glass shattered and a yelp of pain erupted below. Ryan and Gabe bolted to the window. The woman yanked her clawed hand from the shattered window of the guard's booth. The guard toppled to the ground, his face bloodied, as the woman punched the button inside the booth to open the gates.

"Fucking hell," Ryan hissed. When he spoke next, he used the pack bonds. *"Guys, we have a problem! Some woman in a van just breached the main gates!"*

But it got worse as five others leaped from the van's interior, all armed with claws and fangs, their eyes flashing in their twisted faces.

Gabe threw off his gloves and tore from the room, his fangs and claws sharp. He thundered down the stairs and toward the double oak doors that led to the courtyard. A small force had already assembled at the doors.

"Alpha McCready says hello, mutt lovers!" the woman roared from beyond the door. "Your time is over! Step down so the new world can rise!"

Izzie snarled, "How many of them?"

Zach called out from the dining room, "Got sights on them! There's at least—" He yelled in shock and fear as a window shattered.

Ryan shoved past Gabe into the dining hall. Gabe followed and found Zach stumbling away from the shattered window. A cylinder lay on the floor. "Get back!" Zach roared, yanking Ryan and Gabe away. Smoke erupted from the cylinder, and Gabe's eyes streamed. Tear gas. Lungs burning, he stumbled from the dining hall, feeling his way blindly. His chest tightened until he couldn't breathe, hacking and gasping for air.

"Gabe, I've got you!" Max's scent of cinnamon and chilis enveloped him, and arms went around him.

Another window shattered nearby, and Ben hollered, "Everyone fall back!" Clouds of tear gas filled the first floor of the agency, forcing the pack to retreat upstairs to higher ground. Screams of terror and pain erupted from the clinic, and Gabe's heart seized.

"The patients!" They had vulnerable people down there. Would these assholes hurt them? Gabe yanked off his sweatshirt and tried to form a makeshift mask around his mouth. He had to help them.

Max grabbed his arms, his nails digging in. "Don't! You'll get hurt!"

"I have to do something," Gabe said around a cough as he wiped his eyes.

Zach looked out the hallway window and growled, "More coming! Another fucking van full of them!"

Vicenzo and Eddie came charging down the hall, Eddie armed with a silver bat and Vicenzo with fangs and claws.

"Damn, I just wanted to take a nap!" Vicenzo snapped.

Eddie shouted down into the tear gas-fogged stairwell. "Y'all're gonna regret this! Vico's real mean when he doesn't get his nap!"

Rotating his neck, Ryan popped the muscles. "Let's go, you bigoted bastards!"

Gabe unsheathed his claws, his fangs dropping to sharp points. He stood shoulder to shoulder with Izzie and Max, his heart hammering with fear and fury.

Through the cloud of vapor, a woman prowled toward them. She wore a gas mask shaped like a wolf's snarling face. Her claws were several inches long, and a growl rumbled from her like thunder.

Ben chucked his sweater onto the ground. "Think you can come and stir shit up in my agency, warg? Send a message to McCready for me." He flipped her both his middle fingers. He kicked off his pants and dropped to all fours as a wolf, flying toward her like a silver comet.

Gabe threw off his clothes and charged, his roar of fury morphing into a snarl. Fur enveloped him and a wolf's protective rage crashed over him in a haze of red. He hurled himself upon a fully shifted wolf, who was also fitted with a gas mask over its face. The wargs swarmed them, some as wolves, some in their human form with fangs and claws flashing.

Max flew past as a wolf, his red fur blazing like a fireball. He tackled a wolf before it could jump on Gabe. Ben ripped out its throat while Max pinned it.

Izzie roared, "Send him a message from me too!" She slammed her clawed foot into a warg's stomach, and he flew down the stairs, screaming with each step he crashed against.

Eddie shouted, "Duck, Vico!" He swung his silver bat over Vicenzo and right into a masked man's face, cracking the gas mask off his head.

Vicenzo popped up from his crouch, grinning maliciously. "Have a taste of your own medicine, fucker!" He grabbed the stunned werewolf by the throat and hurled him down the stairs into the gas cloud.

"I just really love salami sandwiches!" Ryan shouted.

Gabe spat out his enemy's windpipe. He cocked his head at Ryan. Ben and the others were staring. So were the wargs.

Ryan frowned. "What? I thought we were all shouting random things!" Shrugging, he punched his claws through his boxing glove and swung, cracking a warg across her face.

Zach headbutted a humanoid warg in the face, then kneed him in the stomach when he went down. "It's okay, Ry." Taking a deep breath, he bellowed, "The *Star Wars* prequels are good, damn it!" And when Ryan threw a warg at him, Zach sliced their throat in vengeance.

The wargs lay dead or incapacitated around them.

Ryan shook his head. "Zach, I love you, but you're just wrong."

"Okay, I'm never getting into an argument about movies with you, ever," Izzie said as she blinked at them.

Gabe loved the idiots he called his pack so much.

Ben shifted to a man, blood running in rivers down his body. Wounds knit themselves closed across his bare skin. He yanked his walkie-talkie from his utility belt and spoke into it. "Get the ventilation system working overtime. We've gotta clear this shit from the building. I want all windows opened." Motioning to the pack, he said, "Take their masks. We've gotta get folk evacuated."

Eddie put one on, adjusting it so it fit. "Got ya, boss."

Once he was masked up, Gabe braved the gas, waving clouds of it out of his face. The white smoke obscured his vision, so he had to rely on his hearing. There was a woman gasping nearby, and he followed the sound to an overturned table. She lay behind it, shaking and coughing. Looking at his mask, she screamed, "No! Get away from me!"

"Ma'am, it's Agent Reyes. I've got you. Come with me." Gabe touched her shoulder. She clasped his hand in her trembling fingers, and Gabe supported her since she was shaking too badly to walk. He knew the layout of the manor blindfolded, so he guided her toward where he knew the exit was. The fresh air blew away the vapors as they stumbled outside.

"Mom!" A little boy and his dad ran to greet the woman, hugging her tight.

Gabe left her to their care and ran back inside. He lost track of time as he guided people out of the tear gas and into the fresh air. Fire trucks blared their alarm, and paramedics swarmed the courtyard, tending to people.

Luke sat on the fountain, his eyes wide and far away. "The clinic... they trashed it. How will I treat people?"

Gabe squeezed his shoulder but couldn't find the words. From the outside, the agency looked even worse. Many of the ground floor windows had been blown out, and clouds of gas billowed from them. They'd even set fire to the vegetation, and firefighters swarmed the area to combat the blaze. It was more than just the visible damage that hurt. McCready's people had attacked the only resource werewolves had.

"Everyone's out!" Eddie called, leading a couple of children out the door. Their parents ran to them, hoisting the kids into their arms.

Gabe's eyes stung. He didn't know if he'd cry or scream his despair. Eyes downcast, Max handed Gabe his clothes, having already dressed himself, and Gabe put them on without a word.

An hour passed before the tear gas evaporated. Gabe wandered around checking on patients and fellow staff. He followed Ben inside, trying to brace himself for the damage, but it was so much worse than he'd thought. The clinic looked like a tornado had torn through it; furniture had been scratched, exam rooms raided, medical supplies scattered everywhere. The dining hall looked like a war zone of broken chairs and tables.

Some of the wargs had accessed the elevator and used it to get deeper into the manor and let all the feral wolves out of the kennels, though the wolves had instinctively hidden from all the noise rather than run around creating more chaos. Zach and a few other skilled catchers were rounding them up with catch poles and tranquilizers. Some of those patients had been on their way to recovery. This trauma would only set them back.

The only positive Gabe could see was that aside from the wargs, no one had died, but the injuries their patients had sustained couldn't be treated at the clinic in the state it was in.

Gabe found Ben pacing around the vans in the courtyard. His shoulders were tight, his hands in fists at his sides. Blood dripped from between his fingers where his claws had cut in. Gabe sighed. "Viejo—" He stopped. What on earth could he say to make all of this okay?

Ben knelt, examining the license plates. They were from Alaska. With a snarl, Ben ripped a plate from a van and hurled it into the trees. He let loose a roar that made the birds take flight and Gabe's eardrums rattle, then slumped against the vehicle. His shoulders rose and fell fast.

"Enough is fucking enough," Ben growled low in his chest. Fury burned bright in his eyes. "Enough sitting around being the victims. Enough taking what he throws at us." He shoved past Gabe and stormed back to the agency.

"Ben?" Gabe called, jogging after him. "Hey, wait up! What are we doing?"

Ben whipped around, his fangs sharp and eyes flashing yellow. "What we should have done. We rolled over, Gabe. We gave up and accepted things as they were when McCready became Alpha. That isn't us. That's not who we are. We're fighters, and it's time we remembered that."

Ben walked away, resolution and fury fueling every step.

Repairs began on the agency.

It broke Gabe's heart when people who hadn't heard the news arrived at the gates seeking refuge. They brought their families, young children, older relatives, all hoping to find sanctuary from whatever chaos and pain they were fleeing. But Ben had no choice but to turn them all away and recommend various subpar shelters for them to stay in instead.

"I hate this," Gabe whispered, wiping his eyes as a mother led her little boy away. The child kept looking back, disappointment bright in his big eyes. "We really couldn't have given them a place here, Ben?"

Ben closed his eyes tight. "No. Not if McCready is just going to send another wave of wargs at us. Not when the clinic is still in disarray and we can't even treat those who come to us with injuries or sickness. It wouldn't be right."

Gabe snarled his frustration. "But we have to do something!"

Ben gripped his shoulder. "I'm working on it, kid. I promise."

Shortly after the attack, Ben released a statement to the news, saying, "Aaron McCready struck at the heart of every wolf in this city when he attacked the agency. His message was very clear. He wants city wolves to be helpless and without resources because by choosing to live in peace with humans, we are going against his ideals. I will never stop believing in a world where we can all live as one. And so to Aaron McCready, I say this: we're not going down without a fight. You want a war? You've fucking got it."

His statement went viral and sent a shiver down Gabe's spine. There was no doubt in his mind that McCready would see Ben's message or at least have it relayed to him. Perhaps this was what he'd wanted all along, a chance to get rid of the agency for good.

In the days after their fight with the wargs, Ben was always on the phone or just hanging up, usually with a tired scowl. When Gabe asked about it, Ben surprised him with a smile. "Folk are reaching out. They know if the agency goes, hope is lost for shifters in NYC. They wanna know how they can join and bring the fight to McCready."

Gabe's heart soared. "How many?"

"Too many. Kid, McCready's got a reckoning coming his way. Mark my words."

And the reckoning was coming fast, surging closer with the fury of a typhoon.

November arrived. The moon hung low over the trees as Ben led the way through Inwood Park.

Max yawned and shivered against Gabe's side.

"Not that I don't like a nightly hike in a whole other borough from where I live," Ryan said. "But I'm sure hoping you brought us out here to do something other than stargaze, Ben."

"College basketball was on," Zach added. Gabe chuckled, understanding Ryan's grumbles.

Ben's teeth flashed as he smiled. "Well, I got something a little more exciting than college basketball."

Although surrounded by the smells of trees and soil, Gabe smelled other wolves and humans. He quickened his pace, striding shoulder to shoulder with Ben.

Within a clearing in the woods, a fire roared, illuminating a massive gathering of humans and wolves sprawling into the shadows. There were more people here than Gabe could count, or smell, their scents tangling together. Izzie stumbled into him, her jaw dropping. "Who are these people?"

Understanding dawned on Gabe. "These people are here to join us?"

Max gasped. "No way!" Gabe laughed at the amazed grin that split his face. There had to be over a hundred people here.

Ben shouldered past Gabe, and the roaring bonfire cast his shadow long and tall. "Wolves, human allies!" His voice was like a roar of thunder on the horizon. "You stand before me because you've witnessed the hatred tearing this city apart. It's spreading like a sickness to every corner of the country. Aaron McCready wants to divide us. There's no bigger threat to the truce between shifters and our allies! I ain't gonna sugarcoat it: there will be war. We're putting our lives and the safety of those we love at risk. If there were any other way, I wouldn't ask this of anyone."

Max's fingers tangled with Gabe's and held tight.

"But I believe in a world where werewolves and humans are equals. I've seen that, for everything that sets us apart, we're unstoppable when we come together. And I think that world is worth dying for. Stand with us, as a pack!"

The resounding roar shook the trees to their roots, and the forest came alive with the howling of wolves. A shiver ran down Gabe's spine, raising every hair. He'd never seen humans and werewolves come together like this, rallying for a world where they could live as one people. He clapped Ben on the shoulder, his heart racing in time with Ben's. "Nice, Viejo."

Ben's shoulders shook, and he blinked hard. "If my gramps could see this... Humans and shifters haven't come together like this since the day the Council was founded."

Ryan threw back his head and howled, jumping up and down with Izzie. "Fuck yeah! We could bring the fight to McCready tomorrow!"

To the gathered crowd, Ben said, "McCready's base is on the coast of Alaska. Make your preparations. We will leave as soon as possible. We'll wait for you in Anchorage. It's close to the island but far enough that we shouldn't be spotted by any friends of his. Once we're united, we'll strike."

Gabe's heart raced and he held on tight to Max's hand. It was happening. Only a few weeks ago, standing up to McCready's forces had seemed like a suicidal and outlandish idea. Soon, the might of wolves and humans would storm the shores of Crescent Cove, and McCready's short-lived reign would come crashing to an end.

"Look, Max. Alaska..."

With a yawn, Max leaned over Gabe's shoulder to get a peek out the window. Beyond the wing of the plane, the Alaskan wilderness sprawled beneath them. Gabe wished they'd come under better circumstances. He would love to hunt within the forests without a worry or care in his mind.

"Pretty." Max grunted, dropping his cheek against Gabe's shoulder. "It would be prettier if I wasn't worried we'll die terrible deaths."

Gabe squeezed his hand. "I know..."

In the aisle across from them, Ryan and Zach chatted excitedly while Izzie watched a movie. Behind them sat Ben, Eddie, and Vicenzo. In the row beyond were Kendra and Veronica. They'd crammed as many packmates as they could on a private jet out of New York. Their allies would arrive not long after.

Once they landed, they headed to collect their suitcases. "Everyone else should be here soon," Ben said as he looked around.

"Unless they back out," Vicenzo said, pulling his backpack on across his shoulders as they departed baggage claim.

Max's eyes went wide in worry. "You don't think people will come?"

"It's a lot to ask of someone, to die for a cause you believe in. Don't expect everyone to turn up."

"But they have to. We need them."

Eddie sighed. "Thanks for the pessimism, Vico. We were all gettin' too optimistic here."

"He ain't wrong," Ben said. "But I think our allies know what's at stake if we fail. If we let him, McCready will destroy all the progress wolves and humans have fought so hard to make. The world he wants is one where wolves and humans are pitted against each other, with wolves at the top and everyone else at the bottom. He starts by tearing down the resources we need to keep ourselves safe, then riling up the humans against us."

Vicenzo sighed, rolling his suitcase along the floor. "You know, if he weren't a lunatic, I might even agree with him."

Gabe raised a brow. "You understand his brand of crazy?"

"It's not like he's wrong, right? Humans have oppressed us. I totally get feeling angry over all the shit they've put us through just for trying to exist. He's Alpha, so he *should* stand up for us. All of us, not those he deems superior. If he really wanted to, he could be a force for something good. Instead, he pits us all against each other and divides us." He scowled. "Guy's gotta go."

Gabe blinked at him. "Wow. Think that's the most I ever heard you speak."

Vicenzo shrugged. "Don't get used to it. Just don't want you thinking I'm gonna turn around and backstab you guys."

Ben said, "I second that. If we don't stop him here, no one else will."

"But we can't stop him alone," Max said. "We tried that."

Gabe squeezed Max's shoulder. "Ben made a pretty rousing impression. People will show up." He hoped so, anyway. He knew he wouldn't forgive himself if he sat around and waited for the world to end rather than making a stand to protect his pack. But not everyone shared his motivation. If people believed in their cause, they would show.

They drove from the airport and through the town of Anchorage, but they didn't stop until they were on the outskirts of town. Then they parked and started walking. Ben took the lead through a tangle of woodland. It was hardly a hiking spot; the ground was too uneven and there were no trails. "It'll do," Ben declared, setting down his pack. "Make camp," he called. "We'll be hidden here. McCready won't suspect us until we're ready to strike."

From his pack Gabe unfurled a tent big enough for him and Max. "Never been camping?" he asked, laughing as Max struggled to help set up the tent.

"No. I always wanted to, and now that I'm finally doing it, we're on the brink of war. I guess I should work on my timing."

By the time the sun was setting, the pack had made camp within the woods. Gabe stopped by Luke's tent for his weekly dose of aconitum. The last thing he needed was to go berserk in the middle of a fight again.

Ben declared that everyone should split up and hunt before sundown so they wouldn't compete with any predators at night. Max swallowed, his wide eyes darting around the trees. "Do you think there are bears out here?"

"Probably," Gabe confessed, not liking the idea of crossing one. He removed his clothes, shivering as the chill nipped his bare skin. He offered a smile and draped an arm over Max's shoulders "Don't worry. I'll protect you."

Max scoffed. "Cheesy." He hurried into the woods and when Gabe caught up with him, he'd shifted to a red wolf. Gabe dropped to all fours and did what his wolf had been begging for all day. As a wolf, he bounded into the trees with his mate at his side. The forest darkened and the stars had lit up the skies by the time they returned, each carrying a plump rabbit in their jaws.

The smell of roasting meat filled the woods as the pack gathered around the fire and cooked scraps of fresh kill on sticks. Gabe's rabbit was still a little raw, just the way he liked his meat. For a time, the uncertainty of the coming battle was forgotten. Ryan had bought a cooler full of beers during their drive through Anchorage, and they helped themselves to some local brews. Zach told ghost stories his grandfather used to tell him on camping trips. Surrounded by the pack and with good food and drink, it was hard to have a worry in his head when Gabe retired to the tent.

He settled into his sleeping bag beside Max, their hands touching as the sounds of the wilderness lulled them to sleep.

Over the course of the week, the campsite grew larger and larger. Many of their allies from New York had flown in to join them. Though the day was bitterly cold, Gabe's spirits soared when he emerged from his tent to the news that fifty of their allies were now accounted for among their numbers. Not everyone joined them in the woods. With the conditions growing colder and colder, many stayed in hotels in town.

"Not as big a turnout as I'd hoped for," Ben admitted, taking a swig of fire-brewed coffee. "But it'll have to do."

Gabe took a sip and burned his tongue. "We can't wait a little longer?"

"We gave them a week. The week's up. We can't camp out here forever. The cold will dampen morale."

"You think the pack is big enough to storm that island?" Gabe motioned beyond the coastline, which was visible to them from the ridge. Crescent Cove was a black island several miles off the coast, shrouded by dense trees, rocky and unwelcoming. Gabe had no idea how many wolves lurked within the woods, but he had some idea of what to expect.

Ben said, "I'll be honest. I don't. Then again, we don't know what we're up against. But we can't wait much longer. There's a storm coming in and if we don't end things now, we could be taken out by the weather before we even set sail for the island."

Gabe sighed, breath steaming in the frigid air. "So, what? We're damned if we do, damned if we don't?"

"Sure feels that way..."

A howl within the trees raised the hair on Gabe's arms. He lurched to his feet, and Ben jumped up beside him. Ryan burst out of the trees and came running toward them, spraying snow behind him. "Wolves!" he shouted, breath pluming. "There's wolves! I—I—"

"Whoa!" Ben raised both arms. "Slow down and catch your breath."

Izzie ran over. "Is it McCready? I'll kick his fanatical ass back to that miserable rock he calls home!"

Ryan slumped, hands on his knees. "No. There's only two of them but... Ben, they're a couple of kids." Ryan raised his head, his glasses slipping off his nose. "You should see them. They look real worn down."

Max frowned. "Maybe refugees who couldn't get onto the island?"

"We should offer them whatever we can spare. Food, blankets, a tent," said Vicenzo.

Ben raised a hand, urging them to keep calm. "We'll do everything we can." He motioned for everyone to follow him. "Lead the way, Ry. Where'd you see 'em?"

Ryan galloped ahead. The winds changed, carrying a whiff of unfamiliar wolves to Gabe. He took Max's hand and held tight, needing him close.

Between the trees, they appeared.

"Shit," Eddie muttered. "Look at the poor kids."

A small pup trotted beside a wolf only a little taller than her. The older male wolf nudged the smaller female. Compassion seized Gabe's heart. The kids reminded him of himself and Izzie, with that haunted, lost look in their eyes.

Ben made a wounded noise in his throat. "Poor things. They're so young." He lowered himself to one knee, grimacing when the snow seeped into his clothes. "Hey there. You two all right?"

The pup hid behind the bigger one, tail tucked and ears flat.

The taller pup crouched low. His muscles groaned and popped, gray fur rippling and receding. When he looked up, he was a human boy. He appeared biracial, with African American features, light brown skin, and wavy black hair. He was so thin his ribs stuck out and gooseflesh pebbled his skin. His teeth chattered, but he wasn't shaking despite the cold. Wolves ran hot. The scent of his fear bowled over Gabe.

"I... I know you. Saw you in town buying supplies." His voice cracked, either from fear or the effects of puberty. He couldn't be older than thirteen. "You're the LPA wolves."

"Yeah," Ben said, offering a friendly smile.

"You're here to stop the Alpha, aren't you?"

"We are," Ben said cheerily. "Is that a problem?"

The kid shook his head. "N-no." The pup leaned on his ankle, whimpering. He seemed to draw courage from her and lifted his head higher. "I—I want to help you. That's why I'm here. Me and my sister." He smiled down at the little pup, and her tail wagged.

Gabe smiled to himself. "How do you think you can help us?"

The kid looked at them with a spark in his hazel eyes and said something Gabe would never have expected. "I think I know how you can win against him."

THE KID'S NAME WAS Thomas, though he preferred Tommy. Gabe loaned him a change of clothes and the pack escorted Tommy and his sister back to the camp. They gathered around the fire and Kendra served them rabbit stew. The kid scarfed the stew down while Gabe offered a bowl to his sister.

"She's shy," Tommy said. "She won't shift until she's ready."

Gabe chuckled. "That's okay. Sometimes, being in fur is easier."

The pup dug in, tail wagging as she chowed down.

Tommy scratched her ears. "Her name's Luna."

"That's a good name," Max said, sitting beside Tommy with a bowl of stew. "Tommy, where are your parents?"

Tommy huddled deeper into his coat like he was trying to retreat from the question. "Our mom... she died when I was really little. Luna was just a baby." He swallowed hard. "Hunters."

Across the fire, Vicenzo stiffened like he'd been shocked. Eddie raised a hand like he wanted to reach out to Vicenzo, then put it down, curling his fingers.

Pity squeezed Gabe's heart. "I'm so sorry." These kids reminded him so much of himself and Izzie. Izzie must have sensed his grief because she came up behind where he was sitting and put her hand on his shoulder. "I know what it's like to lose a parent."

Tommy looked at him with wide eyes. "Really?"

Gabe nodded. "Yes. I lost my father when I was exactly your age."

"Was she your only parent?" Max asked.

Tommy shook his head, blinking wet eyes. "We had our dad, but... I don't want to talk about him." His voice quavered with more than grief. The spicy scent of his anger stung Gabe's nose.

Gabe raised both hands. "Okay. You don't have to."

Changing the subject, Max said, "What are you two doing all the way out here?"

Tommy wiped his mouth on his sleeve. "It's a really long story."

Smiling, Gabe said, "That's okay. We've got all night."

Tommy blew out a breath that misted in the air. "I don't know where to begin."

"You told us you knew how to stop McCready," Ben said.

The boy flinched at the very mention of his name. "I think so. Yeah. He... he has to be stopped." His voice quavered, and tears swam in his eyes. "He ruined everything."

Ryan grimaced. "Yeah. He's pretty good at that."

"A-after the hunters killed our mom, they took us away and brought us to the island."

Max tilted his head. "You mean the Cove?"

Tommy nodded. "Yeah. It used to be a hideout for hunters."

Eddie paled, lowering his stew bowl. "Oh man... Don't tell me you two were trapped on that island."

Ben looked at Eddie. "You know about the island's history?"

Eddie nodded. "Yeah, 'course. Every hunter did. It used to be a smugglin' spot where we could trade weapons. Then some hunter clan took it over as a hideout. What wolves they didn't kill, they used to hunt game." Bitter anger filled his voice. "Kind of like my old clan. 'Cept my uncle's wolves hunted other wolves."

Tommy hugged his knees to his chest. "They were training me to hunt. They would have done the same to Luna when she got older, but... but we wolves stuck together and formed bonds to keep from going feral. The bigger, stronger wolves rebelled, and all the hunters were killed. For a long time, we lived in peace on that island. Until..."

"McCready." Gabe sighed, understanding.

"He... he came and told our Alpha the island would be his now. Our Alpha fought back but she... she didn't stand a chance. He turned into this monster. I ran." He wiped furiously at the tears that overflowed down his cheeks. "I took my sister and just ran away. Like a coward."

Luna whined and crawled into her brother's lap. Tommy stroked her dense fur for comfort.

"No." Gabe gripped his shoulder. "You did a good job, Tommy. You protected your pack like a good wolf should." Pride warmed his chest.

Tommy sniffed and held his head higher. "W-we hung out around town, and I saw you guys. I recognized..." He frowned at Ben. "Um... What was your name again?"

"Ben, kiddo."

"That's right. I recognized you from the television. Your agency got attacked by wargs, and you said you were going to fight back. I didn't think you actually meant it, but you really came all this way to defeat the Alpha?"

Ben dipped his head. "That we did."

Tommy wet his chapped lips. "I think I know how you can stop him."

Gabe leaned forward, his hands on his knees. "Tell us."

After Tommy took a gulp of the water Izzie handed him, he stared into the thermos, thinking.

There came a grind of muscle and bone. A little girl with dark skin and a wild bundle of curls sat up on her brother's lap. "Tommy! Let me tell this part!" She smiled big and bright, revealing a charming little gap between her two front teeth.

"Sweetheart, it's freezing out here!" Izzie exclaimed, shedding her coat and running over to Tommy. She threw the coat over little Luna.

Gabe grinned. "Hi. Luna, right?"

"Yup!" she said, popping the *P*. "Hi! I'm Luna. I'm six!"

Tommy laughed embarrassedly. "Okay, Luna."

"There's so many of you. So many wolfies!" she exclaimed. "Tommy, are they our new pack?" Luna craned her head back to look at her big brother.

"Didn't you want to tell a story?" Tommy asked.

Luna pursed her lips, then her big eyes lit up. "Oh yeah. On the island, there's a big, huge monster in the bottom of a well!"

Ryan sucked in his lips to keep from laughing. "I don't remember that part of *Lassie*. Do you guys?"

Eddie took a sip of coffee. "What kinda monster, sweet pea?"

She shrugged. "I don't know." She opened her little arms wide for emphasis. "He's this big!"

Chuckles erupted around the campfire and Tommy explained. "When we were first brought to the island, the hunters told stories about a monster they caught. They said he was too powerful to be killed, and so they locked him up. I found a well in the ruins of an old fishing village at the tip of the island. This voice called out to me, asking for food. The voice freaked me out at first 'cause he didn't sound human but he wasn't mean or scary. He was lonely. Sad. I visited him a lot and brought him food. My pack wouldn't free him when I asked. They didn't think he could be trusted."

Eddie asked, "Was he a wolf?"

Tommy nodded. "The hunters said so, but... they said he was more than that. Huge. A wolf unlike anything they've ever seen."

Eddie whispered, "A berserker."

Gabe's heart skipped a beat.

Max narrowed his eyes. "Is he still there?"

Frowning, Tommy said, "He should be unless..."

Unless McCready got to him. Gabe's stomach churned. Needing to walk off the nerves building within him, he stood and paced away from the fire. Ben and Max followed him. "Ben," Gabe said. "If McCready doesn't know about this berserker trapped on the island, he could be exactly what we need to flip the fight to our advantage."

Ben ran a hand through his snow-flecked beard. "Or this berserker will slaughter us *and* McCready's people."

Gabe growled, kicking up snow as he paced. "We won't know that unless we go out there and speak to him. If he can speak and isn't feral..." There were too many ifs. Maybe this was a crazy idea, but what other choice did they have? "Ben, what can it hurt? We go to that well and just talk to the guy. If he's bad news, he stays. If he wants out, maybe we can work out a deal."

Ben sighed heavily, his eyes full of worry. He gripped Gabe's arms and leaned their foreheads together. "Okay. We'll head out to the island and prepare for an attack once night's fallen. Whether or not the berserker is with us, we need to face McCready before that blizzard arrives."

Ben walked back to the fire and told the pack the plan.

Taking Gabe's hand, Max said, "It has begun."

Gabe squeezed tight. "Stay with me."

"Until the end." Max leaned his head on Gabe's shoulder.

CHAPTER 10

FINALLY WHOLE

Under the cover of darkness, the agency wolves and their allies boarded boats they'd rented in town and took to the churning Alaskan waters. The island of Crescent Cove loomed ever closer, black trees reaching toward the star-strewn sky. If Gabe hadn't known any better, he would've thought the island was deserted until wolves howled across the water to begin their nightly hunt.

Tommy sat in the boat with Gabe and Max. He kept looking back at the opposite shore, gnawing his lip.

Max said, "Your sister is in good hands."

Kendra had taken the little girl to a motel to spend the night out of the bitter cold. His mom hadn't wanted to be apart from Max with the battle drawing near, but he had insisted she take care of Luna. They needed Tommy to guide them to the well.

"You don't have to stay with us," Gabe said. "Just show us to the well. Then you can ask someone to escort you back to Anchorage."

"We've never been apart before," Tommy confessed.

Gabe rowed faster through the churning water. "You've been taking care of her since your mom passed, huh?"

Tommy nodded. "Yeah."

Max smiled. "You've done a great job. You should be proud."

He smiled and averted his gaze. "I've tried my best." Squirming, he twisted his fingers together. "I don't know what we'll do now that our pack is gone."

Gabe squeezed the oars, wishing he could help.

Max looked like he wanted to say something but the boat's oars bumped against the shoreline. "Time to get out," he said, stepping out of the boat. Gabe and Max dragged the boat up the rocky shore to higher ground. The silhouettes of their pack and allies drifted over the water, getting closer until Ben's boat came ashore.

While everyone pulled their boats ashore, Ben approached Gabe, Max, and Tommy. "Only a few of us should find that well. We can't risk attracting a patrol's attention. Tommy, who would you like to accompany you?"

Tommy looked from Gabe to Max. "Uh... I guess you guys."

"The three of you will be okay?" Ben looked between them.

Gabe nodded. "We'll be quiet."

Ben squeezed their shoulders. "If at any point you think this is too risky, you come back. Got it?"

"Gabriel!" Veronica whispered. "Be careful!"

Gabe smiled at her. "I will. We're not going to fight, just to talk to a disembodied voice in a well. Believe it or not, that's nowhere near the strangest thing I've done."

Gripping Max's shoulder for support, Gabe turned his back on Ben and the pack. Max took his hand, and they followed Tommy up the hill from the beach and into the trees. The moon was the only guiding light in the night sky, and shadows played tricks on Gabe. More than once, he thought he saw suspicious shapes in the trees, only for them to be an oddly shaped boulder or a tree branch.

Max jumped every so often, looking around.

"Scared?" Gabe whispered, nudging his shoulder.

His mate gave his head a shake. "Just keep thinking I hear things."

Despite the deep shadows that clouded the surrounding woods, there was no sign of wolves and any scents were stale.

Tommy said, "Wolves don't really come over here. There isn't any game on this island, and my pack did their fishing at the northern end. We always stayed away from the eastern tip because of the Beast of the Black Gullet, as we called him."

Max shivered. "And no one ever tried to free him?"

Tommy shook his head. "Everyone thought it was too risky and that it was better to just leave him alone but we weren't cruel. We'd bring him food and water. Some wolves even worshipped him and thought if we kept him happy and fed, he'd bring us luck. But I think the adults were too scared to trust him."

"Did you trust him?" Max asked.

Tommy hesitated, wrinkling his nose, then nodded. "Yeah. I did. He was... This is kinda dumb, but I sort of thought of him as a friend? Like, we both missed our families, so we'd talk about good times. I liked him, even if I only ever heard his voice."

"Did he tell you what his name was? How he got trapped?" Max took a wide step over a fallen tree and took Gabe's hand to guide him over.

"No," Tommy answered, hopping over a rock. "I had this feeling he wouldn't tell me if I asked. He was more interested in hearing stories about my childhood than talking about himself." He quickened his pace. "Come on. We're close."

They followed Tommy at a brisk pace and the trees became dilapidated buildings, the wood eaten away by moss and rot. The fishing village couldn't have over ten houses. It was years old, but the briny odor of fish still emanated from the barrels overflowing with brittle yellowed fish bones.

"Did the hunters live here?" Gabe asked.

Tommy shook his head. He was hunched over, his hands deep in his pockets and shoulders up to his ears. "No," he said. "They stuck to the other end of the island. Guess they didn't want to be near the wolf they trapped."

Max offered a smile. "It's okay. They're gone and they can't hurt you anymore."

"And McCready won't either," Gabe promised him.

Tommy nodded, but he didn't look convinced. Gabe's heart hurt at the idea of this poor kid relying on himself for so long.

A roar echoed over the treetops. Birds took flight, beating their wings. A chill traveled down Gabe's spine. The roar carried on and on, and Gabe realized—

"He's howling," Max whispered, freckled face upturned to the moon.

Gabe's heart settled, because Max was right. What he'd mistaken for a roar of primal fury was actually a somber howl. It was rough around the edges and wild, but there was an unmistakable note of loneliness that made something twinge in his chest. He touched his breastbone, confused by the sensation. It wasn't a metaphorical pang of heartache. It was very real. Something in that howl reached out to him, imploring him to—

Come. Come. Come.

Someone. Anyone.

Find me.

Please.

I can't take it.

I can't be alone anymore.

PleasePleasePleasePlease—

"Gabe?"

Gabe wiped his eyes, astonished to find they were wet. "Let's go." He forged ahead, following that agonizing howl of heartbreak deeper into the forgotten village.

"Gabe, wait!" Max hissed, lengthening his strides to keep pace.

Tommy jogged ahead, stopping in the middle of the village in front of a well. The black gullet of the well seemed to go on forever. Gabe didn't know how deep the thing was, but he knew what awaited them at the bottom. A big lonesome beast. Gabe sure hoped he was as friendly as Tommy seemed to think.

"Hello?" Gabe called into the well. His echo was the only response he got.

Tommy clapped his hands together. "Let's go."

"Are you sure?" Gabe asked. "You don't have to."

"I want to. I've wanted to see him face to face for years. Besides, he knows me." He worried his lower lip. "I hope he remembers me."

"Me too," Max said, "for all our sakes."

"How do we get down?" Tommy asked, peering into the deep drop of the well.

Max looked up at the moonlight. "I have an idea."

One by one, Max lowered them down into the well using his lunar powers. Gabe offered to go first. Threads of moonlight spilled from Max's fingertips, wrapping around Gabe's middle.

Tommy jumped, his wide eyes darting from Max to Gabe. "Whoa. Is that magic?"

"I'll tell you later," Max said.

The ground disappeared from beneath Gabe's feet and he drifted down into the dark.

The moonlight vanished the deeper Gabe went, and so did the fresh air. The air down here was wet and briny and the only sounds were his labored breathing. Gabe's heart skipped when his toes touched solid ground.

"Max, I'm on the ground," he called, his voice echoing. Gabe winced, feeling bad for whoever had been trapped down here. There was no way to climb out of the well. The berserker was well and truly trapped.

Max and Tommy soon joined him. Tommy gasped when something crunched under the too-big boots he'd borrowed from Zach. "Eww…"

Gabe used the flashlight app on his phone and shone it down. A sea of yellowed bones flooded the stony ground. The whole well reeked of death. Taking a deep breath to calm his churning gut, Gabe shone the flashlight farther down the tunnel. "Oh Goddess…" The tunnel seemed to go on forever with not a speck of light to be seen.

Max gulped and gripped Gabe's arm. "Here we go…"

The three of them set off down the dark tunnel. The way forward was straight at least, with only a few twists and turns but no dividing paths. His sense of smell was overpowered by the damp, mossy odor of the well.

"I hear something," Max whispered.

Gabe held his breath. Each step echoed and the constant drip of water was amplified, but he thought he heard the wind... until he realized the wind shouldn't have sounded like something big drawing in low, rumbling breaths and snarling them out. Gabe's heart went wild, slamming against his chest, but there was something else that pulsed along with his heart. What was it?

Two bright lights appeared at the end of the tunnel. Max gasped, gripping Gabe's arm so tightly Gabe thought he'd snap the bone in half. Tommy froze, the whites of his eyes glistening. Icy dread ran down Gabe's spine because those weren't lights.

They were eyes. Pupilless eyes. Bright and yellow, like traffic lights in the dark.

"Tommy?" Gabe whispered. "How long has it been since you last talked to him?"

Tommy swallowed, his throat clicking. "Uh, I don't know. A few weeks?"

Max choked out, "Fuck. Tommy, I think talking to you was what kept him sane."

Taking one step back, Gabe tried to shoulder Max and Tommy behind him. Max stayed rooted at his side. Gabe wanted to run, all his instincts screaming to go. But if his training had taught him anything, it was that you never ran from a feral wolf—especially when they were as big as a berserker werewolf.

Hand shaking, Gabe shone his flashlight farther down the tunnel. The light caught on an enormous clawed foot the length of Gabe's forearm, each nail as long as Gabe's finger and curved like utility hooks.

A rumble shook the tunnel, and Gabe realized the berserker was snarling at them.

If they didn't deescalate this situation, they were dead.

"H-hello," Tommy stammered. "Hi. It's me. It's Tommy. Remember?"

Gabe raised his phone, shining the light over the tattered remnants of clothes the beast still wore. The thing was huge, his body filling the width of the tunnel, his pointed ears scraping the stalactites and flicking when water dripped on them. Those twitchy ears might have been funny if Gabe weren't terrified he was about to meet his end.

"What do I say?" Tommy whispered.

Gabe forced away his lizard-brained thoughts of *Run, run, run!* and said, "Ask him questions about himself. Try and make him remember his humanity."

"O-okay... What's your name?" Tommy asked. "I never asked you your name."

A growl crawled from the black beast's throat. He hunched over, hiding his snout in his massive clawed hands. Through the gaps in his fingers, the yellow light flickered. "C... C... C-can't remember..." The deep, growling voice was wretched. "Too long. Been trapped here." Snarls and snorts punctuated every word. "O-out. Want out. N-Need out."

"I'm sorry." Tommy's voice was barely above a whisper.

Gabe cleared his throat. "We're going to help you get out of here. Okay?"

"How?" Max whispered.

Gabe had no clue. "Just keep talking. Can you do that? Tell us about yourself. Do you... I don't know, do you have any family out there?"

The beast curled his fingers. Claws raked down his snout and his cheeks, droplets of blood welling to the surface. "Gone. All. Gone. Took me away." A shudder racked the beast's body. "Can't remember them. Faces fading. No. No, no, no..." His eyes flashed yellow. The beast slammed his claws against his head. The yellow light went out, then came back on. "No. Don't forget. Don't forget. Don't!"

"Who took you away?" Gabe asked.

A roar shook the tunnel. Max tugged Gabe back as a stalactite fell from the ceiling and shattered at their feet. The beast slammed his head into the wall. He raked his claws down the stone, shooting up sparks. "He did! His name. What was his name?" The beast panted, strings of spit dangling from his mouth. "Kill him. I will *kill him.*" He whirled toward them, fangs pearly bright in the dark. His eyes filled with yellow.

"Can we run yet?" Tommy squeaked.

Max grabbed Gabe's arm. "Run!"

They didn't stand a chance. Gabe had only made it a few steps when a clawed hand hooked around his ankle. His skull smacked against the ground, an explosion of white blinding him briefly.

"Gabe!" Max's roar filled the tunnel. He leaped in front of Gabe, claws out. A single swipe from the beast sent him flying into the wall.

Tommy screamed, hiding his head in his hands and curling into a ball.

Gabe's heart was ready to burst from his chest as he stared up a long snout and into blazing yellow eyes. The beast blasted him with hot, sour breath. Strings of spit rained onto Gabe's face. Those hooked claws curled near Gabe's ear, the hand itself big enough to crush his skull like a melon. The beast leaned in, and Gabe went cross-eyed as its cold, slimy nose touched his own nose.

Then the beast sniffed him. It drew in a long, deep breath and huffed it back into his face in a hot gust.

Gabe didn't move, not even to blink or twitch a muscle.

The beast huffed in another breath. Its eyes flickered.

Something tugged in Gabe's chest. Something *burned.*

The beast said, "Mi..."

Gabe squinted at him. "What?"

Those yellow eyes flickered. Yellow. Yellow.

Gabe's heart stopped.

Amber eyes stared down at him, an exact reflection of his own eye color.

The beast said, "Mi... jo."

He thought he'd misheard. "What... what did you call me?"

A pulse thumped in his chest like a second heartbeat.

"No," Gabe croaked. Because it wasn't possible. It didn't make sense.

But there was a bond stirring to life in his chest that told him this was real. The bond stretched taut and the beast above him doubled over with a snarl. Muscles rippled and popped. The long black fur shortened, revealing tanned skin. The snout became a nose. The only fur still on him was a long, wild beard.

The man above him was skin and bones. His eyes were sunken, and shadows pooled in the pockets of his skeletal face. His shoulder blades stuck out so sharply, Gabe was amazed his skin didn't tear like paper. His hair had gone silver in places. There was nothing recognizable about him. Not until he opened his eyes and showed Gabe that impossible identical amber.

"It's me, mijo." He touched Gabe's face with a trembling hand. Gabe flinched, but the touch was so tender, it took his breath away.

A tear dangled on the tip of the man's nose. It wobbled and fell, disappearing into his beard. Beneath his facial hair, his lips formed a smile that Gabe would know anywhere.

"It's your father," Manuel Reyes said.

Those three hushed words shattered Gabe into pieces.

"No. No, no, no!" Gabe scrambled to his feet, colliding with the wall. "It's not true. Stop it. Stop it!" His ears rang. His vision warped.

This wasn't real. It couldn't be real. He'd watched his father's blood color the water crimson. Watched as the river dragged his father away. His mother had broken down when she told him the news, telling him his father was dead. All the shattered pieces of his heart knew this man to be dead and gone.

Manuel Reyes was dead, and yet here he stood, gaunt and clad in tattered, moth-eaten clothes, looking at Gabe as if he were a little boy again.

My father's alive. He's alive!

Then the wind rushed in his ears and bony arms caught him just before he collapsed.

"Easy, Gabriel."

That voice, lilted with a familiar gruff Mexican accent, sent his heart into overdrive. He blinked fast to clear his hazy vision, too stunned to speak as his father's face came into focus.

"I've gone crazy, haven't I?" That was the only way this made sense. "All of this is some... some fever dream or something. Or I've died?" Did the dead even have dreams?

Max laughed softly. "No, love. You're alive, and so is your dad."

Gabe lurched onto his elbows and crawled back, suddenly struggling for air to breathe. "No. No, it's impossible. You died! The river carried you away. You were shot. You..." Oh, goddess. He felt sick. His father had been kept prisoner in this dark hellhole for all these years.

"No, Gabriel." Warm hands clasped his. Weren't the dead supposed to be cold, clammy? "I escaped the floodwaters, though Stone's bullet was poisoned. My berserker gene activated to keep me alive."

Gabe blinked hard, a lump in his throat as memories of that horrible day resurfaced, as fresh and painful as if it had been yesterday. "You've been trapped here all these years?" Anguish for what his father had suffered left his voice raw and broken.

"It hasn't been easy." His father's eyes glimmered with tears. His hand trembled as he touched the side of Gabe's neck, just like he used to when Gabe was a boy. "I missed you all so much."

"I thought—we all thought you were dead. All these years, we thought—" Tears burned his eyes and he didn't know if he wanted to roar in fury at the years stolen from them or break down.

"Gabe." Max's voice shook. "Gabe, let him talk."

The devastation in his father's face nearly brought Gabe to his knees. "Goddess. Gabriel, I am so sorry." He'd never heard his father cry before.

Tears left wet tracks down Gabe's cheeks, and he couldn't seem to speak.

"I never should have tried to expose that... that slimy bastard!" Pacing, Manuel tangled his trembling hands in his overgrown hair. "If I'd known how terribly you all would suffer, I wouldn't have dug as deep as I did into Aaron McCready. You have to understand. McCready was determined to silence me. I knew too much. I found out about McCready's connection to the Wargs. If I'd talked, I would have jeopardized his place on the Council, his goals, *everything*. He was desperate to silence me." Manuel huffed out a breath. "You know who McCready is, don't you?"

"Yeah. Yes, I..." A thought came to him. "That day you were away visiting the Council, you were going to tell Hanson about McCready, weren't you?"

"Yes. I thought if I could just get to Hanson and tell him the truth, then the Council would take action. I underestimated McCready's paranoia. He knew how close I'd come to exposing him. John Stone was the piece of the puzzle I didn't see coming. I knew he loathed me, yes. Hated me, yes. But I had no idea he and McCready were cohorts, not until it was too late. All I wanted the moment I escaped the river was to find all of you and let you know I was all right. But I never got the chance."

Gabe swallowed hard. "The hunters?"

"Yes." Manuel breathed. "They took me prisoner when I was too weak to fight back. Brought me to the island. Threw me into this prison."

"Wait," Max said. "All these years, you've been—"

"Trapped. Yes," Manuel huffed. A tear left a wet track down his father's face, disappearing into his rugged beard. "Nothing would have stopped me from coming home to you, Gabriel. To your mother. Your sister."

Gabe tried to take a deep breath and choked on it, sobs shaking his shoulders. "I blamed myself for your death. For years, it haunted me."

His father bowed his head, peering up at Gabe through remorseful eyes. "I'm so sorry, Gabriel."

"I hated myself. I wished I'd died instead of you." His voice broke, tears scorching a path down his cheeks.

His father took a slow step forward, arms open. "Nothing that happened that night was your fault. None of it." Gabe's resistance crumbled as his father grasped his shoulders. He'd never thought he'd hear his father release him from the burden of his grief and guilt. Gabe stumbled into his father's arms. He closed his eyes and for a moment, he was a boy again, wrapped in the safety and comfort of his father's embrace. "I'd give my life again for you. For our family."

For the first time since he was a child, Gabe buried his face in his father's shoulder and clung on as years of guilt and anguish finally fell from his shoulders.

"By the goddess," his father whispered, his eyes sparkling as his hands framed Gabe's face. "You're tall. You must be..."

"Six feet," Max chimed in, smiling widely.

His father laughed warmly. "Like your grandfather. I'm glad you got his height."

Gabe chuckled, wiping his eyes. His father had looked like a giant when Gabe was a kid, but now—he wrapped his arms around his dad and lifted his toes off the ground. His father pulled him into a bone-breaking hug Gabe couldn't escape from and they tussled like they hadn't since Gabe was thirteen. Breathless, grinning so hard it hurt, Gabe motioned Max over. "Pa, this is my mate. Max, this is Manuel Reyes." To Gabe's delight, his father welcomed Max in for a backslapping hug. Gabe laughed, hardly able to contain his excitement.

"Tommy," Manuel said, smiling warmly. "I'm Manuel Reyes. It's good to meet you."

"Hi." Tommy approached, hands deep in his pockets and head bowed. "It's good to finally see what you look like."

Manuel grinned and wrestled the boy into a hug. "You as well. Thank you." He swept the boy's hair from his forehead. "I would have lost my mind a long time ago if it weren't for you keeping me company." A frown creased his brow. "What exactly are you all doing here?"

Max opened his mouth and shut it. "That's a loaded question."

"We came to face McCready," Gabe said.

Manuel's mouth fell open. "Just you? Are you crazy?"

"No, not just us." Gabe's heart skipped a beat. His father was going to see Ben again and meet all his friends in the agency. He could see Gabe's—

"Mother... you need to see her!" Gabe gripped Manuel's shoulders. "And Izzie!"

His father squeezed Gabe's elbows, his eyes wide in disbelief. "Is she here? By the goddess. I've been gone so long. Too long." His father combed his hands through his long hair. "No, no! I can't see your mother! Not like this! I look like shit, probably smell like it too!" Panic gripped his face, and he sniffed at his underarms.

Gabe grabbed his arm. "Come on. She'll faint, she'll be so happy! If she doesn't slap you first."

"Happy? You think so?" His father's hands trembled. "Did she ever...?" He looked away, unable to finish.

Gabe smiled. His face hurt from it. "No. She never remarried."

His father exhaled, blinking hard and wiping his eyes. "You're joking."

"No! Come see for yourself!"

Manuel faltered. "How did you all get down here?" He seized Gabe's arm, his eyes wide and panicked. "There's no way out. I've tried to escape the goddess only knows how many times."

Gabe waved him off. "Relax. We have a way out."

Manuel looked between them incredulously. "How?"

"Don't tell your mother that I screamed when Max levitated me." Manuel stood on wobbly knees.

"I make no promises. That was hilarious," Gabe said.

Manuel sucked in big gulps of air, his face upturned to the fading light of the moon. "Goddess. It feels so good to breathe fresh air again."

Eager as he was to witness his family reunited, Gabe lingered to allow Manuel his first taste of freedom in years.

Exhaling with a smile, Manuel said, "Come on. Let's go."

Gabe pulled him toward the beach, his knees shaking and heart pumping.

They hiked through the woods. On the horizon, a sliver of dawn glowed that couldn't be buried by the gray storm clouds thickening overhead. They followed the ground where it sloped and arrived back on the beach.

Ben sat on an overturned boat, his chin propped up by his hand. His mouth hung open and he snored thunderously.

"Ben?" Gabe shook him awake.

"What the—" Ben lurched to his feet. "Finally, what's going on?" He froze, his bushy brows low over his eyes. His mouth slipped open. "No..." His voice was barely a whisper as he took in Manuel. Gabe grinned and nodded.

"Ben, this is—"

Ben opened his mouth, then shut it. "Manuel. Manuel Reyes. You're... but—"

Manuel held out a hand. "Ben Stroud. Damn. It's good to see you again."

He looked at Manuel's hand, then his face, blinking fast. He reached out slowly as if expecting an electric shock. As he tugged Manuel into a backbreaking hug, Ben's lips trembled beneath his bushy beard. "Un-fucking-believable, man!" Ben's shoulders quivered with sobs, but they turned to hysterical laughter. Manuel laughed with him, and Ben yanked him back at arm's length, taking him in. "*How*?"

"It's a long story." Manuel slapped his shoulder. "Hell, you got old."

Ben barked out a laugh and wiped his eyes. "You're one to talk!" He tugged on a silver strand of hair. "She-Wolf's tits—excuse me, Max—we've got to get some food in you, man!" He opened his backpack and handed Manuel a package of jerky.

Zach ran up to meet them. "What's happening? Did you meet that berserker or—" He jumped as Gabe bounded up to him and grabbed him by the shoulders.

"Zach, meet my father, Manuel Reyes!"

Zach gaped.

Ryan's jaw dropped. "Wait. Wait. Wait. Gabe, is this a joke?" Ryan pointed at Manuel, slack-jawed.

"No, Ry! This is my father!" Gabe squeezed his dad's shoulders. "This is Ryan Kelly and Zach DeShawn."

Manuel held out a hand, and Zach and Ryan were frozen in twin expressions of astonishment.

Gabe figured they'd need a minute.

"Where is she? Where's Veronica? Is Izzie here?" Manuel asked.

Shoving Ryan and Zach out of the way, Ben motioned down the beach. "By the water with our pack."

Manuel exhaled, his eyes wide. He combed his hands through his hair as he followed Ben past the frozen statues of Zach and Ryan. As they neared the shore, Manuel hesitated. "Maybe," he began. "Maybe you should tell her, Gabriel. I don't want her fainting like you did."

Ryan came to life. "Wait, what? Dude, you fainted?"

Gabe rolled his eyes when Ryan sniggered. "Hey, finding out your dead dad's actually been alive for sixteen whole years is a lot."

Manuel tugged on Gabe's arm, urging him to lead the way to Veronica and Izzie. They stopped atop a dune where farther down the beach, Veronica and Izzie sat with a few others around a cluster of tents.

His father panted by his side, eyes wide and wet. "What do I do?" he asked, squeezing Gabe's arm so tight it hurt.

Gabe gripped his shoulder. "I don't know… Let me ease her into the idea. Then you can, I don't know, make some big dramatic appearance."

Manuel nodded, still gazing at his wife with tears in his eyes. "Okay. Sure."

His heart raced. There was no easy way to say any of this, but he went to meet his mother and Izzie where they sat in the sand, making conversation with their human allies. "Mamá, Izzie."

Veronica sprang up. "Thank the goddess you're okay!" Gabe let her hug him even though his whole body vibrated with nervous energy. Veronica smiled at him with a curious tilt of her brow. "Well? Did you meet this big scary berserker?"

"I did." Gabe swallowed, squeezing his fists.

"What's he like?" Izzie asked. "Can we trust him?"

"Yeah! Yeah, we can. Listen, there's something you should know."

His mother frowned, noticing the tremor in his voice. "Are you all right? Can we meet him?"

Gabe squeezed her hands, exhaling to calm his nerves. She was going to think he was crazy. "You already know him." His voice trembled so badly he could barely get the words out. "Ma. It's... It's Papá. He's alive."

She looked like he'd slapped her. "That's not funny, Gabriel." Shaking her head, she turned around to leave. Veronica froze in place, gazing up at the dune. Izzie looked that way and her eyes went wide.

"Mamá," Izzie whispered. Her trembling hand tugged on her mother's sleeve. "Mamá, look. Look! Is that—"

The rising sun spilled across the sand and onto Manuel, who was standing tall at the top of the dune. Veronica stumbled and Izzie caught her. Gabe knew his mother was stronger than him because somehow she managed not to faint, but her face went ashen and her eyes impossibly wide. She turned away, unable to stifle a sob.

Manuel was shaking hard. He could hardly hold her gaze but he tried, blinking back tears. "V," he began, and he slipped in the sand and went sliding down the hill, arms flailing.

Veronica ran, her hair streaming behind her, and Manuel crashed into her arms. She stumbled but didn't fall. Both breathing hard, they gazed at each other. Goddess... the way he looked at her, like she was the She-Wolf herself come to Earth. A lump rose in Gabe's throat. Izzie put her arm around his waist, sniffling.

Veronica's hand settled on Manuel's grizzled cheek. "H-How is this possible? I thought—" Veronica's voice failed her. Tears spilled down her face. She stroked his cheek, and Manuel turned his head, his quivering lips caressing her hand.

"I know. I'm here." Blinking hard, Manuel took her face in his hands. A trembling smile broke across his face. "I'm not going anywhere. Never again."

Veronica threw herself into his arms and they laughed and cried together. Manuel spun her around in his arms as they shared a sweet, lasting kiss. When they finally broke apart, they were drying each other's tears. Gabe's mother smiled in a way he hadn't seen in years.

Manuel turned to Izzie, frozen by Gabe's side, her eyes shining with emotion.

He laughed, wiping his eyes, and grinned. "Isabella," he whispered. "You're all grown up..."

She made a sound between a laugh and a sob, shaking her head in disbelief. Gabe gave her a shove. She walked to her father slowly, but as he opened his arms to her, she bowled him off his feet as she threw herself into his arms.

Max pushed Gabe toward his dad, and as the rest of his family turned to him, whole and happy as they hadn't been in years, Gabe ran to them and enveloped them all in his arms. He laughed like he had when he was a boy, carefree and jubilant, surrounded by the love of his mother, sister, and father.

The Reyes pack was whole again.

CHAPTER 11

BATTLE OF CRESCENT COVE

THE SKIES DARKENED WITH the coming blizzard, and Max's heart raced in anticipation. This time they couldn't fail. McCready had to be stopped.

Ben and Manuel stood shoulder to shoulder observing the trees that led deeper into the island toward McCready and his wargs. Manuel said, "I've been waiting for this day for years."

"I'll bet," Ben said.

"McCready has taken countless lives and hidden from justice behind the Council." Manuel curled his lip. He'd shaved his beard, revealing a face so familiar Max thought he was staring at an older version of Gabe. "He has to be stopped."

Veronica came to stand by his side. "I'll confront him with you."

"No, Veronica. You'll stay here where it's safe."

She snapped, "Manuel Reyes, you'll be lucky if I ever leave your side again. I'm coming with you."

Looks familiar, Max thought with some fondness. *I guess all the Reyes men are overprotective worrywarts.*

Ben whistled. The ground trembled under the paws and boots, and their wolves and human allies assembled from where they'd been hidden within the woods.

149

Manuel's jaw fell open. "Ben, these are all your pack?"

Ben grinned, his chest swelling in pride. "After Hanson's murder and what McCready's done to the country, people are waking up." To his pack, he said, "Our future is in McCready's hands. Tonight we'll take it back with our claws and fangs! The sun will rise on a new world where humans and wolves are equals! Stand with me!"

Lacing his fingers with Gabe's, Max held on tight.

Ben said, "It's time to take the fight to that sham of a Council!" Tossing aside his clothes, he shifted to his silver wolf and charged toward the forest. Their army followed him.

As snowflakes fell thick and fast from the sky, Gabe turned to Tommy. "You don't have to stay. You can go back and be with your sister."

But Tommy shook his head. "I need to do this," he said with determination Max didn't understand.

"It's going to be dangerous," Max said.

Tommy clenched his jaw. "I have to be there."

There was no time to argue. Max grabbed his shoulder. "Stay close!"

"I will!" Tommy said, eyes flashing.

Gabe took off after his father and Max followed, Tommy right on his heels. All around them the army of wolves and humans stormed the forest. The wind howled, and snow buffeted them. The blizzard was coming and fast. If they didn't finish this quickly, they'd be lost in the storm's whiteout.

Howls sent a shudder down Max's spine, and the ground trembled under his feet. Eyes gleamed between the trees. "They're coming!" Manuel roared. McCready's wargs burst from between the trees, fur rippling and fangs flashing. A great black wolf lunged for Manuel and he ducked beneath it. Veronica swung her silver whip, shredding the flesh of any wolves that came near her husband.

Beside Max, Gabe hunched over, growing fangs and fur. With a snarl, he charged and Max and Izzie followed. Max's clothes burst from his body as he shifted, tackling his opponent as a wolf. His fangs sought the soft flesh beneath a thick layer of fur and crunched down.

Gabe yelped, thrashing to escape a wolf with its fangs buried in his hide. Charging, Izzie buried her claws deep in the wolf's belly.

Max's paws churned up snow as he ran, jaws snapping at any who barred his path. The blood of his enemies soaked his tongue as he fought his way through the pack. He broke through their lines and ran, Gabe and his family at his side and their packmates close behind.

A howl from above froze Max in place. On a rocky outcrop stood a beast bigger than any other. McCready pushed off from the edge, slamming the ground with enormous paws as he landed before them, dwarfing them in his shadow. He prowled toward them on all fours, the growl in his throat vibrating the icicles dangling from the snow-laden pines. Silhouetted behind him were more wargs, fangs bared and eyes glowing.

At the sight of Manuel standing tall before his pack, McCready's eyes went wide, his body trembling with a furious snarl. "Manuel Reyes? How?" The roar shook the treetops. "Stone killed you!"

Manuel shouldered toward him, his fangs lengthening and eyes flashing. "No. You tried to hide the truth, and you failed. The world's seen what you are, Aaron McCready, and they won't have it! When your army falls, there'll be nowhere you can run to, no one to protect you. You'll answer for every one of your crimes."

A roar of laughter pulled from McCready's throat. "After tonight, you'll wish Stone had killed you, Reyes!" He raised a claw and Veronica tore out in front of her husband, swinging her whip. McCready bellowed as it licked across his snout, tearing away a strip of flesh, and he bared his fangs in a loathsome grin. "I'll tear your throats out and drink the blood from your carcasses! Attack!"

Manuel shifted and grew to twice his height. Veronica and Izzie gasped when a great black wolf stood before their enemy on two legs, as big as McCready and with a growl so deep it reverberated in Max's chest. When Manuel opened his eyes, they flared amber. He was in control.

McCready sneered in disgust. "A hybrid was never meant to have such power. I'll rip it from your corpse!"

The wargs ran, hurtling toward Max and the others. Ben led the charge, colliding with them. Ben's wolves attacked, hurling themselves upon McCready, their fangs ripping his flesh. The beast battered them away as if they were fleas, but he screamed as a flurry of Eddie's silver bullets pierced his hide.

The ground shook as the berserker warriors collided, fangs tearing flesh and claws slashing. Manuel came crashing to the ground with earthshaking force as McCready grabbed onto his neck. Seconds behind Gabe, Max charged and they hurled themselves upon McCready.

The beast dragged his claws across Manuel's face, and he roared, pawing away the blood in his eyes. Gabe pounced on McCready, but he seized Gabe around the middle and squeezed, making him yelp in anguish.

Terror and fury drove Max toward the beast, driving his snout into a bullet wound that was slow to heal. He ripped into it, and McCready's pained howl made his ears ring. Next thing he knew, Max flailed in midair, held by the scruff in McCready's grasp. The beast threw both him and Gabe, and the wind went out of Max as he collided with a tree trunk. McCready tossed Manuel aside when he came running, and he stormed toward Max and Gabe.

"Stay away from them!" Manuel roared, struggling to break free of the wargs swarming him like ants.

"How does it feel, Manuel?" McCready snarled as he leaned over Gabe's limp body. "You sacrificed so much, but your family will die regardless. I'll make you watch as I rip them all to pieces!" He slammed his paw down on Gabe's ribs, and Gabe screamed as McCready slowly crushed him.

The pain of his aching body brought Max out of his shift. "No," Max croaked, fighting against the crippling pain. "Don't!"

"Stop!" A young voice screamed above the chaos.

And amazingly, McCready did. It was like he'd been frozen in ice. The shock on his bestial face was so human, it couldn't be mistaken for anything else. He turned and towered over Tommy. The boy shivered but glared defiantly into McCready's blazing eyes.

McCready roared, "Everyone stop!"

His wargs' eyes flashed yellow. Like robots, they all froze in place, their eyes empty and glassy.

Max leaned on the tree for support, his knees shaking. He couldn't have anticipated what happened next if he'd tried.

McCready melted from his shift, shrinking down to his normal height. His hand trembled when he reached toward Tommy. "Thomas…" he whispered in a voice so devastated, Max couldn't believe it had come from a monster like him.

Tommy blinked hard. "Hey." His chest hitched. "Hi, Dad."

Ryan shifted. "*What*?" he bellowed, eyes bulging. "Are you fucking serious right now?"

Max thought he'd misheard but after Ryan's reaction, he knew he hadn't.

Gabe sat up with snow in his fur, panting.

To Max's amazement, there were tears in Aaron McCready's eyes. Now that Max was seeing them side by side, the similarities were hard to deny. McCready's pasty skin was nothing like Tommy's warm brown, but their hazel eyes were exactly the same. Tommy had his father's wavy hair texture. His jawline. But that was where the similarities ended. "How is this possible?" McCready whispered, voice breaking. "I thought the hunters killed you."

Tommy shook his head. "They took us away. I thought you'd come for us when you arrived on the island." A tear fell down his face. "Instead, you… you…" Anger thickened his voice.

McCready reached out to wipe it away but Tommy jerked out of his reach. "Oh, Thomas," he whispered, devastation making his voice shake. "I need you to understand—everything I have done is for the greater good."

Tommy shook his head. "Don't you dare try to justify slaughtering our pack! We had a family again, and you ripped them away from us."

He flinched back from his son's anger. "Wait a moment. *Us*? Your sister. Luna."

Tommy's throat bobbed when he swallowed. "Yeah. She's alive, Dad. I raised her all on my own."

Shaking his head, McCready closed his eyes tight. His mouth quivered. "Goddess. My boy. My poor, poor boy. Where is she?"

Tommy hesitated, glancing at Max.

McCready's face twisted, and that familiar hatred was back. He whirled toward Max but Gabe was on his paws and at Max's side in seconds. Ben snarled and prowled toward McCready. "Where is my daughter?" he rumbled, brown fur thickening on his arms.

Max stared him down. "She's safe. We're not monsters. We wouldn't harm children, not even yours."

Panting, McCready came closer.

"Dad," Tommy snapped. "He's telling the truth! Luna's safe."

McCready shook his head. "You know nothing of these people!"

His son folded his arms. "At least they helped us. Unlike you."

McCready flinched.

Ben shifted to a man, blood streaking his pale skin. "Surrender, Mc-Cready, and we will let you see her again."

McCready bared his teeth, his hands in fists. His eyes bulged, his pupils darting from Ben to his son. "We can leave right now," McCready whispered, his eyes locked on Tommy. "You, Luna, and I can go far away from this. We can be a family again."

Max's heart skipped as he watched Tommy's eyes widen and fill with tears. The boy looked so lost, so hurt. It made Max's heart crack in two, remembering the day he'd seen his stepfather, who he'd cared for and admired, raise a hand against his mother. He knew that look of hurt. That betrayal. It had surely been on his own face once.

"I had a family." He took a step back, his whole body quivering. "You... you murdered them."

"I didn't know they had you among them. If I had—"

"You would have killed them anyway!" Tommy roared, his voice shaking. Tears spilled down his face. "You claim you want to help werewolves, b-but you murdered innocent wolves just because they had something you wanted. You're a monster!"

His father shook his head, blinking fast. "You are young. You know nothing of the world. Otherwise you would understand."

"Mom wouldn't even recognize you!"

McCready lurched toward him and Max reacted, yanking Tommy behind him. Gabe snarled, his fur bristling.

"Don't." McCready pointed a trembling, clawed finger at him. "Don't you talk about your mother. I am creating a world where werewolves will never be hunted by humans again like we were. Where we are at the top where we belong! Don't you want that? Don't you want kids your age to grow up never knowing what it's like to lose their family to humanity's cruelty?"

Tommy's expression faltered. "I do," he admitted, wetting his quivering lips. "But this... this can't be the way we go about it." He took several steps back toward the agency wolves.

"Don't do this," McCready rasped, and Max realized he was begging. "Thomas. Don't."

His son closed his eyes tight, tears falling down his face. "Y-you're a monster. You killed my friends. You..." He wrapped his arms around his stomach and gasped, folding into himself. Max stepped backward, not taking his eyes off McCready, and put his arm around the anguished boy. He curled into Max's side, trembling fingers gripping his arm.

McCready's eyes flashed yellow. "Give him back," he snarled, the deep rumbling growl building in him like thunder. "Give my son back to me!"

And all around them, the wargs screamed in ways no wolves ever should. Their yellow eyes bulged. Their bodies jerked and seized. Tommy howled and clutched his head. His eyes flashed a blank yellow, the corded muscles of his neck sticking out in sharp relief as he screamed and screamed.

"What the fuck is going on?" Shaking, Max dropped to his knees beside the boy. "Tommy!" Blood trickled from Tommy's nose. His brown skin turned an ashy gray.

Manuel gasped. "He's killing them."

Before their eyes, McCready shifted back to his berserker form. His roar shook the trees to their roots, and he grew taller than ever before.

Manuel said, "He's using their bonds to steal their life force, to strengthen himself."

Horror nearly made Max sick. His hands shook when he framed Tommy's face. Froth gathered at the corner of Tommy's mouth. "We have to stop him!"

Veronica grabbed Manuel's arm. "Can we do that? Can our bond give you strength?"

His complexion paled. "V, I can't do that. I couldn't just take from you!"

Izzie shook her head. "You won't be taking anything! We're offering. Get stronger and end McCready now. Quickly!"

Shifting to a man, Gabe raced to stand beside his family. Veronica linked hands with her grown children and locked eyes with Manuel. "Do it," she commanded. "We're ready."

Chest rising and falling fast, Manuel grew taller. Fur wrapped around his body, which became taut with muscle. Max couldn't look away from Gabe, waiting to see pain overcome his face, for him to drop to the ground screaming. His mate and his family closed their eyes, each of them gasping softly.

"Are you hurt?" Max called out to him.

Gabe shook his head. "N-no. Feels... warm. For now."

Manuel grew to McCready's height and even bigger, towering over the Alpha of the Council.

Then McCready roared and shot toward him. The berserkers collided like mountains. Blood rained onto the ground, spattering hot on Max's skin. He gripped Tommy's twitching hand and squeezed tight. Gabe, Veronica, and Izzie panted, their hands still clasped. The wind roared around them as the storm turned violent, the snow needling Max's eyes and the wind numbing his face. If Manuel didn't end this soon, he wouldn't be able to go on fighting. The whiteout was coming, and it was coming fast.

Manuel punched his hand out, and McCready grunted as Manuel's claws drove into his stomach and pulled. The beast dropped to his knees, shaking the forest floor. Slowly, he and Manuel shrank down to their original heights, their fur falling off until they were human.

There was a hole through McCready's stomach when Manuel pulled his fist free. Max could see his insides. He looked away fast as McCready collapsed, wheezing gasps spilling from his lips. The wargs around him groaned and shook, too weak to continue fighting. He'd drained them of their life force. Max was amazed some of them were still alive.

The boy gasped at Max's feet, and Max's heart soared. "Are you okay?"

Tommy whimpered but nodded.

Taking deep breaths, Gabe, Izzie, and Veronica unlinked their hands.

Manuel loomed over McCready, his lip curled. "It's over, McCready."

"How..." he rasped, lips stained red. "How could I fail?"

Ryan shrugged. "I would say something about the power of love versus the power of hate and how love's stronger and yada yada, but the fact is—you lost because you suck!" He flipped McCready off.

"Kill him," Ben spat. "We need to make sure he can never hurt anyone again."

Manuel glanced at Tommy, sadness creasing his brow. "Tommy," he began.

Closing his eyes tight, Tommy rolled onto his side. His body quivered with sobs even as he nodded.

Manuel turned to McCready, his claws lengthening.

Gale-force winds slammed into all of them. Max stumbled and would have fallen if Ryan hadn't grabbed him by the waist.

"Holy shit! That blizzard's here!" Ryan shouted, his voice drowned out by the wind.

A wall of white crashed over them. Snow pelted every inch of Max. He dropped to his knees and crouched over Tommy, shielding him. "Gabe?" Max called, struggling to see through the fat flakes that smacked into his eyes. He could hardly see more than the length of his extended hand.

"McCready!" Manuel roared, and Max's heart sank.

"This isn't over, Reyes!" McCready's voice echoed through the whiteout of the storm. "I will take back everything your wretched dogs stole from me!" Bone ground against bone. Thunderous paw steps got farther and farther away.

"After him!" Manuel shouted, but it was useless trying. No one could see or do anything.

The blizzard snatched victory right from their hands.

"No," Tommy whimpered. "No, no, no..."

Max felt blindly for his hand and held on tight.

The blizzard lasted only minutes. Gradually, the gale died down and Max's vision cleared. Everyone around him had been covered in snow. It fell off their bodies as everyone slowly came back to life. Zach helped Ryan up. Vicenzo shook snow out of his black fur and Eddie smacked it out of his cowboy hat. Max ground his teeth when he realized there wasn't so much as a trace of McCready. The snow had covered his tracks.

Manuel cursed as he helped Veronica and Izzie to stand. "He's gone. He'd have swum to shore or taken a boat."

Gabe sat up and shook his head, sending snow flying. "No. Come on, we could still catch up to him." Max was alarmed by how pale Gabe was. He lurched to his feet and grabbed Gabe's arm to steady him when he swayed. Even Izzie's olive complexion had a grayish tinge.

"It doesn't matter. We're in no state to fight." Manuel winced and caressed Veronica's cheek. She was pale too. "I shouldn't have used our bond like that. It took a lot out of the three of you."

Veronica shook her head. "It was worth it, mi corazón."

"Councilman Reyes?" croaked a woman's voice. "By the goddess, is that really you?"

Max whirled around just as a warg stood. Four others found their feet. For wargs, they didn't fit the criteria. Most if not all of McCready's recruits were young. These wargs were weathered, their hair going gray in places.

Manuel turned, his mouth slipping open. "By the goddess. Melanie. It's been years."

Melanie wiped blood from her face. "Indeed it has. I wish we were reuniting under better circumstances."

Gabe growled, though he didn't look threatening with his eyes heavy-lidded with exhaustion. "Any reason we shouldn't kill you?"

One of the other councilmembers raised his hands placatingly. "Please. I know what this looks like."

Manuel said, "Tell me you didn't join that monster of your own volition, Gregor. We only worked together a short while, but you were wolves of honor."

"We still are!" Melanie snapped. "That monster killed or bent the minds of any councilmembers who wouldn't bow to his every whim. He let the strongest live as his thralls. The weaker ones, he and his wargs butchered." She kicked a warg's lifeless face. "Looks like they won't be hurting anyone again."

Manuel sighed. "I'm sorry, Mel, Gregor, all of you. If I'd only told Hanson sooner... But the past is the past. It's time to move forward."

Melanie's lips quirked. "Indeed it is, and I think I have a few ideas about where to fix the Council. No... to remake it."

With the councilmembers in tow, Max followed the agency wolves back to the boats, lost in a fog as battle scenes continued to play through his head. The howls, screams, and cracks of gunfire still rang in his ears. He was afraid to trust in the sudden silence that had fallen over the island when they returned to the beach. Bodies littered the ground, piled one on top of the other, their blood turning the earth to mud under Max's feet. The corpses of shifters in human and wolf form watched him pass, eyes wide and staring blankly, blood matting their fur. He closed his eyes tight but their faces, frozen forever in their final moments, were burned into his mind.

Looking back at Manuel, Melanie said, "When you can, come to Wolf Point. The Council needs an Alpha, and it's clear to me and my fellow councilmembers that your strength befits the title. We'll hold a ceremony to celebrate. It's about time we had some light in this time of darkness."

Gabe gasped. "No way."

"Did you hear that?" Veronica grinned and gripped her husband's shoulder.

Manuel huffed out a breath, blinking fast. "I... Yes, Melanie. I will. Thank you."

Grinning, Ryan clapped Manuel on the back. "How'd we go from McCready's brand of douchebaggery to having the world's first hybrid Alpha?"

"About damn time we had some good news," Zach said, chuckling.

Max grinned. "Congrats, Alpha!"

Face pale, Manuel swayed. "I think I need to sit down." Izzie and Veronica helped him into the boat.

With his hand holding tight to Tommy's, Max settled into a rowboat beside Gabe with Zach at the oars. Ryan gave the boat a push and jumped in beside Zach. As they rowed into the fog, Ryan laid his head on Zach's shoulder and slept. Max wished he could sleep, but every time he closed his eyes, he saw the silhouettes of wolves fighting and dying on the back of his eyelids.

Once they reached land, they searched the shore for McCready's trail. The snowfall had completely covered his escape and stolen his scent.

Tommy shivered, his arms around himself. "So, we're just going to let him go?"

"No. His trail is out there." Manuel patted his shoulder. "I will put together a team to track him down. This isn't over."

Gripping the boy's arm, Max said, "Your dad won't hurt you."

Tommy stayed quiet. He didn't look like he believed them.

The agency wolves returned to the camp for the night and nestled around a small fire. Gabe bumped his shoulder with Max's and for a time, neither of them spoke. Most of the pack slept around them, lying close for warmth.

Vicenzo draped his elbows over his knees, the firelight reflecting in his eyes. "McCready's right, you know. We can't trust them. Humans. Humans destroy everything they touch, and they barely tolerate us. The world would be better off if humans weren't around. If the world was just untamed wilderness again, for the wolves and animals."

Max was unsettled to hear him say so, but he could see his point. "There are other solutions. Killing off humans would cause more problems in the end, especially for our kind. Humans are already afraid of us. We need to show them why they're wrong to fear us, not why they're right."

Vicenzo scowled. "We shouldn't have to prove shit to them."

"Then why are you here fighting for a world where we're equals if you believe humans can't be trusted?"

"'Cause McCready's just gonna make things worse for us in the long run by pissing off humans. Doesn't mean he's wrong, though. He's right to fear them, but he's wrong about everything else. Spare me the lecture, right? I don't care about humans. Never will, not after what they've done to my family." Vicenzo dusted snow from his jeans and walked away.

He made to argue but Gabe nudged him, shooting him a look that suggested he leave the grumpy wolf to himself. Max sighed. "The world's big enough for all of us. That's what I think. So I don't see why we can't share it."

Gabe grimaced. "Vicenzo has a point. It's exhausting, Max. No matter how we behave, there will always be people that look at us and see us as animals."

Max took his hand and squeezed tight. "There are good people in this world. Werewolves and humans. They're the ones that make this messed-up world worth living in."

His mate's mouth quirked into a smile. He leaned his cheek on Max's hair. "I just hope we can come back from this. McCready's done so much damage. Will humans ever trust us again?"

"I don't know, but I think so." Max had to believe they could. He had to believe that this world was big enough for shifters and humans to live in peace. He closed his eyes and nestled into the warmth of Gabe's neck, breathing in the scent of him beneath the blood and sweat. Finally, he found sleep.

CHAPTER 12

CHANGES

MAX HAD NEVER BEEN happier to return to New York City. He couldn't wait to go back to the academy and resume his training, couldn't wait to fall asleep in his own bed instead of a tent.

McCready was still out there, but they'd destroyed the bulk of his forces. They'd done what they'd set out to do, and now they could all return home. Manuel was making plans to rebuild the Council. It would take time to fill all the seats but as soon as he had enough members to spare, he would send out a team to hunt McCready down. Some of the agency's allies had remained in Alaska trying to find a trace of him. They would be in touch with Ben if they had any news.

When the plane touched down at JFK, Max could have kissed the dirty terminal ground.

"Home at last!" Ryan said, arms open wide as if to embrace the whole airport.

Izzie groaned. "I need a huge margarita."

"Sis, same," Ryan agreed.

Manuel was frozen, his eyes darting around. Veronica touched his shoulder. "It must be overwhelming for you."

"It is," Manuel said, jumping when a voice blasted over the PA system. "I haven't been in an airport in years, forget a city."

Veronica squeezed his hand. "Don't worry, I'll make sure you don't eat anybody."

He grimaced. "That's not funny, mi amor. I might."

Gabe chuckled beside Max. "Let's get a cab before my dad murders someone."

His father's breath hitched. "Please, tell me ground transportation isn't the hot mess it used to be."

Max smiled. "Wouldn't be New York if you didn't get an aneurysm trying to get home from JFK."

Manuel's eyes watered, and his lips quivered. "Home. Goddess. I'm going home."

Hugging him tight, Veronica said, "You are, mi corazón, and you will never leave again."

Manuel caressed her hair and sniffed, thumbing away a tear.

Gabe and Izzie grabbed their parents. "Come on," Gabe said, "let's get home before we all get too weepy."

Looking around for his own mother, Max found her holding Luna's hand. Luna kept pointing to everything that caught her attention and saying she wanted to go on another airplane ride around the world.

"What will we do about the kids?" Max murmured to Gabe.

He frowned. "I don't know, Lobito. I think Ben has a plan, though. We'll see."

Max hoped they could do something to help Tommy and little Luna. They were orphans, and they'd been looking after themselves for far too long.

It took an hour to get a ride out of the airport, at least for Gabe and Max's families. The rest of the agency split up into different cars. Ben's ex-mate and his sons came to pick him up. He hugged both his boys, then before he got into the car, he faced the agency wolves. "I won't get too sappy here," he said, "because it's not a luxury we have. This fight with McCready ain't over 'till that bastard's dead."

Zach said, "That's right. We accomplished a lot in Alaska, even if he's still alive, but by taking Luna and Tommy with us, we only gave him more reason to want us dead."

Ben shifted his bag from one shoulder to another. "I don't wanna make you all nervous, but the point is we can't get complacent. We need to be ready to face him when he strikes."

Heart sinking, Max took Gabe's hand, and his mate squeezed his fingers.

Tommy shivered beside Max, the scent of his fear heavy in the air.

"Tommy, munchkin," Ben said.

Luna giggled. "Me?"

"Yeah, you, missy," Ben said, a smile softening his face. "Would you and your brother like to stay in the agency for a while?"

"The agency?" She wrinkled her nose. "Is that, like, a big house?"

Zach grinned. "The biggest house in the whole world."

"Like a mansion?" Luna gasped.

"Yup," Kendra said. "There'll be lots of room for you to run and play, and other wolves for you to meet."

Max lowered his voice and said, "Is that safe, Ben?" The attack on the agency weeks ago still haunted him from time to time.

"The wargs are gone and I've tightened up security. They'll be safe, Max." Turning to Tommy, he said, "Is staying at the agency a good option for you?"

Tommy narrowed his eyes. "It's my *only* option." He sighed. "I mean... Yeah. I think so. Thank you. Will Luna and me... will we find someone to look after us? Like, a family?"

Ben squeezed his shoulder. "I will do everything in my power to make sure you and your sister are taken care of. You will stay in the manor as long as you like. Okay?"

Smiling apprehensively, Tommy bobbed his head. "Okay."

Ben turned to the pack. "Get yourselves settled in. Relax. But this Sunday, I want to have a meeting at the agency to discuss a plan. Okay?"

When everyone expressed their agreement, the time came to part ways at least temporarily. Max nearly fell asleep on the ride home. The moment he and Gabe were back in their apartment, they left their bags in the doorway and crashed into bed. Max curled into Gabe's side, closing his eyes when Gabe kissed his forehead.

Max tried to relax, but his heart kept racing.

"What's wrong?" Gabe asked.

"It feels so temporary," Max admitted. "This victory. This peace. Like it could shatter at any minute." A shiver ran through him, remembering all those dead humans and wolves on the beach in Alaska.

"I know." Gabe ran his hand up and down Max's arm. "I don't want to fight anymore, Max. I just want everything to go back to the way it was before McCready ripped it all up."

Max took his hand. "The moon always rises."

Gabe frowned. "Huh?"

"It's a thing my mom told me when I was a kid. It's, you know, a promise that everything will be okay."

"I kind of like that." Gabe put his arm around Max's shoulders.

"We have each other. Our pack. We'll be okay." Needing to reassure Gabe, Max curled atop him and pressed kisses to his neck. "Anything that comes for us, we're tearing it down," Max growled into his ear.

Gabe's breath hitched. He slid his hands down Max's back and squeezed his ass. Max shivered at the hard, possessive hold. "No one will touch you," Gabe said, his breath hot against Max's ear. "You're mine."

Max bit his lip, his cock throbbing at the claim Gabe had staked on him. He rutted his hips against the bulge in Gabe's jeans. "Mine," he said between pants. Need made his blood run hot. After everything they'd been through, with everything that could still come, Max needed the reassurance of their bond. He needed to know they were alive. They weren't on that beach anymore. They were here in their home, their sanctuary, and for now nothing and no one could touch them but each other.

Max claimed Gabe's mouth in a scorching kiss. The bed creaked beneath him as Gabe sat up, and Max straddled his knees. Gabe crawled back until he hit the headboard, fumbling with the clasp on Max's jeans. "Want you in my mouth, Lobito. Need to taste you."

Max would give him everything he needed. Yanking his jeans down to his knees, Max moaned when Gabe palmed the outline of his cock. He was already so hard, even the slightest touch made his balls tighten. Gabe wiggled down Max's underwear and slapped his hands on his ass and squeezed. Gasping, Max closed his eyes and savored Gabe's touch. Gabe's reverence for his body always made him feel so sexy, so powerful and desired.

"Open for me," Max whispered, caressing Gabe's lips.

His mate gazed up at him, the adoration in his eyes stealing Max's breath. "Anything."

He shivered when their bond burned like the sun in his chest. Wave after wave of love and affection and need flowed through Max, and he realized some of that was Gabe's. The bond between them whispered, *"We're here. We're alive. We're safe. I will do anything for you. I love you, I love you, I love you."*

Tears prickled Max's eyes, and he combed his fingers through Gabe's hair. He closed his eyes again, sighing in bliss when Gabe wrapped his mouth around him and worshipped him. Max stroked Gabe's hair and brushed his thumbs over his cheekbones. He wished he was more limber so he could lean down and kiss Gabe's hair. "Yes," Max whispered, gasping when Gabe bobbed his head, taking him in deeper, faster. "Gabe. That's so good."

Gabe explored Max's upper body, his hands big and warm as they slipped beneath Max's shirt to rub his abs and tweak his nipples until they pebbled. His mate tapped his fingers against Max's lips and he opened for him, licking the tips of his fingers. His balls throbbed in anticipation when Gabe slipped his wet fingers between Max's ass cheeks and found his hole.

Gabe's name escaped Max in a gasp when Gabe pushed inside him. He breathed through the stretch and burn, his entire body welcoming Gabe's fingers like they were an extension of Max's own body.

Beneath him, Gabe moaned around his cock. Looking over his shoulder, Max was delighted when he saw how hard Gabe was just from sucking and fingering him.

"So hot around me," Gabe whispered through their bond, and Max shivered. They'd never used their bond to communicate in bed before, but he liked it. Gabe tongued the slit of his cock, then twirled his tongue around Max's head, flicking and licking until Max's toes curled. *"Love the way you fit in my mouth. Your taste. So fucking good, Max."*

He panted, the caress of Gabe's fingers, his hot mouth, and his dirty words threatening to bring him over the edge sooner than he wanted.

"Fuck my mouth, Lobito. Get yourself off. I'll make you come again when I fill you up and fuck you just the way you like."

"Gabe," Max groaned, gripping the headboard for support. Needing more friction, Max rocked his hips in shallow thrusts. He rolled his eyes back when Gabe moved with him, bobbing his head faster. Max worked his hips, pumping in and out of Gabe's mouth. With each thrust he went a little deeper, a cry escaping him when Gabe caressed his prostate. Max threw his head back, chasing his release until, crying out to his mate, he erupted down Gabe's throat. His hips jerked with every pulse of his orgasm.

Gabe swirled his tongue around him, sucking him in deeper to swallow every drop. Knowing Gabe loved the taste of his cum made him moan. Gabe pulled off him, panting and lips flushed, and Max wiped away a pearly drop from the corner of Gabe's swollen lips. His mate stuck out his tongue and licked it from Max's finger, grinning devilishly when Max groaned.

"You are so fucking hot," Max whispered.

Gabe chuckled. "You're awfully pretty too."

Grinning, Max reached behind him and stroked Gabe's rock-hard length. Gabe's body seized, his hips jerking into Max's touch. He would love to bring him over the edge here and now, but Gabe batted his hand away, smiling playfully. "Not yet. I'm saving this for you." And he rolled them over so Max was the one beneath him this time.

A part of Max doubted he could be ready for another round so soon, but he'd underestimated the effect Gabe Reyes had on his body. Flat on his stomach, all Max could do was moan and whimper as Gabe ate out his hole, tonguing him open and lighting up every nerve ending in Max's body.

"Can't hold back." Gabe panted, his breath hot on Max's most sensitive parts. "Need to be in you, Max. Now."

Max raised his hips high, supporting himself on his knees and elbows. A lube cap snicked open. Gabe slicked himself, the wet sounds making Max bite his lip. His mate pushed in, the pressure immense. Max bit down on the sheets, curling his hands into fists. He gasped when Gabe's pelvis rammed his buttocks.

Gabe moaned above him. "Fuck, Max..."

They both caught their breath when Gabe was in as deep as he could go. The spot where their bodies met burned in the best way. Whimpering, Max rocked his hips, and Gabe lowered himself so his stomach touched Max's back, his clawed hands curling into the sheets by Max's head. Gabe thrust, and Max arched back to meet him, and they cried out together when the sparks of pleasure ignited into a roaring flame.

The bed creaked and groaned, and the headboard slammed against the wall. Max took Gabe's hand and squeezed, losing himself in the passion of their union. With every thrust and reverent gasp of Max's name, Gabe took him far away to a place that was only theirs. A place where there was no pain or uncertainty, a place where no one could ever hurt them. Max never wanted to leave the utopia they created, and when he came messily in the sheets and Gabe's hand wrapped around him and squeezed out every drop, there were tears in his eyes.

In a voice choked with emotion, Gabe whispered Max's name and he shivered when Gabe filled him with his release and his knot. Gingerly, Gabe rolled them onto their sides, his stomach plastered to Max's back. He reached around and touched Gabe's arm, smiling when his mate peppered his shoulder with kisses.

"This is ours," Max whispered, his voice hoarse. "No one can take this from us." He clenched around Gabe's knot, enjoying the delighted shiver he pulled from Gabe. "I'll kill anyone who tries."

Gabe put his arms around his chest and squeezed. "Mine," he growled in his wolf's low rumble.

Max took his hand. "Mine," the wolf said.

THAT WEEKEND, BEN CALLED a meeting at the agency. In the week they'd been away in Alaska, the agency had undergone repairs. The windows had been covered and were being fitted with glass, but most of the work had gone into getting the clinic up and running. The dining hall had been repaired as well, with new tables and chairs. Vicenzo was back to working in the kitchen, and he helped prepare a meal of spaghetti and meatballs for the pack when they gathered around their table.

"McCready's assholes ever mess with my kitchen again, I'm spraying lemon juice in their eyes," Vicenzo growled, slapping a heaping serving of pasta on Max's plate before he stomped over to sit in his own seat.

Manuel and Veronica sat next to each other. "The agency looks even better than the last time I visited, Ben," Manuel said.

"We've grown a lot over the years," Ben said, twirling spaghetti around his fork.

Tommy entered the dining room carrying Luna on his shoulders. They were wearing real clothes now, which made a big difference. Luna crawled down from Tommy's back and screamed, "Max!" She tore across the room and collided with him, hugging his knees.

"Luna," Tommy rebuked her. "You have to ask before you hug people!"

Luna pouted. "I'm sorry."

Max chuckled and patted her shoulder. "That's okay. I give you permission to hug me whenever you want."

"Yay!" She poked her tongue out at Tommy. "Max, I drew you a picture! Do you want to see?"

His heart squeezed. "Really? I'd love to."

She pulled a piece of paper from her backpack and handed it to him.

Scrawled in crayon was a shape Max thought was supposed to be himself, the red hair a giveaway. "You drew me?" He grinned down at her.

"Mm-hmm!" She nodded proudly. "Your hair is the prettiest color I've ever seen."

Max nearly melted into a puddle of goo. "Thank you so much, sweetheart."

Ryan stuck out his lower lip. "What? I don't get a picture?"

"You do!" Luna said, giggling. She pulled more papers from her bag. "I drew all of you."

Zach gasped. "Really?"

Luna dashed around and handed everyone her masterpieces. Ryan showed off his drawing—he had a circle for a head with a goofy smile and glasses. Then he punched Zach's shoulder when he laughed.

Tommy sat down beside Max. "Settling in okay?" Max asked.

The boy smiled. Max noticed there were bags under his eyes. "I'm fine," he said but his heart stuttered. Max hoped he was doing all right. He wanted to ask Ben how the kids were settling in.

As things settled back down, Ben cleared his throat. "First, let me offer my heartfelt condolences to our Alpha-to-be."

Manuel slumped in his seat, and Gabe and Izzie laughed at him. Veronica rubbed her husband's shoulder as Manuel rolled his eyes and clapped with everyone else. "Thanks, Ben."

Ben flashed him a smile. "I'm sure you've all heard Manuel's inauguration is the day before Thanksgiving. That's only in a couple weeks. Plenty of time for people to throw a hissy fit over the Council's first hybrid Alpha. It's already starting."

Everyone's mood sobered except for Luna's, who was trying to cram a whole meatball in her mouth. Tommy made her spit it out and he cut it into bite-sized pieces for her.

Ben held up his phone. There was a news headline displayed there—Riots in Boston Over Council's First Hybrid Alpha. Max's stomach churned, and he set down his fork.

Ryan stabbed his meatball. "Always something, isn't it?"

Crossing her arms, Izzie said, "Too bad. This is happening. They can suck it up and deal with it."

"I agree," Ben said, setting down his phone. "But this is bound to get worse before it gets better. I'm hoping that once Manuel's inauguration is over, things will settle down but for now eighteen people were injured and one person lost their life. This isn't something we can ignore."

Zach grimaced. "Pureblood supremacists had everything they wanted, and now it's been snatched away from them. They want revenge."

"Exactly," Ben said. "We need to be on high alert. Eddie."

Eddie looked up, cheeks full of food. Luna laughed at him, and Eddie fought back a smile. "Yessir?"

"I want you to train our new recruits. You were a hunter, so you know all about how to hit berserkers where it really hurts. McCready's still running around in the wild and we need to be ready to face him in case we get hit again. I put in orders for tons of silver claws, dentures, and weapons. All of our agents will be outfitted with them."

"You got it, Ben."

Max picked at his pasta. "Has there been any word about McCready?"

Ben shook his head. "Not yet. My agents out in the field found his trail but with the weather like it is, any trace of him keeps disappearing, but we know where he's heading."

Max's heart skipped a beat. He was coming here. To New York.

Tommy's complexion went ashy. "He's coming for me and Luna, isn't he?"

Gripping his shoulder, Max said, "We won't let him take you away."

"For now, just keep your wits about you," Ben said, then tucked into his meal.

When Max cleared his plate, he took it to the kitchen. Vicenzo gave him a grunt of acknowledgement from where he was kneading dough. Max left the kitchen and found Ben at the door, who motioned for Max to follow him outside. They stepped out onto the wraparound porch, Ben sitting in a rocking chair while Max sat in a cushioned wicker chair.

"Luna's a strong kid," Ben said, affection warming his voice. "The harsh life she found herself in hasn't brought her down."

Max nodded. "It's because Tommy shielded her."

"Yeah. That boy is something else."

He reminded Max of Gabe, of himself even, shouldering so much responsibility at such a young age. "It's not fair that they lost their family the way they did. And even though their father is still alive, he's an asshole who can't love them the way they deserve." His eyes stung. Their situation tore at him. He knew all too well what it was like to finally have a father figure only for him to betray his trust.

Ben said, "Tommy wakes up screaming at night. He thinks McCready's coming for him, that he's going to kill us all and take him away."

Max gritted his teeth, fighting back the snarl in his chest. He would kill McCready if he laid a hand on those poor kids. He couldn't forget the way McCready had leeched his son's own life force, how Tommy had screamed until his throat went hoarse but had kept on screaming.

"He can't hurt them."

"I know." Ben touched Max's arm. "We won't let him. Max…" Ben paused, his chin in his hand as he gazed out over the grounds of the estate. "Max, they can't stay here much longer. The agency will be the first place McCready looks."

Max swallowed the spike of protective rage, but he couldn't control his wolf's urges to protect the kids he saw so much of himself in.

"I thought being around other shifters would be good for them, but they don't need a huge manor to get lost in or a room full of toys. They need a family, Max. Even just a temporary one until McCready's out of the picture. They can't stay here but I think they would be safer among our agents."

Max nodded. "Have you reached out to anyone about fostering them?"

"I'm working on that. The agency has always helped place homeless werekids with families since they're usually overlooked in human foster care systems. Until a family reaches out, I've asked around our pack about giving them somewhere quiet to stay in the meantime."

"Yes," Max said before he could stop himself.

Ben squinted at him. "I didn't even finish asking."

"Yes." Max turned in his chair to face him. "I'd love to take care of them until they can find a home. They can stay upstate in our house. It's out of the city. They'd be safe there."

Ben arched a brow. "Are you gonna give Gabe a say in this?"

Fuck. Max slapped his forehead. "Yeah. Of course." He couldn't imagine Gabe would say no, but he might if he didn't think they were the right fit. "I'll ask him. I'm sure he'll say yes."

"I hope so. You and Gabe were the first people who came to mind. I'd love to, but I'm too busy with work and my family. Ryan's practically a child himself, and Zach wouldn't know what to do with a kid. Manuel and Veronica are still getting settled. Vico would probably growl at them."

"Gabe and I will be more than happy to take care of them. I'll talk to him."

"Thanks, kid."

Max's heart thumped as he set off, following Gabe's scent of spring flowers through HQ. Gabe would say yes. Unless he wasn't ready to have a house full of kids. Nerves fluttered in Max's stomach as he followed Gabe's scent to Luna and Tommy's room. He peered inside, and his heart melted.

A black wolf lay on a star-patterned rug and on top of him was little Luna, her fingers bunched in his fur and her face buried in Gabe's ruff.

Gabe opened his amber eyes, his tail thumping in greeting.

"Hey," Max murmured, sitting on the carpet beside him. He glanced at Tommy, who was sitting on his bed with his nose in his phone and his earbuds in. "Ben wanted to know if we could watch Luna and Tommy indefinitely. He's trying to find them a forever home, so it could take a while. Would you be up for that?"

He waited, expecting Gabe to speak through their bond. Instead, Gabe stood with a wolfy groan and walked carefully to Luna's bed. He tilted his body slightly so she rolled gently onto the mattress. She yawned but didn't wake up. Gabe grabbed his clothes and padded into the bathroom. When he returned, he was dressed and human. He looked content in a way Max had never seen him before, like he was glowing.

He sat on the floor next to Max, their backs resting against Luna's bed. "There's a problem with that idea."

Max's heart sank, but he nodded and gave Gabe the chance to speak.

Twisting around, Gabe looked at Luna and smiled tenderly. He reached over to tuck a wayward curl out of her face. "I don't know if I'll ever want them to leave."

A smile tugged at Max's lips. "So, can we ask Tommy if he'd like to stay with us?"

Gabe waved at Tommy. The teen yanked his earbuds out, frowning. "Yeah?"

Gabe grinned and Tommy softened, his shoulders losing their tension. "Ben's trying to help you guys find parents who will love you and care for you and your sister."

Tommy nodded. "Yeah, he told me."

"Would you like to stay with us in the meantime?" Max asked. "We're pretty fun."

Tommy blinked, his eyes widening. "I need to ask Luna first but... yeah. I'd like that." A smile lit up his face. "She really likes you guys. She wouldn't shut up about how pretty your hair is, Max."

His sister yawned, sitting up and stretching her arms over her head. Tommy went and sat on her bed. "Luna, do you wanna live with Gabe and Max for a while?"

She rubbed sleep from her eyes. "At their house?"

"Yeah. Would you like that?"

A sunny smile lit up her face. "Yeah! Do you have a big house? Is there a backyard? Can I have my own room?"

Gabe laughed. "Yes, yes, and maybe."

"Yes!" She jumped up and down on the bed.

Tommy grinned at her excitement. Glancing at Gabe and Max, he said, "Thanks, you guys. I promise we won't be in the way."

Max shrugged. "You couldn't if you tried."

He couldn't wait for the day to be over so Luna and Tommy could head home with them.

IT TURNED OUT A lot needed to happen before Tommy and Luna could get settled into their new home. Gabe borrowed a pickup from the agency's garage and the kids climbed in the back seat. They drove from the agency to Dutchess County in upstate New York.

The sun was setting by the time they arrived outside Gabe and Max's countryside home.

Tommy carried a sleeping Luna from the car, moving in a circle to take in the environment. "Wow. This place is so pretty. Must be amazing to shift and run at night."

"It is," Gabe said, slamming the car door. Max lugged a heavy bag of Luna's new toys from the truck bed. His mate opened the door for him and Max set the bag down inside. "We have an extra bedroom upstairs you two can share," Gabe said, flicking on the light.

"Your house is awesome," Tommy said, his voice strained from carrying Luna. "Is it safe around here?"

"Oh yeah," Gabe said easily. "Even the coyotes are pretty harmless."

Max said, "Let me show you your room."

Tommy laid Luna down on the sofa, and she curled into a ball and went on sleeping.

Max showed him where the bedroom was. It was bare for now, but the movers bringing the kids' beds weren't far behind. Jogging down the stairs, Max found Gabe going through their fridge. "Thinking what I'm thinking?"

Gabe rifled through the fridge. "What do kids eat?" He examined a jar of pickles.

"Exactly." Max figured he'd have to run to the store to stock up on kid-friendly snacks and recipe ingredients. "I'll be back."

Gabe's face fell. "You're leaving me alone with them?"

Snorting, Max said, "They aren't going to eat you."

Luna yawned, her curly hair unruly from sleep. "Where are you going?" She hopped off the couch and rubbed her eyes.

"Into town," Max answered. "Would you and Tommy like to come with us?"

She shrugged. "Okay. Can we get pizza?"

Max liked that idea, though he still wanted to do some shopping while they were in town. The kids couldn't live off pizza, after all.

Once all four of them were in the car, Max drove them into town. The village bustled with people out doing their shopping. The streets were dark and the wind was blowing colder. Gabe took the kids to the pizzeria and Max went to the grocery store. He'd asked Tommy what they liked to eat, and he'd told him Luna was allergic to dairy. Though he was at a loss for what to stock up on, he knew someone who knew how to feed kids. He called his mother as he walked along the aisle of boxed cereal.

"Hi, honey! How are you?"

"Good." Max realized this was true. So much had happened since his mother had revealed he'd been adopted and while the truth still ached dully like a loose tooth, he wasn't torn up over it anymore. In hindsight, it didn't seem like such a big deal compared to everything else. He just didn't know how to tell her that, and he didn't want to do it over the phone. "Uh, so, Tommy and Luna are staying with us indefinitely, and I was wondering... What do kids eat?"

Kendra laughed. "Well, let's see... Luna is six, right? That's a tricky age. I remember being so worried you'd starve yourself. You would only eat three things."

Max wrinkled his nose. "Seriously?"

"Yup. Tomato soup, grilled cheese, and sliced apple."

"I don't remember that at all. Sorry. Sounds like I was annoying."

"It sure saved me the stress of meal planning. You grew out of it."

Max plucked a box of whole grain cereal from the shelf. "So is it okay if she eats cereal?"

"Only once in a while and make sure it's at least whole grain. Make sure you stock up on fruits and veggies and lots of protein. Oh, and invite me over sometime. I'd love to spend time with my grandpups. Can I call them that yet? Is it too soon?"

Max smiled. "Maybe, yeah. We'll see." If Tommy and Luna decided they'd rather be elsewhere, Max wouldn't make them stay. Already, the idea of letting them go made his heart ache. He hadn't realized how deep his paternal instincts ran until he found two lost, needy kids he wanted to protect. "Gotta go." He hesitated, wetting his lips. "Mom... thanks for putting up with me."

Kendra laughed softly. "It's my privilege, honey."

Max hung up with warmth in his chest. He had a feeling they would be all right.

THEY RETURNED HOME WITH groceries and pizza. Apparently, Luna's lactose intolerance only extended to dairy when served on its own, but she could have cheese when mixed with other things. They ate together at the table. Around a mouthful of pizza, Luna said, "Are you two in love? You act like a mommy and a daddy."

Tommy muffled his laughter behind his napkin.

Gabe smiled brightly and took Max's hand. "Yeah."

"Oh," she said, picking some cheese off her pizza. "So, can boys love other boys?"

Gabe nodded. "Yup. Girls can love other girls too. Sometimes, a girl or a boy can love more than one gender. Everyone's different."

"Okay," Luna said, wrinkling her nose like she was thinking very hard about this. "Can a boy or a girl be in love with a horse?"

Max choked on his pizza as Tommy doubled over with a snort.

"No," Gabe began slowly, looking to Max for help, but he was trying too hard not to laugh to contribute anything meaningful.

"Why?" Luna asked, and then, "Oh! Because horses can't dance, so they can't dance together at the wedding!" She went back to eating.

Tommy shrugged.

"Are you our daddies?" Luna asked.

Max's heart melted, and his mate parted his lips but no words came out.

Tommy cleared his throat. "Luna, don't talk with your mouth full."

She stuck out her tomato sauce-covered tongue at him, and both Max and Gabe barked out a laugh.

After dinner, Max realized he ought to check and make sure Luna was getting ready for bed, but Tommy was already on it, leading her to the bathroom to brush her teeth. Tommy was more than just Luna's big brother; he was her parent too.

Max saw both kids to their bedroom. The movers had arrived earlier and set their beds up, so Tommy tucked Luna into hers. Max said, "Gabe and I are down the hall if you need anything, okay?"

"Goodnight." Luna waved.

Tommy smiled. "We're all good."

Max left them alone and once he was dressed for bed, he curled up beside Gabe and exhaled.

"Busy kids," Gabe noted, swiping through his phone.

"They're great," Max said, fluffing his pillow and settling onto the mattress.

Gabe smiled. "They're pretty sweet."

"Tommy's so responsible." Max folded his arm beneath his head. "I hope he can trust us to help him take care of Luna. He shouldn't have to do it all by himself."

Gabe turned off the light and Max fell asleep instantly, exhausted from the day. He woke in the middle of the night with a full bladder. Once he'd used the master bathroom, he tiptoed back toward his bed. A noise caught his attention. It had come from beyond their bedroom door and down the hall.

Max left the bedroom and stopped in the hallway outside Tommy and Luna's room. Someone hiccuped and sniffled. "Shh, Luna, shh. It's okay. You're okay."

Heart skipping, Max knocked on the kids' bedroom door. "Tommy? Everything okay?" Luna's sniffles became whimpers and croaky sobs. Max opened the door. The lamp was on and Tommy was pacing the room carrying Luna. She clung to him and sobbed. Tommy turned to Max, his eyes wide and desperate. "I don't know what to do," he croaked. "She's been crying for an hour."

Max's heart sank. "Tommy, why didn't you come get us?"

The boy hung his head. "I didn't want to disturb you."

"What's going on?" Gabe asked, his voice dry and his hair sticking up everywhere. "What's wrong, Tommy?"

"I think she had a dream. She has nightmares sometimes ever since our pack was killed."

Frowning, Gabe went to Tommy. "Luna? Hey, you're okay, chiquita. It was just a bad dream."

"No!" She wailed, sniffling into Tommy's shoulder. "It—it was real! Th-the bad wolves came and hurt everyone."

Max sat on Tommy's bed, and the boy collapsed beside him. Gabe went to sit on Tommy's other side and reached out to rub Luna's back.

"I miss my friends. Why can't we see them again?" Luna's voice broke as she sobbed.

Tommy's lip trembled. "I told you, Luna. They... they died, and when people die, we can't see them ever again."

"Why?" Luna sniffled, rubbing her face on his shoulder. "It's not fair."

Tommy blinked, his eyes wet. "No. It isn't." He looked torn between wanting to cry or fall asleep. "I don't know what to say," he whispered. "Everything I do is wrong."

Squeezing his shoulder, Max said, "No. You're doing everything right."

Gabe gripped Luna's shoulders. "Can I hold her?" Tommy nodded. "Come here, pup." Gabe hoisted the little girl into his arms and let her cry it out on his shoulder.

"Are the bad wolves going to come a-and hurt us?"

Gabe shook his head. "No, pup. No one will hurt you or your brother. I promise."

Max felt his promise flowing through the bond they shared, warm as sunshine. Even though Gabe's promise was meant for the kids, he couldn't help but feel safe as well.

"It's w-warm," Luna whispered, nuzzling into Gabe's chest. His mate's eyes widened, and he looked at Max in astonishment.

Tommy touched his chest, and Max wondered if he'd felt it too.

His throat thickened. Somehow, Tommy and Luna were becoming pack.

Max had an idea. He went to the bathroom and undressed, then dropped to all fours and shifted. His toenails clicked over the floorboards as he nosed open the kids' bedroom door. Luna squirmed out of Gabe's arms and ran, and Max's tail wagged when she threw her arms around him and buried her face in his fur.

"So floofy," she whispered reverently, and she squished his face between her hands. Max licked her nose, and Luna erupted into giggles.

The little girl climbed onto his back, and Max trotted down the hall toward their bedroom. He hopped up onto his and Gabe's bed, and Luna sank into the blankets and sighed. Circling, Max pawed the blankets into a comfortable mound, then lay down with a huff. Luna cuddled against him, burying her little fingers in his fur.

"I wish you could be my dad," she whispered.

Max rubbed his snout against her hair.

The bed creaked when Gabe's black wolf joined them. Tommy lay down between Max and Gabe, resting his hand protectively on Luna's ankle.

"Thank you," Tommy whispered, carding his fingers through Gabe's fur.

Two golden threads wrapped around his heart, and Max knew fighting it was pointless. Luna and Tommy were part of his and Gabe's pack.

CHAPTER 13

HOPE

Luna and Tommy fit into Gabe's and Max's lives in ways Gabe couldn't have expected. At the end of a long day doing agency work, Gabe's spirits soared when he opened the door and Luna ran to greet him with one of her amazing hugs and Tommy gifted him with a smile like sunshine itself. The kids were making the house their own, but it was more than that. Gabe could feel their threads intertwined with his and Max's. They were pack.

Gabe had always known he wanted a family, and he and Max had talked about it. There was a seven-year gap in their ages, but Gabe had never been one of those almost-thirties who felt pressured to have kids, so he and Max had been content to work and live together, just the two of them. Parenthood, or something very close to it, had fallen into their laps when they'd least expected it, and Gabe wouldn't have it any other way.

He could see himself sitting down and eating family dinners with Max and the kids. He wanted to give Tommy and Luna everything they could possibly need to thrive and heal. He wanted to make this arrangement permanent, and he hoped Max felt the same.

The day before Manuel's inauguration, Gabe finished packing his overnight bag for the flight to Wolf Point. He passed the kids' room where Max sat on Luna's bed reading a picture book to her. Gabe's heart just about melted. Seeing how much Max loved Tommy and Luna made Gabe fall in love with him even more.

Luna laid her curly head on the pillow and Max kissed her cheek. "Good-night, sweetheart."

"Max?" Luna gazed at him with those big puppy dog eyes.

"Yeah?"

"Can me and Tommy stay with you forever?"

He hit his head against the doorframe. Why was she so cute?

Max smiled. "I'd love it if you would." He left her nightlight on.

Tommy came out of the bathroom, his face freshly washed. "Good night, Gabe, Max."

Gabe tousled his hair as he passed and Tommy closed the door behind him.

His mate leaned against the door and touched his chest. "My freaking heart, man."

"I know," Gabe said, chuckling as they went into their bedroom. "Can you believe such great kids came from someone like McCready?"

"I know. Must have been their mother's influence."

Gabe wished he hadn't mentioned McCready. The asshole's name soured his mood.

Max pulled off his sweater and rifled through the drawer for a T-shirt. "Has Ben had any word about McCready?"

He thought back to a phone call he'd had with Ben this morning. "Nothing. It's like he's just disappeared." Anxiety made pins and needles tingle in his hands and feet.

"Are you worried about the inauguration?" Max stepped into his sweat-pants.

Gabe gnawed on his lower lip. "No, not really. Every inauguration has insane security—they have to. Governors come from all over. Even the president makes an appearance. My father will be safe. But McCready's still out there. He's coming for us." He blew out a breath. "I'm so sick of holding my breath, waiting for the other shoe to drop."

Max sat on the bed and squeezed his thigh. "I know. But things will settle down. Sure as—"

"Sure as the moon always rises," Gabe said, making Max smile. "I know. There's so much uncertainty, but you and those kids give me hope, mi amor."

"Gabe," Max whispered, "I want to give those kids a home. Here. With us."

His heart soared. "Me too."

Max put his arms around him and pulled him down to the mattress. "I see so much of us in them, you know? Every time I comfort Luna from a bad dream or I make Tommy smile, an old wound from Richard's abuse heals."

Gabe knew what he meant. "They're already ours, Max. They're pack."

"We'll ask them soon."

Hardly able to keep the smile off his face, Gabe kissed Max and for a time, all his troubles disappeared.

THIS WAS GABE'S SECOND visit to Wolf Point this year, and unlike the last time, he was actually looking forward to it. Gabe still wanted to pinch himself. His father was alive, and not only that, he was going to become Alpha of the Council. He'd hardly seen his father at all since they'd returned as he'd been so busy with Council affairs. Gabe was aching for a chance to sit down and talk to him.

The entire agency flew out to attend Manuel's inauguration, including Tommy and Luna. Kendra came too and sat beside the kids. They talked the entire flight when Luna wasn't watching movies. Manuel and Veronica had flown out a day early, and Veronica met them at the airport, greeting Gabe and Izzie with big hugs.

"How are things?" Gabe asked as she drove him, Izzie, Max, and Kendra from the airport. Ryan, Ben, and Zach rode with the kids in the car behind them.

"You mean, are there riots in the streets?" Veronica shook her head. "Things have been quiet. Security is at its highest, so that's probably deterred a lot of troublemakers, but we're expecting protests in the days that follow."

Gabe frowned. "Great."

Veronica rubbed the crease between his brows. "Relax, mi sol. I know things have been hard, but this is a joyous day for werewolves and our family." A sunny smile lit up her face. "Your father's alive, Gabriel. He's come back to us, and we're going to make this country a better place for everyone."

Gabe cocked his head. "We?"

Veronica winked but said nothing more.

Politicians from all over the country were flying in to honor the new Alpha. Security was as tight as at the White House on Inauguration Day. Inside town hall, they walked among the portraits of famous councilmembers from lycanthrope history. Gabe's heart lifted at the idea that his father's portrait would be restored and hung among so many other pioneers of werewolf rights.

In the gathering chamber, Gabe was surprised to see so many seats filled. He spotted Ben's mother and father among many human governors from around the country. There were also new faces Gabe didn't recognize, people who smelled like werewolves and hybrids.

"New councilmembers?" Gabe asked his mother as they took their seats.

"Your father has been hard at work filling the seats vacated by Mc-Cready's supporters."

"Wow," Max whispered. "It sounds like the Council is really going to change for the better."

Around the town, wolves howled. Gabe jumped and Veronica chuckled. "Relax, mi sol. It's tradition. They're acknowledging the new Alpha."

Gabe's heart thumped when everyone rose to welcome Manuel. He strode down the steps, garbed in a luxurious suit. What a difference a few weeks and a new title made. He'd filled out and lost the haunted look of a beast trapped in the bottom of a well. His hair was short and parted neatly, his face clean-shaven.

Manuel walked up to the podium and looked out into the crowd. Gabe smiled when their eyes met, and Manuel's stern features softened into a smile. In a voice that carried through the chamber, Manuel said, "Now is a time of reunification. My predecessor, whose name I will not speak, tried to divide us. He burned the bridge between our people that our ancestors had spent decades building. I can't hope to rebuild that bridge alone, so I extend to you all a ladder. It's one we will build together, piece by piece, until one day we have scaled the divide between our people and reached an understanding that we are all created equal, whether wolf or human."

Izzie leaned her head on Gabe's shoulder.

Manuel said, "Before I introduce my new councilmembers, it gives me great honor to announce the beta I have chosen to lead at my side. Only that title is no longer applicable. A beta's position has always implied they are a station lower than the Alpha, and for this amazing woman, that is simply not true. She is brave and smart. Human, a historic first for this Council, and she has the heart and soul of a wolf. She is my partner in all things in life, my equal in every sense, and I can think of no one better to rule at my side. Please, allow me to introduce your Alpha, Veronica Reyes."

Gabe's mouth fell open and Izzie gasped, looking to their mother in awe.

Smiling radiantly, Veronica descended the steps, her emerald dress swaying around her ankles. The agency wolves went wild, howling and cheering as she took her place beside her husband. Veronica took the mic and said, "Manuel and I pledge to lead this Council forward, never backward, toward a future where wolves and humans can work together to make the world a better place."

Everyone in the chamber erupted into cheers. Gabe's eyes welled with tears of pride for his pack and from the hope that was so palpable in the air he could taste it. Finally, they were stepping out of the darkness and into the light.

THE CELEBRATIONS WENT ON long into the evening. Big-name musicians showed up to sing to the crowds who'd gathered from far and wide outside town hall. Fireworks erupted in the indigo sky. Inside, the agency wolves and the new Alphas feasted on a banquet with more food than even packs of werewolves could eat in one sitting.

After one too many glasses of wine, Gabe went to the restroom. He emptied his bladder, and on the way back to the dining hall, he ran into Izzie. "You remember the way back to the dining room?" Gabe asked, swaying on his feet.

Izzie snorted. "You're so drunk."

"Am not." Gabe hiccuped. She laughed at him.

"Where's the bathroom?" Izzie asked, fiddling with her purse straps.

"Uh... Shit. I don't remember." Gabe scratched his head. "Guess I'm drunker than I thought."

"Children," Manuel greeted, striding past.

"Don't 'children' us, Alpha Reyes!" Izzie wrangled him into a hug.

"Any news on McCready?" Gabe asked.

Manuel grimaced. "He left Alaska some time ago. Ben's agents lost his trail. They found a man dead on the side of the road, ripped to pieces, so we can assume he stole a vehicle. There's been no sign of him for weeks." He gazed out the window over the forest. "There's so much uncertainty, but John Stone is dead and the Council has been remade. It's about time we had some hope, especially for our family."

Gabe's stomach clenched. "Who told you about Stone's death?"

"I did," Izzie said, her breath misting the windowpane. She eyed him apprehensively. "Should I not have?"

Gabe shrugged. "It's fine."

Manuel sighed heavily. "No, it isn't fine that I let myself get distracted by the treason going on in the Council. I should never have left. Time was running out. I knew if I didn't speak to Hanson soon, I'd never get the chance to. I knew Stone hated me, but I'd never have imagined he and McCready were working together. I wasn't paying attention to Stone. It was a mistake. One you paid for." His lips quivered, voice roughening with guilt.

Izzie wrapped her arms around herself. "I still... I think about that night sometimes. The night you went missing."

Gabe tried to ignore the prickle of unease that crawled over his skin. His abduction had happened so long ago, but if he stopped and let himself dwell on it, to reflect on everything that had been done to him in that dark basement, it still stirred feelings of dread and despair inside him. Sorrow. Such sorrow for the boy who'd lost his father, his innocence, to a monster.

"Gabriel, I... I was awake when Stone took you."

Gabe nodded. "I know." She'd told him this a long time ago.

"I heard footsteps outside my door. I smelled your fear and I... I just froze up. I couldn't move. For so long, I couldn't move. By the time I woke up Ma, you were already gone. If I'd just been braver—"

Gabe shook his head. "Don't do this to yourself, Izzie. I could have fought back. I could have screamed. He told me if I tried, he'd..."

"Listen to me." Manuel faced them and gripped their shoulders. "You were children. It wasn't your responsibility to expect a monster to come into your home." A shiver ran through him. "I should have done more. I should have protected you both."

Gabe gripped his dad's arm and Izzie put her arms around him.

"Perhaps if I'd just stepped down from my position on the Council, it would have made all the difference." Manuel's lip quivered. "I'm so sorry. I only wanted to... I wanted to set an example for you kids, to persevere in the face of hatred, not back down because of it."

"We know," Izzie assured him, and she kissed his cheek.

Gabe nodded. "It's not your fault the world couldn't let us be kids, or a hybrid be equal to his counterparts. That's not on us. Never apologize for trying to make the world a better place."

Izzie nodded resolutely. "He's right. That's not who we are. The Reyes pack are fighters."

Swiping away the tears in his eyes, Manuel blew out a breath. He put his arms around Gabe and his sister. "Damn right we are."

Manuel's phone rang. He sighed at Melanie's name on the screen.

"You can take that," Izzie said. "We're not going anywhere."

Manuel answered the call. "Councilwoman Mel—" He stopped speaking. Gabe could hear his heartbeat speed up and he strained to hear whatever Melanie was saying that had made his father so nervous, but it was too noisy.

"How could this happen?" Manuel paced, rubbing his hand over his mouth like he was trying to find a beard to tug on. "Why wasn't I informed sooner?"

Izzie met Gabe's gaze, her eyes wide and full of fear.

"Damn it!" Manuel swiped to end the call. He shoved his phone into his pocket and snarled, raking a hand through his hair.

Gabe cleared his throat. "W-what happened?"

His father's eyes were wide and haunted, like he was trapped at the bottom of that well all over again.

Gabe knew before the words fell from his father's lips like a guillotine.

"There was a sighting."

His ears rang and his knees threatened to buckle.

Manuel's complexion was ashen. "McCready tore through Yellowstone National Park a few days ago. Brought a bunch of wild wolves under his command. He's coming for us, and he's not alone."

"He could be here in days."

Max's throat bobbed when he swallowed, his eyes wide in the dark.

Sleeping peacefully, the kids lay curled at their feet as wolves. Gabe couldn't bear to tell them the news yet. Tomorrow was Thanksgiving, so that wouldn't be the best time to speak either. But they had to know, and soon.

"He's coming for us," Max whispered. "For them."

Gabe blinked away the moisture in his eyes. "Nothing can happen to them."

His mate growled, his eyes flashing. "No. Never."

Gabe moved in, touching his forehead to Max's. "If McCready comes for us, I want you and the kids to be safe. So if anything happens to me, to the pack—"

"Gabe." Max's voice trembled. "Don't."

Gabe cupped Max's cheek. "Listen to me. He told me once he would use what we loved as a weapon. Max... Max, if he ever got his hands on those kids..." His mouth trembled, and he pressed it into a tight line. "If he comes for us, promise me you'll take the kids and go. The She-Wolf's realm might be the only place that's safe enough for them until McCready's dead. So if he comes for us, for them..."

Max took Gabe's face in his hands. "Nothing is going to happen to you or to anyone in the pack. Do you hear me?"

"Promise me, mi amor. For our family."

His mate's lips trembled but he nodded. "Fine. I promise." Max leaned in and claimed Gabe's mouth, the bond between them warm like the sun. "But I'll always come back for you. No matter how long it takes. There's not a thing in the world that can keep me from you."

CHAPTER 14

WE'RE YOUR PACK NOW

THANKSGIVING DAY ARRIVED. MAX usually loved the holiday, but he woke with dread heavy on his chest and his heart racing. He took a few deep breaths. McCready was coming for them, but he wasn't here yet. The pack was coming over for dinner and they could discuss a course of action then. Downstairs, the kids and Gabe chattered lightheartedly, their laughter soothing Max's frayed nerves.

Above all else, Max knew he had to keep Tommy and Luna safe. Their father was a murderer and a monster. He could never be trusted with them. All Max had to do was remember Tommy screaming and thrashing as his father leeched the life from him to grow his own strength, and he was kicking out of the blankets. It was time to start the day and hope for the best.

The cool floorboards gave him a shock, and he checked the temperature. It was bitter cold today. He went downstairs and got a fire going in the hearth.

"Max, breakfast!" Gabe called from the kitchen.

Tommy, Luna, and Gabe sat around the breakfast table, plates of bacon and eggs steaming.

Gabe passed him his coffee, and Max took a grateful sip. "Thank you."

Outside the windows, frost gathered on the grass and the lawn was littered with fallen leaves.

Luna said, "It's Thanksgiving!"

"Yup," Tommy said, cramming some bacon in his mouth.

"What are you thankful for?" Max asked, supposing they should start the day with positivity.

Luna made a show of thinking about it, tapping her little chin. "I'm thankful for... everything."

Gabe chuckled. "That's a lot of things to be thankful for."

"We haven't had Thanksgiving in a long time," Luna said.

Tommy smiled, though his eyes were downcast. "Our pack sometimes celebrated but times were hard, and there wasn't a lot to be thankful for."

Nodding, Gabe said, "I hope this year can be different."

Max closed his eyes tight.

"I think it *is* different," Luna said.

"Why?" Max asked.

She smiled and pointed at him, then Gabe. "Because Tommy and me have a pack now."

Gabe covered his mouth, blinking fast. Max slid his foot over his mate's beneath the table, his own eyes stinging.

"Did that make you sad?" Luna asked, frowning at Gabe.

"No." Gabe shook his head and wiped his eyes. "No, it made me really happy, pup."

"And sometimes people cry when they're happy too," Luna said, like she was remembering something Tommy told her.

"That's right." Her brother poked her nose and made her laugh.

The little girl's joy spread through the bonds tying them together, raising Max's spirits.

Later, when Gabe and Max did the dishes, Max whispered, "I almost told them we wanted to—"

Gabe sighed. "Me too."

"Why'd you hold back?"

Gabe's face twisted. "Because I can't hand them that joy only for Mc-Cready to rip it away."

He squeezed the dishrag, claws dimpling the fabric. "That's why I stayed quiet too."

Beyond the windows, the skies were clear and blue except on the horizon. Those clouds were dark and gray.

THE TURKEY HAD JUST finished roasting when the front doorbell rang. Gabe took the turkey out of the oven while Max ran to get the door. Ben's glower lit up into a smile.

Max grinned. "I thought you might not come."

Ben waved a hand. "No, things worked out with Heather's family. The boys are spending Thanksgiving with her, but we'll all get to have Christmas together." He didn't sound like he was happy to be away from his sons, but he smiled regardless. "Thanks for having me. I brought two kinds of pie." He hefted a bakery bag onto the island counter.

"Of course. Wouldn't be the same without you." Max hugged him.

Ben removed his beanie and stuffed it in his jacket pocket. "I have the agency wolves on high alert. Eddie's got security fitted with silver claws and fangs and protective ear coverings in case he tries to control anybody. He has a pack, Max."

"I know. Manuel told me."

Ben shook his head. "Poor creatures. They're all under his control and we'll have to kill them to keep ourselves safe. It's so fucked."

A shiver of dread ran through Max. "Gabe and I talked about how to protect the kids. I may have to take them to Amaris's realm."

"But we don't know what's there. It might not be any safer there than here."

Max blew out a breath. "I know."

"Have you told them?"

Max swallowed hard. "Not yet."

"You need to. They have to be prepared."

"Hi, Ben!" Luna called, running down the stairs toward him.

"Luna, don't run!" Tommy shouted from upstairs.

"Hey, kiddo!" Ben knelt down to hug Luna when she ran into his arms. "Looking forward to all that turkey?"

"I bet I can eat the whole entire thing," Luna said.

Ben gawked at her. "I'd pay you twenty bucks."

Luna cocked her head. "Only twenty? That's a rip-off!"

Max rolled his eyes. "Don't encourage her."

Seeing Luna so happy and Tommy so relaxed only made it harder for Max to tell them what they deserved to know, but it couldn't be avoided. After dinner. He would let them have a happy Thanksgiving, let them just have this day, and then he would tell them.

In the next few minutes, the rest of the agency wolves arrived. Ryan and Zach brought pumpkin ales and Izzie had made a bowl of cranberry sauce. Manuel and Veronica, the new Alphas, carried in Tupperware full of mashed potatoes and gravy. His mother had made stuffing Max remembered gorging on as a kid until he'd felt like a stuffed turkey. In the living room, the kids watched the Macy's Thanksgiving Day Parade on live TV.

The pack bustled around the kitchen, grabbing plates and transferring the food from Tupperware to proper serving bowls and reheating meals in the microwave. With the food hot and ready to be served, the pack carried their bowls and plates to the table. "Kids," Max called to the living room, "dinnertime!"

Tommy and Luna came running.

"Shouldn't we wait for Ed and Vico?" Ryan asked, sitting down in his chair.

Ben checked his phone. "Eddie's wrapping up training and Vico's on patrol since the kitchen closed early today. They're coming, but not for a while yet."

Luna reached for the plate of turkey, but Tommy grabbed her hand and she groaned. "I'm hungry," she grumbled.

"I know," Tommy said. "But we have to give thanks first."

"So let's get on with it before I starve to death!" Luna exclaimed, making everyone laugh.

One by one, the pack expressed what they were thankful for. Though the sentiments were all different, many were thankful for the new Alphas of the Council.

When Tommy's turn came around, he cleared his throat. "I just wanted to say... thank you, all of you. After we lost our pack, things were really hard. It was just me and Luna. And I did my best to look after her, but some days I didn't feel like I did a good job."

Max's throat ached.

Tommy blinked fast. "But things are different. We have a pack now, and we're not alone. Not anymore. So, thank you."

Wiping his eyes, Max felt overwhelmed by the gratitude that flowed through Tommy's bond to theirs.

Manuel raised a glass. "To pack."

"Here, here!" Ryan raised his glass. The pack clinked their beer and wine glasses together—and cranberry juice in Tommy and Luna's case—and wished each other a happy Thanksgiving.

For a while, all the uncertainty still coming their way was forgotten about. Luna laughed at Ryan's stories about the Thanksgiving meal he'd attended with his family that afternoon. Zach and Manuel talked football while Gabe and Izzie teased each other good-naturedly. At one end of the table, Ben reflected on past Thanksgivings he'd spent with his kids. Veronica and Kendra asked Max about how his academy training was going and if The Slaughtered Lamb had reopened yet. He let them know training was going great, but the Lamb was still closed for repairs.

Luna and Tommy chatted, their faces alight with glee. Their sunny smiles were such a stark contrast to the lost, frightened pups they'd found in the wilds of Alaska. Max gritted his teeth, resolving never to see them in pain or suffering again.

"I understand," Max said. "Mom, I get it now."

His mother turned toward him. Her eyes widened, and she didn't have to ask.

Putting his arm around her shoulders, he stared into her eyes, trying to make sure that she knew he meant this. "Why you did what you did. Why you never told me. You were protecting me." He swallowed hard. "I have to tell them about what's coming, but I... I'm so scared to steal this hope away from them. I'd do anything to make sure they're happy. Safe. So, I get it. I do."

His mother blinked fast, her blue eyes glistening. "I should have—"

Exhaling, Max let the bitterness slide off his shoulders. He'd spent enough time angry at her. "I understand, because I would do anything to protect them." Across the table, Tommy and Luna smiled at each other. "Anything."

She slipped her arms around him, and he rested his chin atop her soft hair and squeezed her tight, making her laugh wetly. "A part of me was scared," she admitted. "If you knew your birth parents, you'd forget about me. You'd stop seeing me as your mother."

Max kissed her forehead. "You are my mother. In all the ways that matter."

She held him tight and planted a wet kiss on his cheek. "Love you, baby."

"You too, Mom." He smiled.

Ben's phone rang. "Oh, hey! Vicenzo's calling. Should I tell him we already ate all the food?" His mischievous smile made Max laugh.

"Oh, Ben, stop it!" Kendra chided.

Ben shushed everyone and took the call.

"Vico, say hey. You're on speaker. Having trouble finding the house?" Ben held the phone toward everyone.

A chorus of greetings filled the room.

There was nothing but ragged breathing on the line.

The good humor around the table drained away. Max's heart skipped a beat, but he told himself it could be anything.

Ben said, "Vico? Speak up. I can't hear you."

Not a word. The breathing got louder. It sounded like harsh pants through a mouthful of salivating fangs.

"Agents. Hello," Aaron McCready snarled. "I hope I'm not interrupting anything."

Max dropped his glass of wine and it shattered, flooding the hardwood in a tide of crimson.

At the sound of his father's voice, Tommy's eyes went wide.

Gabe was on his feet, tipping his chair back onto the floor with a crash.

"No," Ben rasped, gripping the phone so tight his fingers whitened. "McCready. No. I'm begging you." His voice broke, his lips bloodless in his horror.

McCready panted, his voice gravelly and wet as if he spoke through a throat thick with blood. "You know, you really should have known better, Benjamin. Leaving all those wolves alone. You really think some silver and a few earplugs will stop my pack from ripping yours apart?"

"What do you want?" Ben paced, his eyes wide and full of fear. "If you've got a problem, take it up with me! Leave them alone. They did nothing to you!"

"Oh, I do have a problem. Your agents took something that belongs to me. It's only fair I take something that belongs to you. An eye for an eye."

Ben made a choked sound in the back of his throat. "Please, don't."

"Are you listening, Benjamin?" Aaron McCready snarled. He sounded like an animal.

Max gripped Gabe's arm hard.

"Do you hear them, Benjamin? My wolves. Howling for your agents' blood."

McCready fell silent, and through the low buzz of static there came the howling of wolves. But they sounded off. Twisted. Furious.

Feral.

Ben's knees went weak. He collapsed, gripping the table before he could hit the ground.

"Dad, stop it!" Tommy was on his feet and snatching the phone from where Ben had dropped it.

Gabe's claws lengthened, and Max growled beside him, clutching Luna to him as she trembled against him.

"Thomas." McCready's voice held no relief or love, only fury. "You can stop this. You and your sister. All it takes is one word, Thomas. Say yes. Come to me. Bring your sister. We will go away together, and all this death can be avoided."

"No," Luna whimpered. "Tommy, no. Don't let him take us away!"

"Tommy." Gabe grabbed the boy's arm. Tears filled Tommy's eyes. "Don't listen to him. He's lying."

"But what if—" Tommy's breath turned to gasps.

"He's *lying*," Gabe insisted. "He's lost his mind. He'll get what he wants, and then he'll turn around and kill us all."

"Thomas, I promise. Listen to your father," McCready rasped.

Tommy's hand shook, the phone quaking in his grasp. Max touched his shoulder, and Gabe gripped the back of his neck. Together, they pushed waves of comfort through their bonds and into Tommy.

"We're your pack now," Gabe said. "And wolves protect their pack. You aren't going anywhere. We're facing him together or not at all."

"Thomas!" McCready roared.

The boy's eyes snapped open, blazing with fury, and he gasped, "You're not my pack, McCready. Not anymore."

A growl rumbled like thunder. "Then I will make you watch as the ones who stole you from me die one by one."

The line went dead.

Bursting into tears, Luna hid her face in Max's stomach.

Tommy's knees shook and Max pulled him into a hug, his arms around both kids.

The smell of the pack's terror was palpable, a sourness in the back of Max's throat.

"Ben." A voice broke through the ringing in Max's ears. Zach stood by Ben's side, his hand outstretched, but Ben, head bowed and on all fours, shooed him away.

"What do we do?" Izzie whispered, her eyes wide with horror and full of tears.

A snarl filled the air. Ben's claws raked over the hardwood, leaving deep gashes. "What do you mean, what do we do?" His eyes blazed, fangs glistening. In his fury, Ben jumped to his feet, standing taller than any of them. "We stop him. Tonight. Once and for all or we fucking die trying!"

CHAPTER 15

THE HARDEST GOODBYE

No one could get in touch with Eddie or Vicenzo. Gabe tried to tell himself it was because they were busy fighting or perhaps they were holed up somewhere safe. Eddie wore a silver collar that suppressed his wolf. He would be immune to McCready's madness, but he also couldn't shift, leaving him at the mercy of feral wolves.

Please, let them be safe.

Gabe helped Tommy and Luna pack their belongings.

"Will we ever come back?" Luna asked, tears clinging to her eyelashes.

He tried to smile. "I think so."

Tommy picked at threads in the carpet.

To him, Gabe said, "Your father has a connection with you." More so than with Luna.

Tommy nodded, his face twisting in misery. "I was seven when the hunters came. Luna was only a few weeks old." He glanced at his sister. "You didn't have time to form as strong a bond with him as I did, so that's why he's able to get inside my head."

Luna gripped his knee. "You can't listen to him, Tommy. Okay?" Her lip quivered.

He glared down at the rug, his hands in fists. "If I went to him, do you think he would leave everyone alone?"

Gabe sat on the floor beside him. "I don't trust a word he says."

"But isn't it worth the risk?" Tommy snapped.

Gabe shook his head. "No, Thomas. I wouldn't risk losing you for any offer he made. And everyone here feels the same. This isn't your responsibility to fix."

The boy blinked hard, tears bright in his eyes.

An unsettling thought came to him. "Do you want to go to him? To be with him?"

Tommy shook his head, and Gabe's shoulders lost their tension. "Only if I knew he wouldn't hurt you guys. I still..." He hesitated, wetting his lips. "I still remember what he was like. Before the hunters came. He still had fanatical beliefs Mom argued with him about, but he was different. He'd pick me up and spin me around. He did anything to make me laugh. But now it's like that goodness I saw in him is just gone. I hate him for everything he's done, but a part of me still loves him too. The person he used to be."

This wasn't right. It wasn't fair. After everything Tommy and Luna had been through, all the loss and suffering and uncertainty, they deserved only stability and safety. Instead, all Gabe and Max could promise them was danger and fear.

"Are you packed?" Max asked.

The kids nodded sullenly.

"Let's go." He motioned for the kids to follow him downstairs, and Gabe trailed after them.

As the kids went outside, Max gripped Gabe's arm before he could follow.

"Max," he said, his voice a croak. He knew what had to be done, and it was like a knife in his heart.

Max blinked hard. "They need us."

"I know!" he said, his throat thick with grief. "But Max, our friends—" He couldn't continue.

His mate's mouth trembled and he went to Gabe and held him desperately. Gabe buried his face in Max's hair, clenching his jaw to silence the mournful howl building in his chest. His wolf was torn in two. Max and the kids needed him, but he was terrified that he would never see Ben, Ryan, Zach, or any of the other agency wolves again. No matter what had come their way, Gabe had fought side by side with his pack even in the face of certain death. They'd come first, even before his own life. But now he was a father. He had two kids who needed him. He couldn't put the pack first, not this time.

"We have to do this," Max whispered, tears bright in his eyes.

Gabe put his arm around him and stepped outside.

In the driveway, Ryan stood by Zach, ashen-faced. His back to them, Zach clutched the roof of the car for support. Ryan put his hand on Zach's tense shoulder and met Gabe's eyes without a smile or a word.

Kendra stood with the kids, her arms around them while they hugged her.

With tears in her eyes, Izzie hugged Veronica and Manuel.

His chin to his chest and his face in shadow, Ben leaned on his truck. When he looked up, Gabe didn't recognize him. He'd never seen Ben look so small and unsure, crushed under the weight of everything he was asking his family to do.

"I..." Ben said, and his voice was carried away by the wind. He blinked fast and cleared his throat. "I know what I'm asking of all of you." Heads turned and Ben seemed to shrink under their terror, sorrow, and uncertainty, then held his head higher. "I will never ask anyone to do something they don't want to do. You're my family. I love you all." Ben's voice cracked, and he took in a deep breath.

Gabe took a step toward him, and Izzie gripped his sleeve, her face wet and eyes red.

Once again Ben tried for words but all that came out was a choked noise. He raised a hand to his eyes, wiping stubbornly. A lump rose in Gabe's throat.

"I swore an oath to the wolves of the agency. It's mine to uphold, not yours. You have families." In Kendra's arms, Luna whimpered. "People you've reunited with." Manuel hugged Veronica tight. "It's been an honor to know you, all of you. You've given me so much joy." He smiled, but it broke upon his face. "If you want to leave, then say it now. I'll never hold it against you."

Ryan turned his face away into Zach's back with a strangled gasp, and Zach reached around and grabbed his hand, squeezing until Ryan's fingernails whitened. Then Zach pushed off from the truck and turned, walking to Ben and grabbing his hand to pull him into a fierce embrace.

"Damn it, Zach," Ryan croaked, wiping his eyes. He ran to stand with Zach and Ben, hugging them both.

Manuel and Veronica went to them. "I'll gather the Council, Ben," Manuel said, gripping Ben's shoulder. "You were the father my children needed. I will do all I can to ensure the agency's survival."

Speechless, Ben squeezed Manuel's shoulder and pulled him in for a slap on the back.

Max remained at Kendra's side, his eyes wide and full of tears.

Everyone he loved was leaving to fight, and Gabe didn't know if he would see them alive again. He took one step toward Ben, and Ben became a blur through the tears in Gabe's eyes.

"Viejo," Gabe choked out.

Ben blinked fast.

"You know I would. I would fucking die for you. For what you did for my family. For me."

Ben's mouth trembled. His big warm hands settled on Gabe's shaking shoulders. "I know." A tear slipped down Ben's face and rolled into his beard. He sniffed hard.

"But I can't." Gabe gripped Ben's arm to hold himself together. "I can't, not this time. I can't leave them. I can't."

Ben took a step, then another, gathering Gabe's face between his hands. "I know," he whispered, voice thick with pain. "It's okay." He thumbed away a tear on Gabe's face.

Gabe took hold of the front of Ben's jacket to hold himself up as his wolf howled for Max, for his kids, and for the man he'd called father for so long.

"Tell me," Gabe begged him. "Tell me you need me. Just tell me, Ben. Tell me, and I'll follow you."

Ben pressed his lips tight together, his shoulders shaking. "Until you hear from us, you and Max take those kids and you run. You run until one of us tells you that you can stop."

He pulled Gabe into a crushing embrace, squeezing fistfuls of Gabe's jacket. Ben pressed a trembling kiss to his forehead, and Gabe broke apart in his arms.

TEARS BURNED MAX'S EYES as they said their goodbyes.

Gabe and Izzie wept in their parents' arms like children. Izzie was clearly torn, but her parents had pleaded for her to go with Gabe, and she'd crumbled.

Since he'd been focused on them, Max nearly fell backward when Ryan threw himself into his arms. Ryan's tears wet Max's chest, and Max held him tight. Zach came up behind them and wrapped his big arms around them both, burying his face in Max's neck.

"I love you guys," Ryan said with a sob as he went to hug Gabe around the neck, then Izzie.

"You too," Max said, sniffling. "You were the pack my mother and I needed. Our first pack."

Zach's body shook against Max. "I'm so glad you chose us."

Max was too. He would be forever grateful that the agency had come into his life. But he couldn't find the words to say that, and so he cried with them.

Ben hugged Max tight, and Max could hardly see him through his tears.

"Chin up, Little Red," Ben said, his voice hoarse. "If we kick McCready's ass, you'll be the first to know."

Max could only nod as he buried his face in Ben's shoulder.

Walking away from Ben, Gabe's parents, Zach, and Ryan was the hardest thing Max had ever done because it was not a choice he'd ever thought he would make.

Izzie untangled herself from her parents and ran into the car without a look back, her face wet.

"Max," Gabe whispered, his voice raw and wet. "We have to."

The children cried in the back seat of the car, and Max reminded himself that this painful goodbye was for them. Tommy and Luna were worth the pain of leaving his pack behind. Gabe pulled him close and led him to the car. The two of them sat in the second row, the kids in the third, and Izzie sat beside Kendra in the front seat.

Outside the car windows, the pack stood shoulder to shoulder. Ryan held on to Zach, his eyes red from grief, and Zach had one arm around Ryan, thumbing away his own tears. Veronica and Manuel held each other close, united in their pain. Beside them stood Ben, strong even in his sorrow.

For so long, they had done everything together. They'd laughed together, hunted together, fought side by side and sacrificed for each other. Now they were going their separate ways, their fates uncertain.

"We'll see them again," Max said, because his broken heart refused to comprehend any other outcome.

Gabe reached across the space between their seats and grabbed his hand. "We will. We have to."

Kendra started the engine, a shuddery gasp escaping her. Tires crunched over gravel.

His mother drove them away down the dirt road and Max dried his eyes and looked back, desperate for one final look.

They were gone.

THEY DROVE FOR AN hour. Cars sped past on the freeway as they passed a sign that said WELCOME TO ALBANY.

In the seat behind him, Luna and Tommy snored, leaning on each other as they slept.

Max slumped onto Gabe's shoulder, ready to sleep again. "Where are we going?" Max asked. His voice was bone dry.

Kendra glanced at him in the rearview mirror. Her eyes were red and baggy. "I'm not sure. As far from New York State as we can get until... until we know for sure."

Until they heard from Ben and the others, or they didn't ever hear from them again.

Dread consumed Max, and he closed his eyes tight and wished this was all nothing but a bad dream.

They stopped in the city of Albany and spent the night in a cheap hotel in a sketchy part of the city. There were two beds. Tommy and Luna got one, and Izzie and Kendra piled in another. Gabe and Max slept on a few extra pillows on the floor. They watched TV, a comedy, but none of them laughed or even really paid attention. They needed something, anything, to keep their minds off their pack, far away and fighting for their lives.

"Can you feel them?" Max asked, his voice muffled against Gabe's shoulder.

A sigh escaped his mate. "No."

Max sighed too, fear tightening his stomach. "We'd know," he said, not believing that at all. "If anything happened to them, we'd know."

"Would we?" Gabe whispered.

"Yes." Max forced himself to swallow the lie down. He needed to believe that their friends were still alive.

Gabe leaned his cheek on Max's hair and closed his eyes. Max slept.

When he woke, he'd only slept three hours. It was still dark outside. There was a strange burning sensation in his chest, like he had heartburn. At first, Max thought that was what had disturbed his sleep until Luna shouted, "Tommy tried to leave!"

"Why?" Gabe asked, rubbing sleep from his red-rimmed eyes.

"We shouldn't have left!" Tommy paced up and down, fur blackening his arms, his fangs sharp in his mouth. "If we'd just gone to him, this wouldn't be happening!"

"Tommy," Gabe began.

The boy shouted, "I'll leave! I'll go to him, and no one will get hurt!"

"Tommy. N-no. You can't. You can't!" Izzie hugged Luna to her chest, but Luna broke free and ran, grabbing Tommy. "Stop it! Stop saying this!"

"Shut up!" Tommy tried to pull her off him.

Heart racing fast to see Tommy so worked up, Max climbed out of bed. "Tommy. Hey. Stop." He gripped the boy's shoulders.

Kendra led Luna away to the other bed, whispering soothing words to the distraught girl.

Tommy squirmed out of his reach. "We need to go back. We shouldn't have left. If we start driving now, we could make it back before nightfall. We could help them!"

Gabe was biting on his nails, something Max had never seen him do. "I could go."

Terror drove a stake through Max's heart. "Gabe, no."

Izzie lurched to her feet. "Get a hold of yourself!" Izzie's voice trembled, tears sparkling in her eyes. "This isn't what Ben wanted. What our parents wanted."

"Who cares?" Gabe roared. "We just got our family back. We just got Dad back, and we could lose him again! We need to go back now!"

Luna wailed in Kendra's arms. "Stop it. Both of you stop it!" Kendra snapped.

"They're giving their lives so that we can live! We can't dishonor their sacrifice by throwing away our lives!" Izzie retorted, but she seemed to shrink before Gabe's anger as if she hardly believed her words herself.

Gabe looked in Max's direction. "Max, we're going back."

Max finally found his voice. "No."

Shock widened Gabe's eyes. "What?"

"I said no," Max said, though the look of betrayal on Gabe's face sapped the resolve he needed. Luna wailed louder.

A snarl twisted Gabe's face. "What do you mean, no? Max, our pack is fucking dying! We're going back!"

Max's patience unraveled. "I said no! And if you want to go back, then you're going without me."

Gabe took a step back as if Max had slapped him. "Don't you get it?" Gabe panted, blinking fast. "They'll die unless we—"

Kendra roared, "Everyone, *stop*!"

With a wince, Gabe's fur receded; his fangs lost their edge.

Astonished to see his mother quaking with fury, Max gaped at her.

White fur rippled over Kendra's arms. "Tommy, your intentions are noble, but if you think we're going to let you sacrifice yourself, then you're dead wrong. Gabe, you made your choice. Be a man and stick to it. We're all upset and scared, we're divided, but we are still a damn *pack* and we have got to act like it. Am I clear?"

Max turned away, digging his fingers into his eyes. Fuck. He didn't want to cry. If he did, he didn't know how he'd stop. His heart was shattering like glass in his chest.

Gasping, Tommy put his arms around Max and held tight. Luna ran to her brother and crashed into him.

Gabe pressed himself against Max's back and buried his face in his neck. A full-body shudder racked Gabe, and his tears were hot on Max's skin.

"Sorry." Gabe's voice whispered along the threads that bound them. *"I'm sorry, Lobito. So, so sorry. I wish I was stronger. It's too hard."*

"I know," Max thought back, unable to speak as grief unwound him. *"I know. I know."*

He took solace in their bond, in the threads that connected him to Kendra and Izzie, Tommy and Luna. There'd once been more of them; now there were six. They weren't whole anymore, but they were still a pack. They still had each other. Max gripped Gabe's arms and squeezed tight.

Kendra whispered, "I'm going to get the car out of park before someone else decides to take off. We need to keep moving."

Izzie laughed wetly. "Sounds like a plan."

Wiping his eyes, Max sat on the bed next to her and put his head on her shoulder. Izzie kissed his cheek and sniffled.

Kendra left. The bed creaked as Gabe squeezed between him and Izzie. He tousled his sister's hair, and she smacked his hand away with a snort. Gabe's remorseful eyes landed on Max. Taking in a deep breath, Max laid his head on his shoulder. Tommy and Luna joined them, and they sat in healing silence.

When it was time to pile into the car, they joined Kendra. She looked back, arching a brow questioningly. Gabe took Max's hand and said, "Onward and upward, Captain Kendra."

She smiled and opened the GPS app. "Where to next?"

Izzie tipped her head back thoughtfully. "Let's get out of the US and go as far as we can. Maybe Canada."

"Fine by me." Gabe nudged Max. "How about it?"

As long as they were together, Max didn't care where they went.

Kendra pulled out of the parking space and started driving.

They left Albany behind and didn't look back.

THEY DROVE ON INTO the night. The moon was full and bright overhead, the only light on the quiet, isolated stretch of road they travelled.

Something twinged in Max's chest, and he grimaced in discomfort. That strange sensation again.

Gabe rubbed his chest, then frowned. "You felt that too, Max?"

Izzie winced. "So did I. What—"

Something tore across the road ahead of them. Kendra screamed and swerved around it. The tires slipped on the icy road. "Hold on!" she hollered.

The car lurched off the road and the kids screamed in the back seat as the car shot down a hill. Tree branches slapped the windows as they flew over violent bumps in the terrain, and Max would have flown out of his seat if his seat belt hadn't been on. The car slammed into a tree, shattering the front window.

"Is anyone hurt?" Kendra called, picking glass off her lap.

"N-no," Tommy stammered. "Luna, you okay?"

"I think so." Luna panted, her eyes wide and face pale.

The kids stayed in the car while the adults climbed out to inspect the damage.

"Shit!" Kendra hissed. One tire had blown out, and she ran to check the trunk.

Gabe and Izzie loomed over her shoulders. Gabe shone a light into the trunk, and Kendra said, "Someone help me change this tire."

Max hoisted the spare from the trunk and grabbed the jack. "Kids, come on out!" he shouted. With Luna and Tommy out of the car, Max raised the car with the jack. Kendra removed the hubcap and loosened the nuts, grunting and snarling as she maneuvered the wrench.

"What was that thing?" Izzie asked, standing between Tommy and Luna with an arm around them. The kids shivered, their breath misting in the bitter cold air.

"Nothing," Max said. He needed it to have just been a deer or something, even though he knew exactly what it was. A wolf. "It was nothing, okay?"

A howl echoed through the trees. A wolf was going on the hunt. Max waited for the answering howls of a pack. An answering roar rattled the windows. Gabe snarled beside him and Izzie's claws popped out.

A bottle of water on the dashboard vibrated, and ripples formed in the water.

"He's here." Tommy tugged Luna close, his eyes wide in fright.

Gabe grabbed Tommy's shoulder and shoved him toward the car. "Tommy, Luna, get in the car! Lock the doors!"

Whimpering, the kids leaped into the back seat and hid on the floor. Kendra locked the vehicle doors. The earth shook under the pounding of enormous paws, and birds took flight from the trees and flew in front of the moon. Eyes flashed in the dark. Something was coming, getting closer and closer. There was a twinge in Max's chest and it burned like acid beneath his skin, familiar and yet so wrong at the same time.

"Max," Gabe whispered, his face gone white. He gripped Max's arm. "Max, that's—"

A wolf stepped from the shadows of the woods.

Izzie's mouth dropped open. "That's—"

The wolf's eyes opened, and if Max hadn't recognized him right away, the silver eyes would have done the trick.

It was Ben.

And yet...

"Viejo?" Gabe rasped. "What? How?"

Confusion warred with Max's joy even as his wolf growled in his chest. Something was wrong. Something wasn't right.

And then he realized what it was.

The thread connecting him to Ben was *wrong*. It was black. Twisted. Rotten. It burned beneath his ribcage.

Ben reached a foreleg up and pawed at his head. He whined, a long, tortured sound. Writhing, he shook his head and arched his back, snapping his jaws at nothing.

"Ben?" Gabe gasped. Izzie grabbed him hard.

"Stay back," Izzie hissed, eyes wide. "Something's wrong with him. Something's—"

Ben's eyes opened. They flashed yellow, and a growl rumbled from his chest.

"Run!" Ben's voice blared in Max's mind, and he recoiled. *"Run! I'll kill you. He's in my head. You've got to run!"*

Aaron McCready prowled from the woods behind Ben, his eyes burning in the dark. He walked on all fours as an enormous wolf, bigger than the car concealing the kids crying within.

Laughter crawled from McCready's maw. He raised himself onto two legs, slamming his claws down on the roof of the car and leaving a dent. "Good boy, Benjamin. I knew you'd help me find them."

Ben snarled behind them, fur bristling and hackles raised. His eyes burned yellow.

"I'm sorry." Ben's voice was tortured. *"I'm so sorry. I don't want to do this!"*

Gabe's lip curled in fury. "What the fuck did you do?"

Huge claws punctured the roof of the car with a metallic crunch. "Your pack didn't stand a chance against the power of a berserker wolf. I'm sure they've ripped each other to shreds by now. I kept one for myself. Ben may look like a feral beast, but his mind is very much intact. I used his connection to you to track you down. He could feel you, even if you couldn't feel him. And now..." He grinned, baring long fangs. "Now, I'll get to watch him kill you. Benjamin."

Ben stopped snarling. He sat alert and ready. His eyes were yellow orbs, glowing in the dark.

"Kill them all," McCready ordered.

"Ben, no!" Gabe shouted, rounding on the older wolf.

Ben bunched his muscles and sprang, his jaws open wide.

Gabe's clothes fell away in tatters as he shifted, hurling himself upon Ben. They collided in a blur of fangs and claws.

"Gabe!" Max tried to run to him, but Izzie restrained him.

McCready roared at them. "This could all be over quickly, Max. No one must die. Give me what I want."

His heart raced so hard, he thought it would burst. Gabe yelped, pinned beneath Ben.

"Thomas! Luna!" McCready roared. "Come on out now. If you're good, I'll let your friends live!"

"Leave those kids the hell alone!" Izzie shifted with a roar and charged at McCready, leaping onto his back. Kendra snarled, shifting to a white wolf and hurling herself at McCready too. He batted her aside like she was a fruit fly. McCready pounced, colliding with Max. It was like being hit by a furry truck, and he flew off his feet and crashed to the ground.

McCready rose onto his back legs, drew back his paw, and punched through the window of the car. Tommy screamed and Luna howled in terror. The little girl kicked and thrashed as he dragged her through the window. She tumbled to the ground and McCready lunged back inside for Tommy.

"Leave him alone!" Luna screamed, scratching at McCready's legs.

"Get back!" Max reached for McCready with his powers, using gravity to hoist him off his feet. McCready yelped as he flew backward and crashed into a tree, nearly uprooting it. Max ran for the car. "Tommy, come on!" He reached for the boy's hands and pulled him from the car. Tommy scrambled out through the window, and Max hauled him to his feet. He shoved the kids toward the woods. "Run!"

"Thomas, Luna!" McCready bellowed, his roar shaking the ground. "Come with me, and this will be over!"

Tommy's eyes flashed yellow. He gasped and doubled over, clutching his head.

"Yes, that's it." McCready grinned. "You're still mine. My pack. And Luna will be too! We'll be a family again."

Max grabbed Tommy's shoulders. *"Tommy, don't listen!"* He pushed the words across the bond connecting them. Tommy's eyes flashed from yellow to hazel.

Kendra leaped onto McCready's back, driving her claws into his shoulder. McCready howled and bucked her off. *"Go, Max!"* Kendra shouted through their bond. Jumping on McCready again, she fastened her fangs into his shoulder.

Max grabbed Luna's and Tommy's hands and ran, stumbling down the hill below the road and into the dark. The pained yelps and furious snarls of the wolves faded as the wind howled in his ears. A roar shook the treetops. Luna gasped as she ran, tears streaming down her cheeks. "I've got you!" Max assured her, the breath tearing from his lungs. "I've got you; I won't let him hurt you!"

"Max." His mother's frightened voice filled his mind. She was hurting. He could feel it. *"I tried. He's coming. Run. Don't stop running!"*

He wouldn't just run. He would go as far away as he could if it meant keeping his kids safe. As the moon shone down on him, Max turned his face to the moon above and sang.

CHAPTER 16

I'LL COME BACK FOR YOU

THE MOON GAZED IMPASSIVELY at him before the clouds concealed the light.

Nothing happened.

Fuck, fuck, fuck.

He closed his eyes, trying to concentrate. He'd howled. Shouldn't that be enough to open the portal?

"Max, what are you doing?" Tommy croaked.

Max hunched over, his bones creaking and skin rippling into fur as he assumed his wolf form. His heart hammered and if he'd had any doubts, Luna's frightened cries drove them out. He had to do this for the kids. Though no moonlight could penetrate the clouds, Max threw back his head to the darkness above. His throat was tight and at first all he could let out was a small *woof.*

Come on. Come on. He had to do this. For his pups, he had to open a way to Amaris and her hunting grounds. He had to go to the She-Wolf.

Gathering his strength, Max let loose a warbling howl. With his howl, much deeper and louder than the first and fueled with desperation, the sky lit up with bursts of lightning. Thunder snarled, so loud it was deafening.

A burst of light appeared in the center of the woods, swelling bigger and brighter until the light obscured Max's vision.

The trees blew apart all around them, leaving Max and the kids defenseless and vulnerable to the fury of the storm. Max flew off his feet, and Tommy shielded Luna when they fell onto the ground.

The blinding light cast away the surrounding darkness before dying to a dimmer but still luminous glow. A gateway had appeared in the middle of the vast woods, shimmering as if made of mist. Max couldn't look away. The portal was just as impressive as it had been when he'd first glimpsed it only months ago.

As if looking out a window, the portal gifted him with a glimpse of a world beyond theirs—rolling emerald fields of grass, a star-spangled sky, and snow-capped mountains. Before Max's eyes, a pack of wolves ran past pursuing a deer.

Those were the fabled hunting grounds, home to all wolves from eons before they'd learned to assume a human form. Home to Amaris... and Max once too. It looked so picturesque he didn't understand why he'd been so afraid of it for so long.

"What is that?" Luna whispered, awed and frightened.

"A portal," Max said, shifting back, "to the She-Wolf's realm."

"Is it safe?" Tommy asked.

Max swallowed all his apprehension. "Only one way to find out."

A shape plunged from out of the darkness, hurtling toward them. "Tommy, Luna! No!" McCready howled.

Max took Luna's hand in his and clasped Tommy's with his other hand. "Hold on tight!"

Luna shrieked, closing her eyes. Tommy panted, his eyes wide and petrified.

"Gabe," Max thought, *"I'll come back for you. I promise. I promise!"*

"Max," came Gabe's answering cry. *"Max, I—"*

"Let them go!" McCready commanded, and he charged at Max. The ground shook as McCready gained ground.

"Go, kids!" Max cried, and he ran toward the portal, pulling the kids with him.

A blast of freezing air hit him, and Max's stomach lurched like he'd missed a step going downstairs.

Entering the portal turned his insides upside down. A wave of dizziness hit him, as if he were spiraling down a long, dark hole. Freezing cold blasted his skin, paralyzing him. He lay in an indentation in the thick, freezing snow. Tiny daggers of frost pierced his face and eyes. He shifted to a wolf so his dense fur could ward off the cold.

"Max, close it!" Tommy bellowed, hoisting Luna off her feet.

He whipped around and on the other side of the portal, McCready grew closer.

With a jolt of panic, Max lurched to his paws and warbled out a howl. The portal narrowed, closing but not fast enough. McCready burst through, or at least his upper half did. The lower half was stuck. McCready thrashed, clawing at the snow.

"Back!" Max said through the bonds, barking a warning at the kids. *"Run!"*

Tommy grabbed Luna's hand and waded through the snow.

With a groan, McCready pushed himself through the portal, crashing into the snow. The portal closed behind him. McCready bared his fangs in a triumphant grin. "Give my children back to me, mutt," he snarled and threw back his head and howled.

Only to be cut off with a yelp as a snowball crashed into his head.

Luna yelled, "Shut up, you big stupid stinker!" She threw another snowball.

Grinning, Tommy chucked one. "Take that, ugly!"

Max's tail wagged.

McCready sputtered, shielding his face with his claws.

With the moon still high above, Max raised his paws and slammed them into the snow. McCready yelped as gravity crushed him down. A crack split the air, and Max realized with a lurch that his gravity hadn't only affected

McCready. The earth shook as an avalanche of snow came loose from the hill above.

Max ran, leaping through the snow until he was beside Tommy and Luna. The mouth of a cave loomed ahead. *"Inside!"* Max commanded, and the kids made a dash for the cave, Max squeezing inside after them.

McCready's roar of fury pursued them, but it was muffled as snow sealed the entrance. Max didn't care if they were trapped inside, not right now. All that mattered was that there was something between him and the kids and McCready.

"How did you do this?" Tommy panted.

Max shifted to a man and leaned against the wall. "I'm sort of a demigod."

Tommy snorted. "Cool."

Luna huddled next to Max, shaking. "What do we do now? How are we going to get back home?"

Max hugged his knees to his chest. "Once we find a way out of this cave, I'll try to open a way back." Maybe they could leave McCready here to rot in the mountains.

"What if you can't?" Tommy asked.

"We're all alone," Luna whimpered.

Shaking his head, Max said, "No. We're not. I have a family here somewhere. They'll help me."

He hoped so anyway.

The wind howled, impossibly loud in the desolation of the mountains. Max shifted back and curled onto his side, wrapping himself around Luna and making sure she was nestled into his fur. Tommy and Luna assumed their wolf forms, needing the extra layer of fur for warmth.

Max closed his eyes tight and prayed that once the storm was gone, he could take them home.

GABE RAN FASTER THAN he had in his life, crying out to Max through their bond. The blinding light of the portal obscured the surrounding woods. "Max!" he shouted, but he was too far away to catch up to them and join them in the realm beyond. Max and the kids ran into the portal, silhouetted against the light. And McCready leaped in after them. The portal sealed shut behind them.

Gabe couldn't describe the despair that washed over him when the bonds flickered and faded. Tommy's. Luna's. Max's. Gone, quicker than Gabe could blink, leaving only an empty chasm in his chest where his family should have been. His knees shook and he collapsed. He hadn't been prepared for the finality of it, for how quickly they would just disappear. Would he see them again?

He squeezed his hands into fists. He'd let McCready go after them.

Now there was a monster pursuing his family, and he couldn't do anything about it. They were gone, vanished into a realm he couldn't reach no matter how far or fast he ran. He was helpless again, just like when he was a boy underneath Stone's knife. But it was his family under the knife now. His mate. His pups. And he couldn't help them.

A hand fell on his shoulder.

"Gabe." It was Ben's voice. His eyes had lost their feral glow now that McCready was gone. He stood beside Gabe, human, his cuts healing before Gabe's eyes. "I'm sorry. There's nothing you can do."

He didn't want to go anywhere and shook off Ben's hand. He had to wait here for them. He had to be here when they returned, whether that was in an hour, a week, or a month from now.

"Gabriel!" Izzie panted. "You're hurt. We need to get you back to the car. Come on now."

Both Ben and Izzie lifted him to his feet and urged him up the hill toward the road.

Kendra ran to them wrapped in her shawl. "Where is he? Where's Max? I can't feel him anymore. What happened?" Her voice was hysterical with fear.

Ben gripped her shoulders. "He and the kids are gone. They went to the She-Wolf's realm."

Kendra's face went through a flurry of emotions. Relief. Confusion. Sorrow. Fear. "McCready?"

Ben swallowed visibly. "He may have followed them."

She put her hand over her mouth. "What can we do? There must be something we can do!"

Ben held her fast by the shoulders. "They're gone, Kendra."

She was speechless.

"All we can do now is return to what's left of the agency and take care of the ones who are still here."

Anger rose in Gabe. Ben sounded as if Max was gone forever, never to return.

"He's coming back," Gabe said, balling his hands into fists at his sides.

Nodding, Ben furrowed his brows in that uncertain way of his. "I know." He squeezed Gabe's shoulder. "Come on. We need to get back to the city."

Gabe looked back toward the woods. What if Max came back with Tommy and Luna?

Tears pricked his eyes, but he blinked hard against them. Max wouldn't want him falling apart. He had to trust that if—*when*—Max returned, he would come home to Gabe.

Max had to come home. The kids too. Gabe couldn't go through life without them.

They waited an hour for a tow truck to arrive and help them get back to civilization. While they waited, Ben got in touch with Manuel back home and put him on speakerphone.

When Gabe heard his father's voice, tears burned his eyes, and he couldn't speak from the emotions that overwhelmed him.

"We're all right," Manuel said, tired but alive. "I calmed the Yellowstone wolves who survived the fight. They're locked up and awaiting transportation back to the park for now."

Izzie wiped her eyes. "Everyone's okay? Really?"

"Yes. Zach and Ry. Eddie got a bit beat up, but Vicenzo's keeping a watchful eye on him." Manuel's voice cracked when he said, "I can't wait to see you all again."

All of them, except Max and the kids. The joy at hearing his father's voice turned to ash in Gabe's chest.

The tow truck arrived, and police helped drive them to the nearest town. Kendra's old car was beyond repair. While she went in search of a rental, Gabe and the others collapsed into a booth at a diner. Gabe had never been less hungry. All he cared about was Max and the kids, who were farther away from him than they'd ever been, with McCready hounding them.

"Here. Drink this." Ben pushed a mug of coffee that smelled like alcohol under Gabe's nose. "Not peanut butter whiskey, but it'll do."

Gabe took a gulp of the cocktail, and the buzz went straight through his empty stomach.

Ben squeezed his hand, massaging some warmth into Gabe's fingers.

He squeezed back. "I'm so fucking glad to see you, Viejo." A lump rose in his throat, and Ben's eyes looked misty from where Gabe was sitting. He tugged Gabe close so he could bump their foreheads together.

"Me too, kid."

Izzie returned from the bathroom and sat next to Kendra, who was gazing blankly at the menu, her eyes glassy. His sister put an arm around her.

"How are you feeling?" Izzie eyed Ben anxiously. "Feel like taking a bite out of my butt again?"

He flinched. "I'm so sorry. McCready made me track you through our pack bonds."

"We couldn't feel you," Gabe said. "Not until you got really close. Even then, your bond felt... wrong. Twisted. None of us recognized it."

A shiver ran through Ben, and he closed his eyes tight. "It's all my fault. Max is gone because of me. Those poor kids..." Ben's voice broke, and he wiped his eyes.

Gabe gripped his arm. "No. It's the fucking asshole McCready's fault."

Ben set his lips in a thin line and nodded. "Damn straight."

"He shows his face again, I'll rip out his throat!" Gabe's claws cut into the table, and his fangs poked into his lower lip.

"Gabe," Izzie hissed. "You're wolfing out!"

People were staring.

Gabe's heart stuttered. He raised a hand to his mouth, feeling the points of his fangs. "Fuck." He couldn't feel Max or the kids. His wolf was going crazy, the vibrations of a growl building in his throat. His wolf wanted to burst from his skin and hunt. Find his mate. Find his pups. Kill anyone who dared take them from him again.

"Gabe. Easy." Ben's low voice couldn't reassure him.

He blinked fast and forced his claws to retract. They wouldn't.

Ben waved their server over. "Let's eat and get you back to the agency. Being around the rest of the pack will soothe your wolf."

Perhaps, for a time. Gabe kept his hands in his lap to conceal his claws. His breath rumbled in his chest, and his fangs were sharp points in his mouth.

Losing his family was wreaking havoc on his control.

The sooner they got home, the better.

KENDRA DROVE THEM THROUGH Fire Island toward HQ. Leaning out the window, Gabe watched and waited. He had no idea what to expect. Ben had told him there'd been damage but that the manor was still standing. He was afraid of what awaited them.

They rounded the corner and the familiar iron gates opened at their approach. Dried blood spattered the courtyard. Plants had been ripped up. The bodies of wolves lay broken and bloody everywhere he looked. Gabe recognized some of them as Agency wolves.

"So many were hurt." Izzie whispered.

Gabe had never seen the manor so quiet. Usually, it bustled with activity. No ferals howled from the kennels. No one roamed the halls. Even the aroma of food seemed muted compared to the smell of blood that hung in the air.

Ben led them through the clinic. The moans and groans, whines and whimpers of the patients filled the space. Nurses hurried up and down the halls. Doctors jogged from one room to another.

"Were there many casualties?" Gabe asked.

Ben hung his head. "I'm sure Manuel and Veronica saved who they could. I don't remember much of the fight before McCready controlled me." He led the way to a door at the end of the corridor. Familiar scents lit up Gabe's senses, warm threads coming to life in his chest. Gabe howled, and the pack answered from beyond the door.

He'd barely stepped into the room when his father and mother threw themselves into his arms. "Gabe, Izzie!" Manuel cried. Veronica kissed both his cheeks, then rushed to embrace Izzie.

"There's my boy!" Ryan hurled himself upon Gabe, wrapping his arms and legs around Gabe's upper body. Gabe squawked and fell, but Zach caught him, hugging him close.

"Guys," Gabe croaked, hardly able to believe it.

"Let him go, Ry. You're choking him," Zach said, wiping tears of joy from his eyes.

"I'm never letting you outta my sight!" Ryan pressed his forehead to Gabe's, tears clinging to his lashes. "I'm gonna be stuck to you like fucking herpes, mark my words!"

"Hey, y'all," said a voice with a Southern accent, weak but pleased. Eddie lay in bed, bandages wrapped around various parts of his body.

"Shit, man. You look like... shit," Gabe said, laughing and clasping Eddie's hand gingerly. "You didn't lose your head when McCready came."

Eddie smiled, squinting at him through a black eye. "Yup. Silver collar has its perks, but I wasn't much good against a hundred feral wolves."

"It was insane!" Ryan exclaimed.

Zach sank into a chair with a groan. "McCready got in our heads. Without Manuel, we all would have ripped each other to pieces. He howled, and all that feral rage just... went away. Ben, where did you go? We couldn't find you anywhere after McCready ran off."

Ben shook his head. "I need a fucking cellar of booze before I can get into that story again."

"Where's Max?" Zach asked.

Gabe opened his mouth but found himself at a loss for words.

Izzie put her arm around Kendra.

Before they could answer, the door banged open and Gabe whirled around.

Vicenzo marched in armed with a tray. With his lips set in a thin line and his eyes narrowed, he walked stiffly to Eddie's bedside and slammed the tray down next to his bed. Eddie blinked. "Uh. What is this?"

"Soup," Vicenzo stated. "Drink it."

Eddie's lips parted in surprise. He sat up, wincing. "You... made soup? For me?"

"Yes," Vicenzo said through gritted teeth. His cheeks were bright red even through his tan.

Ryan covered his mouth to hide his grin.

"So you can get better." Vicenzo crossed his arms over his chest and looked at something on the wall over Eddie's head. "And next time, don't come at a pack of feral wolves with that toy crossbow of yours! You can't shift. You should have been on the defensive."

"I was saving you, stupid," Eddie retorted, his face reddening in indignation. "Your earbuds came out and you went all feral; I had to carry your furry ass away from the horde of werewolves trying to eat you."

"I only went bonkers because I was trying to keep a certain wolf who can't shift from getting his throat torn out!" Vicenzo snapped.

Ryan began snorting with laughter. Gabe's mouth twitched at the mental image of Eddie carrying a wolfed-out Vicenzo over his shoulder.

"It sounds like you boys saved each other," Kendra mused innocently.

Eddie flushed and picked up his soup. He took a sip. "Wow. That's good, Vico."

"Whatever." Vicenzo gritted his teeth and looked away with a scowl. "Just heal up, would you? Or I'll have to save your ass again if McCready comes back." He frowned, glancing at Gabe through narrow blue eyes. "*Is* McCready coming back?"

Gabe opened his mouth and shut it, hopelessness clawing at him. He didn't know if McCready would return. Or if he'd ever see Max and the kids again.

Izzie said softly, "Max took the kids into the hunting grounds. McCready, he followed."

Zach's eyes widened.

"Shit," Ryan whispered, looking at Gabe in understanding. "But they'll come back, right? They have to!"

Gabe closed his eyes tight, and his claws punctured his palms. His wolf panted beneath his skin.

Manuel gripped his shoulders. "Let's get you back upstate, Gabriel. You should be somewhere that smells like your mate right now."

Exhausted, Gabe said goodbye to the others, wished Ed a speedy recovery, which was likely since Vicenzo was staying near the estate, and let his mother and father take him home.

WHEN MAX WOKE UP, the roaring of the wind had died down to silence. Tommy and Luna were awake and getting dressed with the clothes they'd discarded before they shifted. Max rummaged in his pack and changed into his sweater and jeans. It was time to figure out a way out of the hunting grounds.

"I think he's gone," Tommy whispered. "I don't hear him anymore."

"Maybe," Max said, tugging on his boots. "Knowing him, he's trying to find a way around to reach us." He was tense with the knowledge that

McCready would never give up on trying to find them. "Come on. Let's find a way out. I can feel a draft." Once they were out, he wanted to open a way back. If he were by himself and McCready weren't hunting them, he might have gone in search of the She-Wolf for answers, but he couldn't think about what he wanted.

Max held Luna's hand and Tommy followed him deeper into the cave. The draft got stronger, and Max breathed in deeply, chasing the scent of cold, fresh air.

"I can see light!" Tommy said, but Max grabbed the boy before he could lurch ahead.

"Let me go first," Max said, lowering his voice.

The rays of light grew brighter. Max made the kids wait behind a boulder and forged on ahead. He couldn't smell McCready, but he needed to play it safe. He stuck his head out into the open. They'd crossed the mountains through the cave. The mountain trail sloped into a valley of vibrant greenery.

"Okay," Max called. "You can come on out."

"Wow!" Luna exclaimed. "We're so high up."

Tommy gawked, taking in the view. "Look at the moon."

The moon hung low in the sky, bigger and brighter than Max had ever seen it. Without city lights, there was nothing to block out all the stars that blanketed the indigo sky. Green and purple auroras swirled overhead. Below the mountain range was a sprawling green valley with rolling, tree-covered hills for miles and bright blue rivers flowing from the mountains.

All the despair he'd warred with overnight was dispersing like a stormy cloud bank. There was hope yet, so long as he was strong enough to persist, and he would be strong—for his kids and for his mate a whole world away, waiting for him to come home.

I'll come home, Gabe. I promise you. We'll see each other again.

"Can you try to open one of those portal things?" Tommy asked.

"I can," Max said. "I can't imagine I'll have any trouble with the moon so close."

Luna gazed up at him, her hands bunched. "Do it, do it!"

Max cleared his throat. He cupped his hands to his mouth and howled until he ran out of breath. Tommy looked every which way, and Luna looked ready to burst with anticipation.

Nothing happened.

Frustration made Max's cheeks flush. The moon was out, and he howled. Was there some sort of parameter he was missing? He undressed and shifted to his wolf. Taking in another big breath, he howled again, wincing when his voice cracked. Nothing happened. "What am I doing wrong?" he muttered after he'd shifted back.

"What did you do last time?" Tommy asked, pacing.

Max shrugged into his sweater. "I was really desperate. Maybe that has to be a factor?" He knew jack shit about portals.

"So we're stuck here?" Luna slapped her little arms to her sides.

Max shook his head and forced his frustration away. He had to be the optimistic one for the kids. "No. We'll find a way. I..." An idea came to him. "I think I know someone who may be able to help us get home."

Luna rolled her eyes. "We're totally stuck here."

Max knelt and touched her shoulders. "Hey. Number one, you're *way* too young to roll your eyes at me. Okay? Number two, I promise I'll help us get home to Gabe and the pack. Okay?"

Her lip quivered. "You swear?"

Max touched his forehead to hers and let his promise surge through their bond. She gasped, then closed her eyes and smiled. "I promise," Max said.

She hugged him, and he scooped her up and gazed into the valley below.

They might be stuck here but in the meantime a voice was calling out from within. Somewhere in that sprawling green valley, Amaris was waiting for him, and whether or not she wanted him, he was coming for her. He only hoped she wouldn't turn him and his kids away. The answers to all his questions could be within reach, and he was as excited as he was trembling with nerves.

Whether he truly had been unwanted or left on Earth for some other reason, he would know soon enough. Even if his worst fears were confirmed, knowing wouldn't break him. He had a pack in another realm awaiting his return and as soon as he could, he would run to them and hell itself wouldn't be able to stand in his way.

CHAPTER 17

YOU CAN STILL BE STRONG

THE MOON GLOWED BRIGHT, never waxing or waning. The sun never rose, and it was dark at all hours, making it impossible to tell how long they'd been in this land of eternal night. Max wondered if time in this realm even existed. The thought scared him. What if he returned to Gabe and discovered that twelve years had passed? He decided he'd rather not think about that possibility.

They'd left the mountains behind some time ago and Max had never been so relieved. Their pace was slow since the kids were hungry and tired easily. Max's own belly was cramping but as a full-grown wolf, he could go longer without food. Fortunately, there were plenty of rivers to fish from. Luna didn't like the smell of fish, but she was hungry enough that she ate plenty anyway.

The valley itself was lush and vibrant with the occasional cool breeze to keep things from getting too warm. He couldn't tell what season it was. Up in the mountains it was as cold as the harshest winter, but in the valley it was green like summer. This world looked like his, but it was different. Were there summers and winters, or was this realm untouched by the seasons, frozen in time?

Max was in awe of the sky; it was easy to forget his worries and just look up at the stars. The moon was so close, dominating the night sky and illuminating the land in silver moonlight. He couldn't see Earth. He didn't know in what pocket of the universe this realm dwelled or if it was visible among the galaxies through a telescope. It was easy to feel alone.

We've never been so far apart, love.

Max felt Gabe's absence in every ache of his heart.

The silence was broken as somewhere far away, wolves howled to the moon. Max sat up, both hopeful and unnerved. There was a pack nearby. A roar answered them, one that filled Max with dread.

Luna woke with a gasp.

Tommy bolted up, his eyes briefly flashing yellow. "He's close. I can feel him."

That roar sounded like McCready's savage voice. The wolves howled again and this time something about their voices was unhinged and aggressive. They sounded as feral as one could get. McCready had brought a pack under his control.

Tired as he was, there was no time to sit around. Max knew he had to move. Grabbing the kids' hands, Max urged them to move and fast. The howls of the pack grew louder, pursuing them deeper into the hunting grounds.

GABE DREAMED HE WAS running through impenetrable darkness. Screams and howls still haunted him as in the dream, he fought his way through werewolves, following Max's voice. *"Hurry!"* he told himself, but his legs couldn't run fast enough. A bright light blinded him as Max's silhouette approached the portal. Gabe couldn't reach him; he was running as slowly as if his legs were trapped in quicksand. Only then did he realize his legs had been chewed off below the knee. He turned and encountered the eyes of a familiar beast gnawing on the bone of his leg. Familiar, because the wolf was Gabe.

"You'll never reach him in time. Give in to me. You're weak. I'm strong. I can help him."

But Gabe was too afraid to give in. He feared if he did, he'd never come back. There had to be something left of him for Max to love when he returned.

"Stop fighting me!" Pain tore into his leg as the bone cracked and snapped under powerful jaws. The wolf tugged him close, standing over him with blood raining down from his snout to spatter Gabe's face. *"Surrender to me. Only I can help him. Let me out."*

When Gabe opened his eyes, he lay in an empty bedroom he vaguely recognized as his own. His gaze flitted around the room that blurred in and out of focus. Max's scent hung heavy in the air and in a moment of wakeful forgetfulness, Gabe felt for Max's side of the bed and encountered cold, empty space. He sat up, looking around fruitlessly to catch sight of his mate. The silence of the room mocked him.

They'd disappeared so quickly, as if they'd never been part of this world to begin with, leaving behind painful reminders of their existence. His claws dug into the bed, shredding the sheets. As if sensing his despair, the animal wanted to come out while he was too weak to stop it, just like it had done whenever he was desperate and scared, a predator circling prey as it kicked and thrashed in the throes of death.

No. No. I'm in control! I'm—

His fangs lengthened as hoarse pants tore from his throat. He couldn't cave. He wouldn't forgive himself if Max fought his way back to him only to be reunited with an empty shell. He needed to be there for the kids when they came home. If they—

The spur of doubt left him wide open, a soldier in the enemy's line of fire who was blinded by a smoke grenade. Fur sprouted on his arms, his fangs snapped, and his claws pierced the mattress. Something between a howl and a scream tore from his throat. He drove his claws into his side, trying to fight off the invasion of his body.

The door banged open, and the smells of other wolves made him snarl, his fangs bared. "Get. Out," he said, seething. His voice was guttural. He didn't trust himself not to hurt anyone in this state. Rolling over, he bit down on his pillow, getting a mouthful of feathers.

"Gabriel!" His mother's voice was frayed. "It's all right. Everything's going to be okay!"

Fury tore a snarl from him. His hands turned to paws. The smells of the pack accosted him. This was his den. His territory. They had no business being here. Whirling toward the intruders, the wolf's body quivered in fury and fear. Their faces were warped and distorted. If he didn't attack, they'd do it first. They'd outnumber him, overwhelm him. Kill him.

He sprang from the bed, charging toward them. The windows rattled with the force of a deafening roar. A beast came toward the wolf, shaking the floorboards with each step. Yellow eyes blazed as the beast towered over him. "Stand down." The commanding voice made his eardrums vibrate. The wolf's fury died. He could not oppose the demands of such a powerful beast, even if he wanted to. "You will not take my son from me. Stand down!" The roar of a berserker bowled over the wolf.

Two paws slammed onto the ground on either side of the wolf's head. He shuddered, his tail tucked and ears flat. As furious and scared as he was, he knew when he was outmatched. He wouldn't dare oppose such a king of beasts. The wolf rolled over with a growl, exposing his belly.

When Gabe's eyes opened, he was naked and lying on the floor. He couldn't remember how or why but bile had left a bitter taste in his mouth, and he couldn't stop shaking. "Gabriel!" His mother's trembling hands clasped his face. Tears glittered in her eyelashes.

"Mamá?" Why was she crying? What had he done? Arms flew around him, cradling his head to his mother's shoulder. She trembled, and Gabe put his arms around her. He didn't have to guess. He'd lost himself, like he had when he'd been a boy, his scars still healing from John Stone's knife and a hole in his heart where his father used to be.

Izzie gaped at him from the doorway, her eyes wide and distressed.

"You're burning up, mi sol. Go back to bed." Veronica helped him stand and brushed sweaty hair from his face as he stumbled back to bed. He collapsed, feeling like he was falling when he closed his eyes. A large rough hand settled on his forehead. His father stood over him wearing a smile that didn't mask his worry. Gabe hated that he'd put them through such a stressful ordeal.

"Sleep, Gabriel. Once you're better, I'm going to help you. I promise."

Gabe didn't know if there was any helping him. The wolf wanted out, and Gabe had never been able to stop him before. Not without Max. "Can't."

Manuel cupped his cheek. "I can. And I will. You think I didn't suffer? I wanted to die after I was torn away from you, Izzie, and your mother. There were days when I wanted to give in, to forget, when my beast spoke as loudly as my doubts. But I didn't. You are still in control. None of your pain defines you. You can still be strong. I will help you."

He clasped Gabe's hand and held tight. Gabe squeezed back, but he could hardly keep his eyes open. "Okay. But you have your work cut out for you, Papá…" He laughed softly, unable to stay awake. He breathed in the stale smell of Max on his pillowcase and let sleep take him.

CHAPTER 18

A WOMAN SO WILD

Wolves howled not far behind him. McCready was still in pursuit.

"Wake up." Max gently shook Tommy awake.

Tommy jumped, his eyes wide. "Is he here?"

Max shook his head. "Not yet, but we have to keep moving."

The boy nudged Luna. "Luna, we have to go."

His sister, leaves caught in her curls, whined in protest. Max hated to make her get up. They'd walked so much yesterday. "Can't," she croaked. "I'm hungry, and my legs hurt."

"I know," Tommy said. "Here, you can ride on my back."

Rubbing her eyes, Luna climbed onto his back piggyback style. She laid her head on his shoulder.

Max rose on aching legs, shivering when rain coursed down his body. His eyes were bleary with exhaustion, but he had to keep going. If the pack caught up to them, Max needed to be strong enough to protect the kids.

They hiked through the woods, Tommy grunting when he stopped to adjust Luna's position on his back. Through the trees, an odd noise made Max pause. It sounded like... throat singing? "Whoa. Stop." He thrust out a hand to make Tommy stop.

"Wh-what is that?" Tommy sniffed the air.

"I don't know." Max urged him behind a tree. "Stay put. I'm going to check it out."

"Max," Luna whimpered, but he offered her a smile he hoped was more reassuring than he felt.

Confused and unsettled, Max put his back against a tree and cautiously peeked out into a clearing ahead.

Despite the downpour, a sinewy figure stood under the deluge, her face upturned to the moon. Rain dripped off her leather ensemble. A curtain of sleek red hair tumbled down her back, flowing in the wind. Her milky skin was so fair it glowed in the dark. She chanted in a language he was unfamiliar with until he realized it was mostly just snarls and howls. Such animalistic sounds raised the hair on his arms.

The woman danced, jerking her body as if she were being electrocuted and making those unsettling snarls. It might have been funny if it weren't so eerie. She spun, drawing a circle in the dirt and scattering flowers over the marks. Still chanting, she lifted the limp body of a rabbit to the moon and tore out its throat with her teeth with a blood-curdling scream. Blood dribbled down her chin and smeared her mouth.

Max hid behind the tree, petrified. He'd never seen a woman so wild before. Gathering his courage, he lurched from behind the tree and froze, transfixed as the woman levitated, her hair flowing around her. She opened her arms and spun as weightlessly as if she were underwater.

She has the same powers as me!

"Wow," whispered a girl's voice.

Max jumped. "Kids," he hissed, annoyed when he realized they'd come up the hill behind him. "I told you to stay."

Tommy glowered at him. "What if she attacked you? Me and Luna can fight too."

"Yeah!" Luna sneezed.

The woman stopped chanting, startled out of her meditation. With a shriek, she fell onto her back in the mud.

In a flash, she was on her feet. Her eyes locked on to them before Max could hide, and they blazed with anger. "Who do you think you are? Interrupting my prayer! I should—" Suddenly, she fell silent, her eyes widening until they seemed as big as the moon above. The next thing Max knew, she had thrown her arms around him and crushed his head to her chest in a bone-breaking embrace.

Max screamed. Because what else could he do? The kids screamed with him and hid behind a tree. So much for having his back.

"Maxwell! You're here, you're here!" She squealed, shaking him in her arms like a rag doll until he was dizzy. "I've been waiting so long!"

"Let go! How do you know my name?" Max kicked and clawed himself free, dragging himself across the ground in his attempt to escape, but she pounced on his back.

"Get back here, silly wolf! Don't ruin this moment for me! Whoa! You smell amazing! So many smells!" She sniffed his neck, his underarms, then tried to sniff his groin. Max kicked her away and scrambled back until he collided with a tree, panting. She gasped, her hands over her mouth. "Oh, I'm so sorry! Is that not how you greet people where you're from?"

How did she know he was an outsider? "Not unless they wanna get arrested! Who are you?"

She looked hurt and pouted at him. "Seriously? I'm a red wolf. That isn't enough of a hint for you? I thought big brothers were supposed to be wiser."

Max's retort died in his throat, and he blinked, his mouth flapping wordlessly like a fish. "You're my...?" She had the same orange eyes, red mane, and a smattering of freckles.

She sat up, radiating energy. "Okay, let me help you out. Is your mother Amaris?"

Max nodded.

"Great!" She smiled so cheerfully, Max wouldn't have guessed he'd just watched her tear out a rabbit's throat with her teeth. "Oh, we're getting warmer! Is your father Mani?"

"I don't know who my real father is. My adoptive father was—"

"Brian, right?"

Max was floored. "How do you know what his name was?"

"All right," she went on, not giving Max time to adjust to the surprise, "so Amaris is my mother too, and she's only had one mate her entire life. Mani. So that would make you and me—siblings! Just from a different litter."

Max was silent, too stunned to speak. "Wow." His voice cracked. "My sister... You're a seer?"

She nodded, her bushy curls bouncing. "Yup! I know so much about you."

"That's not creepy at all," Max mumbled. "Wait. So you know who I am and that we were coming."

"Yup! You and the little ones." She waved at the tree they hid behind. "Come out, guys! I'm friendly, I promise."

Slowly, the kids came out of hiding. "Hi." Luna spoke from behind Tommy's legs.

"Hi, pups. What are your names?"

"I'm Luna. This is Tommy."

She smiled at them. "I hoped so much I'd meet you guys soon."

"Are your visions usually wrong?" Max asked.

"Not always," she responded. "I knew you would eventually come looking for Mother, but not when. My visions are never clear. That's why I leave the pack from time to time to do rituals. The rituals help me see more clearly into the future."

Max wet his lips, unsure if he wanted an answer. "Do you know a lot about me?"

She smiled and shook her head, scattering raindrops. "Just bits and pieces. I know that you've been through a lot. I've seen glimpses of your world and all its struggles between lycanthropes and humans. It's beautiful but harsh. I know you have a mate. He's very handsome from what I've glimpsed."

Max's mouth twitched. "He is."

"I want to hear all about your world! The sights, the smells—the food!" She did a little somersault in excitement, gliding easily through the air like a fairy without wings. "I know what your favorite is. Steak, and pieces of elk pressed between those fluffy mushrooms..." She sighed dreamily. "It all looks delicious."

"Mushrooms?" Max snorted. "That's bread."

"What's that?"

Max shrugged, at a loss. "I'll tell you later." He realized in all the commotion he hadn't learned her name. "Who are you?"

She slapped her forehead. "Ugh! Of course. I'm Thebe. Don't worry, Maxwell, I'll take you to meet her."

"Who?"

She looked back in disbelief, showing her fangs in a big grin. "Silly. Mother, of course!"

Max's heart soared. Perhaps a silver lining would come out of this after all. "You can call me Max."

She giggled. "All right. Max it is."

GABE'S FEVER BROKE OVERNIGHT. He woke drenched in sweat, but the dizziness and chills had finally subsided. He drew himself from bed and stopped as he nudged something with his foot—one of Luna's toys, a little stuffed wolf. Everything in this house reminded him of the kids and Max, a constant reminder of what he'd lost.

Drying his eyes, he forced himself out the door. The floorboards were cold under his feet, the house still and quiet. He shivered, tying his robe tighter. He hoped wherever Max was that he and the kids were warm. Downstairs, Manuel sat at the breakfast bar drinking a steaming mug of coffee.

"Feeling better?"

Gabe poured himself some coffee and shrugged. The mug warmed his fingers, and he took a few meager sips, careful not to burn his tongue.

The corners of Manuel's mouth turned up in a tentative smile. "Don't give up on Max yet. You know he's fighting to get back to you."

Gabe tried to smile but his lips felt heavy. He'd never doubted Max before, and he wasn't about to start now. "I know."

"Gabriel." His father's tone was serious. "We need to talk about what happened last night." He barely remembered anything from last night. That usually meant something bad. He squeezed the handle of his mug, hating that he'd caused trouble for everyone. "Do you often lose control like that?"

"Ever since Stone abducted me, I've had trouble controlling my wolf," Gabe responded. "I got real protective of Izzie to where I'd lose it if I thought anyone was a threat to her. I had nightmares about Stone, and I'd wake up in a terrified rage. It only got worse after I was separated from Max for a year while hunting Stone. After McCready took control of the Council, my wolf became restless again. It only happens if I'm feeling helpless or desperate. Like... like when Stone had me." Gabe exhaled shortly, realizing that he'd barely drawn a breath since he'd started speaking. The hand holding the mug trembled, and he quickly set the coffee down.

Manuel observed him without speaking, his expression carefully guarded, but tears glistened in his eyes. Gabe looked away fast, unsettled to see his father so emotional. "I blamed myself for a long time. About what happened to you." Gabe cleared his throat, fixating on the patterns in the marble countertop. His father sniffed and the scent of his guilt made Gabe's throat ache. "But I got over that, told myself I'd make you proud, and looked after our she-wolves for you."

Manuel huffed, blinking fast as he stared at his hands lying still against the countertop. "You took on so much responsibility. Mijo, I never wanted to leave our family."

"I know," Gabe interjected. "You didn't have a choice."

Manuel studied the countertop, his coffee forgotten. "So, based on what you're telling me, you became reliant on your wolf to ease your anxiety and self-doubt. Do you feel like you aren't strong enough unless you surrender to your inner beast? That unless you give in to him, you won't be able to protect those you love?"

"Yeah. Exactly." Gabe tipped his chin toward his chest. "And... and recently, I awoke my berserker gene."

His father looked up sharply, eyes wide. "When?"

"It happened in Vermont when I confronted Stone for the last time and again when I challenged McCready. The first time I was sort of in control, but the second time... I could have killed everyone around me."

Manuel frowned, gazing at him over his coffee. "Since then?"

"I've been taking sedatives. I had to. The shit I could do in that form..."

"I know. That power and rage can be terrifying. Those with the berserker gene lose all control when those they love are threatened or when they feel especially volatile. However, the only way to master your berserker gene is to stop running from it and face it head on. I can help you with that." He downed the last of his coffee with sudden vigor and offered Gabe a cheery smile. "Get dressed. We're going on a road trip." He jumped up, suddenly bursting with vim and vigor as he smacked Gabe's shoulder and jogged past.

"Where we headed?"

"Up into the mountains. I thought a nice camping trip would do us some good, so make sure you pack what you need."

He didn't have time to ask anything else before his father hurried up the stairs, humming in his excitement. Gabe laughed softly and gingerly drank his steaming coffee. He didn't know where they were going or how a road trip would help, but he certainly wouldn't say no to some fresh air among nature.

By the time Gabe was dressed, most of the pack was rousing. Veronica cooked up some bacon, and Izzie scrambled eggs. Gabe was grateful to have his family close by for support. They were all eagerly awaiting Max's return with him.

Kendra nursed a cup of tea on the patio. She was staying with Gabe and his family in case Max came home.

"Where to?" she asked, sizing up Gabe's backpack.

"A camping trip with Pops."

She breathed in deeply. "It's the perfect day for it." She had bags under her eyes and her hands fumbled with the tea mug. Sighing, she looked away.

"Wanna come with us? You look like you could use a bit of relaxation."

She smiled. "No, that's all right. I'd like to be close by. Just in case."

Gabe's chest tightened; butterflies fluttered through his stomach in anticipation. "Yeah. Just in case. I probably won't be gone long but if—if he comes back..."

"You'll be the second to know, right after me." She took his hand, her skin cold. "I know. Things are so uncertain right now." Gabe squeezed her hand tight, trying to hold himself together. She was already worried enough without dealing with his worries on top of hers. "But I believe he's safe, Gabe. He's gone to meet his mother and his birth family. They'll protect him and the kids, I know it."

Would Amaris truly protect Max after she'd abandoned him? He forced a smile on his face and tried to ignore his worries. "He better tell me everything when he gets back."

Manuel tossed his backpack in the back seat of his car. "Ready, mijo? Let's rock and roll."

Gabe gave his mother-in-law one final squeeze then hurried to join his father in the car.

The house disappeared among windswept farm country as they drove. Gabe rolled down the window and leaned his head out, enjoying the crisp breeze. The skies were clear and such a deep blue Gabe felt he could drown in it. For all that was wrong in the world right now, nature was untouched by its troubles, thriving with breathtaking beauty around him.

Manuel pulled over to park at the start of the hiking trail. They walked the trail, their boots clumping over leaves and sticks. Nothing could shatter the blissful quiet of the woods. Gabe breathed in deep and sighed in contentment. The air was so pure in the countryside he sometimes wondered how he could go back to the stink of the city, though to a wolf the city had its own engaging smells.

Manuel ventured off the path. Gabe followed, knowing their inner beasts would guide the way home. After walking for some time among the trees, Manuel dropped his backpack and helped himself to some water. Gabe brushed some ants off a log and sat, taking a deep gulp of water too.

His father reclined, his hands propped behind him, and turned his face upward to an ocean of blue sky. "What sets werewolves apart from beasts is the balance we walk between our animal and human nature. If we're too human, we lose that connection to our inner wolf, but if we're too reliant on our beast, then we risk losing ourselves. Gabriel, the only way you can move past this is if you find that balance within yourself."

"I don't know how."

Manuel's mouth twitched. "That's what I'm here to help you with."

"All right!" Gabe pushed himself up. "What are we gonna do?"

"First, we'll do some deep breathing. You need awareness, focus."

Gabe deflated. He'd thought maybe he'd have to punch a tree or something, work out all that wolfish energy. "Okay. What am I focusing on?"

"Sit down, preferably on a flat surface. I'll explain."

Gabe sat pretzel-legged on the soil and drummed his fingers on his knee.

"You need to show your wolf that you're in control. Confront him, challenge him and win."

Gabe wasn't sure he understood. "You mean literally? How's that possible?" The only time he'd ever been cornered by his inner wolf was after he'd believed Max had died. "I mean... it happened once before. I thought Max had died and it broke me. It's hard to explain what happened. The wolf was so close to the surface I could see him. He towered over me, tried to make me go feral. It was freaky."

Manuel's stare was knowing. "The wolf pulled you into your inner world. It's a place within us where both our human and animal spirits reside. I've glimpsed it in my despair."

"I thought I was hallucinating or something."

"No, it's a very real and frightening experience. But that sort of encounter is something shifter monks all over the world meditate each day to find within themselves. It's very possible for you to get there without succumbing to despair or fear. With constant practice and focus."

Gabe swallowed. "That'll take forever."

Manuel's lips quirked, and he hummed thoughtfully. "Maybe not. Berserkers have mastered that balance between wolf and man. All werewolves bow to their dominance; some will do it whether or not they're willing. You probably know by now that the howl of a berserker is difficult for any werewolf to refuse. Yours is likely no different. When's the last time you took your sedative?"

"Last Monday."

Manuel nodded thoughtfully. "We'll give it a few days for the sedative to leave your system. Then, I'll howl, and your wolf will respond to it. He'll surge to the surface."

"No way, Pops. Last time that happened, I lost my head. I turned on Max and made my friends hurt each other. I couldn't control myself!"

"That's why I'm here. If you lose control, I'll be here to ground you. This is a good chance for you to practice resisting your wolf."

Gabe shook his head. "Are you crazy?" He barked a laugh. "I can never be trusted in that form. I could hurt you!" That was just impossible. Without Max and the kids, his grip on his wolf was slipping by the day. If his family didn't come home soon, he imagined he'd go feral within a few weeks. "Maybe you should just leave me in the woods. I can't be fixed. After everything that's happened to me, I'm too broken." The shame curled his fingers.

Manuel grabbed his shoulders and shook lightly. "Mijo, you are not broken. Cracked, maybe, but never broken. Your struggles with control began after what that monster did to you. There's a place inside you that has never fully healed. We need to find the root of that pain, not hide from it. You need to find that boy who was taken away in the night, the boy who was hurt, and face him. You can be strong. You can put your demons to rest."

Hadn't he said something similar to Max long ago? He'd held Max tight and told him they'd vanquish their demons together, and Max had done it. No matter what shit life threw at him, Max rose above it. Gabe wanted to be strong like Max, worthy of being his equal.

Gabe sighed, still unsure but too stubborn to quit. "All right." He grinned. "You're on! But don't get mad at me if I lose my head and take a bite outta you."

Enough was damn well enough. He wanted to be better for Max and for his pups when they finally returned home to him.

CHAPTER 19

THE LAST PRECIOUS MEMORY

Training to master both his wolf and his humanity was much less interesting than Gabe had thought. His father instructed, "Sit on the ground. Take deep breaths in and out."

Gabe remained standing, a river gurgling behind him. "I thought we were training."

Manuel snorted. "If I attempt to control your wolf now, you won't be able to fight me off."

"Try me."

Manuel shook his head and shot him a stern look. "Do as I tell you. You need to find inner focus, and being among nature is a good place to start. Our wolves naturally feel right at home in the forest. He'll be close but not close enough. If you focus, you can sense him, and that focus may give you an edge over me."

"What sort of edge?" What would an edge do, make him hover off the ground like the monks from the Monastery of the Moon?

"Enough for you to control him."

"You make it sound easy," Gabe said. A thought occurred to him. "When did you first shift into your berserker form? Why didn't you use your abilities to kill Stone when you could?"

Manuel turned his face to the sky. "My great-great-grandfather had the gene. He was not a good man. Surely you've heard the stories in our family of a terrible beast who abused his kin and hunted innocent people." He shivered.

Gabe recalled his abuelo telling ghost stories about a huge bipedal beast with a hunger for blood. Those stories had given him nightmares.

"Sometimes I felt this intense rage inside me. If I was stressed or afraid. If anyone threatened my family. But nothing ever came of it, and I was relieved. I didn't want to be like my ancestor. After Stone shot me, my desperation to return home to all of you caused the gene to awaken. Shifting to a berserker saved my life, but without my family to ground me, I was unable to shift back for many, many years. I could only turn back when I was reunited with you in that well."

Gabe grimaced. "Will this even work? What if I can't assume that form again?"

With a juvenile roll of his eyes, Manuel patted the leaf-strewn soil. "Just humor your old man. We'll know in time."

"If I wanted to meditate, I'd have gone to a monastery," Gabe grumbled, plopping down on his ass.

Manuel chuckled. "If we had time, I would send you to one. But Max could return any day now, and McCready might follow. Even if they don't return as soon as we'd hoped, your control is slipping. We need to be ready for either scenario."

And so it began. Gabe closed his eyes and took deep breaths. It wasn't unpleasant, at least; the rich smell of soil and leaves combined with the sweet smell of grass was soothing. Contentment warmed him and he knew his inner beast was appeased by the natural surroundings. However, Gabe's mind kept wandering. Had Max found the She-Wolf by now? Were the kids okay? His stomach twisted into knots.

A stick rapped him on the head. "Ow!"

"Focus. Find a rhythm in your breathing and stay on course."

Gabe fought the urge to throw the stick across the clearing. "This isn't exactly thrilling. My mind—"

"—is wandering, I know. That's fine, but if you catch it wandering, focus on your breathing. Start again. Deep breaths in through the nose and out with the mouth." He demonstrated for emphasis, his hands upon his knees and his face to the sky. Gabe screwed his eyes shut and resisted the urge to grumble. He took in a slow, deep breath and released it. His father's voice came to him. "Be in the moment. Listen to the wind in the trees, the scents of the forest."

Gabe focused on his breathing and tried to "be in the moment" by noticing the smells. The wind carried the smell of the sweet flesh of a deer to his nose. A bird cried out among the trees and the wind whispered through the leaves. What kind of bird was that? A blue jay? A robin?

"Focus, Gabriel."

Gabe gritted his teeth. "Thought you told me to be in the moment."

"Balance, mijo. Find that balance."

Thirty minutes later, Gabe's toes twitched, and his mind was bouncing around like a monkey in a jungle. With a growl, he lurched to his feet and kicked a stone into a tree. "Why is it so hard to focus?"

"It takes time."

"We don't have time! McCready could come back any time now!"

Manuel sighed and Gabe winced, hoping he hadn't disappointed him. "Let's take a break. We can do some hunting, make camp."

GABE LAY BENEATH A blanket of stars that night. His father slept nearby but Gabe couldn't relax. The venison dinner was a lump in his stomach. His legs twitched restlessly, and he gave up on trying to sleep. He crawled out of his sleeping bag and sat on top of it, closed his eyes, and breathed in and out. His mind was calmer. He'd run off a lot of anxious energy during the hunt and he was tired, and his mind no longer felt like an unchained beast.

He opened his eyes and realized he'd fallen asleep during his breathing exercises. Golden rays of dawn shimmered through the trees, pooling warm on his skin. He stole away into the trees to take a quick leak and returned to focus on his breathing once more. In the early hours of the morning, even the forest was still asleep.

Silence rang in his ears and focusing was easier when his mind was still fogged from sleep. He lost track of time, letting his breath come and go and wrangling his mind back if it wandered. It was tedious and frustrating, but his determination kept him on track. He had to do this. For Max, for Luna and Tommy, and for himself, so he could give them his all and be strong for his pack.

So for the next week, he set aside time to breathe and focus. Some days were easier than others but he was noticing even minor changes, like the way his body was loose and relaxed afterward and that he felt calmer after having put aside time for himself. He wasn't there yet, but he was making progress.

"Sometimes when I close my eyes, I can see him. Yellow eyes winking at me in my mind, then they're gone," Gabe explained after dinner. The sun was setting on a scarlet-tinged horizon, staining the forest a bloody orange. "I'm breathing and suddenly, I hear him breathing too. Like he's right there next to me and I could reach out and touch him. Unless that's you pranking me."

Manuel pulled a strip of meat off a rabbit bone and chewed. "Good. That's very good."

Gabe drummed his fingers on his kneecap. He hadn't taken the sedative in his backpack for a week. "Can we give it a go?"

Manuel shrugged. "Sure. If you have trouble, there are other steps we can take. But we'll discuss those later."

Gabe set aside his bowl. "Let's do this."

"Hold your horses. First, do your breathing exercises. If you see him again, then we can give it a go."

Gabe worried he would be too excited to really focus. He sat and closed his eyes, trying to focus on his breathing. The minutes went by, and he struggled to keep from guessing how much time had passed and to keep from getting frustrated when he realized how long it was taking. Behind his eyelids, the forest darkened as the sun disappeared. Perhaps they wouldn't get around to their first attempt tonight, but there was always tomorrow, Gabe told himself bitterly. His chin drooped to his chest, and keeping his eyes closed had never been easier as sleep encroached.

His breath deepened, and then he realized someone was panting in his ear. There were no hot puffs of breath, but the sound was close. The breathing was deep and hoarse, a growl lurking just beneath the surface. The wolf was nearby. His fingers hadn't turned to claws, and he hadn't grown fangs, but his chest felt tight, heavy, as if something deep within were pressing its paws up against his insides.

"Papá." Gabe's voice was gravelly with a growl. Manuel stirred by the fire, in and out of sleep. His eyes widened and Gabe figured he must look strange with the beast so close to the surface yet under his command.

"This is promising," Manuel said, hurrying over.

Gabe laughed, the sound a bark.

"Can you feel him?"

"Yeah. Chest is tight. Feels hard to breathe. If I close my eyes, I can see him. Holy shit, I can hear him breathing."

"Keep him tethered, Gabriel. Don't let him take control." Manuel removed his clothes, and the change came over him. An enormous wolf with black fur towered over Gabe on two legs. The wolf said, "Get ready. Stay focused. Don't let him take the reins. Bind him. Imagine a cage or a heavy chain."

Gabe squeezed his fists together and tried to keep the wolf in his mind's eye. He imagined a cage with steel bars around the wolf. "Got it."

"Get ready."

Gabe had thought he was prepared but as the berserker's commanding howl reached into his soul, the restraints he'd built around his inner beast threatened to crack. His knees buckled; his hands flew over his ears. He gnashed his teeth. Fur sprouted on his arms; his fangs came out.

No! I'm in control! I'm in fucking control!

The wolf hurled itself against the iron bars of the cage, eyes blazing. *"Let me out. You will let me out. Without me you're weak. You need me!"*

No. I don't. You don't control me, you don't— The bars cracked and came loose. Gabe imagined a chain around the wolf's neck, hauling it to the ground. The links cracked and crumbled as the wolf snarled, *"Mine! You are mine!"*

One by one, the links fell away, and the beast charged, flying right at him. A snarl tore from the wolf's throat and the man in him was gone. The king of beasts towered over him, commanding strength and obedience, but the wolf would not be controlled. He bared his fangs, ready to fight, to kill.

"Let my son go, wolf." The berserker snarled. The roar drove a stake of terror through the wolf's heart. "You have no control over me! You will let my son go!" The beast bore down upon him, snarling, asserting raw power the wolf had no hope of matching. Against his will, his legs buckled, his tail tucked, and he bowed his head. He snarled his fury, but he couldn't hope to stand against such power.

Gabe's eyes flew open. His body was drenched in icy sweat. His arms and legs were heavy, and he struggled to stay conscious. The fire crackled nearby, chasing the chill from his skin. He didn't need to ask what had happened. Disappointment was like bile at the back of his throat. He slowly sat up, head throbbing. He struggled to catch his breath, too fatigued to move. Anger broke through the fog in his mind. He'd failed again. He wanted to fall back down and never get up.

"How do you feel?" Manuel stood across the fire, wide-eyed and nervous.

Gabe couldn't answer.

"For your first attempt, you did well. You fought hard. It's encouraging."

"My first attempt? That wasn't it? You made him submit!" Gabe hated the idea of going through that over and over again. "What is the point of this?"

Manuel tossed a stick into the fire. "You must be the one to make him submit. Not me. I'm here to bring you back when you lose control, but you can't be reliant on me. You must own him without my interference."

"I can't do this." Gabe slumped, his forehead to his knee. He felt so small beneath the towering trees, vulnerable to the wind's icy chill that seeped into his bones.

"You can." Manuel gripped his shoulder. "You fear him, don't you?"

Gabe swallowed. "Of course I do. I could hurt someone. Lose myself."

"That fear of yourself, of what you endured when you were a boy, is what's holding you back. A berserker cannot fear, not if he has something he needs to protect. You must accept him, Gabriel. Accept your scars. Your pain."

"Easier said than done."

"I know. But that is the only thing I can think of. Your determination to protect those you love is there, but you fear yourself. You're holding yourself to very high standards, but these things take time."

Gabe shook his head, blinking hard. "I haven't been in control of my wolf for years. Maybe I never will be."

His father didn't answer. Boots crunched over twigs and stones. Manuel touched his arm, tracing a long, pale scar. Stone's scar. "You've been through hell, mijo. No one would blame you for giving up. It's true, there are some scars that go too deep and maybe that's true in your case."

Gabe's throat ached. He hated that he'd let his father down, that he couldn't be as strong as he was. "Disappointed?" He blinked a tear from his eyes and wiped it away fast. He couldn't look his father in the eyes.

"No. I only wish I'd been able to protect you from so much hurt." His father's voice broke, and Gabe didn't have to look at him to know he was wrestling with his own emotions.

"Would it be all right if I was broken? If I was weak?" Gabe wished he hadn't asked. He held his breath, scared to know the answer.

"I don't believe you are. I don't look at you and see the things you do. No one does. You've been through so much, but you're not broken. You had to pull yourself out of a dark place and you've got the scars to show for it. You're stronger than you think you are."

Gabe swallowed, drawing his knees to his chest. He wanted to shy away from his father's touch, tender and reassuring against his hair. He felt undeserving of it.

"But if you want to give up, then that changes nothing. You're my son, and I'll accept all of you."

Gabe couldn't speak, willing himself to keep it together as his father held on tight to his shoulder. For a time neither of them spoke. Gabe watched the firelight dance against the trees, the shadows weaving to and fro.

"I'm sure your mother's already told you," Manuel said, his voice slightly hoarse. "But it needs repeating. Nothing that happened that day was your fault. I made the choice to die for you, and I would do it again for all of you."

He remembered how scared he'd been when McCready had come for Luna and Tommy. He would have given his life for theirs without question. The only fear he'd felt was for them. Not even the thought of dying had frightened him. All that mattered was that Luna and Tommy were safe.

"Do you want to go home, Gabe?"

He wiped his eyes, unsure how to answer. He didn't know that he could ever control his wolf and become the berserker his father was. It still seemed impossible, but the thought of giving up was harder. "No."

"Then there's something else we can try, but in the morning. Get some sleep. You'll need your strength."

G ABE'S STRENGTH HAD RETURNED overnight. His father was up and waiting for him by a brook a short walk away from the campsite.

"We going fishing?" Gabe asked. "Or are you gonna smack me with a trout if I act up?"

Manuel rumbled with laughter. "Actually, this brook reminded me of a place we used to visit. Do you remember Uncle Felix?"

"He owned a farm, right?" Gabe remembered the farm well and the little brook below a stone bridge he'd loved to go splashing in. "I loved that place. The smells of all the animals and hay, running in the woods with you and Ma." He smiled for the first time in days. "I remember I shifted and went running through the brook, then came tearing back into the house like a hurricane! I got mud everywhere and got water all over Felix. Ma was so embarrassed." He'd been crushed when Felix sold the farm.

"Hold on to those happy memories, mijo. All our happiest, most meaningful memories tie us to our humanity. That's why, when we're at our lowest or away from those we love, it's harder to keep the wolf under control. For all your suffering, you have so much to cherish."

Gabe smiled, his heart fluttering when he thought of the LPA and Max, Tommy, and Luna. "Yeah, I do." But he sensed a deeper meaning to his father's words. "Why are we here?"

Manuel stopped on the bank of the brook and dropped his pack in the soil. "I'm going to bring out your inner wolf again. You're going to fight him using a memory this time. The happiest, strongest memory you have. It should keep him from overpowering you, and you'll be able to take control."

Now that sounded easy. There were so many happy memories to choose from: the day Izzie was born, joining the LPA, the first time he'd smelled Max's scent, their first kiss, the moment Luna and Tommy became pack... "All right. Let's do this."

Once Manuel had shifted to a wolf, he stood on his two powerful hind legs, towering over Gabe. It was hard not to be intimidated. "Get ready," his father's baritone rumbled. "Think of the happiest memory you can and hold on to it tight. Visualizing helps too. Imagine the brook, the trees, what the weather was like. Live in that memory."

Gabe's heart raced and he closed his eyes, trying to recall that day on the farm. Warm summer sunlight, the trees lush and green, the water cool and crisp between his toes as he ran, chasing after a frog. A howl shook the treetops. The sun disappeared behind the clouds and left him shivering. The frogs had stopped croaking; the birds had fallen silent. The water became uncomfortably warm. Then the clear water ran red, staining his skin crimson. Leaves died and fell from the trees.

Shaking, Gabe turned upstream. The corpses of his mother and father lay twisted beneath the underpass of the bridge, flooding the water with their blood. He tried to scream but no words would come. Beneath the shadows of the bridge, furious yellow eyes blazed at him and bloody paws waded through the brook as the wolf came closer.

The black wolf ran, and Gabe tried to run but he couldn't go fast enough. Fangs pierced his back. He screamed, and then the scream was muffled as he fell beneath the water. It tasted like pennies as the wolf's paws held him under.

Gabe's eyes flew open, and he gasped for air, lying flat on his back on the forest floor. He exhaled his relief.

"What happened?" Manuel knelt by his side. "The wolf took over again."

"I tried"—Gabe panted—"to imagine the farm. But... it went so fucking wrong. There was blood in the water. The trees were dead."

"Shhh." His father's hand on his shoulder steadied him. "It wasn't real."

"Will he do it again?" Gabe felt sick with worry that the wolf would corrupt his happier memories with Max and the pack.

"He? Gabriel, this is your doing."

"No, it isn't," Gabe snapped. "I'm not traumatizing myself on purpose!"

"Whether or not you're aware of it, you are putting up internal defenses. Were you afraid just now?"

Gabe scoffed and flung up his hands. "I don't know! Maybe… maybe I was afraid I couldn't overpower him?"

"Then that's why the memory failed, because of your own self-doubt." Manuel extended a hand. "Come on. Get up. We'll take a break and try again later."

But later was no better. Gabe tried imagining the day he joined the LPA and went out to a big dinner with Ben and his family. Instead of celebrating with Ben and the others, the restaurant had been torn apart by a hurricane, and no matter how loud Gabe screamed, Ben wouldn't come for him. He'd been buried alive, and he woke up shaking. Manuel decided they'd better rest for the remainder of the day.

Gabe slept little. He thought of some of the happiest moments of his life, and his and Max's mating ceremony was high up there. But he was afraid the wolf would taint it.

"Don't hold back," Manuel said, helping Gabe to his feet after a third failed attempt. He'd imagined the day of Izzie's birth and still shuddered to recall the things he'd seen. "You can do this, mijo."

Gabe tried to set aside his fear and recalled his and Max's ceremony. The way he'd looked in that tux, the joyful smile on his face as they met beneath the floral arch. The moon high in the sky, glimmering on Central Park's great lake. But it wasn't strong enough. Max's skin turned deathly pale, and horror gripped his face. Gabe couldn't move a muscle, frozen, unable to scream as Richard came at Max with a knife, driving it through him while he could do nothing but watch.

"I can't do this anymore." Gabe rinsed his mouth in the brook, splashing his face to get rid of all the sweat. Bile was still bitter in his mouth.

"I know it's hard. You need to believe in yourself, as cheesy as that sounds." His father motioned for him to stand. "Well, you didn't transform these past few times. The memory was powerful enough to keep the wolf at bay. Let's keep trying."

He didn't know what he had left to give. He'd tried his and Max's first kiss. That had ended badly and still made him shudder. He'd thought of the day he met Zach, but that hadn't worked either. He got another idea, though he was aware of just how wrong this one could go, and he went ahead and tried it.

"Well," Manuel said, "you didn't shift that time either. But you look pale. What did you think of this time?"

"I'd... rather not say." He'd remembered the night he and Max had claimed each other as mates. Except they'd torn each other apart. He sighed, ready to call it quits.

"Try going farther back, maybe. To your childhood. Things like your first day of school, or—"

Gabe shook his head so hard he thought he'd rattle his brain around. "Most of my childhood memories turned pretty bitter after I thought you were dead." Gabe fell silent. There was one memory. It wasn't a happy memory, but...

But maybe that wasn't what he needed. Instead of hiding from his painful memories, perhaps all he needed was to let them in. Gabe exhaled. Oh, he was not looking forward to this.

"What are you thinking?" Manuel cocked a brow.

Gabe was sure this one would fail too, but he couldn't shake the idea from his head. "I wanna try again."

"Are you sure? We can rest."

"No. Let's try again. One more time for today."

Manuel nodded. "Very well."

The howl echoed through the forest. Gabe held on tight to the memory, remembering the rain on the windowpane, his soccer-patterned bedsheets, the stomachache from one too many of his mother's delicious tacos. His father's smile. His last smile.

Stone's hand around his mouth, cold and smelling of mud. The dark basement, littered with fallen bricks and dead insects. Blood trickling from countless cuts on his arms. A wolf stepped from the shadows. It morphed from Stone's black wolf to Gabe's and back again, over and over until it was distorted.

"Mommy and Daddy didn't want you anymore," the wolf said. "This is where they send little hybrid boys nobody wants anymore."

The wolf came for him, smelling of blood, and carrion breath blasted his face. Gabe wasn't paralyzed. He whirled and locked his arms around the wolf's neck. They struggled. Paws flew at Gabe's face, claws shredded his pajamas, and frothing jaws snapped at his neck.

He seized a brick and hurled it at the wolf's head. The wolf recoiled with a yelp and Gabe charged. His arms flew around the wolf as they fell, hurtling into a black abyss. The wolf thrashed and snapped but Gabe pinned the beast beneath him, panting. Gabe's strength waned. The struggle couldn't continue much longer—one of them would have to surrender. He clasped the wolf's flailing limb, feeling the raised skin rough with scar tissue, and his chest tightened. He wouldn't hurt the wolf. He was tired of being hurt by himself.

His arms went around the wolf's neck and held tight. They caught their breath, the wolf's body vibrating as he growled. "Weak. You're weak. You need me. Let me out." The wolf snarled in his ear.

Gabe expected a bite at any second, but he held the wolf close. "No. I'm not. What happened with Stone wasn't my fault. I was a kid. There was nothing I could have done. Nothing." The wolf growled in protest, breath hot against Gabe's neck. "I'm not weak. I'm not helpless. Not anymore."

He caressed the wolf's fur. The wolf's growl rumbled to silence. Gabe swallowed, pushing the words out before doubt could steal them away. "I'm sick of fighting with myself. I'm done with all the doubt and self-loathing. Tired of wondering if I'm strong enough to protect the ones I love." He buried his face in the beast's fur, running his fingers gently over scar tissue. "I am strong, and I'll get even stronger, but I can't do it alone."

The wolf wriggled free, his lips pulled back in a snarl. "Won't bow to you! Lose everything if you take control. Lose mate. Lose pups. Won't let you!" The wolf morphed into John Stone. "You're nothing! Weak, stupid half-breed! I am in control!" The wolf-Stone abomination grew before Gabe's eyes until it towered over Gabe's head. But Gabe wasn't afraid of this amalgamation of his doubts and fears. For all its fury, the wolf trembled with fear, its tail hiding between its legs.

"I'll never let anyone hurt me again, or my pack. Including myself." Gabe lunged, wrapping his fingers around the wolf's snout and tugging it close to stare into its wide, wild eyes. "I'm done being afraid. Do you hear me?" His voice echoed into the abyss. "I am in charge now! I'll tear down anything that threatens my pack!"

The wolf shrank before his fury. No. The wolf wasn't the one getting smaller. Gabe was the one growing, taller and taller. With a whine, the wolf hid its fangs, its ears flattened and head hung low. The wolf was like a frightened pup now. It flashed, morphing into a frightened boy covered in blood and back to a wolf again.

The boy whispered, "Pa died because of me. Because I was too weak. Because I let myself be taken away. It was my fault. All my fault." Tears streaked the boy's cheeks.

Gabe felt for him, felt for the frightened child that still lurked inside him burdened with scars. Pulling the shivering boy close, Gabe embraced him. "No, pup. No, it wasn't our fault. I'm sorry that you were hurt. I'm so sorry for all the pain and fear and heartbreak. But it's over. It's over."

He held the boy in the dark until the child stopped shaking. Gabe's arms fell to his sides and the child shifted. The wolf looked into Gabe's eyes. With no sound of protest, the wolf lay down and exposed its throat.

THE FIRE CRACKLED, AND smoke billowed toward the sky. "Did you think of anything in particular this time?" Manuel asked. Gabe hesitated, unsure of what to say. He took his time, chewing venison while he gathered his thoughts.

"You," he answered.

Manuel's brows quirked in surprise. "Really? What memory was this? Soccer practice? Those were always fun."

"That's the thing—it wasn't a happy memory. We had it wrong. I was trying to fight my wolf. Trying to overpower him. Beat him into submission. But that's not what I needed. I needed to forgive myself. Because I hadn't. Not even after we found you."

Manuel blinked fast, lips trembling. "And this sad memory helped?"

"Yeah. It was the last time I saw you before Stone took me away."

Manuel stared into the fire, a sad smile on his face. "I remember. You were so angry because Izzie wandered off, and you wanted to be a man, not a big brother."

"Yeah. But you came in and put some sense in my head. You told me a wolf protects his pack. Then you smiled and said good night. And that was the last time I saw you smile."

For so many years after his father's death, or what he'd thought had been his father's death, the last memory of his father's smile had been like a knife twisting around in his chest. Over time, the grief had faded to a scar, and reuniting with his father had mended the hole in his heart.

"That's a very sad memory," Manuel said softly. "For a long time, it hurt to remember that night."

The lump in his throat tried to silence Gabe, but he pushed on, his voice thick. "Yeah. It was for me too. But it was the last memory I had of you. It became so precious to me, even though it was painful. So that's what I thought of. I guess it worked."

He'd had to face down his most painful memory and he had found healing. He wasn't sure if it was enough to make him a powerful berserker, but he knew even before his father told him that Gabe hadn't shifted during the last encounter with his wolf. For the first time in his life, he was in control of his doubts and fears. That was all that mattered.

"Did you forgive yourself, Gabriel?"

Turning his face to the stars, Gabe exhaled easier than he had in years. "Yes. I did."

Manuel blinked, his eyes glistening. He clasped Gabe's shoulder and held tight, and nothing more needed to be said.

Chapter 20

A Song of Family

THE MOON LIT UP the night sky, so big and bright Max thought he could reach out and touch it.

Thebe roasted a rabbit over a fire nearby, humming lightly. Max still couldn't believe he had a sister. He wanted to know all about her, wanted to ask if she would like to come back with him to Earth. He would love for her to meet Gabe and Kendra, but he didn't want to alarm her.

She watched Luna and Tommy sleep. "Why would this McCready fellow want to hurt such sweet kids?"

Max's heart ached. "I don't think he wants to hurt them, but he doesn't have their best interests at heart. He's consumed with rage at the state of the world. He wants werewolves to be at the top, no matter the cost. You know, I think in his mind he's doing this for the greater good. He wants to protect werewolves from being hurt the way his family was hurt, but the way he's gone about it is... misguided, to put it mildly. And even then, he only cares about protecting full-blooded wolves."

"Sounds like a nice guy," Thebe chirped.

Max swallowed, suddenly eager to move on. "McCready pursued me, and he's already found a pack here and possessed them. You're sure Amaris will take us in, even knowing the danger?"

"Of course she will. We'll be there soon."

Max ripped up a handful of grass and exhaled to ease his nerves. "Do we have any more siblings?"

Thebe grinned, nodding. "A lot of them have already left to form their own packs. Mother and Father were trying to have another litter before I left. They should have been born by now. I've been meaning to go back and visit them."

"Did she ever mention me?" Max asked.

Thebe stared up at the moon, a smile playing on her lips. "Not really. I mean, she told me about you and that you were in another realm, but never why. I think whatever happened that separated you two was painful for her. But whenever I told her about any visions of my big brother on Earth, she'd look so relieved. Even though you two were far apart, she was thinking of you a lot."

Max smiled, warm from head to toe and so relieved. He couldn't wait to see her and finally understand why he'd been abandoned on Earth. Distant howls drove away any pleasant feelings. Thebe stood, looking to the north where they'd fled from the pack.

Luna yawned and stretched. "Grumpy wolf is on the move!"

Thebe said, "We better get going."

They set off at a brisk pace, and though Max longed to sleep, the adrenaline gave him the burst of energy he needed to keep moving. Thebe pointed east. "See there, between those two mountain peaks?" On the horizon were two mountain peaks, one taller than the other and close together. "They're called the Twin Fangs. My pack lives just below those mountains. It's a day away. We'll be there in no time."

The Twin Fangs loomed over the highlands, and the smell of other wolves hung thick in the air like fog. Fresh tracks marred the dusting of snow on the grass, stiff and frozen beneath the thin layer of frost. They were close now. Thebe stepped in front of him. "Let me take the lead. They know me. Wouldn't want you to take a bite in the butt. That would be an embarrassing way to meet your family."

His family. Max's heart soared. He was so close to meeting his birth family, so close to finally learning about a part of his history. Howls echoed over the frosty hilltops. The Twin Fangs pack had scented them on the breeze and were coming to investigate. Max's heart thundered in his chest. Their voices were so familiar. They could have been any wolves, but Max's heart knew them. Because he'd dreamed of them. He'd ached for them. He'd waited and wondered and feared and now, oh *now*, it was finally about to happen.

Max tipped back his head and answered the call. His voice shook and broke and he ran out of breath. He cupped his hands to his mouth and howled again. Though his voice was human, they'd undoubtedly recognize the call of a fellow wolf assuring them he'd come in peace and inviting them to meet, as if they were old friends who'd parted. He wasn't afraid. These were his people. His family.

And then one of them howled back. And this one… this wolf's song reached right into Max's heart. Warmth bloomed in his chest. The igniting of a bond, long since extinguished. Max's eyes were wet, and he shook fiercely but not from the bitter cold.

"Max, wait up!" Thebe called, but Max couldn't stop. He wouldn't, not now. His skin was itching. His heart wouldn't stop racing. He had to run. Now, now, *now!* He had to see. He had to meet them. He had to know their names, their scents, their stories, and hear their songs.

Would they accept him? Would they even know who he was? He hadn't realized he'd left Thebe and the kids some ways behind, his feet moving of their own accord, carrying him ever closer to the howls of his kinsmen. Despite the cold, he removed his clothes and left them lying in the dirt. His feet became paws, carrying him easily over misshapen and uneven ground.

The wind stung his eyes and numbed his throat but he howled nevertheless. He sang the song of his pack, of his family, until he was hoarse and breathless, his lungs heaving with each breath. His paws sprayed snow as he ran. He slipped, his claws scrabbling in the icy grass. He collapsed, panting on the hilltop. Shaking snow from his eyes, he looked to the woods, waiting, watching, and the world held its breath.

Then from the woods they appeared: red pelts as vibrant as flames lighting up the trees as they strode from the shadows, orange eyes glowing like torches. They walked as one, each step perfectly in sync. There were three of them, two small wolves with fiery pelts and a red wolf as big as a horse leading them, his fur tipped with silver and his face lined with battle scars.

"That's him," Thebe whispered, laying a hand on Max's fur. "That's Mani."

The patriarch of the pack, he carried himself regally, each step poised and deliberate. Then he met Max's stare and the humanity in those orange eyes stole his breath. There was warmth there, recognition, and so much surprise. Mani knew him, and Max knew Mani too.

Because he was Max's birth father, and Max would have known him anywhere from the song that flowed into his head and heart.

"Son. My son. By the Moon. My son is home. He's home!"

The relief, the joy in his father's song made Max's eyes burn. Deep in his chest, something woke up, beating in time with his heart. The bonds of family, long dormant, were coursing through him. Mani strode forward, his shoulders rippling, his nose stretched out as he sniffed at the air. Max wanted to leap to his side and sniff him, run and play with him like a pup, but he held himself back.

The old wolf tipped his head back and let out a deep, warbling cry that reached into Max's soul and filled him with joy. *"Answer it."* The deep, wizened voice of his father filled Max's mind. *"Match it with your voice, my son."* There was a tremor in this voice, so hopeful.

Max looked down at his paws, trying to summon the nerve. A paw print marked the snow at his feet, nearly hidden by frost. Max fitted his paw over the print, and it fit perfectly, not an inch out of place. These were his people, his family, and he belonged here. Max threw back his head to the skies and sang as his father had done, and Mani answered it with his own song.

Then Mani was running. His father was running to him, and Max could hold back no longer. They bounded to each other, circling and sniffing, a flurry of wagging tails. Mani's eyes gleamed with unshed tears when he reached out and bumped his nose to Max's forehead.

"Welcome home, my son."

The welcoming melody of the pack filled the sky, and they sang a song of family beneath the snow-peaked mountains.

WOLVES HOWLED WITHIN THE woods, their voices carried away by the wind that swept the sides of Manuel's vehicle. Other werewolves, Gabe thought, going for a late-night run in the woods and burning off all that wolf energy. The sky had darkened while he napped, and the lights of the town of Millbrook winked below the road. Gabe couldn't wait to be home. He desperately needed a bath and a shave after a week in the woods.

A part of him had been hopeful Max and the kids had returned, and his stomach had fluttered like a butterfly and spread ripples of excitement through him. Then he'd called home shortly before his nap and realized they hadn't returned, and the disappointment had eaten him alive. He didn't know how portals worked except what he'd read in fantasy books. For all he knew, maybe Max had returned... but twenty years in the future or in the past. Or across the country. Or—

"Chin up, mijo. They'll come home."

Gabe looked out the window at the dark woods silhouetted against a canvas of starry skies. The waiting was killing him. He needed to see Max now, pull him into his arms and never let him go, hear Luna laugh and see Tommy smile. *Damn.*

"I need to make a stop in town. Your mother wants milk." Manuel drove them through town and parked outside a convenience store, stifling a yawn. At this hour the only person in the parking lot was a homeless man begging for change outside the store as they entered. The aisles were mostly vacant of people as they walked. Manuel grabbed some milk, and Gabe's stomach ached with hunger, so he snatched a protein bar.

By the registers, a group of five guys milled around the coolers, browsing packs of beer. Gabe sniffed and caught the scent of wolves, soil, and leaves. These guys were so loud they hurt his ears, laughing and wrestling and baring their fangs at one another. They'd been for a run in the woods by the smell of them; they practically stank of rowdy wolf energy. Perhaps it was because he was too tired to match their energy, but they made Gabe uncomfortable. As they caught sight of him and his father, however, he found a new reason to worry.

Their mirth turned to hostility as they glared at Gabe and Manuel, and they all fell abruptly quiet except for one, a blond with a heavyset face and icy blue eyes. He tilted his head back arrogantly and showed his fangs. "Whoa. You mutts reek of humans. You're killing my buzz."

Gabe's jaw tightened. If he weren't so tired, he might have snapped back a retort. Manuel just smiled and dipped his head. "Evening." He walked around them toward the register. His father didn't falter, setting the milk down and offering the uncomfortable-looking cashier his card.

"Go back to Mexico!" the blond jeered, slathering the word Mexico with a stereotypical accent.

Gabe whipped around. "Maybe you should go back to the woods if you wanna act like an animal."

The boys cheered, their faces alive with cruel mirth. The blond's jaw worked, an arrogant sneer curling his lips.

"Gabriel, enough. Ignore them. They're stupid boys," his father muttered.

"No, they're racist, hybrid-hating assholes."

"True." Manuel chuckled.

"You say something, mutt?" The blond took a heavy step closer.

Manuel said, "No. Have a good night." He grabbed the milk and walked to the door.

Gabe stayed, too angry to move. His blood was roaring, and he was pissed. His mate and son and daughter were gone. He'd take any excuse to punch an asshole in the face. The blond lumbered closer, thumbs sticking out of his pockets as he rocked back on his heels. "You called me an animal like that's a bad thing. I'm more wolf than you hybrids will ever be." His packmates cackled, feeding off the fury tightening Gabe's fist.

"Gabe, let's go home!" Manuel called, his voice implying he wouldn't take no for an answer.

These assholes were bristling for a fight. Gabe took the high ground and turned toward the register.

"Good dog!" The blond's harsh voice drew laughter from his friends.

Gabe gnashed his teeth and threw the protein bar back in the box. "Can't believe you let assholes like that into this store," he said, marching past the employees, who didn't respond. The sliding doors opened with a *whoosh* and Gabe walked beneath the streetlamps toward the parking lot. He was so mad he hardly felt the night's chill on his skin. His father put the milk in the back seat.

"Pick your battles, Gabriel. They're not worth the trouble."

Gabe gritted his teeth. "I know."

His father's eyes narrowed. Gabe turned as five figures strode toward them, cast into shadow. They quickened their strides, their arms spread wide as their claws came out. "Get in the car, now." Manuel wrenched open the door. Gabe desperately wanted to have at it with them, but they were outnumbered and he didn't want his father getting hurt because of him. Hurrying around to the other side, he jumped in.

Mocking howls echoed through the parking lot as the boys broke into a run, sprinting toward the car. Manuel started the engine, and the car rocked as one boy hurled himself against the window, pounding it with his fist. His teeth flashed in a savage grin, his eyes wide with adrenaline. The boys surrounded the car, banging on the windows, hurling themselves against the doors, and rattling the handles. Hands pounded down on the roof.

Grimacing, Manuel stepped on the gas and swerved abruptly, knocking two of the boys off their feet. He took off toward the road and another boy rolled off the windshield and tumbled onto the asphalt, leaving scratch marks on the glass. Gabe exhaled, his heart pounding. He grinned. "That'll teach 'em."

A pale face leaned over the windshield, his fangs bared. Manuel panicked and lost control of the wheel. The ground sloped as they flew off the road and hurtled down a hill as brambles snapped under the wheels. Manuel braked just before they hit a tree and the front bumper touched the tree trunk. "Okay, mijo?"

Gabe nodded breathlessly, his heart rate going wild. Manuel tried to reverse and cursed. "Damn. There's something in the way. Stay here." Before Gabe could argue, Manuel slammed the door and ventured around to the back of the car. In the rearview mirror, five figures came running down the hill, briefly illuminated by a streetlamp. Gabe snarled, "Sons of bitches. Hey, Papi, watch out!" He lurched from the car and ran.

His father hoisted a small tree by its branches and pulled, trying to tug it out of the way. Gabe grabbed the tree trunk and tried to help as brambles rustled and the raucous voices grew closer. Snarls and snaps made Gabe whirl around as the wolves came charging out of the undergrowth, their eyes blazing and fangs bared. The wolves circled them, snarling and bloodthirsty and snapping at their ankles mockingly.

A gray wolf charged at Gabe, and though Gabe extended his claws, Manuel was seconds ahead of him. He hurled himself in front of Gabe and yelled as the wolf's jaws clamped around his arm and brought him to his knees. Gabe's blood ran cold and for a moment he felt helpless. He couldn't let his father be hurt again, not because of him. And from that resolve, something woke up inside him, something powerful that harnessed his fear into a storm of fury.

His clothes stretched and ripped as fur sprouted thick across his body and his fangs lengthened to sharp points. The wolves suddenly backed away, growling defensively. A roar tore from his throat, one only a beast could replicate. The wolf released his father's arm and stepped back. Gabe's arms swelled with power and when he stood, he was taller than the car, casting his shadow over the wolves.

Somewhere along the line, he'd shifted to a wolf, but this form was different. He still felt like himself, wild but in control, his fury a typhoon he could unleash whenever he wanted. He stood on two legs, towering over the wolves who backed away shaking, their tails between their legs. Not a single one could muster a sound.

Gabe spoke, vibrating the ground under his feet, his voice hardly more than a growl. "You puppies wanna fight a real wolf? No? Then how about you run home before someone gets hurt?"

Whimpering, the wolves turned and fled through the brambles and up to the road. Gabe saw them off with one final roar for good measure, flexing the muscles in his arms in pure euphoria. "Adios, amigos!" he hollered.

Man, this was awesome! He wanted to smash through some brick walls just to prove he could. Howling, he reached behind him and hurled the tree away from their car. He could stay in this form forever, but he was getting tired and wanted to go home. Like sinking into a warm bath, the change came over him and he shrank back to his regular height and muscle mass, his fur disappearing to leave his arms bare and pink.

"You okay, Papi?" Gabe asked, reaching over to check on his wound. His father was shaking, his eyes wide and mouth agape.

"Gabriel. You did it. You did it!" His father, grinning through the tears in his eyes, clasped his shoulders and shook him.

Gabe smiled at his excitement. "I know. It was amazing!"

"My son, a berserker from Norse legends! By Amaris, you did it!" His father wrestled him into a backbreaking hug. Gabe laughed and held him tight. He closed his eyes and sensed his wolf close to the surface, tired but content.

"Max has to come home," Gabe whispered, his throat thickening. He couldn't wait to show him the strides he'd made toward mastery of his inner wolf. He hoped he made his mate proud.

CHAPTER 21

NEVER UNWANTED

MAX PANTED CONTENTEDLY, BREATHLESS from running and playing with his siblings and Mani, his father. Luna and Tommy pranced around as wolves, chasing each other and Max's siblings. He'd finally met his father. The thought made his tail wag all over again.

Mani had appeared stern and imposing but like most wolves, he had the heart of a puppy inside. He took the lead, his head held high while his pups jumped and ran beside Max. Mani presented as a wolf, but Max smelled a human within him. His pups didn't appear to have learned how to take on a human form yet.

The pups weren't quite pups. They were nearly full grown and there were two of them—twins River and Anders. The two of them harassed their father.

"Pops, I'm hungry!" Anders butted his head into his father's shoulder. *"Give us some food!"* He licked at his father's mouth, trying to make him regurgitate food.

Mani snapped at them. *"No! Fool pups. You're old enough to catch your own prey!"*

River whined, his tail wagging playfully. *"That's too much work. Come on!"*

Their sister growled lowly. *"Idiots. Leave Dad alone."*

Mani growled too and they let up with the teasing. *"No good pups... Have to learn how to hunt for yourselves someday. Your mother spoils you."*

"Max, Max! Have you hunted?" River bounded up to Max and nipped at his face, tugging on his fur.

"Yeah. It takes some practice. I could teach you guys."

"Really? Yes! Can we hunt a bear? No! A musk ox!"

Anders pounced on his brother. *"You can't even catch your tail. How are you supposed to take down a musk ox, you big idiot?"*

Max wagged his tail. *"Maybe we'll start off with something small like a rabbit."* Max loved the idea of hunting with his siblings.

Mani sighed. *"Don't let them boss you around."*

"Where are we going?" Max bounded to keep pace with his father.

"To meet your mother, of course. She'll be so excited. For so long, we didn't believe we'd ever see you again. This is... such a surprise. We hope you'll decide to stay."

Thebe woofed and tilted her head. Mani's tail wagged and he gave her a lick. *"You too, Thebe. We've missed you. It's good to have you home."*

Max hesitated, looking down at his paws. He couldn't stay. His true home was in a whole other realm, and though he was overjoyed to meet his family, his heart ached to be reunited with Gabe and the others.

The air warmed and became dense with mist. An eggy smell permeated the air. Warm pools of water were scattered across the tundra, bubbling and steaming. Max gasped. *"A hot spring! I've heard of these! We have them on Earth too!"*

"Earth?" River cocked his head. *"What's that?"*

"It's where I'm from." Max bent his nose over the hot spring, and though he disliked the eggy odor, he enjoyed the warm moisture that steamed up his fur.

"What else do they have there?"

"Loads of stuff. Cities and towns where lots of people live. In the cities, there's food from all over the world."

River's eyes went wide. *"Food? What kind?"*

"Meat and vegetables, all made in different ways. Bread and sweets... uh, what else?"

"Sweets? What are they like?"

"They're sugary. Kind of like... honey. You guys have honey, right? You find it in beehives."

River licked his lips. *"That's what that golden stuff is? I love that stuff!"*

Anders grinned wolfishly. *"Oh, River knows all about honey, don't you? Got your face stung so many times, it got all swollen."*

"Shut up, it was worth it."

Max trotted to keep up with Mani, saying, *"You guys should come on a trip with me to Earth once you learn to take a human form. You'd love it."*

"Keep up, pups! Don't keep your mother waiting," Mani called. Yipping excitedly, Anders and River bounded ahead, pouncing and chasing each other.

Mani suddenly stopped. He shifted before Max's eyes to a wild-looking man with a broad, hairy chest and long braids tied back into a ponytail that ended around the middle of his muscular back. His scarred face was lined with age and streaked with a dusting of war paint, and his eyes were hard. Beneath a bushy beard flecked with silver, his thin mouth twitched into a smile. "Go on, enjoy the springs. Anders, call your mother."

Max shifted and shivered as the cold air nipped his skin. He dipped a toe in the warm water and sighed. "Kids, do you want to soak in the springs?"

"I'm tired." Luna yawned.

Thebe nudged the little girl, her tail wagging. *"Come on. I'll show you and your brother where the den is."*

His sister led the kids away and Mani trailed behind, ever watchful.

Max sat and the water came up to his waist, submerging him in blissful heat. Anders howled to call Amaris and Max's stomach fluttered as his heart raced. He hadn't thought about what he would say when he finally met Amaris. Would she be happy to see him? He hoped he didn't make an idiot of himself.

An answering howl echoed across the tundra. It was possibly the most beautiful sound Max had ever heard. The power and grace in that howl made him barely repress the urge to howl back, but his brothers didn't even try, howling along with abandon. He squeezed his fists and found his breath was stuck in his throat.

It was happening. He was about to meet his birth mother, about to finally understand the pieces of his past that had been unknown to him for so long. He wished Gabe were here to rub his shoulders and keep him calm, smiling that megawatt smile as he laughed at Max's nerves and assured him all would be well. So instead, he closed his eyes tight and exhaled and told *himself* all would be well. When he opened them, he gasped. The aurora borealis shimmered across the night sky, coloring the hot springs an emerald green as it danced and weaved.

The grass rustled behind him and when Max turned, she was there, bathed in the emerald lights of the aurora. She walked as if she were striding on air, a long red mane of glimmering hair drifting around her slender waist in the breeze. Her ivory skin seemed to glow, and she possessed an ethereal grace, otherworldly in her beauty and elegance. Her face was lined and wise with middle age, a dusting of silver in her hair like the first frost of winter. She wore the skins of a polar bear around her and for a moment Max was intimidated. Only an incredibly powerful wolf could bring down such a big beast.

Her eyes were like orbs of warm flame, the same shade of orange as his. As their eyes met, Max was at a loss for words. He stood, forgetting he was buck naked, his mind a blur as he tried to speak. Amaris's lips trembled, something between a laugh and a sob spilling from her lips. Tears glimmered in her eyelashes. Max blinked, realizing he was close to tears too.

"Son. Oh, my son," she whispered, her voice frayed with emotion. "You're home. I'm so happy you're home."

MAX SPENT THE REST of the evening with his family. Under Amaris's guidance, the pack hunted down a herd of musk ox. Max had never seen the beasts before; they were huge and covered in dense hair with sharp horns spiraling from their thick skulls. Amaris set her sights on the young ones grazing near their parents. River nipped playfully at Anders, but Amaris made them focus with a growl. The pack closed in on the herd and the oxen drew close, forming a circle around the young and vulnerable. Max hesitated under the steely black eyes of a lone male standing to defend his herd.

The pack worked together for an hour, tempting the ire of the ox by running in close and doubling back out of range of those horns when he charged. The herd panicked and ran, and Amaris spotted an opening. She threw back her head and howled, and a shock wave rippled over the tundra.

As if struck by a hurricane, the musk oxen flew off their hooves and tumbled over. Max charged in and grabbed a young ox by the neck. Anders and River tackled it while Amaris and Mani kept the other oxen at bay. Max tore out the young ox's throat and with a growl, Amaris urged his brothers away from the ox's dying thrashes. Elated but exhausted, Max dug in and ate with his pack.

His brothers bounded back to the den in high spirits. Thebe had stayed back to babysit the pups.

Amaris led the way to the pack den nestled among sprawling pine trees, her furs dragging over the grass. She offered Max some furs skinned from bears to wear since he was shivering.

Amaris went to sit beside a bundle on the cave ground. Nestled within the furs were four pups only a few weeks old. Amaris removed her furs so she could shift and lie among them. They nestled against her stomach to eat.

"Aww," Tommy whispered. "They are so cute. Can I touch them?"

Amaris rumbled approvingly. Tommy touched one pup, running his fingers over the short soft fur.

"So cute," Luna cooed. She gently petted a pup.

Mani smiled down at the pups, adoration softening his gruff features. Luna snuggled against Tommy and in a few minutes they fell asleep. Amaris joined them at the fire once she was done feeding the pups.

"I see you have pups of your own," Amaris remarked, gazing tenderly at the kids as they slept.

Max nodded, warming his hands by the fire.

Mani chuckled. "Don't be shy, boy. Talk to us."

He was afraid to meet Amaris's gaze. She was his mother, but she was also the She-Wolf, a goddess among his kind. "Uh, sure. What would you like to know?"

"Everything! What's your life like on Earth? What brought you here to us?"

"Okay... Well, I have a mate named Gabe. I'm friends with the agents of the Lycanthrope Protection Agency. We help protect werewolves against discrimination. My mother's name is Kendra."

"Kendra..." Amaris's eyes lit up in recognition. "I remember her. A kind woman with so much love in her heart, love for a child she could never have. Of all the families I saw in my visions, I knew she would be perfect for you."

"She is. She took me in since she couldn't have kids of her own." Max trailed off, wondering how to ask what he desperately wanted to know. When he glanced up, Amaris had looked away and was staring into the fire with a hard-to-read expression.

"You do a lot of fighting in the LPA?" Mani asked, his eyes alight with interest.

"Not really. Why?"

"You're covered in scars. Got the look of a fighter about you."

Max laughed. "No, I'm really not. My life... it wasn't always easy. My adoptive father left when I was a baby, so my mother raised me alone. She found another mate, a shifter named Richard. He wasn't a good person. He..." Not wanting to get into it or make Amaris regret her decision to leave him on Earth, Max wrapped his fingers around his wrist where one of his scars was, hiding it. "But I met Gabe and the LPA. They took me in, and it's been one big adventure after the other."

"Yeah? And what brought you here, to us?" Mani asked.

"Um..." Max couldn't help feeling unsettled when Amaris rose suddenly and left the cave to stand outside. She'd smelled distressed. "I'll tell you in a moment." He followed Amaris, wrapping the furs tightly around himself as the cold chased away the warmth of the den. She stood beneath the moonlight, her face upturned toward the night sky.

"Amaris?" He still hadn't decided if he should call her mother or not. "It's okay. Really. Life's so much better for me now. I wouldn't have changed a thing."

"No, I understand." She raised a hand to her face, and Max smelled the salt of her tears. "You carry so many scars. You've suffered so much, and I wasn't there. You must hate me terribly."

His heart lurched. Maybe he had once, but seeing how guilt-stricken she was had quickly erased the anger he'd once carried. He wanted to hear her out. "Why would you think that?"

Sighing, she walked the path to the hot springs. Mist warmed the air as they approached the pools. "I abandoned you. I should have been there to make it easier. I promise you, Max, if I thought you would have had an easier life here with me, I would never have left you on Earth."

"Why did you?" Max watched his tone carefully, hoping he didn't sound accusatory, because he wasn't angry. He just had to know.

Drying her eyes, Amaris faced him. "The winter of your birth was the harshest we've seen. Prey was scarce and packs invaded one another's territory looking for food. A pack invaded the den, smelling the prey Mani caught for me. I... I tried so hard to keep you all safe, but I had just given birth. I was too weak from labor."

Her voice became pinched with grief, and she had to fight to get the words out. "There were too many. They... t-trampled my pups. Crushed them, all of them, and by the time Mani arrived and drove them a-away, it was too..." She closed her eyes tight, her face streaked with tears. She took in a deep breath and continued, voice shaky, "I lost all of them except for you. I was so afraid, Max. My milk supply was drying up, and I knew if I didn't do something, you would freeze or starve."

"So you took me away. To Earth." Max's own voice was choked. He'd imagined so many reasons he'd been left on Earth; that he'd been unwanted had been the likeliest reason, and he'd been so afraid to know the truth.

"I knew I had to send you away, but I didn't know who I would leave you with. I let my visions guide me, each one showing families in need, but only one werewolf truly spoke to me. I sensed in her so much longing and sadness, so much love she couldn't give but wanted to. So I left you with her. You were my son. My only surviving child. I knew I had to, but giving you up was the hardest thing I've ever had to do." Her hand trembled as she clasped Max's own shaky hand.

"But I knew you'd be safe with her, and that was all that mattered. Things got better in the valley. Prey returned. The fighting stopped. I wanted to go back for you, but in my visions, you were happy with your mother. She loved you. It wouldn't have been fair to take you away from that. I made the choice to stop receiving visions of you so I could move on and let you be happy where you were. It was hard, Max, but I told myself again and again that it was for the best. I've thought about you every day since then. But you were happy." Her gentle fingers caressed his cheek, wiping away tears he didn't realize had fallen. "What's wrong?"

Max swallowed, trying to hold himself together. "I just worried. That maybe you didn't want me. Or..."

She laughed softly and cradled his face in her hands. She nuzzled her forehead to his. "You were never unwanted, Max. Never."

He quickly wiped away his tears, feeling as if he could breathe more easily now. "Can I ask you something?"

"Of course." They sat together in the grass beneath the rippling aurora borealis.

Max cleared his throat. "One night, I was abducted by a cult. They tried to sacrifice me. I was terrified, so I prayed to you and my lunar abilities... woke up."

Eyes wide in horror, Amaris shook her head. "*That's* why you called out to me? Oh, Max. I didn't know. All I knew was that you were trying to reach me. For all I knew, you had found out about your heritage and wanted to come home. Of course I answered when you called to me. But you never came."

Max wet his lips, his stomach clenching as he fought for the nerve to ask. "My stepfather tortured me. Tried to break me. Then, he tried to have me sacrificed. You really didn't know?" Had she known and not done anything? He wanted to give her the benefit of the doubt, but he had to know.

Ruddy brows furrowed. "No. I swear it to you. I had no idea you were suffering. Not until today." She wiped her eyes.

His shoulders loosened and when he smelled her tears, a wave of guilt washed over him.

"He knew I was different. That my red fur made me unique. He thought if he hurt me, he could open a path to you."

"If I'd known you were being hurt, Max, I would have broken every promise I'd made to myself to keep a distance. I would have brought you home."

It soothed him that she hadn't known about his suffering and sat idly by. "You know... Even if you had revealed yourself and offered to take me away, I wouldn't have gone."

"Really?"

Max nodded. "I couldn't have left my pack behind. I've suffered, sure. I've been hurt. But what I've gone through only strengthened the bonds with the family I found."

Sighing softly, she said, "It pains me that I cannot live up to your expectations of me. To your kind I am all-knowing but I assure you, I'm not perfect."

"Really?" Max couldn't shake the image of this woman as an all-knowing deity.

"Yes. I may be a goddess to your people, but Max, I'm not infallible. Or else I could have protected you and your siblings. All I could do was bless you with the strength you needed to survive your trials when you prayed to me and hope that was enough. Hope that, in time, you would find your way back home." She laughed, a hand to her mouth. "I know, this isn't your home, and I'm a stranger to you. I'd never ask you to choose us over your pack. But I want you to know..." Her hands trembled when she took his, but there was strength in her touch when she squeezed his hands. "You will always have a home here."

Max swallowed through a tight throat, gratitude blooming in his chest. "That's all I wanted since the moment I realized where I came from."

Now that his most pressing question had been answered, Max felt he could breathe more freely. In its absence, more questions stirred within him.

"So is it true what the people of Earth say?"

Amaris smiled. "What specifically?"

"That you nursed Remus and Romulus, that you wanted wolves and humans to live together as equals?"

Amaris let out a tinkling laugh. "Yes, yes, and the ordeal with the moonblade was quite true, though I imagine humans have exaggerated a bit. Remus invaded my realm and came quite close to killing me, but Romulus stopped him."

"So you must have felt when John Stone tried to breach your realm, right?"

"Who?"

That was a long story. "There was a night on Earth when the moon turned red and was eclipsed. He forced open a portal to your realm."

She shivered, clutching her chest. "We saw the light of the portal. Felt the wrongness of what was coming, and then... I felt you. You were so close, for the first time in years."

Max swallowed hard. "I saw you through the portal. All of you. I knew you, but I didn't know why."

"This Stone person, is he still a threat?"

"No, thankfully. He thought wolves and humans shouldn't coexist. He hated hybrids like me for 'dirtying' wolves' supposedly pure connection to you."

She scoffed. "Though wolves and humans are different, I always believed wolves and humans had the ability to thrive together."

"Really? Why?"

She smiled. "Because I fell in love with one." She looked back toward the cave at Mani, grinning and laughing with his pups. "Long, long ago, I ventured into the human world and came upon a beautiful human man bathing in the river. I was taken with him at once and shifted to a human so I could speak to him. He was shocked at first, but the more I visited his village, the more he opened up to me.

"Over time, we fell in love. Despite our differences, he wanted to be part of my world and accepted my bite. I saw the beauty a werewolf and a human could create together, so I gave the packs that left my hunting grounds the ability to take the forms of humans so they could live in peace, and created druids from the trees to protect them from harm.

"Of all my creations, one druid was special. Atticus, King of the Druids. I created him from an oak. He was powerful indeed, and he shared his gift of magic among humans. But the power I'd given him went to his head. He grew arrogant, and his power over humans led them to fear and hate magic, no matter if they were good or evil. He... was one of my greatest mistakes. It's a good thing he is gone."

"Yeah, the whole druid thing didn't really work out," Max admitted.

"No. I couldn't have foreseen how terribly he would mistreat humans and wolves. If I'd known..."

Max gazed at her, astonished.

"What?"

He shook his head. "Nothing. I just always imagined you as this all-knowing force. Flawless. No mistakes."

She laughed softly. "How I wish that were true. I have made many mistakes, Max. The druids were one such mistake. Once I set them free with the wolves, I lost all control over their actions. But there's no going back. The druids are gone now and the one last coven remaining has hidden their magic for generations for fear of persecution."

"Wait, *what?* There's one final coven?" Max was intrigued.

"Yes. But it isn't my place to identify her and her family."

Max's curiosity was piqued. "Do I know her?"

She smiled. "Not her specifically, but you know her grandson. He is... unaware of his heritage, from what Thebe's visions have shown. But who knows, maybe he will discover it for himself someday soon. That's all I will say."

Max sighed. He'd be making wild guesses about that one for a while.

"Despite the loss of the druids, have my wolves fared well on their own? I only receive visions of their lives in bits and pieces."

"Things aren't perfect. Werewolves are still mistreated and judged, and some werewolves have got it in their heads that they're superior to humans."

Amaris looked away, disappointed. "I see. Was I mistaken, then, to believe in a world where differences can be celebrated and embraced?"

Max didn't believe so at all. "No," he assured her. "I've seen just how bad things can get. These scars are from hybrid hatred. But there's still so much good in the world too."

A thought occurred to him, and he doubled over from laughing. "Oh man, if those fanatics knew you had a human mate!" Clutching at his sides, he couldn't stop laughing. He caught his breath, tears pricking his eyes. Amaris was smiling at him. Max wheezed, wiping his eyes. "It's just so stupid. The irrational hatred. Werewolves have made huge strides toward equal treatment, and humans are helping us. So you were right. That world you dreamed of, that you believed in, it isn't impossible. We're getting there every day."

She smiled her relief. "I'm so glad. Still, where you're from is so complicated."

Max swallowed hard as he was hit with guilt. "Amaris, you're in danger. Someone pursued me into this realm. His name's Aaron McCready, and he's bringing a pack with him. Tommy and Luna are his children, and he wants them back."

"But they're yours."

Max touched his chest, feeling the kids' bonds. "We are bonded. I'll do anything to keep them safe."

Amaris's scent soured with worry. "How far away is he? Do you know?"

"Not far enough. He could be here any day now."

Amaris drew her furs tighter around herself. "This is terrible. I have pups in the den. River and Anders are still learning to hunt. Mani and I can fight and well, but I worry for the rest of my pack."

Max balled his hands into fists. "Amaris, you won't face him alone. I brought him here—accidentally," he added quickly when her eyes widened. "He jumped in through the portal after me. If I can find a way home, I can bring my pack, and I know they'll gladly fight with you."

Amaris tilted her head. "'If?'" She chuckled. "Let me guess, the portals confuse you."

Max groaned, his ears hot. "I have no idea how to open one back! I did it fine the first time."

Laughing, Amaris put her arm around his shoulders. "It's quite simple, I promise. I'll teach you."

Something twinged in Max's chest. A sudden flare of anxiety hit him. "It's Luna. Something just happened!"

They ran back to the den, but something was wrong. The den was empty except for Luna, sitting beside the whimpering newborns.

"Luna? Where is everyone?"

The little girl looked up. There were tears in her eyes. "Where did you go?" She sniffled, crossing her little arms. "I called for you and you didn't come." Her lower lip quivered.

"I just went for a walk with Amaris. What happened sweetheart?" He didn't see Thebe anywhere which was odd. She'd been stuck to the kids like glue. Maybe she was helping Tommy with something.

Before she could speak, there came a thundering of paws behind them. *"Mother, we heard other wolves!"* Anders said through the bonds.

Max's heart sank.

Mani stormed out of the trees with River, his fangs sharp and claws out. "The boys and I were tracking them. There's a whole pack of them. Twenty, maybe more. They're only a mile away from the territory."

Amaris growled lowly, her eyes blazing like fire. "That must be McCready. He's pursuing Max and the children."

River and Anders growled.

"Max!" Luna said, tugging on his arm.

"Just a moment, sweetheart." Max hung his head. "I'm so sorry. I promise, I'll get my pack and help you guys face him. Amaris, can you show me how to open a portal back home?"

Amaris said, "How did you get to my realm the first time?"

Max shook his head. "I don't know. I was desperate. I howled and it just... happened. What am I missing? I shifted, but even in my wolf form I couldn't open a portal back home. Do I need to click my heels together and chant, 'There's no place like home'?"

"No..." Amaris said, not getting his reference in the slightest. "I want you to howl, Max, and when you do, I want you to picture who you're going to. It's not enough just to howl. We howl to begin a hunt. To warn away strangers. Sometimes, we howl because it makes us happy. Howl to your pack. To your home. Close your eyes and think, Max. Think of your pack, and the portal will show you the way home."

"Max, listen!" Luna began.

"Luna, I need to focus so I can get you and your brother home. Okay?"

"But—" She looked worriedly from him toward the woods.

"I'll talk to you in a second, Luna. I promise." Something was wrong, but Max had to focus on opening a way home. Taking in a breath, Max closed his eyes. He thought of Gabe and his scent, flowers and springtime. Of Ben. Veronica and Manuel. Zach and Ryan. Eddie and Vico. Izzie. His mother. Of that very first meal he'd eaten with them all, filet mignon. How they'd welcomed him as one of their own. How they loved him, and how much he loved them. He missed them all so much, and he had to see them again.

He tipped his head back and sang to them. He poured all his longing and love into his song.

A light flashed behind his eyelids. When he opened his eyes, a portal had materialized. Through the shimmering portal was a manor surrounded by rolling waves and warm sand. "It's the HQ," Max said, hope flaring bright within him as warmth tingled in his chest. The bonds stirred. His pack was so close.

Amaris touched his shoulder. "Well done. To return, all you have to do is think of us, and we will be here to greet you."

"Max!" It was Thebe's voice, but it was strained with fear. She came crashing out of the woods.

"What is it?" Max asked, alarmed to see Thebe so out of breath, her eyes wide.

Sucking in a gasp, Thebe said, "The kid. Tommy."

"Tommy's gone!" Luna erupted. "I t-tried to tell you, but you wouldn't listen!"

Max's heart sank to the pit of his stomach. "What do you mean?" He knelt and touched Luna's shoulders. "Honey, take a deep breath and tell me where he went."

Luna sobbed in great, wrenching gasps but she tried to do as she'd been told. "He said... he said if he went away, you wouldn't get hurt. The pups wouldn't get hurt. He s-said it was the only w-way to save everybody."

Dread left Max cold all over. "How long ago did he leave?"

"I don't know," Luna whimpered, collapsing into his arms.

Max glared at Thebe. "Why weren't you watching him?"

"He said he was thirsty and asked me to go get some water from the river! When I came back, Luna told me he'd run off. I tried to track him but I lost his trail."

Max took a deep breath and exhaled through clenched teeth. "I've got to bring the pack here now so we can get him back."

Amaris grabbed Thebe's arm. "We'll follow his scent from the den, Max. Maybe we can catch up to him while you get your pack!"

Relief flooded Max's chest. "Thank you, Mom."

Amaris's face softened into a smile. "Go on, son." She shifted to a red wolf, furs pooling around her paws as she took off into the trees. Thebe ran after her with Anders and River barking in pursuit.

"Stay here with your granddad, little one." Mani guided Luna to him.

Luna reached for Max, but he said, "Stay here. I'll be right back! I'm getting Tommy back, Luna. I promise."

With that pledge burning in his heart, Max turned toward the portal and charged through.

CHAPTER 22

THE FINAL CONFRONTATION

IT HAD BEEN MORE than two weeks since Max and the kids disappeared into the portal.

Ben had told Gabe to keep himself busy, and Gabe had tried. Unable to stay in their empty home anymore, he'd spent more time at HQ. He'd just returned from a catcher job with a feral caged in the bed of an agency pickup. Capturing ferals was a lot easier as a berserker. With a growl, he could calm their fear or anger and make them relax enough to go where he needed them to.

HQ had undergone more repairs since both the attack by the Wargs and the Yellowstone wolf pack. The smell of blood was finally fading, but Gabe still couldn't shake all those dead wolves sprawled across the courtyard from his mind. What he wouldn't give for this messed-up world to finally have a semblance of McCready-free normalcy.

Once Gabe dropped the feral off in the kennels, he went in search of food. Ryan, Zach, and Izzie were in the dining hall drinking coffee and chowing down on breakfast sandwiches. Gabe could sense Ben some-where, probably in the office. "Hey," he said, trying to keep his tone light as he settled in beside them.

"Morning," Izzie said around a mouthful of sausage, egg, and cheese.

"Our parents around?" Gabe asked.

"Walking around the garden," she answered.

"Mornin', y'all," Eddie said, settling in across the table. Gabe noticed he'd recovered from the attack.

"Sup!" Ryan said. "Vicenzo's magic soup of lurve work wonders on you?"

Eddie smacked Ryan's hair with his hat, making everyone chuckle. Gabe's mouth attempted a smile, but it was hard.

"No word, huh?" Zach asked, nudging his shoulder.

Gabe just sighed.

"Hey, knowin' Max, he just got done kickin' McCready's ass, and he's hangin' out with his ma," Eddie said, tucking into his bowl of oatmeal.

His heart squeezed. He wondered if Max had found his biological mother. If he'd learned all he wanted to know. If he was happy. Goddess, he missed his mate so much. He hoped the pups were okay.

"I know we're sloppy seconds," Ryan said, patting Gabe's arm. "But come on, man. We gotta pass the time. Let's hit a bar or something. Go running as a pack. Raise your spirits."

"Not sure I'm up for that," Gabe admitted.

Ryan frowned, scratching his chin. "Okay. I got an idea. I'll count to three and snap my fingers. If Max isn't back by then, then we're gonna do something fun. Okay?"

Gabe shrugged.

"Okay..." Ryan inhaled and exhaled.

Zach snorted. "What are you—"

"Shut up, Zach, I'm manifesting Max!" Ryan sat pretzel-legged in his chair, his palms touching. "One, two, three!" he said, clapping with each count. Then he closed his eyes and snapped his fingers.

A flash of light burst outside the window. Squeezing his eyes closed, Gabe assumed it was a burst of lightning until he realized it wasn't raining or anywhere near dark enough for lightning to be that bright. Realization clamped around his heart, and his eyes flew open.

Zach grabbed Ryan's shoulder. "Bro."

Ryan was slack-jawed. "No fucking way."

Bright light squeezed through the curtains. Gabe charged from the table and yanked them wider apart, blinking at the flare of light shimmering in the courtyard. Some of the people in the cafeteria ran to the windows, but others screamed and hid under the tables.

Within his chest, the red thread of Max's bond awoke, interweaving with Gabe's own bond. "Max," he whispered, blinking back tears. "Oh, Max." He bolted from the dining hall and into the lobby.

Ben thundered down the stairs, claws and fangs at the ready. "What in the blistering ball sack—"

"He's back!" Gabe cried, unable to contain himself. "He's back!" His sneakers slapped the pavement as he hurtled into the courtyard and toward the gates. "Open them!" he hollered. The gate guard looked paralyzed.

"Do it!" Ben shouted, the rest of the pack assembling behind him.

The gates flew open. Gabe tore down the road toward the portal, squinting against the light.

Someone stepped from the portal and in front of the light. Within his chest, his wolf howled, *Mate, mine!*

Another song answered his, and the bond between them burned like fire.

"Gabe, Gabe, Gabe!"

Max bounded toward Gabe and Gabe ran to meet him, opening his arms. Hurling himself upon Gabe, Max wrapped him up in his arms and legs. Gabe clung to him, gasping into his shoulder as a wave of emotion cascaded over him. Max's hands stroked all over him, clasping his hair, then his cheeks, while crushing their lips together in a desperate greeting.

Gabe's entire body shuddered with joy, his face wet with tears.

When they broke the kiss, they were both gasping.

He couldn't let Max go and crushed him to his chest. "You're never leaving me again."

Max sniffled, nuzzling into his neck. "You told me to go!"

"I know, and if I ever say anything so stupid again, hit me." Gabe pushed his mouth against Max's, breathing in deep and savoring his scent of cinnamon and chilis, pack and home. "I need you, Max. I can't go through life without you. You're my mate. My partner. My everything."

"I know," Max whispered, stroking his hair. "I know."

"Tell me everything." Gabe panted, framing Max's face in his hand. "What was Amaris like? Is McCready gone for good? The kids—"

The kids weren't here. Gabe relinquished his hold on Max and looked every which way.

"Where's Tommy and Luna? Did they stay behind?"

All he had to do was look into Max's face to know something was terribly wrong. "Max?"

Max's mouth quivered, his eyes impossibly wide. "Where's the pack? We need them. All of them."

His knees wobbled, his heart racing out of control. "Okay. Okay, come on." He grabbed Max's hand with his, and Max nearly crushed it in his grip. They headed back down the road and nearly ran right into Ben and the others.

"Max!" Kendra cried, tearing toward them. He opened his arms and caught her when she crashed into him. Max crumpled into her arms and held tight, whimpering, "Mom, Mom, Mom..."

Then Ryan and Zach crushed Max in a group hug.

"Guys, let go!" Max squawked.

"Never!" Ryan wailed. "I'll never let go, Jack!"

"Come on, share the love," Ben grumbled, putting his arms around all three of them and knocking Ryan's and Max's heads together.

"Guys, stop! It's urgent!" Max wriggled free. "We can do group hugs and Ryan can cry later."

"Hey!" Ryan wiped his eyes. "I am *not* crying! It's allergies. I'm allergic to emotions."

"Max, where are the kids?" Veronica asked, out of breath as she and Manuel came to a stop beside the pack.

"The munchkins stayed with Granny?" Vicenzo asked, wiping his flour-covered hands on his apron.

Max took in a gulp of air. "McCready followed us through. He's bringing a pack of possessed wolves to Amaris's territory and—and Tommy got it in his head that he could save us all by going to McCready."

"Shit." Ben growled. "Well he's definitely your kid with all his self-sacrificing tendencies, Max."

"That fucking guy and his possessed wolves," Ryan said, rolling his eyes. "This is, what, the second time? Come up with something original already."

Kendra unsheathed her claws. "If he harms a hair on that boy's head—"

"Is Luna safe?" Izzie asked, her eyes flashing.

"Yes," Max said. "My sister has her—yes, I have a sister. It's a long story! We need to go now!" He led them up to the portal.

Vicenzo blanched. "Hey, is that thing really safe?"

"Yes!" Max put a foot in and out. "See? It'll take us directly to the She-Wolf. Come on. We need to end this once and for all."

Vicenzo balled his hands into fists, panting. "Here goes!" With a shout, he charged and leaped through, tumbling into the grass on the other side. "Oh fuck!" he shouted, his voice warped. "That did *not* feel good."

Eddie rolled his eyes. "Big baby!" He ran through.

Then Manuel grabbed Veronica's hand and they crossed into the portal.

Izzie and Kendra nodded at each other. "Let's go kick this fucker's ass!" Izzie charged.

Kendra exhaled. "What she said. Cursing's not really my thing." Taking in a deep breath, she jumped through.

Once Zach and Ryan and Ben were through, Gabe's stomach fluttered and he clasped Max's hand. "Let's go!" Max ran, leading Gabe after him. Gabe wasn't prepared to feel like his insides had turned upside down as he stepped through, though, and he tumbled onto the tundra grass where he was promptly sick. "Fuck," he croaked, spitting out a noxious mouthful of puke.

Max helped him up, saying, "You'll get used to it."

Ryan, his face pale green, lay crushed under Zach. Izzie groaned as Ben helped her up just before he doubled over and retched. Sitting up, Ryan looked around, taking pictures with his phone. "Holy shit, holy shit! We're actually here! Look at the moon!"

"Yeah. It's great." Zach grunted, clutching onto a tree for support. His bronze skin had a greenish tinge to it.

Manuel rubbed his back. "I'm too old to be jumping through portals..."

Gabe turned and gasped, stunned by the woman coming toward them clad in furs with a flowing mane of glorious red hair he recognized at a glance. Ryan dropped his phone and Ben grabbed onto Gabe's shoulder. "Tell me you're seeing that too." Gabe nodded numbly. "Shit. What do I say? Should I look her in the eyes? Shit, Gabe, we're about to meet a goddess." His mouth had gone too dry to speak.

"Whoa..." Manuel whispered and bowed his head in reverence.

The She-Wolf smiled at them. She was too beautiful to be anything other than a goddess. She greeted them, her voice warm and welcoming. "Max's pack, I presume? Welcome, all of you. I wish we had time for proper introductions, but it will have to wait."

Ben cleared his throat. "Yes, ma'am. Goddess. Uh..."

"Just Amaris will do."

Ben straightened his back like he was addressing a sergeant in the army. "All right. Amaris. Have you found the boy?"

Frowning, she shook her head. "No, but we have his scent. Thebe, River, and Anders, my children, are trailing him right now." A howl commanded their attention. Amaris's eyes widened. "It's Anders. Come, quickly!"

Amaris bounded ahead and the pack followed her to the border of the mountain among the snow-laden pine trees.

"Where's Luna?" Gabe called, his throat going numb from the cold. "Is she safe?"

"Yes! She's with my mate in the den with the pups," Amaris assured him. "Should McCready break through our line of defense, I've instructed him to take the pups and go as far away as he can."

Gabe's heart sank. "That won't happen." The thought of the kids being orphaned yet again made his heart break. "We'll stop him now. Here."

Amaris rumbled out a growl. "Yes. We shall."

The ground ascended to a hill. The deep snow slowed their ascent, and the breath tore from Gabe's lungs with each step. Finally, the ground evened out into a cliffside that overlooked the valley far below.

His stomach turned over. The pack prowling toward them was at least twenty strong, their growls like a rumbling of thunder. At the forefront was the hulking Aaron McCready. At a glance, it was clear McCready was losing himself as he prowled on all fours, too feral to stand up. His pupils were consumed by blazing yellow, and his body shuddered with savage fury. However, there must still be some of the man in him because he grinned when he spotted Gabe and the others.

"Hybrids in this holy place," McCready snarled. "Disgusting. You've fallen so low, Amaris. I will delight in killing the greatest traitor to all werewolf kind."

"I will never let you harm my family or my son's family!" Amaris said.

"Where is Tommy?" Max snarled as red fur sprouted across his face. "If you've hurt him, McCready, I swear I'll rip you to pieces!"

His heart beating hard, Gabe flicked his gaze from one snarling, possessed wolf to another. Tommy. Where was Tommy? He searched within himself for the bond and found Tommy's thread. Goddess, the boy was terrified. His fear made Gabe's heart race faster.

"Tommy!" Gabe called. "Come out!"

"No. No. No." Tommy whimpered across their bond. *"Go away. Can't you understand?"*

Ryan clutched his chest. "Shit. Poor kid."

"I did this to keep you all safe. Please, just leave!"

"Thomas, don't be shy. Say goodbye to your little friends," McCready crooned, his voice a mockery of a father's love. He shifted to the side, and standing behind him was Tommy McCready. His brown skin was pale, his face wet with tears.

"Dad," he croaked, but he wasn't looking at McCready. He was looking at Gabe and then at Max. "Please. Leave me. I can convince him to go. I can. No one has to get hurt."

Max shook his head. "That isn't happening. We will never let you go."

Ben touched his chest. "You're pack, kid. We can all feel it. You and your sister. We don't leave our pack behind."

McCready snarled. "They lie, Thomas. All they want is to use you against me. If you weren't my son, they wouldn't care about you at all. They hid behind you, thought you and your sister could save them from my wrath."

Tommy blinked fast, his hands in trembling fists. "McCready. Please. Let's go. Isn't this what you wanted? Me?" He touched the beast's brown hide. McCready's yellow eyes flickered. "I'll be here. I'll keep you from going feral. We can be a family again like you wanted. Just don't hurt them."

McCready snarled again, leaning into Tommy's touch. "No. Not without Luna. Why didn't you bring her?"

Tommy squirmed under his father's burning glare. "S-she didn't want to come. I couldn't force her. McCready, please. Let's just go."

More snarls vibrated McCready's body. "I won't leave her here. It isn't fair. It isn't right. First the hunters took her from me. Now you dogs want to take her, too! Thomas. Get her. Bring her to me and then we'll go far away."

Tears spilled over from Tommy's eyes. "She didn't want to come!"

"She's a child. She doesn't know what she wants! Thomas. I swear if you bring her to me, I will do whatever you want."

Tommy hunched over. "F-fine. I'll get her. I'll—"

Gabe took a step forward, then another. "No. No, Tommy, you won't."

Tommy gasped, his eyes blazing. "Why? Why are you all doing this? Why would you all risk dying for me and my sister?"

"You know why." Gabe tapped his chest, trying to smile in the face of the fear tearing through him. "You can feel it. You're pack, Thomas. That's why."

"Just let me go! He'll kill you. All of you! I'll lose my family *again*. I can't." His body shuddered with grief.

McCready raised a clawed hand and held it against Tommy's neck, the razor tip dimpling Tommy's skin. "I am your family. You feel it, don't you?" To Gabe's horror, Tommy nodded. "I do too. We're still connected. In blood *and* in bond. Whatever you have with them can never compare. I am your father. They are nothing to you."

Tommy's eyes flashed yellow.

Gabe and Max started forward. McCready's wolves roared at them, their mouths salivating and their fangs snapping.

Needing to reach the boy, Gabe took Max's hand and together they pushed waves of comfort and love into their bond and through to Tommy.

"Everyone," Ben commanded, and his bond surged within Gabe's chest.

Tommy's yellow eyes flickered, his shoulders rising and falling faster.

McCready snarled. "He is *mine*."

Max said, "McCready's wrong, Tommy! It *is* different. He doesn't love you. Not like we do."

With Tommy's life on the line, each wolf in their pack took a moment to tell Tommy what was in their heart.

Gabe said, "A wolf protects his pack."

Zach said, "But he doesn't do it alone."

Ryan said, "We protect each other, always."

Izzie said, "We chose you, and you chose us."

Kendra said, "In bond or blood, it doesn't matter."

Veronica said, "Pack is more than that."

Eddie said, "If you let us, we'll give you a home. A fresh start."

Vicenzo said, "I know it's hard after everything you've lost. But you gotta give this a chance."

Manuel said, "We'll fight for you, no matter what you choose. We'll bring you home."

Finally, Ben said, "We love you, kid. Do you believe that?"

The yellow in Tommy's eyes burned brighter. McCready snarled a laugh. He fed off of Tommy's bond and used it to force himself onto two legs, pulling himself from feral madness. He roared, the sound bowling them all over and making Gabe's ears ring.

The wolves kicked and thrashed, howling in anguish as he leeched from them and drew their strength. His hate seemed unstoppable, but if Gabe knew anything, it was that there was only one force that could rival hate. And so he poured all his love into the bond tying him to Tommy. Wave after wave of pack and love coursed through him and into his son.

Tommy's eyes flared bright like the sun.

"I love you, too," he whispered. *"All of you. That's why...* that's why—"

McCready screamed, doubling over in agony. He clutched his chest. "Our bond! You shattered it. Why, boy?"

Tommy's eyes lost their feral light. "I don't need you," he snarled. "I never needed you."

"I'm your father," McCready spat the word.

The boy's claws lengthened. "No. I already have a family."

"Thank you. Thank you. All of you."

It sounded like goodbye, and Gabe moved before he could think. "Tommy!"

Max's scent soured with terror. "Tommy. Tommy, no!"

Thomas McCready hurled himself upon his father. His claws punched into McCready's chest, and his fangs found his throat. He slammed into McCready, and the berserker howled in pain and lost his footing. His legs slipped over the edge as his enormous arms wrapped around Tommy.

The entangled wolves disappeared down the steep drop into the valley below.

MAX SHOT TOWARD THE cliff's edge, calling the moonlight to his fingertips.

A horde of possessed wolves ran to meet him and Gabe.

Amaris's howl shook the forest to its roots. As a red wolf, she leaped in front of him, shaking the ground. Before Max's eyes she shifted but didn't stop there, growing bigger and bigger until she towered over them and dwarfed them in her shadow. Something hot singed Max's arm. Embers fell from her red coat, which Max realized was aflame. Fire burned in her orange eyes and smoke curled from her snout.

"What the f—" Ryan began.

Amaris threw her head back and screamed to the night sky. The sound had Max clutching his ears, fearing they'd bleed and rupture. The moon changed from blue to a hateful blood red, staining the land crimson. The stars burned bright, shooting across the night sky and hurtling toward Earth and the hunting grounds. Max gasped as a meteorite plummeted from the sky, crashing down into the woods. The trees smoked and burned.

As flaming meteorites set fire to the forest, the wolves of the LPA and the hunting grounds met the possessed pack in battle.

Max only had Tommy on his mind. While the agency wolves fought McCready's thralls, Max levitated himself above the fighting and flew toward the cliff's edge.

Please. Please let him be all right.

He expected to see blood smears far below. Instead, Tommy and McCready clung to the rock face with their claws. Tommy slipped, his claws shooting up sparks as he slid farther down the cliff wall. McCready fell and caught himself on a protruding rock, yelping when his back cracked against the surface.

"Hold on, Tommy!" Max called, shooting out his hand. He let himself fall, soaring toward Tommy.

The boy cried out in terror when he lost his grip on the rocks. He fell, but Max called upon the moon and suspended Tommy in midair. Keeping himself levitated, Max reached out and caught Tommy's hand, hauling the boy in close and wrapping him in his arms. Max kicked his legs, pushing them back toward solid ground.

Gabe peered over the edge above them. "Max! Hang on!" He knelt, reaching out.

"Watch out!" Tommy cried.

McCready leaped from the outcrop, clawing his way up toward them. Max only had time to brace himself. Blunt fangs snapped around his ankle and tugged him down. Max gnashed his teeth, snarling through the pain. "Tommy, hold on to me!" he shouted, and then they plummeted toward the ground. The wind roared in Max's ears, drowning out Tommy's terrified cry.

Clutching onto him with one arm, Max thrust out his hand and, inches from the ground, he, Tommy, and McCready lurched to a stop. They suspended, Max's nose just brushing the grass. He let go, and the three of them hit the ground with grunts.

Snarling, Max kicked McCready in the snout. The wolf bit down to the bone, his eyes wild and crazed.

"Get off!" Tommy shouting, lurching to his feet. He charged and swung his claws at McCready's face.

McCready stumbled back with a shrill cry, wiping blood from his eyes. "You made your choice, boy," he snarled, rounding on Tommy. "You'll die with them!"

Tommy backed away and tripped over a tree root, and McCready roared and bunched his muscles to pounce.

There were no thoughts. Max's body moved all on its own, and he lurched from the ground and put himself between them. Shoving up his hand, he propelled Tommy out of the way with a pulse of gravity magic.

McCready pounced, his jaws open wide. The berserker crunched down where Tommy would have been, his fangs ripping clean through Max's arm and shaking him like a rag doll. Max flew off his feet and his back slammed into a tree. He was too paralyzed to even scream as McCready turned to face him. Between his teeth was an arm.

My arm? Is that—that's my—

Blood poured across his chest, warming his body as his temperature suddenly plummeted. He shuddered, wanting to scream but unable to suck in even a pinch of air. The arm lay in the snow. He told himself to curl his fingers, and the command went into the empty space where his arm should have been. His heart roared in his ears, and he couldn't breathe.

"Well done, Max." McCready prowled toward him, his shoulders rippling. Blood dripped from his fangs. "How does that arm of yours feel? I'll take off the other one, even things out for you!"

Panic nearly paralyzed Max. He forced it all down in order to fight, to survive, to protect Tommy.

McCready flew off his paws and soared, smashing into a tree. Max levitated him once more and hurled him. Another tree's roots creaked when McCready plowed into the trunk. He tried to throw him again, but McCready pushed off against the tree Max had thrown him into and leaped toward him. Max grunted, crushed beneath a bulky mass of muscle.

"No!" Tommy roared, his voice turning into a wolf's snarl. He leaped fully shifted onto McCready's back and snapped his jaws around his pointed ear. Blood rained down McCready's face. He screamed and tossed Tommy off, revealing the stub of his missing ear. The boy crashed into a tree with a yelp, his paws twitching feebly.

"Don't you fucking touch him again!" Max bellowed, and he brought McCready to his knees with gravity. He thrust his bloody stump toward the tree, forcing away the sheer terror at the amount of blood staining his entire arm red. He might not have his arm, but it didn't matter. He didn't need it. He could still fucking do this.

"Max! Max! Hang in there, you hear me?" Gabe's voice cried out to him through their bond, but Max feared he would be too late.

McCready bared his teeth in a grin. "It's not every day one can boast they killed the son of a goddess. You've made my night!"

Snarling, Max jerked his arms back, spattering himself with his own blood as he pulled on the ropes of gravity with all his might. McCready had no time to move out of the way as a tree came crashing down on him, raising dust around them. Max pushed himself up, gasping for air.

Fuck, he was losing too much blood. If he could shift, he could speed up the healing process. He dropped to all fours, willing the shift to come. Spasms of pain rolled through him as the blood from his stump soaked the ground. The shift was slower than it had ever been.

With a roar, McCready rolled the tree from his back and stumbled, his hind legs shaking. Max heard the bones snap and crack as they mended. McCready's eyes burned as he set his sights on Max. He bunched his muscles and sprang—only to be knocked out of the air when a huge black blur collided with him.

Towering over McCready was an enormous black wolf with blazing amber eyes and scars twisting across bulging muscles. Though his form was monstrous, Max would know those eyes and scars anywhere.

"G-*Gabe*?" Max croaked, recognizing the beast from the hilltop in Vermont. He'd done it. He'd *finally* done it. Max swore if he survived the next few minutes, he was kissing the hell out of Gabe Reyes.

Gasping, McCready tried to stand, only to recoil as the beast stood on his back legs and let out a roar that made Max's eardrums rattle. McCready stared at the beast in a mixture of awe and fury. "Reyes. A fucking hybrid has no right possessing such a majestic beast." He let loose a furious roar. The madness in it pulled at Max's mind, threatening to drive him feral.

But Gabe only shook it off, his lips curling around his fangs in a savage grin.

McCready's ear flattened and his tail dropped. He took several steps back. "No. *No.*"

"I am a hybrid," the beast growled in Gabe's voice. "But I'm more than you ever thought we could be."

For the first time since Max had known him, fear left McCready's eyes wide. Gabe threw back his head and howled as McCready turned to run. The wolf staggered, clawing at his ears, then went completely still. His jaw worked and his eyes darted around, but he seemed incapable of moving.

"Turn around," Gabe commanded.

Shaking, McCready obeyed. He had no other choice. "Thomas," he groaned. "Help me."

Max couldn't look away, spellbound but terrified of what came next. "Tommy," he croaked, "Don't look."

Gasping, Tommy turned his face into the trunk of a tree.

"You... you fucking hybrid." McCready panted, frothing at the mouth. "I'll kill you. I'll kill your pack. I'll burn your whole world to the ground!"

Gabe lunged, seizing McCready's head between his enormous claws. "No. You'll never hurt anyone again!"

McCready's scream choked into gasps and gurgles as Gabe's huge jaws clamped around his neck. Blood poured down his twitching body and pooled under his flailing paws. Bones snapped, the sound echoing in the forest, and Gabe ripped Aaron McCready's head from his neck. It rolled across the ground, the eyes wide and staring vacantly. The light within those haunting yellow eyes died like the flame within a jack-o'-lantern. The body crumpled to the ground, twitched, and fell still.

Max's whole body shook and for the first time, he was afraid as Gabe turned toward him, bestial and unrecognizable. He shivered under those burning eyes, fearing they would turn wild and yellow like they had in Vermont. As Gabe's body shuddered from the growl in his chest, Max feared he'd lost him to bloodlust for good.

"Don't be afraid of me, mi amor. Please." The beast's voice broke. "I did this for you. For us. So I could keep us safe. I'm still here. I'm still yours."

Max was speechless. Before him stood not just a wolf—the heart of a man still beat within him. Gabe had done it. He'd found the peace he'd needed within himself to finally take charge of his inner wolf.

Max was so proud of him.

He tried to stand, to go to him. His vision spun, and the ground hurtled toward him. "Max!" Big furry arms caught him just as he fell. "Max, don't move. Your arm, it— What happened?" Max raised a trembling hand, caressing the beast's face. It looked up from beneath a mop of fur. Its eyes were rimmed with black, the pupils a brilliant amber and radiating utter adoration.

Max laughed, his arm trembling as he wound it around the wolf's neck. "I love you, Gabe Reyes. I always have."

Gabe's enormous arms shook as they went around Max's shoulders, drawing Max into the warm bulk of his body. Joyful whines turned to sobs as Gabe shifted to a man, holding Max with wild desperation as if they'd die if they parted again. Max realized he was crying too, his face damp with tears, but he couldn't stop smiling.

Because it was over. It had ended here in these woods in a realm far away, and despite it all, he and Gabe were here. Together, just as Max had hoped, because that was how it was meant to be.

"Max? Are you okay?"

He realized he was still shaking but only partly from relief. A chill gripped his body.

"Max... Hey! Open your eyes!"

When he obeyed, Gabe swayed, splitting into eight versions of himself.

Max's breath came in short gasps. Icy sweat rolled down his body. He collapsed against Gabe's chest, his vision darkening at the edges. He was sure his arm should have healed by now, but it went on weeping blood.

Exhaustion weighed on him. He needed to rest, just for a little while.

He closed his eyes, unable to keep them open.

"Max. No, no, no. Max!"

CHAPTER 23

THE MOON ALWAYS RISES

MOONLIGHT PRIED BENEATH MAX'S eyelids. Sleep had formed a crust over his eyes. He raised his hand to wipe them, only to encounter empty air. The thin pale stump of his arm sent a shock through his system. He rotated it, looking up and down his arm to make sure he was really looking at a part of his body. His arm below the elbow was completely gone, but Max swore he could still feel his fingers. He closed his eyes, trying to breathe through the surge of panic.

"Lobito!" Gabe's voice filled Max with relief. He leaned over Max, his worried face coming into focus. "Are you all right? Do you need anything?"

"Water," Max croaked, his throat bone dry.

"You got it!" Gabe grabbed a stone bowl with water rippling within. He gingerly lifted Max's head and tipped the bowl against his lips.

He gulped down every drop. "Thank you," he said, no longer sounding as dead as he felt.

"Max? Max!" a little voice cried. Luna hurled herself onto his stomach, knocking the wind out of him.

"Easy, sweetheart!" Thebe hovered over Max, her eyes wide in worry.

He recovered quickly, sitting up and putting his arms—arm—around her. A pang of loss went through him. He shook it away and kissed Luna's black curls. "Hey, kiddo. How are you?"

"I was so worried." She sniffled, her face streaked with tears. "What happened to your arm? Does it hurt?"

Max shook his head. "No. I feel fine." It wasn't entirely a lie. The stump wasn't bleeding anymore, and it had healed.

"Really?" Her puppy dog eyes swam with tears.

"Yeah. Really." He kissed her button nose and she put her little arms around him.

Unwilling to let her go, Max got his feet beneath him and held Luna under the butt with one arm. "Hold on," he said with a grunt. Luna wrapped her arms around his neck, squeezing his waist with her legs. Thebe used her levitation magic to help him stand. "How long have I been out?" he asked.

"Just a few hours," Thebe said.

Gabe took Luna from him and held Max's hand in his.

They followed Thebe out into the light. His heart quickening, Max asked, "Was anyone hurt?"

"Not seriously," she told him.

Gabe said, "My dad subdued the feral wolves."

Out in the clearing, a fire roared. Amaris's pack and the agency wolves gathered around the bonfire where a whole ox roasted over the roaring flames. Izzie shot to her feet the second Max met her gaze. "Max!" She ran to his side and enveloped him in a hug. "Guys, he's up!"

The rest of the pack found their feet as Gabe and Izzie escorted Max over. Despite his exhaustion, Max still smiled when his mother hugged him tight.

Tommy watched Max with wide, distraught eyes.

He motioned him in, and Tommy collapsed against his chest. "I'm so sorry," he whimpered. "Your arm... it's my fault."

Max shook his head. "I'd do it again."

"I know." Tommy sighed, sounding exasperated. "And I'd do the same for you."

Max tried to touch Tommy's cheek with his hand before he remembered it was gone. That hurt more than he was ready to reflect on. "We'll never be put in that situation again, Tommy. McCready's gone. He's gone forever."

Tommy sighed his relief and nuzzled into Max's chest. "It's over. Finally, it's over."

"Max, come and eat!" Ben called, holding out a bowl of stew, the meat plucked freshly from the roasted ox.

He joined his pack around the roaring fire. Mani played a lute he'd crafted from wood himself while Anders and River howled along. Next to Max, Ryan and Zach laughed and joked. Eddie tapped his foot to the beat as Veronica and Manuel danced. Ben got stew in his beard, which made Izzie laugh. His head laid back against a tree, Vicenzo looked totally at ease. Then Kendra and Izzie got up to dance with Luna, who was making up her own dance moves.

Gabe looked at him from across the fire and extended a hand. Max almost went to him but stopped himself. The stump of his arm throbbed and he knew he wouldn't be able to hold Gabe in both arms when they danced. The realization of what he'd lost cleaved through him and suddenly he felt miles away from the celebration. He looked away from Gabe but not before he noticed the frown on his face.

Later Amaris's pack and Ben's pack helped bury the dead. The wolves who had been under McCready's control and survived were allowed to stay and mourn their pack. The packs howled as one and then they dispersed. Max sighed, looking around at what had been broken: the trees had been uprooted and those that remained were charcoal black, and the tundra was punctured with craters from fallen meteorites. Prey animals had fled, and soon the pack would have to follow or risk starvation.

Gabe's arm went around his shoulder. "The forest will heal."

"In time," Max agreed.

Ben walked up to them, his face weary with exhaustion, and the rest of the pack followed. If possible, his beard had even more white hair after their ordeal in the hunting grounds. "Think we've stirred up enough shit for the day, guys. Wanna head home?"

Ryan rolled his shoulders. "Yeah. Think I've had enough of traveling through realms to last a lifetime."

"I'm tired," Luna declared. "Can we go home now, please?"

Max looked back at his siblings and birth parents. "In a moment." He walked over to them.

Amaris was nearby, stroking the head of the guilt-stricken matriarch of the pack McCready had controlled. "You weren't yourself. You will not be punished for that monster's cruelty."

Whining, the wolf went to stand with her pack.

Amaris sighed. "How terrible. It's good McCready was finally stopped before he hurt others."

"Would you like me to stay until you all get settled somewhere?" Max asked. He thought he would in a heartbeat, to make sure they were all right. But his heart cried out for his own pack, and for a moment, he was torn in two.

Amaris laughed and touched his cheek. Mani's arm went around Max's shoulders, and he said, "Lad, we'd love for you to stay. But you don't have to. This pack's weathered loss before, but we know we're strong if we stand together."

"Are you sure?"

Amaris said, "Go home, Max. Be with your mate and your pups." Max wanted to, but his heart broke as she drew him close. Before he could pull away, Amaris touched his wrist and compelled him to stay for a moment. "Treasure those pups, Max. Treasure every moment."

He pulled her into his chest for one final embrace. "I will, Mother. I'll see you again, all of you."

With a caress of his cheek, Amaris stepped back and howled, opening a portal home for them.

"Max!" He turned as Thebe ran into his arms, expelling the wind from his lungs as she hugged him.

"Are you staying?" Max asked. "You don't want a little peek at Earth?"

"Yes, this is my home." Her orange eyes glittered with tears. "But don't worry. I'll visit you someday soon. I'll look after Mom and Dad for you, and the twins and the pups. Don't worry."

Max was disappointed to see her go, but his heart was fuller knowing she'd stay to look after the pack. "Thanks, Thebe." He held her as tightly as he could with one arm. It was hard to let go, but he did it anyway, drying his eyes on his sleeve as he went to meet Gabe and the others at the portal. He looked back one more time at the twins, Thebe, Mani, and Amaris with the bundle of pups in her arms. Their howls wished him well. Max cupped his hand to his mouth and howled back.

Though he was saying goodbye, Max knew it wouldn't be forever, and he wasn't sad. How could he be lonely again when he had one pack in one world and one in another? With a final smile, Max took Gabe's hand and stepped through the portal.

THE AGENCY HQ WAS quiet and dark when Max and the others returned to Earth. Ben stopped in the courtyard. "Guys," he said, and they turned to him. "Let's keep everything we saw between us. Right?"

Eddie tipped his hat. "No problem there, sir."

Zach scoffed. "I mean, no one would believe us anyway."

"That's what you think," Ryan said. "I'm gonna write a book about this, you'll see."

"I'll be the first to call you crazy on the internet," Izzie said, clapping him on the shoulder. "Now, I need to go to bed. 'Night!"

"Yeah, me too." Vicenzo yawned. "I've had enough socializing for a lifetime, so don't blame me if I act like I don't know you freaks for a month or two."

One by one, they split off to their rooms to sleep, at a loss for words after their adventure in the hunting grounds, though Max sensed that this journey into the unknown had only deepened their bonds. They'd been a part of a world their kind could only imagine, and Max knew it had changed him forever. Perhaps the rest of the pack too.

Gabe held Max's hand as they walked the dark trail to the bungalows. Kendra carried Luna, who was fast asleep, and Tommy swayed, looking dead on his feet. Once they were inside their bungalow, Gabe opened up the fold-out bed for Kendra, and the kids piled into the guest room.

After he'd brushed his teeth, Max went to check on the kids. The door creaked when he opened it. Kendra sat on Luna's bed telling her a story about a unicorn, a dragon, and two princes, or something like that. She fell asleep and Kendra kissed her plump cheek.

"Good night, dear," she said to Tommy, caressing his hair.

"See you tomorrow, Grandma." He nestled into his pillows.

Kendra wiped her eyes, a smile bright on her face.

Max grinned, his heart impossibly full.

His mother stretched and yawned, and Max put his arm around her and walked downstairs to the living room.

"Is it bad that I'm holding my breath?" Max asked, the stairs creaking beneath them. "I can't believe he's gone for good."

"I know. It's hard to trust this relief after how many obstacles we've faced," Kendra said. She sat on the sofa bed and Max joined her, the springs creaking.

"How's your arm?" She eyed his stump.

Max squirmed, wishing he could hide it. "Fine." It felt numb, like the remaining limb had fallen asleep, but he really didn't want to talk about it.

"Good," she said, but she didn't sound entirely convinced.

"It feels weird," Max admitted. "I know—things could have been so much worse. I shouldn't complain."

"Oh, honey, stop that." She rubbed his shoulder. "You're entitled to feel however you want. It's a lot to adjust to."

Max swallowed hard. "Can we talk about something else?"

"Of course." Her scent was still tinged with worry, but she let it slide. "McCready's gone, Max. We have two Alphas on the Council, new councilmembers. They'll work together with human governors to ensure prosperity between wolves and humans. Maybe now humans and shifters can finally take a deep breath and heal as a community. We can unify." She sounded so hopeful.

"I don't know if we'll ever fully heal from this. People are more mistrustful of shifters than before."

Kendra rested her head against his cheek. "Time, Max. All in time."

"The moon always rises, right?"

She hummed happily. "Exactly."

Max closed his eyes, ready to sleep. Gabe would have to carry him upstairs.

"What was she like?" Kendra smiled knowingly. "Amaris. Your mother."

"My birth mother," Max corrected. He still didn't know how to describe her, all fiery protectiveness and gentle and loving at once. "She was... indescribable," he said lamely. He smiled at his mother. "But so are you."

"She seemed lovely. I wish we'd had more time to talk. Perhaps another time. Did she tell you what you needed to know?"

"She wanted to protect me, so she gave me to you." Max smiled. "She loved me, always."

"Oh, Max." She blinked away tears. "That's wonderful."

Max closed his eyes and put his head on her shoulder, reaching for her hand and holding tight.

"Didn't you want to stay?"

"I did," Max admitted. "But my place is here with the pups and Gabe. The pack. With you."

Kendra put her arms around him. "I'm proud of you, Max."

He would see them again someday, and until then his heart was fuller than it had ever been.

MAX WOKE IN THE night to an unbearable itch where his arm used to be. The bed was empty, so he supposed Gabe was awake somewhere in the bungalow. Now that he was alone, he allowed himself a growl of frustration. He could still feel his arm, so it freaked him out when he looked down only to encounter the skinny nub of his stump.

He felt stupid for mourning a lost limb of all things. He was lucky to even be alive. Yet he couldn't deny the ache of loss. Time, like his mother had said. He would need time to adjust to his missing limb. Surely, the stump wouldn't itch or tingle forever, right? Eventually, his brain would catch up to the fact that his arm wasn't there anymore, and he'd stop trying to curl fingers that weren't there or put an arm around the people he loved. He was afraid to shift. How would he walk on three legs as a wolf? He knew animals could adjust to a missing limb, but still he worried.

He couldn't be a burden to his pack. The uncertainty gnawed at him, and Max gave up on trying to sleep. He kicked the blankets off and put his feet on the cool floorboards. He reached out his stump to steady himself on the dresser, cursing when he remembered his stupid arm wasn't there. He wondered if it had been burned with McCready's body. That was a chilling thought. He forced it away.

Not sure where he was going, Max wandered aimlessly downstairs. He paused, noticing Gabe in the kitchen below the railing. His mate was nursing a glass of his favorite whiskey, his back to Max while music played quietly from his phone's speakers. Gabe set the glass down and turned, likely sensing Max the way Max always sensed him. He smiled, though there were bags under his eyes.

"Couldn't sleep?" he asked.

Max shook his head.

"Is your arm—"

Max winced. "Fine," he said. "I wish everyone would stop asking me about it and looking at it—" He cut himself off. Gabe's eyes were wide and hurt. "I'm sorry." Max's throat thickened.

"No, I get it." Gabe frowned. "Not losing your arm. I mean, I get how frustrating it must be. But Max, you know no one sees you any differently. You're still our pack. You're still strong."

Gabe's words washed over him, submerging him in the comfort Max hadn't known he needed. Eyes misting, Max went to him and put his hand on the back of Gabe's. The stump of his arm twitched when he tried to put it around Gabe. Another pang of loss went through him, realizing once more he'd never hold Gabe with both hands again.

"Talk to me, mi amor."

He buried his face in Gabe's chest, his throat thickening when it shook beneath him. He couldn't speak. He felt like the feral, terrified red wolf Gabe had found under a bush in the park years ago. So many feelings warred within him, and he didn't know what to say, how to describe how he felt.

Gabe's arms wrapped around Max, crushing him to his body. He buried his nose in Max's hair and didn't speak. He swayed them side to side to a song playing low in the background, kissing and stroking Max's hair. With a gulping breath, Gabe said, "I'm so fucking glad you're okay. You scared me, Lobito. You really did." He laughed, the sound full of joy and relief.

Gabe pulled back to kiss Max's forehead as he gripped his face between his hands. "Can I?" He ran his hands down Max's arms, and Max nodded. He kissed his fingers, then the stump of his arm. "Max, talk to me. You can tell me anything. I'll never judge you."

He swallowed hard. "I…"

Gabe gazed at him, patient as a saint.

Max parted his lips and summoned the words from the deepest, darkest place in his mind. "I don't…" His voice came out a croaky whisper. "Want to be a burden."

Gabe's wide eyes glistened with tears. "To me?"

Unable to look at him, Max hung his head. "Or anyone." Tears fell fast down his face. "I don't want anyone to see me differently."

Gabe thumbed away his tears, pain bright in his eyes.

"D-do you?" Max asked, forcing himself to meet Gabe's eyes. "Do you see me differently now? Do you think I'm weak?"

"You're not." Gabe's voice was sure and steady despite the emotion in his eyes. He framed Max's face in his hands. "I have never thought you were weak, Max. Not when you were feral the night I met you. Not now. You lost your arm protecting our son. How could I ever think you weak for that?" To hear his worst fears denied overwhelmed Max with relief and gratitude. He hadn't realized how much of a grip his doubt had held over him. "You're so strong, mi amor. So beautiful and amazing. You're my life, Max. Nothing's going to change that."

With Gabe's arms around him, the cracked pieces of Max's heart formed some semblance of a whole. When he wound his arm around Gabe's neck, Max could swear he felt the ghost of his hand curling in Gabe's hair.

His mate touched their foreheads together. "Nothing can break us, Max. Not John Stone. Not Richard. Not that year apart. Not McCready and his Wargs. And this sure as hell won't change a thing." He caressed Max's stump. "You and me, we built one hell of a foundation."

Max smiled. It was hard to hold, but the joy budding inside him burned brighter than it had in a long time. He stood on his toes and kissed Gabe, his heart singing when Gabe leaned into him with a needy sigh.

They swayed slow and steady, like they'd danced when Gabe had come back to him after a year apart, their hearts weary and cracked. Like they'd danced at their mating ceremony, overjoyed and full of hope. Max whispered Gabe's name between kisses, the very first word he'd ever spoken to Gabe, giving it back to him in the hope that he would understand.

They'd pulled each other from the brink of feral despair time and again. He would always come back for Gabe Reyes and Gabe would come back for him. It was what they did for each other.

And that wouldn't ever change.

CHAPTER 24

EPILOGUE

TWO YEARS LATER

"TIME HEALS, MAX. SURE as the moon always rises," his mother had told him. "Things won't always be so difficult."

Max hadn't believed her, not for a long time. But whether he was learning to dress himself again, or cut his food, or regaining the strength he'd lost in his residual limb, he'd come to realize day by day that his mother, like always, was right. Things got easier.

Thanks to cooperation between governors and the councilmembers, crimes against werewolves were ticking down, the numbers lower than they'd been in years. Without McCready there to inspire them and with the Council and human governors working hard to repair the bridge between their people, bigots were retreating under their rocks. The new Alphas had shown that they cared for everyone equally, whether they were humans, hybrids, or full-blooded wolves, and the wolves they'd assembled had proven to be honorable and just.

Things were still shaky between humans and werewolves around the country, but New York State had come together after McCready's uprising. During the most recent mayoral election, the lycanthrophobic bigot running for mayor had attempted to divide people by rehashing outdated stereotypes and othering werewolves, claiming that only he could protect the city from the beasts. The city had rejoiced when he'd lost, and the first hybrid mayor had been elected, promising that she would unite werewolves, hybrids, and humans because they were stronger together. Max's mother had cried during the entire live broadcast of her inauguration.

There would always be challenges ahead in Max's personal life and in the wide world, but each day Max was learning to adapt to them, thanks to his prosthetic arm.

Max and his mother had had their trials over the years, but their bond was stronger than ever before. She had been there by his side day and night, telling him about all the amputee success stories she'd read about and helping him with chores around the house. Max tried to ignore the sting of shame, the nagging voice that said he was supposed to be taking care of her now that she was getting older. He felt like he was an infant all over again.

When he voiced those thoughts aloud, she smiled tenderly and took his hand. "Don't be silly. I'm your mother, Max. It's my privilege to help you."

Warmth bloomed in Max's chest. Maybe she hadn't given birth to him, but that didn't mean a thing. When he needed her, she was there. She'd always been there. She wasn't perfect. She'd made mistakes, but so had he. They were both human. Well, mostly human.

Max kissed her hand. "Thank you, Mom."

He didn't miss the way her heart skipped a beat or the tears in her eyes that she blinked away. "Of course, baby." She squeezed his hand tight. "Any time."

Family were the people who stayed and who had your back when times were hard. That was what truly mattered.

WHEN MAX LOOKED BACK on his life over the past few years, he couldn't believe how much had changed. For the longest time, he'd been lost, and he and his mother had gone it alone. Then Richard forced himself into their lives and turned their world upside down. When all felt lost, Gabe had found Max scared, alone, and hurt beneath a bush, and everything had changed. Meeting the agency wolves had changed his life for the better. They'd inspired him to give back to those who'd rescued him, and so Max had become a trainee at the Lycanthrope Academy.

Now he was graduating top of his class. Usually, academy trainees required four years of intense training. Max graduated in three. He didn't let his amputation slow him down. He wanted to use his success to inspire other disabled folks to strive toward their own dreams.

The pack treated Max to dinner at his favorite restaurant to celebrate his upcoming graduation. When Ryan showed up, things got... interesting.

"Oh, Ryan's here!" Izzie waved from her seat.

Zach looked toward the doors, his brow furrowing. "Who is *that*?"

Towering over Ryan was a muscular man, a shifter by the scent of him. Max did a double take, looking from the stranger to Zach. "Hey." He lowered his voice and nudged Izzie. "Is it just me, or does that guy look like a clone of Zach?"

Izzie looked at Zach, then at the guy by the door. "Oh my goddess. They do look alike!"

Max couldn't unsee it. The man was tall like Zach, had the same skin tone and face shape, the same short afro. He was the spitting image except for his fashion sense.

"Is he wearing purple crocs?" Zach looked offended. "With neon green socks? Seriously?"

Gabe wrinkled his nose. "Did they hook up?"

It sure smelled like it.

Zach snapped his head in Gabe's direction. "What?" There was a growly undercurrent to his voice.

Ryan gave them an uncomfortable smile as he approached the table. "Hey, everyone."

The big guy grinned. "Oh my goddess, it's the whole crew! Ryan talked about y'all for two and a half hours. Barely gave me any time to talk about my glorious self. I feel like I know y'all already. Let me guess: pretty boy, amber eyes, perfect hair. I bet you're... Greg." He pointed at Gabe.

Max shoved food in his mouth so he wouldn't laugh.

"Yup," Gabe said, popping the *p*. "That's me. Greg. That's my name now, everyone."

"I knew it!" he boomed. "Score one for Jackie boy!"

"And you are?" Max asked.

Ryan shuffled his feet. "So, uh... everyone, this is Jack."

Once again, everyone looked from Zach to Ryan's date.

Gabe's lips trembled like he was trying not to laugh. "Nice to meet you, Jack. This is Zach."

Zach stuck out his arm stiffly and shook. "Hey, man."

"Good grip," Jack remarked, bobbing his eyebrows.

Izzie masked a laugh as a cough. "How wonderful to meet you, Zach—I mean, *Jack*."

Ryan narrowed his eyes at her.

"How'd you meet?" Zach asked through gritted teeth.

Ryan coughed. "Oh, you know. Around."

Jack laughed. Everyone winced. His laugh sounded like a goose being strangled. "Oh, he's such a little prude, this one. We met on Howlr. You know. The gay hookup app for shifters?"

"Really?" Zach asked, his voice nothing but polite. "How nice." He stabbed his fork into his shrimp scampi.

Jack grinned rakishly. "Yup. I let him eat my shrimp scampi, if you know what I mean. All night long."

Max and Gabe coughed loudly. Luna blinked innocently at Jack.

Tommy frowned suspiciously. "He's not talking about pasta, is he?"

Jack waved. "Hello, kidlings!"

Needless to say, Ryan broke up with Jack before the end of the evening.

Max got the impression Zach was very happy about it.

GRADUATION DAY ARRIVED ON a beautiful summer evening. The ceremony took place on Bryant Park's great lawn. Max couldn't wipe the grin from his face when he accepted his degree. Ben and his father Jonathan, the LPA's founder, stood shoulder to shoulder on the stage. Eyes shining with pride, Ben presented the badge he'd gifted Max four years ago on his birthday.

Jonathan said in a deep voice, "Congratulations, Agent Gallagher. Thank you for your service."

Max blinked away the sheen in his eyes when Ben pinned the badge to his chest. He held his head high and looked him in the eyes. "Thank you, Ben. For everything."

Ben's eyes shone. He opened his arms and Max stepped into his embrace, wrapping his arm around his back. "Love you, kid," Ben rumbled, ruffling Max's hair.

Max squeezed him. "You too." His heart had never felt fuller.

He laughed as his friends loudly howled and cheered for him from the audience, and he found himself overwhelmed with love and gratitude. Ryan waved from where he'd jumped piggyback style onto Zach's back, and Zach winked at him. Eddie whistled, his green eyes sparkling with happiness, something Max had never thought he'd see after the man's rough life. Even moody Vicenzo managed a smile. His mother was crying into her new boyfriend's shoulder as Manuel, Veronica, Izzie, and Gabe piled into a group hug. Tommy had little Luna up on his shoulders, and they were wearing T-shirts that declared "My Dad Graduated!"

It was no use trying to stop the tears of happiness that dampened his cheeks or the huge smile that broke across his face as he gazed at all the people he cherished in the audience.

Once, it had only been him and his mother, alone and frightened.

Now, Max couldn't believe what they'd found together.

GABE WOKE ON A warm midsummer day. The birds sang beyond the windows and crows cawed.

"Morning," Max mumbled.

"Morning, Agent Gallagher." Gabe planted a kiss on Max's cheek.

He sighed happily, hooking his arm around Gabe to tug on his hair. "I can't believe we went on our first job together."

Gabe nuzzled into his neck, smiling when he remembered how effortlessly they'd worked together to catch that feral wolf. "You've come so far, mi amor."

"I know. I'm awesome."

Gabe laughed. "And humble. So very humble. Your head's gonna get fat."

Max turned, parting his lips, and Gabe smacked a kiss on his mouth.

"What time is it?" he asked, his voice pleasantly gravelly from sleep.

Gabe checked the time. "Six."

He did a happy wiggle. "The kids are still asleep then."

Gabe closed his eyes, listening. "Yup. Quiet as mice."

"Perfect. Then we have time for you to give me my graduation present." Max rolled over and sprawled on his back beneath Gabe, looking at him with pure desire in those beautiful orange eyes.

Gabe growled low in his chest. "Oh yes, of course. How could I forget?" He slipped his hand beneath the blankets and stroked the hard line of Max's erection. Max shivered beneath him, tipping his head back, and Gabe sucked a kiss into the hollow of his pale throat. "Anything you want, Agent."

Max groaned quietly, fisting Gabe's hair to encourage him.

"Tell me what you want." Gabe licked a line from Max's Adam's apple to his clavicle, then introduced his fangs to Max's skin, leaving little love bites.

"I want you inside me," Max said, panting. "Want your cock."

Biting his lip, Gabe ground his hips down on Max's. They groaned when their cocks rubbed together through the cloth. Max bucked against him, and Gabe saw stars. Suddenly, he found himself flipped beneath Max. Max sat up and Gabe helped him tug off his boxers. Gabe licked his lips at the sight of Max's cock, then reached out and clasped it in his hand.

Max whined above him, rolling his hips into Gabe's dry strokes.

Gabe yanked open the drawer and handed him lube. "Get yourself ready for me, Lobito."

"Anything." Max slicked his fingers and reached behind himself. Gabe knew the moment he pushed in because Max bit his lip and whined.

Unable to hold back a satisfied growl, Gabe slowly stroked Max's leaking cock. "You look so sexy. Bet you feel amazing, so hot and tight for me."

Max panted while he fucked himself with his fingers. "Oh, fuck. Feels so good. I want your cock in me. Filling me up. Want your cum."

Sitting up, Gabe touched his fingers to Max's lips. "Wet them for me." Max did, suckling on Gabe's fingers like they were Gabe's cock. Feeling between his cheeks, Gabe slipped his wet finger inside Max's tight heat, squeezing past Max's finger on the way in. Arching his back, Max cried out, "Oh, fuck!"

Growling, Gabe stretched his fingers. "Feel so good. So tight and hot. You take our fingers so good. Makes me wish I had an extra cock so I could fill you to bursting." He crooked his finger, brushing Max's prostate. Whimpering, Max rocked his hips, riding their fingers. When their lips met in a messy kiss, they both growled. Their tongues tangled, their lips exchanging snarls and gasps.

Gripping his cock, Gabe slicked himself with lube. "Max. Fuck. I need to be inside you. Now."

Max squatted over Gabe's erection. Never looking away, Max lowered himself down. He tipped his head back, groaning his gratification when he finally got what he wanted. Max's tight, hot walls squeezed around him so perfectly.

Max leaned over and covered Gabe's mouth with his, stifling those sweet moans as he bounced up and down on Gabe's cock. Gabe bit his lower lip, his claws raking up and down Max's back as their bodies came together.

The bed groaned in protest under their frenzied movements, and Gabe knew they'd be needing a new one soon.

Max tossed his head back, flushed and desperate. "More, Gabe. Fuck. Give it to me." In response, Gabe raised his hips and pounded up into his mate's incredible heat. Craving more of those sweet sounds, he slammed into Max as deep as he could. He didn't give Max time to recover before he snapped his hips up and drove back in, coaxing a lovely hoarse cry from Max's lips.

Eyes glowing, Max jerked himself in time to Gabe's pounding thrusts. His mate was close, his soft whimpers and moans became a crescendo that filled each corner of their room. With a shout of Gabe's name, Max shot all over Gabe's chest and stomach, his thighs quivering as he rode up and down through his orgasm.

Those hot, velvety walls squeezed Gabe's orgasm out of him, and he filled Max's body with his release. When Max collapsed into his arms, Gabe caught him and held him tight. "How was your present?"

Max kissed his cheek. "You're the best present I'll ever ask for."

"So cheesy." Gabe's heart melted. He closed his eyes and nuzzled into Max's neck.

"Tired already?" Max asked with a giggle, and Gabe's heart grew wings at the sound. He covered those smiling lips with his and swept sweaty ginger locks from Max's face. Sighing contentedly, Max rubbed his stump up and down Gabe's side. With a kiss to Max's forehead, Gabe rolled them to their sides and draped a leg over his waist, every muscle slack and relaxed. He could have fallen asleep at once, but Max said, "Gabe, we have to get ready for the party."

He planted a kiss on Max's cheek. "I wish I could stay inside you all day."

"How about all night?" Max gave Gabe's rear a squeeze as Gabe stumbled out of bed.

"I'll make breakfast," he said, grabbing a wet rag from the bathroom to clean them up with.

Max yawned. "And I have to clean up around the house."

He glanced at the clock. In four hours, the guests would arrive for Luna's eighth birthday party. It was time to begin the day.

Once they'd showered, Gabe dressed and went downstairs. "Morning, Reyes pack!"

Tommy grinned. "Morning, Pops!"

"Morning, Dad!" Luna waved.

He dropped a kiss onto Luna's hair. "Good morning, birthday girl!" Gabe scooped her off her feet, kissing her cheek until she graced him with those deep belly laughs that never failed to make him smile. "Oof, you're getting bigger every day!" He set her down and rubbed his back.

"I'll be as big as you!" Luna said, pushing herself onto her toes.

"Yeah, right." Tommy cackled.

"Don't tease your sister. Now, who is hungry?"

"Me!" Luna thrust her hand up.

Gabe showed Tommy how to make pancakes. The teen groaned when his came out burned until Gabe showed him how to flip them at just the right time. "Bud, we gotta shave this thing you call a beard." He flicked the facial hair on Tommy's face.

"Hey, I like it."

Luna stuck out her tongue. "It looks stupid."

"Does not. Here, catch." He flipped her a pancake. It landed on the floor.

"Tommy," Max scolded lightly, striding down the stairs. "What did we tell you about flipping them?"

Tommy smiled his charming smile that made Gabe want to give him the world. "Do it more?"

Max sighed, his shoulders shaking with laughter. They gathered around the table for a family breakfast. After they'd eaten, Luna got to watch cartoons while Tommy helped them clean the house. Gabe dusted the picture frames, smiling when he cleaned Tommy's and Luna's framed adoption certificates. He ran his thumb over the glass: Luna Gallagher-Reyes and Thomas Gallagher-Reyes McCready.

"I'll make McCready a good name," Tommy had told them, and Gabe might or might not have shed a few tears. He knew if anyone could bring honor and goodness to the McCready name, it was his son.

They'd just finished cleaning when the grandparents arrived. Veronica squealed and ran to spoil her granddaughter. "Happy birthday, chiquita!"

Gabe checked his mother's bloated shopping bag. His mouth fell open. "Mamá! Are these all toys?"

"Not *all*. Did you see the dresses I bought her? They are so cute!" Veronica hugged Luna.

"Dress*es*? Plural? Oh no." This girl was going to be so spoiled.

Manuel looked ready to pass out, the bags heavy under his eyes. Gabe frowned. "Sure you're up to this?"

"Of course! My flight was just later than I thought. I couldn't miss Luna's birthday." Manuel watched Veronica hug Luna and Tommy. "Wow. I can't believe it."

Gabe chuckled. "What? That they survived this long?"

"They just grow up so fast. I still remember your eighth birthday." A dreamy look filled his father's eyes.

"How's the Council, Alpha Reyes?"

Manuel hung his jacket on the rack. "Good, good."

Veronica said, "We're focusing a lot on building better relationships with humans after all the damage McCready did. Like Kendra says, give it time, but I'm hopeful."

Kendra arrived, bright-faced and lively. "Hey, birthday girl!"

"Granny!" Luna ran into her arms.

"Hey, Kendra." Gabe embraced her, then cocked a brow. "How's your man?"

Kendra had been dating a human named Ronaldo for two years. He was the manager at Kendra's favorite restaurant, and he'd waited on her table during a staff shortage one day. They'd hit it off and been together ever since. Beaming ear to ear, she showed off the sparkling engagement ring on her finger. Gabe swept her into his arms. "Congratulations!"

Max smiled. "I already knew. Now you and I can talk about how gross he and my mom are together. Look at them!" He showed Gabe a picture on his phone of Kendra and Ronaldo being cutesy.

Kendra shooed Max away. "After he proposed, he and I had a lovely cuddle session after the full moon while I was shifted."

"Mom, gross!" Max shrieked, grinning playfully and covering his ears.

With the whole pack coming, they needed more food, so Veronica and Max got to work in the kitchen making fajitas.

The house smelled of Mexican spices by the time Ben arrived, and he opened his arms so Luna and Tommy could pile in for a hug. He was so preoccupied with the kids, he forgot to say hello to Gabe. "Have to say, when I found you beating up a pack of pure-blooded bullies, this wasn't the life I expected for you," Ben said, popping open the bottle of wine he'd brought and pouring Gabe a glass.

"Me neither," Gabe agreed. There'd been so much darkness in his life, it was good to finally have some light.

Ben gripped his shoulder, his mustache tilting as he smiled. "I'm proud of you. You pulled yourself outta all that despair and made something beautiful out of it. Max too. That's commendable."

Gabe's neck warmed. He raised his glass. "That's all you, Viejo." Ben had saved his life the day he took a chance on a lost and broken kid. Before they could get all misty-eyed, Ben suggested they drink and soon after Izzie arrived.

"There's my niece!" she cried, scooping Luna up and twirling her around. "Get over here, nephew!"

"Hey, Aunt Izzie." Tommy hugged her.

She set a box on the counter. Inside was her specialty tres leches cake, and for Gabe and Max, she'd brought a bottle of tequila. "Figured you guys need to relax every once in a while."

They carried the food up the hill to the bigger table outside while Kendra chased Luna around the lawn to keep her away from the cake. Zach and Ryan finally arrived, clad in hockey jerseys and full of winning team spirit.

Eddie and Vicenzo arrived not long after and before long the table was full to bursting with rowdy pack members.

Just in time for lunch, a portal opened and Thebe rushed out, wrapping her arms around Max. Amaris and Mani accompanied her, smiling brightly, with Anders and River jumping at their heels.

Eddie gaped. "I ain't ever gonna get used to the fact that we're cool with an actual goddess."

Then everyone dug into the food. Afterward, they sang "Happy Birthday" and Max took pictures when Luna blew out the candles.

Thebe tried a bite of cake and her eyes widened. "Okay. I think I love Earth."

Gabe asked, "Any more visions?"

"Of you guys? Sometimes. Zach and Ryan, though? Oh yes. Sometimes I catch glimpses of Ben too. Oh! And those guys, Eddie and Vicenzo."

Gabe's eyes widened. "Really?"

"Yeah. Just bits and pieces. But from what I can tell, you guys have more adventures coming up."

Gabe sighed. "And here I was, thinking we could catch a break."

"But don't take my word for it. It's pretty obvious your lives are going to be exciting for a long time."

While Max talked to Mani and Amaris, Gabe sought out Zach. He found him standing on the front porch and chatting with Vicenzo, who for once was smiling. "Damn," Gabe said. "Someone pinch me! You can feel joy after all!" He pinched Vicenzo's arm and earned a smack on the shoulder.

"Yeah. You guys are entertaining, at least." Vicenzo rolled his eyes and walked away

Zach smiled at Gabe's approach, watching as Luna ran around on the lawn chased by Izzie. "Can't believe how big she's gotten. It's crazy, man."

Gabe shook his head. "Tell me about it."

"Uncle Zach!" Luna squawked. "I found a huge butterfly, but it flew away. I wanted to show you."

Gabe knelt with a smile, opening his arms to pick up his daughter as she ran over. The little girl was wearing a cowgirl hat Veronica had bought her.

Gabe handed her over to Zach.

He grinned. "Hey, big girl! Like the hat!" Luna nuzzled into Zach's chest and he froze, wide-eyed. He blinked fast, his eyes misty. He rubbed Luna's back, and she wriggled away to chase after Tommy, who was bounding around the yard as a wolf.

Gabe asked, "What's up?"

"This is what I saw," Zach murmured. "Back in London, when I asked that seer if you and I were together in the future. This is the vision she showed me. The little girl was Luna all along. Not my daughter."

Gabe couldn't read his expression, but he hoped things were good between them. "We are together, Zach. Maybe not in the way you thought, but we are together. And you can still have someone to love you like you deserve."

Zach wiped his eyes, and the warmth in them assured Gabe that yes, they were good and they always would be. "Either way, I got what I wanted." He grabbed Gabe's shoulder, squeezing tight as he passed. Gabe smiled, relieved. He turned and saw Ryan transfixed as he watched Zach walk away. He honestly wondered how Zach hadn't caught on yet.

"You ever gonna tell him?"

Ryan jumped, his cheeks coloring. "No. There's no way he sees me the same way."

"Come on, you gotta be better than Will." He and Zach had dated for a year before Will had abruptly called things off a few months back.

"Fuck that guy," Ryan grumbled.

"Fuck that guy," Gabe agreed. "He's free now." He nudged Ryan's shoulder. "Seems to be feeling better too. Now's your chance."

Ryan's eyes went wide. "You think?"

"Come on, man. If you don't tell him, I will!"

Ryan exhaled, tapping his foot rapidly. He swigged the last of his beer. "Yeah. Yeah! I'm way the hell better than Will! Fuck it, if he could go out with that jerk, he'll go out with me. Right? Right! I'll tell him. I'll ask him out—tomorrow. Or next week."

Gabe rolled his eyes. "Just as long as you do it before the world ends." He hoped Ryan would finally have the guts to reach for his shot at happiness. It couldn't be more obvious they were meant for each other.

As the moon rose, the pack met in the woods beneath a star-streaked sky. Amaris was the one to start it, shifting to a red wolf and throwing her head back to the sky. Her graceful howl coaxed an answering cry of happy howls, even from Eddie, though his howl was very much human. To Gabe's delight, Luna shifted to a wolf and squeaked out an adorable howl with confidence. Max put his arm around Gabe's shoulder, nuzzling into his neck as he laughed.

One by one, the pack took off into the woods with Luna nipping at Tommy's heels. Gabe watched with pride as she ran, then pounced on Kendra and Ryan, chased Veronica and Manuel, and howled with Zach and Izzie. Max removed his prosthesis in preparation for his shift.

Smiling, Gabe kissed Max's forehead, speechless at the amount of love he felt for his pack.

"I told you, didn't I?" Gabe cleared his throat, voice rough with emotion.

"Told me what?" Max ran a hand across his cheek.

Gabe moved back to look at him, nuzzling his forehead to Max's. "I told you long ago that we'd put our demons to rest together. Remember? I didn't really believe it could be done. I thought I'd live with this void inside me forever. But, Max... *Max*..." The pride he felt for Max, for the family they'd found and the life they'd made together, took him by storm.

His mate pulled him close. "I remember." A fond smile tugged at Max's mouth. "But I wasn't sure back then. I was lost, afraid to trust."

"Me?" Gabe asked.

Arm falling from Gabe's waist, Max took his hand. "That the pain had an end. That I'd be able to smile and laugh like I had before. That it would all seem like a bad dream one day." He exhaled, his breath warm against

Gabe. Max grinned, his eyes bright and lips trembling. "But it did. Time heals, like my mom says, but I think loving you did too."

Gabe gripped Max's arm and pulled him close, overwhelmed with the love he felt for him. "We did it, Lobito, " Gabe whispered. "We did it."

Underneath the light of the moon, Max leaned in and kissed him. "Come on." He smiled radiantly as they parted. "Let's show that pack how to howl."

Gabe grinned. "Let's howl at that moon!"

With their pack at their side, Gabe and Max ran among the trees chasing shooting stars across the sky. When they could run no more, they lay beneath a blanket of stars and howled a special song only wolves could understand. A song of love, family, and pack.

Gabe and Max finally got their happy ending, but what's next for the agency wolves? Ryan discovers a family secret, and Zach (finally!) realizes Ryan's feelings for him.

The Lycanthrope Protection Agency #4 – The Moon Over The Oak.

THANK YOU!

Thank you for reading! If you enjoyed, please consider leaving a review on your preferred platform of choice. Indie authors like me depend on word of mouth reviews like yours. Additionally, please consider recommending this series if you enjoyed it! Thank you again!

WANT A FREE EBOOK?

Sign up to my newsletter to receive a free prequel to The Lycanthrope Protection Agency series, Before Moonrise. This novella features forbidden love, friends to lovers, possessive werewolves who adore their mates, and sexy times on a beach, in a barn, and a broom closet just to name a few locations. Additionally, you'll receive bonus content, cover reveals, and news about new releases. What are you waiting for?

Sign up now at www.CJRavenna.com!

ABOUT CJ

CJ Ravenna loves to tell stories where the ordinary meets the extraordinary. Her books often feature an explosion or two, possessive and protective werewolves who adore their mates, steamy and swoony romance, and of course a happy ending. Connect with me on:

My website: cjravenna.com

My Facebook group: Ravenna's Ravens

Instagram: @cjravenna

TikTok: @cjravenna

Goodreads: goodreads.com/cjravenna

Bookbub: bookbub.com/authors/cj-ravenna

ALSO BY CJ RAVENNA

The Lycanthrope Protection Agency Series
Before Moonrise (Jin & Marcus. Newsletter exclusive)
To Hunt A Moonborn Beast (Gabe & Max)
Child Of The Moon (Gabe & Max)
The Moon Aways Rises (Gabe & Max)
The Moon Over The Oak (Zach & Ryan)
Redemption Under The Moon (Ben & Isaac)
Fire and Moonlight (Eddie & Vicenzo)